TANGLED SKIES

Suzanne Cass

S C

STORM CLOUD
PRESS

Tangled Skies

Storm Cloud Press, Perth Australia

Copyright © 2022 by Suzanne Cass

Edits by Tanya Saari

Cover by Vikncharlie

To my sweet Dune, who filled me up with unconditional love.

CHAPTER ONE

Bindi Takao pressed her foot on the gas pedal and urged the car to go faster. She was going to be late. Her yellow Ford ute, nearly as old as she was, rattled and complained as it built up speed, not used to hurtling down the road so fast. Her side window, open to let in the breeze, began to rattle alarmingly inside the door frame, and the noise was enough to bring Bindi back to her senses. Even though the road was dead straight, it wouldn't do to kill herself just to get there on time. Releasing her foot, she unclenched her white-knuckle grip from the steering wheel, and leaned one elbow out the open window. She just had to accept her fate. Bugger. She really didn't want to miss Daisy's bridal shower lunch, but a quick look at the clock on the dash told her she was already running half an hour behind time.

Dry scrubland flashed past on either side of the car, the view familiar, relaxing her a little. The rains would come soon and turn this brown land to verdant green. But Bindi loved this country, no matter the weather. Each season had its own issues, the dry brought heat and dust and desiccation, and the wet brought impossible humidity and flooding, but also renewal. So completely different from the cooler climate of the mountainous landscape in her home country of New

Zealand.

All the women at Stormcloud Station had been looking forward to this event for weeks. Bindi couldn't remember a time when the entire cohort of ladies at Stormcloud had been on an outing together; perhaps it'd never happened before. Daisy's marriage to Dale at the end of the month was a huge occasion.

Bindi could hardly believe it; she was wearing makeup for the first time in forever. And a skirt. Short and floaty with hot-pink stripes. Up until now, she'd had no occasion to wear it, and it'd hung in her wardrobe with the tag still attached. She tamped down on the uncomfortable knot twisting in her guts. She was twenty-five years old; it shouldn't be this hard to wear a skirt. Give her jeans and boots any day of the week. Simple and practical, they were the two mottos she liked to live by. Put her in a dress and she somehow felt vulnerable. Thankfully, she wasn't one of Daisy's bridesmaids—that job had been given to Skylar and Julie—and Bindi didn't envy them one bit. The dove-gray, silk dresses Daisy had picked out for them looked wonderful, but Bindi just knew she'd be having heart palpitations if she'd had to wear that kind of slinky sheath.

Everyone else had gone into town an hour ago, Skylar detouring past the outstation to pick up Daisy. But Bindi had stayed behind to put the finishing touches to lunch. Everything was ready to be served to the guests, the meal was a simple one, idiot-proof, as Skylar so bluntly put it. Bindi almost had to push Skylar out the door, she was such a perfectionist; she hated to leave her kitchen in anyone else's hands. Bindi didn't blame her, Skylar was an amazing chef, and her creations were renowned across the top end of Queensland as some of the best gourmet food to be found anywhere.

Bindi had left the meal in the hands of Alek and Dale, with

strict instructions on the timing and order of service. Surely they couldn't muck it up too badly. Could they?

A curve appeared in the road ahead, and Bindi slowed her vehicle to take the bend. She was nearly halfway to town, only twenty minutes and she'd be on the main street of Dimbulah. Should she call Skylar and let her know she was running late? A quick glance at her phone in the cradle on her dashboard told her there was no reception, so that was out of the question. Cell phone coverage out here was patchy, at best.

Something caught Bindi's eye. What was that? A shape struggling beside the road. All long legs and bony head.

Oh, no.

An animal was caught in the wire fencing beside the road.

As Bindi slowed her car, she saw it wasn't just any animal.

A young foal struggled feebly as a mare stood by, showing the whites of her eyes and pawing at the ground. It was Madonna and her new filly, Melody. They'd gone missing two days ago, and all attempts to find the pair had been fruitless. Until now.

Madonna should be renamed Houdini, because she had a knack for getting out of her stable, lifting latches, and biting through ropes.

Bindi slammed on the brakes, and her car fishtailed to a stop. She pulled onto the verge and was out the door before she had the seatbelt all the way off. And nearly fell on her ass as her sparkling, silver heels caught in the gravel. Bugger, what a day to be trapped wearing her new heels and a skirt. The next time she went to a fancy luncheon with the girls, she was going to wear her boots, Skylar and her airs and graces be damned.

But wait.

She ran back to her car, and rummaged around on the floor of the passenger seat amongst the discarded wrappers, a

3

couple of unwashed T-shirts, two travel mugs, and a six-pack of water bottles and found her old pair of cowboy boots. There were holes worn in both soles, and she'd thrown them into her car until such a time as she could find the money to fix them. They might be worn, but she loved these boots. The leather was soft and comfy, and they fit her feet perfectly.

Her fingers fumbled with the straps of her sky-high heels, and she hopped first on one foot and then on the other as she dragged on her boots.

"Hang on Melody, I'm coming," she called to the distraught filly. A scorching breeze tugged at the long strands of her loose hair, but she had nothing to tie it back with, so, she swept it into an unbound ponytail and tucked it down the neck of her sleeveless, silk shirt as she took off across the road again.

Skidding to a halt a few feet in front of the fence, Bindi dragged in deep breaths as she surveyed the scene. The poor animal had her head thrust through two of the strands of wire near the top and every time she reared back in fear, the wire caught in her short, little mane. But even worse, two of the wires at the bottom had snapped and one strand was wrapped tightly around the filly's front fetlock, and as she struggled, it bit deeper into her tender skin. These fences were meant to keep in cattle, not horses. The Stormcloud horses were all held either in the stables at the back of the lodge, or in a specially built paddock with wooden railings to keep them from hurting themselves. How in God's name Madonna and Melody had found their way into this paddock was beyond Bindi's reasoning.

She reached a hand out and the foal showed the whites of its eyes and whinnied with fear, Madonna answering with her own snort of unease.

"Oh, no, you poor baby," Bindi crooned, keeping her voice low and comforting. Melody was a month old and had only been halter-broken so far. Bindi wasn't even sure how she was going to get close enough to the filly to help her. She was still a little wary around most humans. And neither of the horses were wearing a halter now, so how was she supposed to lead them, even if she did get the filly free?

Out of the corner of her eye, she caught movement farther up the road. A sleek, black pickup truck was barreling toward them. It slowed as it approached, pulling off to park in front of her yellow ute. This was no local farmer stopping to lend a hand, not by the looks of that vehicle. Great, this was the last thing she needed, tourists—or even worse, city slickers, stopping to gawp at her misfortune. She gritted her teeth and stood up, ready to ask them politely to be on their way. Nothing to see here. They'd only get in the way and upset the horses even more.

Instead of the gaggle of brightly dressed sightseers, however, a tall figure eased out of the front seat, dressed in black jeans, black-collared shirt and, most surprising of all, a black cowboy hat to finish the ensemble.

What the...? Well, he might not be a tourist, but he sure wasn't dressed like any farmer she knew around here. He looked more like the cocky cowboy out of an old-style western movie.

"Everything all right?" he asked in a low, gravely voice, an obvious American twang adding to his drawl.

"No, everything is not all right," she said tersely. "You wouldn't happen to have a pair of pliers on you?"

The man considered her for a few seconds and for some stupid reason, she felt her face heat as his stare travelled the length of her body.

"Well, have you got a set of pliers, or not?" she barked, her mind already spinning with other ideas on how to free the filly. Now was *not* the time to be wondering if he liked what he saw.

Rather than answering, he turned and paced back to his pickup and Bindi snorted her disapproval. The guy was leaving. Well, good riddance. Putting the stranger out of her mind, she swiveled to look at Melody again, cooing more mindless noises, while she tried to work out the best way to get her free.

Holding out her hand, she murmured encouragements and slowly advanced until she was close enough to touch Melody. The filly pulled back as far as the wire would allow, as Bindi's fingers landed on the soft spot between her ears, but she made more soothing noises, and moving as slowly as she could, eased her hand down to run it gently along the horse's neck. The filly was trembling with fear and pain, and Bindi wanted to scoop her up into her arms and whisk her off to safety. But safety was a pipe dream if she couldn't get the filly loose first.

A low voice behind her left shoulder almost made her startle, but she forced down her reaction, not wanting to scare Melody further. "Use this to cover her eyes," a voice as smooth as velvet told her. A piece of clothing appeared in front of her; a black T-shirt, if she wasn't mistaken. So, the stranger hadn't left after all. "It'll help keep her quiet while we work on her leg," the steady voice continued. Bindi was conscious of the man standing right behind her, his presence setting all the hairs on top of her arms to tingling.

Without turning around, she took the shirt, and ever so slowly, draped it over the filly's eyes, tying the corners underneath the horse's hard little cheekbones. It worked. The baby horse stopped struggling and stood there, head down in defeat. Why hadn't she thought of that?

"Thank you," she breathed, stepping to the side, away from the man's discomforting proximity.

"No problem." He also took a step back and flashed her a winning smile. Wow! Winning smile was an understatement;

it almost blinded her.

"I don't have any of those plier things you asked for." He raked a dark eyebrow upwards. "But I do have a small wire-cutting tool on my Leatherman, if you'll let me take a look." He pulled a large multi-tool set out of his pocket and gestured to the wire still wrapped around the filly's hoof.

Who was this guy?

There was a swagger in his stride and a hardness in the line of his jaw. Bindi stared into eyes the color of amber liquid, the breeze carrying the aroma of his masculine aftershave to her nostrils. He had a self-confidence about him, an aura that made her want to lean into him. Draw his scent right into her lungs. And perhaps run her tongue down the tanned stretch of his throat, just to see what he tasted like.

What the hell…?

Hastily stepping to one side, she kept her hand on Melody's neck and made room for the man to hunker down and get to work on the wire. Madonna was still standing a few feet away, but she seemed to realize they were only trying to help her baby and had stopped pawing at the ground.

"You must do things a little different here in Queensland," the man drawled conversationally, not looking away from the twisted mess of fencing. She liked his honey-toned twang, it reminded her of something dark and sweet, like molasses or butterscotch.

"How do you mean?" she queried.

"Where I come from, most cowgirls I know don't wear short, pink skirts and barely-there tops while they rescue horses from fences." This time he tipped his head up to stare at her, his gaze traveling appreciatively up her legs, lingering as he got to the low cut of her top.

"I was on my way to a party," she replied defensively. "Why? Where do you come from?" she demanded.

He doffed his hat, amber eyes crinkling at the corner. "Mack Diaz at your service. Straight out of Montana, the land of the Big Sky country."

Bindi was hit with sudden comprehension.

"You're Mack?" She should've realized. Of course, he was. If she hadn't been so caught up with Melody, she might've worked it out sooner. "We weren't expecting you for another three days."

Mack grunted, and, with one final snip, he cleared the last of the wire from the filly's fetlock. He stood and met her gaze. "You must be from Stormcloud Station, then, if you know who I am." The filly stood, shivering slightly, but not trying to get away because of the blindfold still around her head. Bindi ran a soothing hand down the baby animal's neck.

"Yes, I'm the chef's assistant," she replied. Bindi didn't understand the part of her that wanted to cringe as she said this. She'd always been terribly proud of her work with Skylar. Without her permission, her mouth blurted, "But I also help Steve and Dale with the horses when I get the time." For some reason, she wanted Mack to know she was as competent with the outdoor duties as much as the indoor side of station life. Although, why she wanted this cocky cowboy's respect, she had no idea. "I'm Bindi, by the way," she added belatedly.

"Hello, Bindi. Nice to meet you." He flashed her another brilliant smile and held out his hand for her to shake. Taken by surprise, she slid her hand into his and had to stomp on the sudden flash of heat caused by his work-roughened fingers inside her own. At least that proved he was telling the truth about one thing; he was a cowboy, after all. "Well, it's lucky I am early. How were you planning on getting the filly and the mare back to the station on your own?"

Wait, she hadn't thought that far ahead. Oh, just bloody awesome. Now she was stuck with this new cowboy, and two horses who needed rescuing. The wind chose that particular moment to blow in hot swirls across the road, lifting her skirt and making it flutter higher up her thighs. She caught the hem and held it down so he didn't catch an eyeful of her underwear. *Never wearing a skirt ever again,* she decided.

The next thing she knew, he'd rolled up his sleeves and gently picked up Melody, easing her long-limbed body through the wire and holding her against his chest. For all his suave dress sense, he had no qualms about getting down and dirty with the filly. It eased her misgivings about this newest cowboy a tiny bit.

He turned toward her yellow ute and she couldn't help but let her gaze wander down his figure. He was lean, lithe like a cat, but there was surprising strength in those arms, as he carried the foal as if she weighed nothing at all. She hurried across the road after Mack to let the tailgate down, and found an old blanket to spread out, so he could ease the foal into the truck bed, making sure to keep the blindfold securely in place.

"Easy," he crooned to the foal, wrapping the edge of the blanket around her vulnerable body. But all the fight seemed to have drained from Melody, and she lay as meek as a lamb in the bed.

Madonna whinnied desperately from behind the fence.

"Don't get your knickers in a knot," Bindi called to the horse. "We're going to take care of her."

"What do you plan to do with the mare?" Mack asked, still leaning into the rear bed.

"I'm not too sure…" She pursed her lips, thinking hard. "There's a service gate a little way up the road, we could bring her through there. But I don't have anything…" She trailed off as Mack began undoing his belt, the big-ass buckle glinting in the sunlight. What in the hell was he up to? Mack held the belt out to her, and she stared at it as if it were a snake about to strike.

"It's to tie around her neck, so we can lead her," he said, tawny eyes narrowing at her obvious unease.

She snatched the belt from his hand and said, "Good idea. I've got something we might be able to use as a lead rope in my car." She had an ancient stock whip that old Neville had given her when she'd left her first job as a rookie jillaroo up at Nelson's Park cattle station in the Northern Territory when she was only seventeen. He'd made her promise to learn to use it, and she had become fairly proficient with it over the years. It was tucked behind the driver's seat because she didn't want to lose it.

"I'll sit in back with the filly and lead the mare, while you drive, if you like?" Mack had already jumped into the rear tray and settled himself with one elbow on the wheel arch and the other on the filly's flank. "We can come back and collect my vehicle later."

"Right." But Bindi didn't move. She knew she was staring, but she couldn't help it. Who was this guy? So sure of himself. Were all American cowboys the same? Because if they were, she didn't want to meet any more.

CHAPTER TWO

Mack Diaz gazed into Bindi's thick-lashed eyes, trying to decide if they were merely brown, or something darker, like perhaps ebony. She was so much smaller than him, petite, with heavy, straight, black hair hanging down, partially covering her dark, exotic features.

That short little skirt. God, she was killing him with those taut, brown legs that never seemed to end. And the sleeveless, silky top that clung to her curves, highlighting breasts that would—

"You're going to do what?" Her sharp words brought him back with a jolt. She was still staring at him. The makeup and the party clothes—marred only by a battered pair of boots—couldn't hide the fact that she knew her way around the horses, her work-calloused hands a testament to hard work. And was that a scar he saw high up on her left shoulder? Interesting. He'd like to know where she came upon a scar like that.

He eased his leg beneath him, working out the twinge in his thigh. He'd been driving too long without a break. It always ached after long periods of inactivity.

"I'll sit in back, while you drive." It seemed the only logical way to do things. She knew the roads and the way back to the station.

"It's a long way to lead a horse…" She looked unsure.

He couldn't help it, his gaze traveled to that delicious mouth as her top teeth bit down on her bottom lip.

"It'll be fine. And the mare will follow us just about anywhere, as long as her foal is in the back of the car."

The look on her face went from unsure to determined. "You could be right," she mused.

Of course, he was right. Growing up on a ranch in Montana, he'd spent his life around horses and cattle. He didn't want to make a bad impression on his first day, however, especially on someone as pretty as Bindi. Striking, dark eyes fixed on him as she considered him for another moment. A flash of light sparkled off a tiny diamond nose stud as he she turned to stare back down the road, as if willing someone else to come along and help her. Anyone but him, it seemed.

He studied her while she hesitated. Cute. She was sassy and gorgeous, and he decided he might like working at Stormcloud a little better if she was there. Before he returned to Montana and the Pro Bull Riding circuit, that was.

Six months. That's what he'd promised Dean. Well, Dean had said six to twelve months, but Mack was set on the minimum stay. His boss at Stargazer Ranch had cajoled and sweet-talked, and even threatened until Mack had finally agreed. They were short a stock hand at Dean's sister's ranch in Australia, Stormcloud, Dean told him. Their leading hand, a guy named Wazza, had left a few months ago, and they hadn't had a chance to replace him. Dean had said it'd be good for Mack, give him a new perspective, give him time to heal—which Mack didn't need, he was healed enough to do what needed to be done. Mack knew his father was behind the plan to send him to Australia. Dean and his father were good friends, it was one of the reasons Dean had employed him at Stargazer, as a favor to Mack's father. Which still grated; he didn't need anyone's charity. But he and his father had fought constantly when he'd returned to the family ranch to recuperate after the accident. They'd almost come to blows a few times, so Mack had begrudgingly agreed when Dean had offered him a job as a horse wrangler on his luxury ranch. That'd been a year ago, and even though Mack wouldn't admit it, his time at Stargazer had been beneficial to him, both physically and mentally. He wasn't so sure how this stint at Stormcloud would turn out, however.

"Here, you can use this as a lead rope." Bindi handed him a coil of leather. He'd been so caught up with his musings, he'd hardly noticed her walk to her door and pull out the…he uncoiled the leather to see it was some sort of bullwhip, if he wasn't mistaken. Impressive. It'd be even more impressive if she knew how to use it. He raised an eyebrow in her direction, but she was already stalking toward the driver's door. "I'll stay as close as I can to the fence line. Madonna should follow us to the gate. I just hope she doesn't try and jump over it or something stupid."

He hoped the same thing. Bindi started up the battered old car—Mack thought it might even be older than him, the color reminding him of a ripe banana—and he glanced at his sleek, black truck. But seeing as how he'd only passed one other car on the road since he'd left the last town in his wake, he thought it'd be pretty safe. He hoped it'd be okay to leave it there, all his prized possessions were in that car, including his chaps, protective vest, bull rope and bells.

He'd bought the truck sight unseen before he left Montana. Had the guy deliver it to the Brisbane airport for him. It was everything he liked and trusted in a vehicle; a large, black, shiny Chevy Silverado, a truck he recognized from home. But the farther north he drove after leaving Brisbane behind, along the country highways and back roads, the more he got the feeling his car didn't really fit the vibe out here. Too late, he'd bought the car, and he wasn't about to swap it out for one of those smaller, dirty-white utes that everyone seemed to drive.

He watched Bindi through the thin slit of the rear window between the cab and the tray as she turned on the ignition and put the car into gear. Her long hair had come loose from the neck of her shirt, hiding her features behind a curtain of black silk. For a fleeting second, he wondered if her hair would be as soft as it looked. What would it feel like if he tangled his fingers at the nape of her neck, bunched that hair into his fist so he could tug her head back and kiss that pouty mouth of hers? He bet she'd taste good. All clean and wholesome, but with a hint of spice.

Bindi eased the pickup—were they called pickups here? He had no idea—around in a gentle U-turn, and drove along the gravel edge of the road, as close to the fence as she could get without dropping her tires in the shallow ditch running alongside. Madonna trotted toward the car, nostrils flaring as she caught the scent of her filly. Arching her neck, she lifted her legs and frisked along the other side of the fence, tossing her head to show her displeasure at being on the wrong side. The mare was a gorgeous, rust-red color, almost too red to be called a chestnut. With large, muscular forequarters and long slim legs, she was the perfect picture of a horse in her prime. Although he'd never seen one in person, Mack guessed she was one of the famed Australian Stock Horses bred to withstand the tough Australian conditions. Dean had mentioned that his new boss, Steve, bred these horses. He wondered if he'd be allowed to ride her. He'd love to see how different she was to the quarter horses they used at home. The filly was a similar color, although slightly lighter, and her hide shone like copper in the sunlight. They made a beautiful pair, mother and daughter.

His gaze traveled past the horse jogging beside them, out to the flat, open plains beyond. This sort of reminded him a little of the grass plains of Wyoming, but it was so much more...untamed. And with stunted trees breaking the skyline now and then. This country was parched, almost hungry. Dean had warned him that North Queensland went through something called a wet season around this time of the year. But he was yet to see any sign of rain. It was as dry as a chip. And as hot as a blasting oven. It got hot in Montana during summer, but nothing like this. It was going to take some getting used to.

The car came to a slow halt, and the filly made an effort to sit up at the change in motion. He lay a hand on her bony shoulder, holding her down until she stopped struggling. Bindi leapt out of her car to open a rusty gate and he only had time to briefly appreciate her gorgeous legs beneath that skirt, before she had his belt wrapped around the mare's neck and was holding her hand out for the bullwhip.

Bindi handed him the makeshift lead rope once it was attached, and he let the mare dip her head into the tray to sniff her foal. Once she was satisfied her baby was safe, she lifted her head, liquid, brown eyes holding his as she lipped at his outstretched palm, showing him she trusted him. Horses were special creatures. As long as you had their trust. He liked most horses more than he liked most people.

"You're good with her," Bindi said, almost as if she hadn't believed him earlier. "She likes you."

"I know." He tipped his hat and raised a cheeky eyebrow.

Bindi huffed out a small snort and said, "I'll drive slowly. Just tap on the window if you need me to stop."

"Will do," he replied, settling himself more securely beside the foal. There wasn't a lot of room on the bed with the filly's long body and spindly legs taking up most of the space. He kept most of his concentration on the mare as Bindi moved slowly onto the road, making sure the horse would lead properly. But she came willingly enough, trotting steadily beside the car, ears pricked forward and head held high. She really was a gorgeous piece of horseflesh. Mack was keen to meet his new boss, Steve. If he could produce this sort of premium stock, he was a man after Mack's own heart.

The trip took around thirty minutes, the mare trotting obediently along beside the car. She'd hardly even raised a sweat by the time Bindi turned the car down a wide, well-graded driveway. Mack was fleetingly diverted by a set of impressive, wrought-iron gates marking the entrance to Stormcloud Station, but then he was nearly tugged from the truck bed as the mare took it into her head to pull away; obviously sensing they were nearly home and eager to get back to her stable and a fresh bag of hay.

The driveway curved through more open woodland, and went up over a small rise and suddenly the land turned green and vigorous. A large body of water sparkled off to the right, surrounded by lush vegetation and tall trees. Peeking through the thicker vegetation, Mack made out the shapes of a couple of small cabins scattered along the length of the lake. Then the main lodge appeared at the top of a green expanse of lush grass leading down to a modern pool set at the edge of the lake. Dean had told him that Stormcloud was the Australian equivalent of his own luxury ranch. The station had twenty luxury cabins and enough activities and gourmet food to fulfill their rich guests' every whim. This lodge wasn't on such a grand scale as at Stargazer, only a single story instead of double, and a less-flamboyant soaring roofline, but it fit perfectly into the landscape, its wooden walls and subtle lines echoing the low hills and red earth surrounding it.

The road curved past the front of the lodge and a man suddenly appeared at the top of a wide set of stairs, shirtsleeves rolled up to his elbows, a dishcloth in his hand,

and an apron tied around his middle. The guy was young, about Mack's age, taller and broader in the shoulders. He took in Mack and the mare he was leading in one sweeping gaze. Mack worked through all the names Dean had given him and decided this was probably the owner's stepson, Dale, the leading hand. But if that were the case, what was he doing in the kitchen?

"Bindi, what's going on?" the other guy demanded, never taking his eyes off Mack.

Bindi stopped the car and called through the open window. "I found Melody stuck in a fence. Her front leg is pretty cut up. Can you let Steve know? I'll take them both up to the stables and meet him there."

"Righto," the man replied. His gaze finally stopped scrutinizing Mack and went to Bindi. "Who's the guy in the back of your car?" he asked.

"Oh." Bindi jumped and turned to stare at Mack through the small rear window, as if she'd almost forgotten he was there. "This is Mack, the new guy from Stargazer."

"Righto," the man said again, but narrowed his eyes at Mack before he turned to go back inside. Mack squared his shoulders and tilted his chin a little higher.

Madonna let out a loud whinny and pulled on the lead rope, impatient to get to the stables, which must be around the back of the lodge, judging by the direction her pricked ears were pointing. The little filly had hardly moved for the whole trip, clearly defeated by her struggle in the fence.

"Almost there, my girl," Bindi called through the window. She glanced back at Mack, an unreadable look in her eyes, then edged the car forward, up the hill and through a cleared section toward a set of buildings higher up the slope. Wooden fences and the edge of a large shed built out of iron sketched themselves through the canvas of tangled trees. Bindi stopped the pickup out the front of the large open side of the shed. These must be the stables, but they didn't look like any Montana barn he was used to.

"I'll take her." Bindi was already out of the car and gently taking Madonna's lead from his hand. "Are you able to carry Melody inside?"

"Sure." He waited until Bindi turned away with Madonna before he levered himself to his knees, letting the sharp pain in his leg subside, and then maneuvered himself awkwardly out of the tray. Just as his feet hit the red dirt, a voice sounded behind him.

"Bindi, Dale just told me what happened. Thank God you found her when you did."

Mack turned in time to see a man in his mid-fifties striding toward him. This must be Steve. He was closely followed by the guy who'd greeted them on the stairs. Shit, he hoped his new boss hadn't seen that moment of weakness. His leg was fine as long as he kept moving. It was only if it was immobile, or scrunched beneath him in the rear tray of a ute, that it caused him pain.

"And thank you for helping her." Steve reached out a hand to shake Mack's. "Helluva way to start your first day on the station, but we're more than grateful. I'm Steve, and this is Dale." Mack shook both men's hands. Steve had a warm, genuine handshake, as did Dale, although Dale's was slightly less benevolent. Dean had told him something about his new boss, so he already knew that Steve was a fair man, rock-solid, with a sharp mind and passion for bringing cattle farming to a more sustainable level in the twenty-first century.

"Mack Diaz. Nice to meet you, sir." Mack touched the brim of his hat, including Dale in his address. "I'll bring her in, if you'll show me where you want her." He turned back to draw the foal into his arms. Mack didn't want to relinquish the filly quite yet. He'd started the job, and he'd like to finish it.

Steve led him inside and opened the door to a stall. Mack lay the filly down in the thick layer of straw, the blindfold still around her head. Then he stood and backed away so Steve and Dale could take a look at their filly. "Good job," Steve said, patting Mack on the shoulder before he knelt in the straw.

It was nice to get out of the heat of the blazing sun. He could feel the beginning of a headache coming on. Not good.

Out of the corner of his eye, he saw Bindi lead the mare into the stall next door.

"This is going to need stitches. We'll need the vet," Steve said. Mack had already decided the same thing on the ride in the back of the car. He was pleased to see that Steve wasn't one of these slap-dash cowboys who thought they could heal an animal themself. He treated his animals with respect and care.

"I'll call Bill." Dale stood and pulled a cell phone from his back pocket. "I hope he's not on some job hours out of town."

"Me too," Steve replied with a grimace, but Dale was already striding away down the length of the stables, phone to his ear. "I'm going to let her up so she can suckle from her mother," Steve said, turning his attention back to the foal. "The bleeding has just about stopped and it'll help calm both her and the mare."

Mack nodded his agreement. It was what he would've done. He watched as Steve helped the filly to her feet and Bindi led the mare into the stall. Madonna snuffled her baby and then turned to let her stumble toward a teat. Dale arrived with a bag full of hay, which he hung on a hook on the wall, and Madonna tugged out great mouthfuls of food.

"Bill will be out in an hour, or so," Dale reported.

Mack leaned against the outside of the stall, easing his leg a little as he did so. His head was beginning to pound, but he tried to ignore it.

"We're going to have to figure something out with these latches," Steve said as he watched the mother and baby settle in. "We can't have her getting out and risking her filly again."

"I might be able to help with that," Mack said. "We had a couple of escape artists on our ranch, too. My father found a neat invention online that might work here."

Three pairs of eyes all turned to study him. "Thanks," Steve finally said. "That'd be most appreciated. This mare and her little filly are going to be worth a pretty penny if my hunch is right. They're the start of my breeding program, and I don't want either of them to get hurt."

"I can see that," Mack agreed.

"I'll wait here for the vet," Steve said. "Dale, you'd better get back to the kitchen. Alek and Aaron will be going mental, having to deal with lunch service all on their own."

Dale grimaced, but squared his shoulders and nodded. "Yeah, will do. When are Skylar and the rest of the women due back?"

"Skylar promised to be back by five so she can finish the prep for dinner," Steve replied.

Dale's heavy sigh indicated it wouldn't be soon enough for his liking. "Righto, I'm going back to the fray." With that, he gave the mare one more quick glance, and strode out of the stables.

Mack mentally reviewed his list of staff at the station and decided that Skylar was Steve's stepdaughter, as well as head chef at the resort. By all accounts, she was something of a genius when it came to crafting gourmet meals. Which didn't interest him. Give him a rare steak and a heap of fries any day of the week, and he'd be a happy man.

Steve turned his concentration to Bindi, who was cooing to Madonna and lightly stroking the soft spot just below her ear. He raised one eyebrow in speculation. "Bindi, I know you were supposed to be at the bridal luncheon, but now you're here…" Steve didn't finish his question.

She looked startled for a second, as if she'd been lost in thought, her world narrowed so that the mare was the center of her universe. It seemed this girl really cared about her horses. "Oh. Ah… I guess there's no point in me heading back to town now," she sighed. "So, yes, I'll help you. I just need to go and change." Mack hid his disappointment; he really appreciated her outfit. Steve had said she'd been headed into a bridal luncheon. That must be where the rest of the Stormcloud women were. Dean had mentioned something about an upcoming wedding at Stormcloud, but those sorts of things didn't interest Mack, so he'd let most of the details wash over him.

"Would you mind showing Mack to his quarters?" Steve asked, as Bindi turned to leave. "Sorry, mate, normally I'd give you a tour of the place myself, welcome you in and see you settled. But, with Melody like this…"

"Not a problem," Mack insisted. "The filly comes first, I fully appreciate that." Being shown to his room was actually a good thing. He'd kill for a nice cool spot to rest his head for a few minutes. His headache was getting worse, it felt like his forehead was being squeezed in a vise.

Bindi flicked him an indecipherable glance, then said, "Sure, follow me."

He pushed away from the wall, keeping his head steady and eyes directed forward; every move caused a sharp pain to knife through his brain. But he painted a winning smile on his face. No one needed to know. He just had to make it to his room. Half an hour lying down in a dark place often worked wonders.

"Sorry you missed out on your party," Mack drawled, following her flirty little skirt and gently swishing hips out of the stables and down the hill, the sight helping him to forget about his headache for a second.

Bindi glanced back at him over her shoulder. "Yeah, it's not often all the girls have a get together. It's impossible to leave Stormcloud unattended, even for a few hours. We've got twenty resort cabins and we're over half-full. The guests need to be fed and entertained. But Julie was determined that Skylar have a special day. So, she sweet-talked all the men into filling in for a few hours, so we could have our party."

"Nice," Mack drawled again. "And Julie is…?"

"Oh, sorry, I keep forgetting you don't know everyone yet. Julie is Steve's daughter. She works here, helping Daniella deal with the administration side of the resort, but she also helps with the guest activities and in the kitchen, as well. Aaron, her boyfriend, is the station chopper pilot."

"Wow, this really is a family venture, isn't it?"

"Yeah, I guess you could say that." Bindi had led them down the hill toward the back of the lodge, but now she veered away toward a long building on the right. It, too, was made of the same wood planks and iron roof, with the same attention to detail and subtle design.

"This is the staff quarters." She skipped up a set of stairs and held open the door for him. "We're lucky here, everyone gets a room to themselves, and the quarters are nearly as luxurious as the main lodge. This is definitely the nicest place I've ever worked at." Bindi prattled on as she led him down a long hallway with doors leading off on the left and right. It was cooler in here, which was a small mercy. He heard something about the two bathrooms at the end, with towels and linen in the cupboards next to them, but his thoughts were becoming foggy as the pain took over his brain. Would he find painkillers in the bathroom? He didn't want to ask.

Bindi had stopped outside the last door on the right and was looking at him expectantly.

"What?" It was all he could do not to lean his head up

against the cool drywall, but he managed to remain upright.

"This is your room." She gestured to the open door. He stepped inside and pretended to look around.

"I'd better get back to the kitchen. Come inside when you're ready, and I'll introduce you to the others." Bindi offered with a small frown. Could she sense something was wrong with him? "We can go and retrieve your car once lunch service is over, and things quieten down a little."

"Thanks, will do." Mack hoped his answer didn't sound as stilted as it felt. "I'll freshen up and be in soon," he added.

Bindi finally shut the door behind her, and Mack eased himself down onto the bed, placing his aching head in his hands. Shit. He'd hoped he was over the worst of the headaches by now. They'd been getting less frequent. He hadn't had one in nearly a month. He supposed the jet lag wasn't helping. Nor the long, two-day drive up here. He thumped the bed with his fist, but that only made his head pound harder.

CHAPTER THREE

"That's right, you're doing great," Bindi called to the woman on the horse beside her.

"Are you sure? I feel like a sack of potatoes flopping around up here." Petra giggled, and then grabbed for the pommel of the saddle as she nearly lost her balance. Chico gave a gentle snort. The part-clydesdale horse was used to beginners bouncing along on his back. The older woman was trying her best, but she clearly wasn't cut out for horse riding. Her riding helmet kept slipping sideways, and Bindi reached over and tightened it for her. The poor woman was only out here to please her husband, Franco, who sauntered along on his horse up at the front of the line, talking to Mack. At least Franco could ride, which was one silver lining to her day.

"Nah, you're getting the hang of it real well." Mack dropped back to come along the other side of Petra, and Bindi ground her teeth together.

She didn't need his help. She was doing fine, thank you very much. He was supposed to be tagging along at the back, not interfering with every little single thing she did. And not leading the ride, for God's sake. This was only his first full day at Stormcloud. Steve had said she was in charge. This guy was no replacement for Wazza, not in Bindi's books, anyway. Mack had a long way to go before he came anywhere near Wazza's knowledge and experience. But Stormcloud had been down a crew member for the past few months, ever since Wazza and his new ladylove, Kee, along with Kee's daughter, had moved to Cairns. Steve seemed to think Mack would slot right in and be able to pick up things quickly. Bindi had her doubts.

She also missed Wazza and his laid-back attitude. He was generous and caring, a rare commodity amongst the rough and tumble men who often worked on these stations. Steve had chosen well with Wazza, and she knew she was probably biased against any replacement. While Bindi had never seen him in a romantic light, they'd been close friends. Kee was one lucky woman. But at least Wazza and Kee would be back for the wedding, bringing Kee's gorgeous little daughter, Benni, with them.

"Keep your hands down lower." Mack reached over and covered Petra's hand with his to show her what he meant. "That's right, so they hover just above the horse's whither. That helps you keep your balance better, see?" The woman glanced at him and gave a girly giggle. These were all things Bindi had said to Petra not five minutes before. But for some reason, Mack's teachings seemed to have an impact, as the woman kept her hands down like he instructed, instead of letting her arms flap around like a hapless chicken.

Surely Petra wasn't flirting with Mack. Was she? She was twice his age, if she was a day. But Mack seemed to have that effect on every female he met. Especially with that amazing, wide smile of his.

Except her.

She was determined not to be taken in by that startling grin and that cowboy swagger.

Bindi nearly threw Chico's lead rein at Mack in disgust. If he was so good at teaching the older lady, then he could take over.

If only he wasn't so good looking, she might even succeed in putting him beneath her notice. Mack shot her a cheeky grin over the top of Petra's head and it was all Bindi could do not to grin back.

Damn him. She was going to ignore his sexy seduction techniques, if it was the last thing she did.

"How are you going back there?" Bindi called over her shoulder to the other couple following along behind. Secretly, she wished Mack would drop back and talk to them. Perhaps even take up the rear, where she didn't have to look at him anymore. The other couple were younger, staying at Stormcloud for their honeymoon, and they only had eyes for each other. At least they'd both done some horse riding before, and were capable of handling the horses themselves. Sam and Leah. They were so cute, and so in love. If only true love could be that simple.

Normally, Steve led these expeditions, but he was still caught up fretting over the filly, so he'd asked her to lead this small group of four guests to the top of the escarpment this afternoon. Bindi loved getting out of the kitchen, and as long as Skylar was happy to let her go, she always jumped at the chance to go riding.

And that'd been her feeling today, right up until Steve had told her that Mack was coming along too.

Bindi wasn't really sure what she had against Mack. It was nothing she could put her finger on. Everyone else seemed to like him, it was just her. He was just so...arrogant wasn't quite the right word. Self-assured. Extroverted. Nope, that wasn't it. She kept coming back to that word, cocky, because that was the best way to describe him. He fit that stereotype of a cocky cowboy to a *T*. Even down to his slow drawl and the way he tipped his hat to all the ladies in that old-fashioned way. Steve had mentioned that Mack was a pro bull rider, had even won a few championships over in America. Maybe that's where he got his swagger. Maybe all the bull riders were like that. Although, Bindi had never paid them much heed whenever she'd attended a rodeo, too much sweat and testosterone for her liking.

Although, he had lost a bit of that swagger yesterday afternoon. She was sure something had been wrong. When she'd shown him to the staff quarters, he'd seemed to go quiet all of a sudden, face slightly pale and sweaty. She'd wanted to ask him if he was fine, but he'd practically shoved her out the door. Then, when he'd arrived in the kitchen nearly an hour later, there'd been no sign of that moment of weakness; he'd flashed his winning smile at everyone and charmed them all with his tawny eyes and easy humor. Bindi had shrugged it off as her overactive imagination. Thankfully, Steve had asked Dale to take Mack and retrieve his vehicle from the side of the road. Bindi didn't fancy being cooped up in a car with Mack, not even for the short drive back to where she'd found Melody. But then she remembered Mack had begged off early, not even eating dinner before he went back to his room. His excuse was that the jet lag was catching up to him. But he'd already been on the road for nearly two days on the drive up here, so Bindi wasn't sure how solid that reason was.

Dale and Julie had taken the rest of the guests out to the old, abandoned gold mine for the afternoon. She'd watched the convoy of ATVs wind their way down the path behind the lodge as she made her way to the stables. But the newlyweds, along with Franco and Petra, had wanted to do something different. A ride up to the escarpment normally took less than two hours, and the view from up the top was spectacular. Bindi carried all the makings for afternoon tea in her saddle bags; she had some of Skylar's delicious brownies and a thermos of hot water for tea and coffee. Simple but effective.

Her gaze slid to Mack atop his horse, Picasso—named because of the big patches of white and brown covering his piebald hide—watching the easy way he sat in the saddle, the innate understanding that seemed to flow between him and the gelding. At least he had one thing going for him; it was clear he loved horses and could ride well. Why had no one else ever looked so damn good riding a horse? It was as if Mack could turn even that simple act into a sensual experience. At least he wasn't wearing all black today, but that didn't mean he wasn't still dressed like he'd just stepped out of a western movie. He swapped out his black shirt for an equally flashy dark-red one with silver buttons. He wore the same slim-fitting black jeans as yesterday, and topped off his ensemble with what Bindi was starting to call his bad-boy black hat. And his boots—don't even let her start with his boots. A dark mahogany, to match his belt most probably, and made from what looked to be butter-soft leather, inlaid with delicate, tooled designs, they were the best-looking boots she'd ever seen. He was a show pony, through and through. With a snort of self-derision, Bindi tore her gaze away from him. Glancing down at her own boots, she decided hers were much more practical. Her second-favorite pair were well-worn, plain, brown leather, they were dusty and had seen many miles of hard work. She was proud of her boots. Which reminded her, she really should get her favorite pair fixed, sooner rather than later.

As if Mack seemed to gauge her darker mood, he quickened Picasso's pace and re-joined Franco in the lead. Bindi watched his back from beneath the brim of her hat. Something about him niggled at the back of her brain. He reminded her of someone. That attitude, that easy charm, it made her think of… She gasped. Mack reminded her a little of her older brother, Kai. Not in looks—both she and her brother were part Maori—but something in his demeanor, the way he seemed to take life by the scruff of the neck and laugh in the face of the devil all at the same time.

Bindi shivered. The scar on her shoulder itched with a half-forgotten memory.

Perhaps that's why she'd taken a dislike to Mack.

Kai was dead now. But she'd never forget him. Never forget what he'd done to her.

Clicking her tongue, she urged Sahara into a faster walk. The palomino responded with a frisk in her step, she was ready to stretch her legs, and all this slow plodding was making her antsy. Bindi knew how she felt, she longed to lean over the mare's withers and let her wind up to a full gallop over the flat plains to their right. But she had responsibilities, and so did her horse. They needed to get Petra and the rest of their small party up to the top of the escarpment safely. And it was time she took the lead. The path up to the top was often hard to find, created by Steve for his guests alone on this particular trek. There was a road that went all the way to the top also, but it was much longer, following the gradual upward slope along the spine of the escarpment, and was used mainly by the ATVs, or a four-wheel-drive, if need be.

"Are you ready for a bit of a climb?" Bindi asked Petra, not really waiting for her answer, tugging the lead rein to keep Chico up with her. "I'll take the lead," she called, using her authoritative voice, bustling past Mack and Picasso. Petra was jolted out of her complacency, giving a little squeal, and grabbed for the pommel as she nearly slipped sideways again. Bindi held in a sigh. Some people were a natural when it came to horse riding and some people just weren't cut out for it, no matter how patiently you coaxed them.

"Lead on." Mack swung his hat off his head, and let her through with a flourish. She stared at him. If this was his form of chivalry, well… She wasn't quite sure how to take it.

American cowboys sure did things a little different to Aussie men.

An enormous bottle tree which loomed on the left, marking the start of the path they needed to climb, and she turned Sahara onto it. The rest of the way up the escarpment was spent coaxing Petra to stand up in her stirrups to take some of the weight of poor Chico's back so he could clamber up the rocky path. Looking over her shoulder now and then, she checked to make sure Franco and the other couple were handling the steeper terrain. Mack had taken up position at the end of the line, encouraging Leah and Sam not to drop too far behind. Which shouldn't surprise Bindi, because he had worked at Stargazer before he came here. So, he must know how a horse trek with inexperienced riders was supposed to go.

"Are we there yet?" Petra puffed.

"Nearly," Bindi replied. "You just wait, it's worth the climb, I promise."

"I hope so. Remind me to take the ATV trip next time, will you," she said, wiping beads of sweat from her brow beneath the helmet. Bindi thought Petra was only half-joking.

Ten minutes later, they crested the last rocky outcrop, and the ground flattened out beneath the horses' hooves. Bindi led the way toward a cleared area, shaded by a stand of ironbarks. As they drew rein, she heard Petra's intake of breath.

"Oh, wow, you weren't kidding." The older woman's eyes bulged as she took in the vista, now visible as they broke through the last tree line blocking their way.

The escarpment dropped off in a dramatic cliff face twenty meters in front of them, with a hundred meter drop to where the flat floodplains spread out like an olive-and-red patterned carpet below.

She helped Petra dismount, and tied both their horses to a

makeshift railing Steve had created from a fallen sapling. "Go and take a look," Bindi urged. "I'll unpack the saddlebags and set up smoko for you all."

"Franco, you have to see this," Petra called to her husband, who was just dismounting from Captain, the other part-clydesdale. He removed his helmet and wiped the sweat and dust from his face, which was going an interesting shade of red. Most guests weren't used to this Queensland heat, and she was going to need to keep an eye on him; the last thing they wanted was for him to keel over with heat exhaustion.

"Why don't you and your lovely wife take a seat on that large rock over there?" Bindi pointed to a flat rock a little way back from the edge of the cliff, still in the shade of the branches spreading above. "Here, drink this." She handed him a bottle of water she'd plucked from her saddlebags. "I'll bring you over some refreshments soon."

The next ten minutes were spent in a flurry of helping Sam and Leah dismount, making sure their horses were tied up securely so they didn't wander off, and setting up the simple afternoon tea on a second flat rock next to Petra and Franco. To her surprise, Mack took charge of the horses for her, running his expert eye over them all to make sure all were sound and none of them were overheated.

"What's smoko?" A voice drifted over her left shoulder as she poured hot water into the row of mugs she'd set up on her natural stone table. She turned to see Mack regarding her from beneath the brim of his black hat, one eyebrow quirked up in a question mark. She hadn't been ready for his presence so close to her, and his smoldering gaze hit her right between the eyes, sending a shock of heat to her gut.

She laughed a little too loudly to cover her reaction. "I keep forgetting you Americans have no idea of our Aussie slang. Smoko is another word for afternoon tea. You know, when we take a break. Back when everyone used to smoke, the old ringers would light up a ciggie or two."

"A ciggie?" His confusion was comical.

Franco came up and slapped him on the back. "You know, a cigarette. A cancer stick. Smokin' a tab. Light up a smoke. You young men know nothing nowadays." He shook his head and reached for a plate and one of Skylar's famous brownies. Bindi was glad to see his glowing-red face had subsided to a more natural color.

"Riiiight." Mack drew out the word in his slow drawl. She handed him a brownie on a plate and gave him a cheeky wink. This guy had a lot to learn. But she carefully moved to the other side of the rock table, putting distance between her and his sexy drawl that was doing funny things to her insides.

The ride back down the escarpment was pleasant enough. The four guests chatted between themselves and Mack rode at the back of the pack, while she led the way home. It gave her time to think about what else she needed to do this evening. Skylar had been happy to give her the afternoon off, but she knew that as soon as she set foot in that kitchen, it'd be all guns blazing to make sure the evening meal was perfect and served on time. She hardly noticed how quiet Mack had become as they rode down the dusty road and into the stables.

Busying herself with the guests, she showed them how to unsaddle their mounts and turn them all out into the adjacent yard for a much-needed drink and where Steve would come and feed them later on this evening. Then she waved the guests goodbye, promising to see them all at dinner that night, and began to unsaddle Savanah. Out of the corner of her eye, she saw that Picasso had been left tied to the railing, still fully saddled. Where was Mack? What the hell did he think he was up to? He couldn't just slope off like that and leave her with all the work. The cheek of the man. She stormed down the length of the shed, carrying Savanah's saddle, peering into each stable. Where had he gone? Was he already on his way to the staff quarters? When she found him, she was going to give him a piece of her mind. And Steve was going to hear about this. Steve didn't take kindly to slackers.

Turning into the tack room, she dropped the saddle onto a storage rail and turned to head out of the stables to go and find that... Hold up. A figure morphed out of the gloom in the corner of the tack room.

"Mack, is that you?" she demanded.

"Yep. Sorry, just give me a moment." His voice sounded funny, weak, like it was traveling over a long distance.

Her boots tapped over the wooden floorboards as she moved closer to the man huddled in the corner. He was crouched down, head leaned against the side of the shed as if using it for support, hat dropped haphazardly on the floor beside him.

"What's wrong?" Concern replaced the anger in her chest, and she reached out to touch him. His shoulders were rigid, and a slight trembling ran through his body.

"Nothing. I just felt a little dizzy, that's all. I'll be fine in a second."

Dizzy. Why would Mack feel dizzy? Was he heat stressed? Damn, she should've taken more care to see he drank lots of water as well, not just the guests. Newbies to the Queensland heat were often stunned by the effect it could have on them.

"You might have heatstroke," she explained gently. "Wait here, I'll get Dale to give you a hand down to your room. And I'll—"

"No! I don't have heat stroke," he ground out between gritted teeth.

"Then what...?"

"Jesus, I hate this," he spat. "I should be able to conquer

this."

"Conquer what?" He wasn't making much sense.

"Please don't tell anyone. Especially not Steve." Mack's hand was like a brand on the skin of her forearm as he reached over to grab her. She stopped, startled by his touch, and startled by his intensity.

"I'm not…"

"Please, Bindi." He lifted his head and speared her with tawny eyes. Right at that second, he reminded her of a cornered lion. Dangerous. And beautiful.

Damn the man to hell. How dare he ask her to keep such a secret? But his stare remained fixed on her face, drilling into her brain, affecting her body, affecting her ability to think clearly.

She huffed out a breath. This didn't feel right, but she'd agree. For now.

"Fine, I won't tell anyone what I saw here today. On one condition."

"What?" he asked warily. She could tell how much he hated the fact that she'd seen him in a moment of weakness.

"That you tell me what's going on with you. I need to know everything."

He nodded once, then pulled himself up the wall until he was standing. She picked up his hat and handed it to him, watching him like a hawk in case the dizziness came back. "As long as you promise not to tell anyone else."

"I promise," she agreed.

"You drive a hard bargain."

She sighed and uncrossed her fingers behind her back, making a silent mental note that if this happened again, she *would* be telling Steve. Mack was a danger to himself and to the station if he couldn't control whatever was happening to him.

CHAPTER FOUR

Mack sat back in his chair and patted his stomach. "Man, that was some damn fine cooking." He smiled winningly at Skylar, who was seated at the other end of the table.

"I'm glad you appreciated it," she replied, ducking her head just as her blue eyes met his. Then she flicked a guilty glance at the guy sitting next to her. Mack knew he had that sort of effect on women, and most of the time he was barely aware of it. But when he wanted to impress, he turned the charm wattage up to high. Skylar was one good-looking woman. And he wanted to get on the good side of anyone who could cook like that. But she was also off-limits. She was head-over-heels in love with the guy sitting next to her, it was obvious from a mile off. Nash was the local sheriff—no, sheriff wasn't the right term, what'd they called him? Senior Constable, or something. Anyway, Nash's blond, surfer good-looks didn't fool Mack in the slightest. The man's steely eyes fixed on him, not challenging, as such, but in a way that made Mack understand he wasn't going to get away with anything around this guy. Nash was a man to be respected, and Mack was fine with that.

He'd half expected to slowly starve to death here on this station after Dean told him the head chef was renowned for her gourmet meals. He'd never been a fan of gourmet food. A simple man, with simple tastes, was how he liked to think of himself. But he'd been pleasantly surprised. The main meal was a thick chunk of perfectly cooked beef, bred on the station, of course, with homegrown roasted beetroots of all different colors, and a salad of some interesting vegetables that Skylar had called warrigal greens. Much like English spinach, they had a slightly bitter taste that went surprisingly well with the meat. The beef had been tender, melt in his mouth, but it was the sauce that made the dish spectacular. Some kind of Kakadu plum and red wine jus, that was so delicious he could've almost picked up the plate and licked it clean. The entrée had been something called yabbies, which reminded him a little of large prawns, with a subtle garlic mayonnaise. And the dessert had been a red-velvet sponge cake topped with chocolate and wattleseed mousse, sprinkled liberally with round nuts called macadamias. Supposedly, these were native Australian ingredients. He didn't really care where they came from, they were damn delicious, and he was so full he was fit to burst.

Tonight was his first night eating with the Stormcloud crew; the staff usually ate with the guests, all seated at the long tables in the great room. Last night he'd gone to bed early, saying he was suffering jet lag, but really he'd been trying to get rid of the last effects of that damn headache. But that's been nothing next to his embarrassing episode in front of Bindi this afternoon. He shot her a glance, but she was talking to the honeymooning couple on her right.

Tonight, he'd quickly learned that Daniella didn't like hats to be worn inside. He'd also learned that Daniella ruled the resort with an iron fist, at least the running of the lodge and the guest side of things. She was one formidable lady, nothing like Dean's wife Naomi, who used charm and home-spun kindness to achieve her goals. Daniella was all cool efficiency and well-groomed style. A complete contrast to Steve. But after watching them for most of the night, it seemed that opposites really did attract, and they complemented each other's strengths and weaknesses well.

Skylar, Bindi, and Sasha, the receptionist chick whom Mack had only met quickly this morning, served the meal, while everyone else chatted to the guests and ate the delicious food. Once everyone else was fed, the three women joined them to eat before dashing away to get dessert ready. Then they'd rejoined them once dessert was served. His gaze had followed Bindi as she walked between the tables, drawn by the sway of her hips, until he'd brought himself up short and forced himself to chat to Franco sitting on his left.

Now everyone sat around the tables, replete and talking happily. As Mack's gaze roamed across the room, taking in the happy chatter, he decided this station was more like Stargazer Ranch than he'd first envisioned. The similarity wasn't in a physical sense, as the two ranches couldn't be more different, one was dry and dusty and the other surrounded by verdant green mountains often covered in snow, but it was in the way the staff and family formed such a tight-knit crew. There was genuine respect and friendship here. Dale was sitting with his fiancée, Daisy, his arm draped casually around her shoulders. Dale would take over the station one day, but there was no arrogance or entitlement in the man's demeanor. Indeed, from the short time Mack had known him, Dale was generous and hard-working. The couple were due to be married in less than a month, and Daisy struck him as the most laid-back bride-to-be he'd ever encountered. She was a dark-haired beauty, reminding him a little of Bindi, and she met his eyes with a searching gaze, as if there was a wisdom there beyond her years.

Dale had recently been made leading hand at Stormcloud after Wazza had moved on, and now he was marrying this gorgeous woman. As an added bonus, Steve was building the couple a cabin on the property as a wedding present. Construction was due to start right around the time of the wedding, in a secluded spot some distance around the side of the escarpment. Close enough for Dale to get to work in a hurry if he was needed, but far enough away that they had their privacy. Mack didn't envy the guy, he was a true believer that everyone walked their own paths, but he certainly seemed to have it all together. The perfect life.

Farther down the table, Skylar, the lady with the amazing chef skills and her beau, Nash, also sat with their blond heads together, but when he asked Skylar something, she answered him with a dazzling smile that lit up the room, then leaned in and kissed Nash on the mouth, in an open show of affection. Supposedly, they owned a hobby farm down the road a way, and there was a rumor in the air—he'd overheard Sasha talking to Alek this morning—that these two would be the next to tie the knot.

Then there were Julie and Aaron. Julie was Steve's only daughter and had moved to the station not long ago, supposedly to get away from the city. Every family had a comedian, and it seemed this family's was Julie. The few times Mack had seen her, she was always telling jokes and flitting happily in and out of rooms, like a bright butterfly. Aaron was also a newcomer to the station. Big, broad and taciturn, nevertheless his eyes lit up whenever Julie was around, losing that wary edge. Like right now, Julie let out a peal of laughter at something Daisy had said and then fell against Aaron's side in a fit of giggles. He nudged the top of her head with his chin and gave a soft smile. It seemed that love was definitely in the air at Stormcloud. Which was a good thing. This place was filled with strong couples who'd make sure this station endured and flourished.

Daniella got up and announced they'd be serving after-dinner drinks out on the veranda for those guests who'd like to join them. Alek, the Polish activities manager, who Mack thought had taken a bit of dislike to him as he seemed to think he was the only ladies' man around here—had jumped up and gone to arrange some board games for the guests who wanted to join in. Mack wasn't worried about Alek, he'd come around in the end. Anyone with half a brain could see Alek was keen on Sasha, and while the lady was pretty, she wasn't his type. When he looked at Sasha, there was no chemistry. Unlike when he looked at Bindi. Her striking, dark-eyed gaze had his blood turning to molten lava in his veins. But he wasn't here to fall in love. Get through this half-year as best he could. Get back into bull riding if possible. And get back to Montana and into next year's pro circuit. Those were his goals. His dreams. His ambitions.

"So, Mack, I hear you're pretty good at riding those bulls." Steve's words jerked Mack from his musings. Was the guy a mind reader? Most of the staff had remained seated as the guests left the table to move to the verandah. Steve sat on the opposite side of the table, a little farther down, flanked by Dale and Daisy, to his left.

"Yeah," Mack drawled, keeping his surprise under wraps. "I'm not too bad." He sat back farther in his chair.

Steve made an amused sound. "I think it's more than that. Dean tells me you made it into the top rankings a few years running. That's pretty impressive."

Conversation continued to buzz around the table, but Mack was aware of other people tuning into what Steve was saying. Dale raised his head to fasten a curious gaze on him, as did Bindi, who was seated closer to Skylar and Nash.

Mack lifted a shoulder in a shrug. "I was in the top ten two years running," he admitted. And if it hadn't been for the accident, he might well have been standing as number one on the podium last year. But Mack let none of the bitterness show on his face.

Steve speared him with his indigo gaze. "Dean also said you'd be keen to give the Aussie circuit a whirl."

"That I would, sir," Mack said with a grin, carefully avoiding looking at Bindi, who had suddenly narrowed her eyes at him. Shit, he hoped she stuck to her promise not to mention his little episode this afternoon up at the stables.

"Our rodeo season normally runs from April to November, during the dry season," Steve added.

Mack had heard something along those lines, as well, and so he nodded in agreement. He'd put his plans on hold, not expecting to be able to ride until next year. Which had him champing at the bit, but there wasn't a lot he could do about it.

"But you might be in luck. I heard the Cairns rodeo was postponed this year because of a Covid outbreak amongst the riders. They've rescheduled it for the first weekend in December, assuming the weather stays dry. Are you interested?"

Was he interested? It was like all his prayers had been answered at once. "Hell, yes." Then he realized what he'd said. "Sorry about the cussing, sir, ma'am," he said in a hurry, tipping his head in Daniella's direction. But she wasn't listening, she was directing guests to the best chairs outside and chivvying Alek to hurry setting out the games. Mack was still studiously evading Bindi's gaze, but he could feel her hot stare boring into the side of his head.

His mind was already churning with ideas and plans. He'd driven through Cairns on his way up to the station, and it was less than two hours away. Depending on the rodeo schedule, he'd probably need to stay overnight, as most of the bull riding took place in the evening; it was the main event and people wanted a good show. Would Steve even give him the weekend off? He was the new recruit, and he wouldn't be due any leave just yet.

"Come and have a chat with me later," Steve said, breaking into his thoughts. "We can look up the program on the internet and talk logistics."

"Yes, sir." That sounded promising. It sounded like Steve was going to let him go.

"Oh, and, Mack," Steve stood, but then loomed over the table, glowering at him.

"Yes, sir?"

"Stop calling me sir. I'm just Steve. Okay?"

"Oh. Yes, sir—Steve," he hurriedly corrected himself. That might take a little getting used to. Mack had been brought up to respect his seniors. Hell, he still called his father, sir. But if that's what Steve wanted, then that's what he'd get. They did seem to be a lot more relaxed here in Queensland.

The rest of the staff still seated at the table seemed to take Steve's departure as a signal to get up and leave, as well. Chairs scraped on the flagstone floor and the conversation got louder.

Bindi brushed by his chair and whispered, "We need to talk," as she picked up his plate.

He'd almost forgotten about her in his excitement at perhaps getting a ride on his first bull since the accident.

"Let me give you a hand," Mack said, loudly enough for everyone to hear. He stood and began collecting plates from the table.

"Thank you." She picked up one last plate, and he trailed her toward the kitchen.

The kitchen was empty, as he followed Bindi's lead and placed his stack of plates on the countertop.

Bindi rounded on him as soon as his hands were empty. "You can't possibly be considering riding a bull at the moment." She looked at him like he belonged in the loony bin. Which perhaps he did. But he wasn't passing up this opportunity.

"Why not?" he asked nonchalantly.

"Because of what I witnessed in the tack room today. That's why not."

Mack waved his hand as if shooing away a pesky fly. "That? That was nothing. I'll be fine. It was just a touch of jet lag."

"You were not fine," she said, hands going to her hips, eyes sparking fire. He liked her like this, all hot and volatile. The fire in her eyes was reflected in the sparkle of her cute nose ring. "And what if you get dizzy while you're on top of the bull?" she continued, distracting him from staring at her face.

"It's not going to happen. I am completely focussed when I'm riding a bull. Nothing gets to me." It was true. It was almost like he went into a Zen state when he mounted a bull. Nothing around him mattered. His focus zeroed in until it was just him and the bull. Maybe it was the adrenaline, or the competitive edge, the need to win at all costs.

"You told me yourself that you can't control this thing." Her voice took on a high-pitched squeak, and Mack suddenly hoped no one else could hear them. "And you still haven't told me exactly what's wrong with you. You promised, remember? I know it's not jet lag," she growled.

"Yes, I remember. And I will. But I haven't had a chance to get you alone since this afternoon."

Her hands still rested on her luscious hips, but some of the heat seemed to go out of her eyes. "I can't believe you can be so blasé about this whole thing. Your health could be at risk. What if something happened to you and you're all alone in Cairns? With no one who knows what's wrong with you?"

"Well, why don't you come with me? If you're so worried about my health." The words were out of his mouth before he knew what he was saying.

"I'm not going to the rodeo with you," she hissed. "You

need to—"

"Why not?" Skylar rounded into the kitchen, carrying a handful of wine glasses. "You're long overdue for a break, Bindi. I think that's a great idea."

Bindi spluttered, as if she couldn't quite believe what Skylar was saying.

"It's only two days. I can cope without you for that long. The resort is winding down now anyway, we're not as full as we usually are, because we're getting ready for the wedding," Skylar continued.

"Thanks, Skylar, but..." Mack could see Bindi's brain was spinning with excuses as to why she couldn't go.

"Don't you think it'd be a great idea for Bindi to go to the rodeo with Mack, Dad?" Skylar spoke over the top of Bindi's head and Mack turned to see Steve enter the kitchen.

"I don't see why not." Steve sauntered into the kitchen, followed closely by Daniella. "I can't remember the last time you took a break," he added, frowning slightly at Bindi.

"Oh, that's fine, I don't need a break, really—"

"I agree," Daniella stated, interrupting Bindi. "As long as you don't mind, Mack?" She speared him with her perceptive gaze. If he didn't know any better, he might think there was something else going on here.

Mack had been ambivalent at first, but the idea was growing on him. He didn't need anyone to go with him, he'd always been quite capable of doing things on his own. But it sounded like Bindi hadn't had a holiday in a long time, it might do her good to get out and about. If he won, well, then he'd have someone to celebrate with. And even though he hated to admit it, he liked Bindi. It wouldn't hurt to get to know her better.

"Sure, I'd love for Bindi to come with me. She can show me the ropes," Mack replied easily. They might think that an Aussie rodeo was different from what he was used to, but at the heart of it, most bull riding comps were the same. Well, the basics were, at least. You stuck on your allotted bull for the full eight seconds, and as long as you did it with style, you were a winner. But if Bindi was there to help him navigate the cultural differences, then that was fine by him, too.

Bindi still hadn't closed her mouth since Daniella had interrupted her, and she looked from Mack, to Skylar, to Steve, bewilderment on her face.

"Good. Glad that's decided," Skylar said, giving Bindi's shoulder a friendly pat as she walked past into the hallway. But the quick look Skylar shot at Mack from beneath lowered lashes made him sure she was up to something. Was she playing matchmaker? Well, he'd be damned if he was going to be a sucker for her plans.

Bindi glared at Skylar's retreating back. Then she turned her irate gaze on him, and he got the distinct impression she wasn't happy with the turn of events. He didn't think she outright disliked him, but he was getting the vibe that she didn't approve of him. Even though he was attracted to Bindi, and even though he liked a woman who provided a challenge, he didn't need any complications in his life right now.

He let out a quiet sigh. What sort of mess had he got himself into?

CHAPTER FIVE

Bindi was seething inside. But she let none of her disquiet show. How had she just been railroaded into going to a rodeo with Mack? She still wasn't quite sure how it'd happened. Steve and Daniella had taken seats at the kitchen counter, and Daniella was showing her husband something on her iPad. Skylar had disappeared back into the great room, but she'd return soon enough.

And Mack was just standing there with that grin on his face. She wanted to smack him. How could he have agreed so readily to take her with him? They needed to talk, preferably somewhere private. She needed to get to the bottom of these dizzy spells. Perhaps they were harmless. And maybe he was correct, they posed no impediment to him riding a bull. Just the thought of it made her shudder. She'd been to plenty of rodeos in her time, but she usually avoided the bucking bulls. Too much sweat and blood and tears. And danger.

"Come with me." She beckoned him with her little finger.

"Yes, ma'am." That cheeky grin got wider.

"Don't call me that," she growled. "I don't like it."

Mack didn't answer her this time, and she didn't turn around to gauge his reaction.

Where could they go where they wouldn't be interrupted?

She had an idea this might take a while. The staff quarters had a common room, but Sasha or Alek could walk in on them there. Down by the billabong would be quiet, but they might be spotted by Daniella if she came out to the veranda to see if the guests needed anything. It'd have to be the stables. Steve normally went up there to check on the horses before he went to bed, but that'd be an hour or more from now. The stables were her safe place; the horses a balm to her soul. She often went up there to converse with them when no one was watching.

She stalked up the hill in the dark, only the sound of Mack's silver-toed boots on the gravel behind her telling her he was following.

They reached the holding yards without speaking. Bindi turned around to face Mack, but he was a mere shadowy presence in the dim night. A light was on in the tack room, but its glow barely reached this far outside. Shit. She hadn't really thought this through properly. What was she doing bringing a man she hardly knew up here to be alone with him? In the dark. She took a step away and unconsciously wrapped her hand around her shoulder, covering the scar she knew lurked below her sleeve.

No. This was Stormcloud. She was safe here. And even if this man was practically a stranger, he wasn't Kai. Even if he reminded her of him. She was safe. She had to keep reminding herself of that.

"Right. Spill it," she demanded, hoping her voice didn't have the edge of nervousness that was turning her stomach to jelly, leaning her shoulder against the fence in a show of nonchalance.

Mack gave a deep sigh and mirrored her move, leaning against the fence, but thankfully keeping his distance.

"I'm pretty sure what you saw today was a one-off. It won't happen again. I haven't had an episode like that for months now," Mack said into the darkness between them.

He wasn't making much sense. "You're talking in riddles. Just tell me what happened."

Sahara came up and poked her muzzle through the gap in the fence, hoping Bindi might have brought her a tasty morsel. She let the mare lip her fingers gently, but didn't take her focus from the man in front of her.

"Well?" she demanded, when he still didn't answer.

He drew in a deep breath and reached over the railing to pat Sahara's neck. "It was the third-last meet on the calendar. I was at a rodeo in southern Texas. Sitting at six-hundred and eighteen points. If I won this one, I was guaranteed a top seven spot, with a good crack at becoming world champion. I'd drawn Nightmare as my bull."

"There's a bull called Nightmare?" Bindi couldn't help herself.

He chuckled. "Yes, and he lived up to his name that night. He was my worst nightmare. My bull rope slipped, and I lost my grip. He bucked me off into the fence."

"Oh. God." A cold shiver ran down her spine, her laughter dying in an instant. "Were you hurt badly?"

"I guess you could say that. My right femur was broken in two places where the big brute stepped on me, and my skull was fractured when I hit the fence. I spent two days in an induced coma."

"Oh, no," Bindi whispered. She couldn't find the words. What a terrible thing to have happened. She could barely imagine this vibrant, gregarious guy in a coma. He was so full of life. He didn't deserve that sort of fate.

"But that was two years ago. I've recovered now. The doctors say I'm as good as new. I wanted to get back onto the PBR circuit, but no bastard would sponsor me. I blame Clarissa." The last part was said in such a low voice, Bindi hardly caught it. Who was Clarissa? A friend? A girlfriend?

What was he implying? He'd nearly died, and all he wanted to do was get back out there? She'd never understand men. And this man in particular seemed especially crazy.

"So, the dizzy spells…they're what? An effect of the brain injury?"

She saw him grimace in the half-light. "Brain injury is such a definitive term. I don't like to classify—"

She gave a snort of contempt. What else was a fractured skull and two days spent in a coma, if it wasn't a brain injury? This man was suffering a severe case of denial.

"But, yes, the dizziness and the headaches are an aftereffect of the knock to my head," he went on in a rush, perhaps sensing she was about to unload on him again. "And like I said, they were getting better. I *was* better."

His gaze fixed on hers, imploring. He may be in denial, but there was something else going on here, too. Something more than mere ego and a desire to win at all costs. It was almost as if his version of self-worth was wrapped up in being able to ride a damn bull.

"Does Steve know any of this?" she asked wearily. But it was a question Bindi needed answered. Because her boss may not realize he'd taken on such a liability. Was it her responsibility to tell him if he didn't? Oh, God, she didn't know.

"You ask a lot of questions," he said, taking a step closer, resting his hand on the top railing, right above her head.

"And you need to answer them. If you want me to keep your secret, then I need to have all the details." She was *not* going to let him distract her by moving nearer.

"Fair enough." He took another step closer, so he was looking down at her. She kept her eyes level with his chest, refusing to look up. Even though the air seemed to crackle in the space between them.

"Dean told Steve that I had a fall and broke my leg, but it's mended now. Also, Dean knows about the coma, but he doesn't know the extent of my...headaches. Dean never asked, and I never told him. Perhaps he's extending me a professional courtesy. In my world, you don't ask if a guy can handle his problems, you trust that he's doing the best that he can, and leave it at that."

"Yeah, well, in my world, they call that stupid arrogance," Bindi huffed. This conversation was going nowhere fast.

And his nearness was turning her traitorous mind to other thoughts. Amorous thoughts. The kind where he leaned down and captured her lips. The kind where she tangled her fingers in the hair at the back of his neck to pull him closer. The kind of thoughts she hadn't had in a long time.

She tipped her head back to look at him. But that was a mistake, because she was suddenly trapped by his stare. Eyes lit by the faint glow from the tack room, she could see the smoky shine of hunger in them. He'd never hidden the fact that he appreciated how she looked. He definitely flirted with her every chance he got. But this was more. Dangerous. Almost predatory. And God help her, she knew she should look away, so he didn't see the same hunger reflected in her gaze. But she was trapped. His mouth curved up in a sexy smile, and she knew he'd figured out she was attracted to him, too. More than attracted. It was like a carnal pull she had no resistance to.

Sahara's head poked back through the railings, looking for attention, filling the space between them. The horse broke their laser-like connection, and Bindi took a step backward, as if released from some physical restraint. Her breath was coming fast, and her heart was beating erratically.

"I'll keep your secrets, for now," she said, turning on her heel. She needed to get away from Mack. He could find his own way back to the staff quarters.

"Thank you," he called after her. But he was wise enough

not to follow her down the hill. Which was a good thing, because she was walking so fast, she was almost running.

* * *

"I think Mack is hot. Don't you think he's hot?" Skylar straightened from where she'd been peering into the oven, and cocked her head toward Bindi.

Bindi merely rolled her eyes and continued mixing the cake batter.

When Bindi didn't answer, Sasha piped up from her spot at the other end of the countertop. "Yeah, he certainly looks fine in his black jeans. And those eyes…Oh. My. God. He has the most come-to-bed smolder I've ever seen on a guy," Sasha was helping the two of them sort through a pile of Skylar's best recipes, trying to find the perfect wedding cake for Dale and Daisy's big day.

But Bindi was beginning to doubt Sasha's motive for joining them in the kitchen. What the hell were these two up to? Was this some kind of ambush? Bindi didn't like the idea they were trying to matchmake her to the American cowboy.

"Don't you think, Bindi?" Sasha asked sweetly.

"Not really," Bindi replied, keeping her focus on the batter as she spooned it into the cake tin.

"Oh, really?" Skylar said. "That's a shame. You could really have some fun this weekend in Cairns with him. But, I guess if you're not into him…"

"I'm not into him," Bindi replied, trying to hide the fact she was grinding her teeth. She was only going to the rodeo under duress, and she wanted to make sure everyone knew it. Steve had asked her to go to show him the way and introduce him to Cairns and the people of the top end, and she was doing it to please Steve, that was all.

But after her chat with Mack last night, she also understood the full extent of his injuries, something Steve wasn't privy to. At least Steve's instinct had been right, someone needed to be there to look after him, but not only in the ways Steve envisaged. Bindi felt compelled to go, to make sure he survived his first encounter with a bull after his accident. What if he suffered another episode while he was up on the bull? She hated feeling like she was somehow responsible for Mack's physical wellbeing. Hated feeling like the responsibility had been thrust upon her without her agreement. But then, she *had* been stupid enough to ask for the truth, and now she knew the truth, she couldn't put that genie back in the bottle. She'd gone over and over the reasons she shouldn't go to Cairns all morning in her head. And she kept coming up with the same solution to the argument. Logically, her head told her Mack was old enough to look after himself. But the completely irrational side of her, the one where her feelings overruled her head, was nagging that she'd never forgive herself if he got hurt and she wasn't there to help. God, why did she have to get sucked into other people's problems all the time? She was such an idiot.

Looking up, she noticed both of the other women were staring at her. "If you think he's that hot, why don't you go for him?" Bindi said to Sasha, and then immediately regretted her outburst. Sasha frowned and looked down at her pile of papers. Everyone knew Sasha was keen on Alek. Everyone but Alek, that was. He was either as blind as a bat, or too chicken to act, because it was obvious Sasha would jump into his arms, if he could only get up the courage to ask her.

She sighed and picked up the bowl. Mack had only been here three days, and he was already driving her insane. There was no need for her to take out her exasperation on Sasha. "Have you found anything suitable for a wedding cake?" she asked, hoping to change the subject.

"Yes, I've found a couple that might work." Sasha picked up the journal and flashed it in Bindi's direction.

"We'll come and look," Skylar said, waving at Bindi to

hurry.

The cake tin was full, and Bindi scraped down the edges of the mixing bowl, putting the last dregs into the tin. Then she handed it to Skylar, who put it in the oven. The passionfruit-and-fig cake was for Julie and Steve to take out for smoko this afternoon; with most of the fresh ingredients homegrown, of course. They were taking a group of guests over to North Paddock to check the health of the cattle, as well as the level of feed. Steve was thinking of moving the herd soon to spell the pasture. If the cattle were allowed to stay too long in one place, they'd eat everything in sight, killing a lot of the annuals and perennials, and the paddock could take years to recover. Steve liked to rotate his cattle and keep some paddocks free for at least a season. It was one of the reasons Stormcloud ran less stock. Because Steve wanted to keep his pastures healthy, and encourage the wild species to flourish, not denude the plains completely, like some of the lesser-informed pastoralists were wont to do. Bindi was keen to learn as much as she could from Steve about living and farming on this land while having as small an impact as possible. One day, she might even buy her own little piece of land, and when she did, she wanted to run it as sustainably as possible. She'd been saving up, building up a little nest egg for herself. Whether she bought that land in Queensland or back in her home country of New Zealand, was still an undecided issue.

Bindi and Skylar each took up a position, flanking Sasha as all three stared at the recipe book. This was Skylar's holy grail. A collection of her favorite recipes she'd accumulated over the past ten years, most of them using native bush foods.

"How about this one?" Sasha turned to the page she was marking with her thumb. "Macadamia nut and finger lime cake with burnt butter."

"Mm, that one is lovely and moist," Skylar murmured.

"We could do three layers and cover it in a rustic white icing with native wildflowers on each tier."

"Nice," Bindi agreed.

"Or this one." Bindi licked her finger and turned the pages to reveal a delicious-looking pavlova. "Lemon myrtle meringue with mango and macadamia nuts," Sasha sighed. "This one looks amazing."

"It is good," Skylar agreed. "But it might be a little tricky to serve. Especially if it turns out to be a scorcher that day."

Bindi agreed. The wedding was in three weeks, a few days before Christmas. Dale and Daisy had purposefully set it at the beginning of the wet season, because Stormcloud always shut down over that period. It was usually too wet to do much else, and flooding often hindered travel, so guests found it harder to get in and out of the station. They also needed the time to rest and recuperate, along with the countryside. And wet season was also incredibly hot and humid. Skylar was right, a cake based on egg whites and cream might not fare so well.

"Okay. Well, what about this one?" Sasha turned all the way to the back of the book. "A bush fruit Christmas cake. It uses quandongs and ground pepper berries, with toasted wattleseeds."

Skylar raised a speculative eyebrow, her blue eyes sparkling. "I think you found it, Sasha. This is perfect. We can cover it in a more traditional white royal icing and have it dripping in wildflowers. It'll survive the heat better than any other cake, too. I think Daisy will love it." Skylar sounded excited. "I'm going to start gathering the ingredients today. I'd like to make a sample for Daisy to taste before we commit. Dale loves anything I cook, so he's easy." Skylar waved her hand in the air as if her brother were an afterthought in this whole wedding bonanza.

"He'd be eternally delighted if his cake was made of a pile

of your pumpkin and wattleseed scones," Bindi joked, and they all laughed. Everyone at Stormcloud knew how much Dale loved his sister's scones. Loved everything Skylar made, if the truth be told. But he seemed to have an uncanny knack of smelling if there were scones in the oven from miles away. He'd been known to sneak into the kitchen when he was supposed to be out working and snaffle the hot scones straight off the baking trays while Skylar's back was turned.

Almost as if he'd been summoned, Dale suddenly appeared in the doorway leading off the hallway.

"Did I hear someone mention my favorite food?" The corners of his mouth turned up in a hopeful smile.

"Sorry, bro," Skylar replied. "Not today."

Mack appeared in the doorway behind Dale, and Bindi didn't hear the rest of what Skylar had to say. She hadn't seen Mack since last night at the stables. After he'd told her the truth about his accident. After...whatever it was had passed between them. She wasn't prepared to say it was almost a kiss, because it wasn't. By the time she'd reached her room, her heart rate had slowed, and she'd almost been prepared to believe she'd been carried away by her stupid imagination. She was just tired and overwrought by Mack's surprisingly harrowing story. That was all. Once she was safely tucked in bed, she could easily dismiss her feelings as misplaced and juvenile.

But one look at Mack standing there, hands on hip, smiling that wicked smile, and her disloyal heart was galloping a million miles an hour again. There was nothing juvenile about the images that were playing through her mind right now. On purpose, she turned her back and pretended to be busy at the sink. But she tuned back into the conversation, none-the-less.

"What have you got for smoko, then?" Dale asked. "I'm taking Mack out to help me fix a cracked concrete slab beneath the water trough out in the Portico's Paddock. We need something to keep our strength up."

"I've got leftover muffins from this morning," Skylar said. "Or I can get you some banana bread out of the freezer."

"We'll take the banana bread," Dale replied, after a second weighing up his options.

"Right, then." Skylar bustled around the kitchen getting smoko ready and chatting to Dale about the wedding cake they were thinking of making.

Suddenly, there was a voice at Bindi's shoulder. Mack had snuck up next to her without her noticing, and she jumped, almost dropping the plate she was washing.

"Afternoon," he said in that low drawl that turned her spine to liquid.

"Hi," she replied, pleased to hear her voice come out normal.

"Steve's given me…us…the go-ahead to take off to this rodeo the day after tomorrow. Are you still coming?"

Now was her chance to back out. She screwed up her mouth in a grimace, but the words wouldn't come. She was committed to this venture, whether she liked it or not. Bindi didn't trust herself to answer, so she nodded her agreement, scrubbing at a particularly tough stain on the plate.

"Good." He leaned in a little closer, and Bindi got a faint whiff of his cologne mixed with dust and horse sweat from his day's work. It was delicious. She held her breath, denying that her traitorous mind had even gone that far. "I want to leave early, so I can check out the lay of the land, get my bearings before the ride. Can you be ready by six?"

Six am? That was ridiculously early, especially since seeing the main event wouldn't take place until around seven that night. "Sure," was all she said. He must really have meant it when he said he wanted to get the lay of the land. She glanced up and could see he was deadly serious. A small voice told her that maybe she'd misjudged him. He might have a cavalier attitude when it came to his health, but when it came to riding a bull, he wanted to get it right.

Her gaze locked with his, and for a second she was lost in their tawny depths. Were those flecks of gold she could see scattered through his irises? She leaned in closer to get a better look. Mack's hot breath flowed over her cheek and her eyes drifted down to his lips. A firm, strong, top lip dusted with a scattering of two-day growth, quirking upward with a knowing smile.

"Mack, you coming?" Dale's voice cut through the kitchen.

Bindi jumped, dropping the plate into the water. Shit. What *had* she been doing? Out of the corner of her eye, she saw Mack nod in assent to Dale.

"See you ladies tonight," Mack said, and he was gone from her side.

She didn't dare turn around, instead fishing the plate out of the sudsy water.

"See you," Skylar and Sasha chorused, and belatedly, Bindi joined them.

Had anyone seen her strange interaction with Mack? She hoped they'd all been busy getting smoko ready.

Fleetingly, she closed her eyes. When she opened them and turned around, Sasha was smirking at her.

Oh, yeah, they'd seen it all right.

What was she going to do? She didn't want to be attracted to Mack. Hell, she didn't even think she liked him. She'd never been this confused about her feelings for a man in her life before. It was high time she got herself under control and stopped this silly infatuation.

CHAPTER SIX

Mack backed his truck into the parking spot and turned off the engine. He drew in a deep breath, filling his lungs with all the familiar rodeo smells coming through his open window. Dust rose in a halo around them from the dirt parking lot on the outskirts of the fairground. Cars lined up for as far as the eye could see. This was clearly a big-ticket event in this part of the world. A man in an Akubra—he'd learned that's what they called the cowboy hats here—and chaps strolled by, leading a black horse. Judging by the deep Western saddle and the decorative breast collar, the horse and man were possibly off to partake in the barrel racing, which was due to start in half an hour.

Farther down the line of vehicles, a woman coaxed her horse down a float ramp; the gelding flighty and nervous, reared twice before she got him under control. He saw a couple of kids in the distance, each sucking on a cloud of bright-pink cotton candy. The roar of an enraged bull sounded somewhere in the distance, probably one of the bronco bulls being loaded into the yards for tonight. The bull ring would be in the centre of the fairground, it always took pride of place, no matter how big or small the rodeo was. And that was where he needed to be.

God, he'd missed this.

"Are we getting out?" Bindi's voice beside him made him jump. He'd been so absorbed by being back at a rodeo, he'd forgotten she was there for a second.

"Yeah," he drawled. "Just getting my bearings, that's all."

"Right." Bindi flashed a dark-eyed glance his way, and he suddenly wanted to know what she was thinking. He wasn't afraid to get back on a bull, if that's what she thought. This was something he'd been looking forward to for two long years. "Where shall we start?" She unbuckled her seat belt and opened her door, waiting for him to do the same.

The two-hour drive to Cairns had been an uneventful one. Bindi had been waiting for him in the staff common room at six am on the dot. Most of the staff were already up and about, or soon would be. She'd climbed into the passenger seat without so much as a word. Every time he tried to start a conversation, she'd answered in monosyllables, unless it was a question about which direction to take next. Like she was intentionally shutting him down. After a few attempts to find out more about her, Mack had also descended into silence. It was fine by him if she didn't want to talk, he could concentrate on thinking about his ride tonight. But that hadn't stopped his gaze from straying sideways to take in her trim legs, encased in tight-fitting, blue denim, or wandering up to where the slight swell of her breasts were visible in lower-than-normal cut of her white, V-neck shirt which bared her smooth, brown shoulders, showing a hint of that scar. Bindi was one appealing woman. It was a pity she was giving off all those don't-touch-me vibes. On another day, he might well have taken up that challenge and hit her with the full wattage of his Diaz charm. But he was here to ride a bull tonight, and so he didn't take her standoffishness as the challenge he might normally have.

This time, he'd paid more attention to the passing

countryside than he had on the way out to Stormcloud. He saw it through slightly different eyes, now that he'd ridden through it on horseback and experienced it firsthand. The flat plains stretched out all around them were dry and dusty, waiting for the rains he'd been told would come soon to spring everything to life again. But as they'd approached Cairns, the road sloped upward, taking them over a low mountain range, and it was almost like they'd crossed the threshold into a completely different land. On one side of the range, the trees were spindly and brown, although becoming denser, with more undergrowth. Then, all of a sudden, they were running down the other side, crossing a bridge, and the vegetation turned to jungle before his eyes, crowding in on the road, lush and bright green. When he'd driven through Cairns on his way to Stormcloud, he'd been vaguely aware that the town was set in the tropics, but now that he drove with clear eyes, this place was more like paradise, reminding him of his short holiday to Hawaii one time. How could these two places exist almost side by side? Stormcloud with all its red dirt and withered, brown grass, and this coastal rain forest, so rich and verdant?

"Do you want to check out any of the agricultural events?" Bindi turned to look at him hopefully, breaking his contemplations. Her hair was up in a loose ponytail today, instead of the more functional long plait he was used to. It suited her, softened her exotic features, made her seem younger and more vulnerable. Her nose stud sparkled in the morning sun, drawing his gaze. "I wouldn't mind taking a look at the woodcutting," she added. The faint sound of axes pounding into a block of wood drifted on the breeze, somewhere over to the left, near the main entrance, which they'd passed by on their way to find a park.

But he had only one thing on his mind. "I'd really like to look at the arena. Get acquainted with some of the bulls." He was at a severe disadvantage coming to this meet. He was completely unfamiliar with any of the bulls, didn't know which ones had the big reputations and which ones were considered the easy rides, like he would've if he'd been back on the PBR circuit in the US. He recognized a couple of the names of his other competitors on the list, but only because they'd come over to try their luck on the Aussie circuit when they'd crashed out in America.

When Mack had called the event coordinator to see if there were any spots on the list for a latecomer, the guy on the other end of the phone hadn't hidden his surprise. They never normally got new riders once the season started, and definitely not this late in the draw. Mack had explained that he'd be joining the list properly next season, but wanted to try his hand while he had the chance, blow out some cobwebs and show the top runners a thing or two about style and stamina. His tongue-in-cheek arrogance had the desired effect, and the man had told him to come on down to Cairns, as there was a bull with his name on it, just waiting for him. He didn't mention that he probably wouldn't stay on to see out the whole season. But you never knew, if he did well in the early events, maybe he might stay the whole twelve months, like Dean wanted.

With all the odds stacked against him, he did have one thing going in his favor; he was pretty much a complete unknown on this circuit, which might work to his advantage. They wouldn't see him coming until it was too late. He'd never admit it to any other living soul, but he was aiming for top prize tonight. If he'd said that to any of his brothers, or even his father, they would've laughed him out of town. And they might be right. Mack hadn't ridden competitively in two years. What on earth made him think he could just jump on the back of a bull and take up right where he left off? But Mack had a feeling. A good feeling that things were going to go his way tonight.

"No problem, it's this way." Bindi jumped out of the car, placed her hat on her head, and gave him a flat stare. For a split second, he considered changing his mind and asking to see the woodcutting, just to see that bright spark come back into her eyes. Just to spend some time with her, when she wasn't glowering at him. But that wasn't why he was here.

He locked his vehicle and followed Bindi as she weaved through the throng of tightly packed cars. The crowds increased as they got closer to the arena. Mack could feel the buzz in the air. The drone of an announcer's voice filled the air, as he called the start of the barrel races, and the crowd surged, eager to get a good view. A set of bleachers hugged one side of the metal barriers, and this was where most of the spectators were headed. He followed Bindi's tan Akubra and blue jeans through the throng of people, until they came up against the metal railings marking out the arena. She rested her chin on the top rail, and watched the horse and rider in the middle intently. Mack did the same, rising on the balls of his feet in anticipation, but instead of focussing on the action inside, he checked out the lay of the land. A row of tents and awnings adorned the opposite side of the arena behind the railings; this would be the food vendors and market stalls. Mack's gaze caught on the neat row of pens farther around to the left. The bull pens. A set of heavy, slab-sided metal gates guarded the entry to the pens, waiting for the command to be opened and let loose a whirlwind of angry bull.

Mack was also interested in the state of the ring. This would be where he'd ride later tonight. The ground would be well and truly churned up by earlier events like the barrel racing, and the bareback bronco riding, but that was a good thing, as it'd break up the earth and soften the landing. Not that he was going to fall, not tonight. The original soil looked to be some sort of sandy loam, which was also good, as it wouldn't pack down too hard. The organizers had then topped it with another few feet of fresh sand. It was a good-size ring, bigger than most he was used to in the US, which would give the clowns more room to maneuver, to direct the bull away from him if he did happen to land on his ass.

"I'm hungry," Bindi said. They hadn't had a proper breakfast before they left, he'd been in so much of a hurry, they'd only had time to stop past the kitchen and swipe a single muffin each. "Do you want to get something to eat?" She tipped back her hat and squinted her brown eyes against the bright sunshine.

After a moment's consideration, he replied, "Nope. I'll eat a little later. I'm going to introduce myself to some of the boys over there." He nodded in the direction of the bull pens to a group of men milling in the shade of a temporary tarpaulin. He thought he recognized Billy Scadden, who'd ridden in the PBR four years ago, then disappeared from the circuit. Perhaps it was time to go and announce his presence.

"Oh, right. Okay." Bindi tried, but didn't quite succeed in hiding the disappointment on her face.

Shit, why did he suddenly feel like the villain?

"How about we meet up back here for lunch? You can show me the best places to eat. Let's say midday?"

"Sure, whatever. I'm going to watch the woodcutting, see you later."

Mack wasn't sure exactly what Bindi had expected from this trip. Perhaps she thought he'd need her to hold his hand. Or perhaps she thought this was some kind of mini holiday. But neither of those things was true for him. He could see it in the way she narrowed her eyes at him, that she was still worried he might come down with another dizzy spell. But he was fine. Perfectly fine.

He watched Bindi turn and weave her way through the crowd, her neat curves swaying nicely in those tight, blue jeans. Then he noticed the appreciative glances some of the other men threw her way and something in his chest tightened. He almost called her back, changed his mind and told her he'd go with her. But she disappeared into the crush of humanity, and the moment was lost. He needed to keep reminding himself that he wasn't here for Bindi. He was here to ride.

Of its own accord, his gaze strayed in the direction Bindi had disappeared, and he cursed his own weakness.

* * *

Mack's pulse thrummed through him, and his breathing sounded like a mini tornado to his own ears. He was the twelfth rider in tonight's lineup, and next up to ride. He'd drawn a bull named Sugar Baby, but he had no idea whether the bull was ornery or not, as the name meant nothing to him.

He stood on the bottom rung at the back of the bullpen and observed the rider before him give the nod to open the gates. His heart rate accelerated as he watched the bull explode from the pen, launching himself many feet into the air. For a second Mack was astride that bull along with the other rider, feeling every twist, turn and jerk. His guts squeezed at the thought, and a spasm of vertigo threatened to overtake him. He suddenly felt ill and grappled for the top railing, as a memory of the fence rearing up and the sickening crack as his skull hit the wood, unfolded in his mind.

No.

He ground his teeth together, forcing his breathing to slow. He wasn't going to let this beat him. The first ride after the accident was always going to be a watershed for him, but he was determined to get this over with so he could move onward. And upwards.

Mack tuned the other rider out, tuned out the noise of the crowd and the announcer's tinny voice over the loudspeaker and focussed on what he knew. Something familiar. His final gear check before he mounted up. Gloves; he pushed down between each of his fingers, one after the other, making sure the gloves were as tight and firm as they could be. Chaps. To help him grip the bull's sides and safeguard the vulnerable skin of his inner thighs. Hat. Mack banged it harder onto his head. His mother would call him a fool for not wearing a helmet tonight, but it was what Mack was used to. Some of the guys wore helmets, but it wasn't compulsory. Mack knew he looked more the part with his black cowboy hat on. Protective vest. He yanked on the front to make sure the zipper was secure and slapped at the panels that shielded his ribs and lower torso. Mack had removed all the sponsorship badges from his vest, leaving glaring bare patches where they used to be. Clarissa had made sure that he'd lost all his sponsors after his accident. The bitch. She never admitted it, but it could only have been her. She had a vendetta against him, and did everything in her power to make him pay. But he couldn't let that worry him now. Soon enough, he'd garner more sponsors, maybe even after his ride tonight.

Fleetingly, he wondered if Bindi was sitting in the bleachers watching the meet, like she'd promised. It'd be nice to know she was there. Nice to know someone was rooting for him. Normally, he had any number of people calling his name, urging him on, stroking his pride. This was a whole new world, and he needed to remember that.

It was time. The announcer called his name, and the spotter beckoned him over the railing. Mack dropped all thoughts of Bindi and Clarissa and his family, and stepped up onto the wooden platform beside the bull pen, handing his bull rope to the spotter to fit underneath the bull's belly.

Then he was lowering himself over the bull's back and everything shifted, the boom of the announcer melted away, the voices of the guys around him in the chute became a buzz in the background. He locked those memories of his fall into an impenetrable safe in his mind, determined not to let them out until this was over. It was just him and the bull. This was what he knew. This was what he lived for. Mack raised his hand in the air and nodded. The chute flew open, and the crowd roared. Sugar Baby came out bucking, twisting his immense bulk in the air, then landed and spun, kicking out his hind feet.

Mack was pitched from side to side as the bull tried his best to rid the unwanted rider from his back. He was slightly taller than most bull riders; the short stocky ones had a lower center of gravity, but Mack knew how to stick on a bull, come hell or high water. And he wanted this one. Bad. Squeezing his thighs together, he counted the seconds in his head along with the announcer. *"Three. Four."*

All he had to do was stick on this beast for eight seconds. A tiny amount of time in the scheme of things. But eight seconds could have been eight thousand the way Sugar Baby bucked, jarring his arm almost out of its socket every time he landed.

"Come on, you sonofabitch, show me what you got," he ground out between clenched teeth, and dug his heels into the bull's muscular sides. As if the bull heard him, he doubled his efforts to dislodge him. *"Five. Six."* He was almost there. The bull pitched forward, and then dropped his hindquarters with a gut-wrenching jolt. *"Seven."* Mack's free hand whipped through the air, trying to regain his balance, but he could feel himself sliding, his left leg losing position.

Mack sailed through the air, managing to get his feet underneath him just in time. Clowns rushed in from all sides, distracting the bull while Mack made his escape. He hadn't heard the buzzer. Had he made the eight seconds? Leaping onto the bottom railing, he climbed the fence, searching for the scoreboard at the same time.

Yes. He let out a whoop of joy. He'd made the eight

seconds. But it wasn't all about timing. Points were awarded by two judges to the bull for its efforts as to how difficult he made it to stay on his back, as well as for the contestant's style. Even before his score had been posted, Mack knew he wasn't the winner. Sugar Baby had been ornery and big, but he wasn't the meanest bull by any means tonight. Other bulls had showed a much stronger bucking action. Add to that, Mack's lack of riding over the past two years, and he knew his style score would be lower than he was used to.

"Seventy-nine points," the announcer bellowed, and Mack let out a sigh of relief. Not enough to win, but it put him in fifth place on the winner's board, and he was okay with that. For now. It wasn't a bad start. "Not a bad score for this formerly unheard-of rider," the announcer continued. "My instinct tells me we haven't seen the last of Mack Diaz, not by a long shot."

Mack couldn't help the smile that crept over his face. He landed on the ground outside the bull pens, and a number of guys came up to congratulate him, Billy Scadden amongst them.

He'd been right, it was Billy he'd spotted with the crowd this morning. And Mack knew the exact second Billy recognized him as he'd approached the group. The man had a protruding nose and a thin mouth, which turned down in a grimace of distaste as he saw Mack coming. The emotion was a fleeting one, and he'd just as quickly extended his hand and painted a welcoming smile of surprise on his face, but Mack hadn't missed the look of dislike.

Billy smacked him on the back and said, "Great ride, dude." Mack knew he was only acting so magnanimous because Billy had come second tonight, with a score of eighty-eight points.

Mack wandered away from the well-wishers, floating on a cloud of euphoria. He'd done it. Conquered his demons and completed his first ride since the accident. He searched the crowd for Bindi's face, but he could see no sign of her. Shit, she hadn't watched him like she'd promised. Something cold settled in the pit of his stomach, bringing his feet back down to earth with a thump. He wanted to go and celebrate, but what was the point of celebrating on his own?

Perhaps she'd gone back to the car to wait for him. He needed to take his stuff back to his truck, anyway. He headed toward the parking lot. Everything looked a little different in the dark. Large spotlights had been erected atop tall poles to light everything from above, but there were still deep shadows in many places. The plan was for them to sleep in their swags next to the truck, and then head home tomorrow morning, after taking another wander around the fair. Mack had been surprised at Bindi's plan, he was used to crashing at a local hotel, but she'd said this was the way most people did it here in Oz. That was fine with him. Once she'd explained that a swag was an Aussie version of a bedroll crossed with a small tent, and she'd borrowed Dale's swag for him, Mack was almost looking forward to trying out this new challenge. Perhaps he could unroll his swag beside Bindi's. Who knew? He might even be able to persuade her to give him a kiss or two. Kissing Bindi might be a very nice distraction, indeed. Those full, lush lips would be sweet and soft against his.

Wending his way between the parked cars, his mind was so preoccupied with the exact tilt of Bindi's mouth, Mack didn't see the other guy until he almost barreled into him.

"Whoa, sorry, man." Mack had to tilt his head back to stare up at the other guy's face. Even in the dark, Mack could see he was huge. With massive shoulders, like a weightlifter, and a big, ten-gallon hat rammed on his head, keeping his features in shadow.

"You Mack Diaz?" the man barked.

Immediately, Mack's hackles rose at the tone in the other

man's voice. "Who wants to know?" he shot back.

"I got a message for ya." The big man leaned in closer. With cars on either side of him, Mack's only form of retreat was backward. But he wasn't frightened of this big goon.

"Oh, really," Mack drawled, feigning disinterest. "Well, I don't care for your tone, so if you'll just let me past—"

The man reached out and took hold of the front of Mack's protective vest in a vise-like grip. "You listen up, and you listen good," the man growled into his ear.

Mack bunched his fists at his side, ready to fight if he had to, searching the surrounding parking lot for help. But they seemed to be alone.

"Stay away from the circuit. You don't belong here. Don't ride again, or bad things will happen. Got it?"

What? Was this guy crazy? He was threatening him. But why?

"Who's the message from?" Mack demanded. "And what —"

"You don't get to ask no questions," the man growled back. "Just heed this warning, that's all."

The big guy turned to go, and Mack called after him, "Well, you can just tell your boss, or whoever, that you don't frighten me. I don't intend to stop riding. I'm going to get back in the ring and I'm going to win this Aussie circuit next year. Then I'm coming back to take the US championship, as well."

The man glanced back once, scowling, then disappeared between the cars, moving much more quickly than Mack might've guessed, given his bulk.

Mack stood in the parking lot, mind whirling. Who was trying to warn him off riding? And why? Surely, it couldn't be Clarissa. Could her reach extend all the way to Australia? How did she even know he was here? And why would she try to stop him from riding? Did her contempt of him run that deep? Did she despise him that much, that she'd try and stop him at any cost?

Clarissa was the CEO of her daddy's multi-billion-dollar company, Bettdorff, a very lucrative betting app Daddy had created a few years ago. The company was trying to break into the over-hyped sport of bull riding, by sponsoring riders. She'd seduced him with her sexy ways, and her offers of a large sponsorship, and tempted him into her bed more than once. He'd enjoyed her company, and enjoyed her wealth and influence. Enjoyed the extra money her sponsorship offered. Then, one night, she'd tried to subtly persuade him that it was in his best interest not to win the next round. She wanted him to cheat. To throw the contest, so her other sponsored rider took the honors, instead. There was a lot of money to be made by unscrupulous people betting on the outcome of each competition.

He'd refused to do it and torn up the contract, storming out of her office. That night, he'd had the accident and hadn't ridden again—until now. Mack had his theories that the accident wasn't really an accident, at all. But no one seemed to believe him.

Bringing his mind back to the present, he stared out at the parking lot, which was really just a large paddock set aside for the show every year. Where the hell was his truck? Standing on tiptoe, he tried to see over all the vehicles to find his Chevy. Problem was, all the cars were big, four-wheel-drives, and he was having a hard time pinpointing his location. When they'd parked this morning, it'd been in the second to last row, near a fence. Finally, he thought he saw the fence and made his way toward it.

Grumbling to himself, swearing he was going to find that big goon and let him know with his fists just how much he wasn't afraid of him, Mack wove between the cars, searching for his vehicle, unzipping his vest as he went, and adding it

Suzanne Cass

to the pile of gear in his hands.

He rounded the back of another car and there was his Chevy; his hunk of a black truck really did stand out in the crowd of white utes.

Two shadowy figures stood next to the rear wheel of his pickup. Was that Bindi? It sure looked like it. And who was the guy standing next to her? Surely, she hadn't hooked up with someone? He strode forward, ready to find out what she was up to.

Bindi raised her hand and slapped the man across the face, then screamed when the guy grabbed her by the throat and thrust her back against the car.

What the hell? He broke into a run.

CHAPTER SEVEN

Bindi struggled to breathe. Wrapping her fingers around the man's large hands, she tried ineffectually to pull them away from her throat, but he merely grunted and tightened his grip. Her mind struggled to make sense of the previous few minutes.

Bindi had been sitting in the bleachers, watching the bull riding, just as she'd promised Mack she would. It was everything she'd thought it would be, stressful, dangerous, and full of testosterone-filled men and their egos. But it was also nail-biting and thrilling, as everyone around her held their breath, watching as each rider was successful, or failed to make the eight seconds. It was even exciting waiting for Mack to mount up. They called his name and Bindi had sat higher in her seat, craning her neck. There he was, clambering up onto the platform.

Bindi's heart had plummeted as she watched him.

Mack wasn't wearing a helmet.

His black Stetson was pulled down over his forehead, so she could only just make out his eyes.

How could someone who'd already suffered a head injury be so reckless?

Admittedly, some of the other riders also only wore a

cowboy hat, but the majority so far had all been wearing protective headgear. Clearly, helmets weren't mandatory, otherwise all the riders would have them on, but surely Mack should be wearing one?

She'd been so gullible, she'd never even thought to ask him about it. She'd just assumed he'd be sensible. But she was fast finding out that Mack and sensible were two words that didn't go together. Part of the reason she'd come to Cairns with him was to make sure he wasn't alone, so that if he suffered another dizzy spell, she could be there for him. Now she just felt stupid and betrayed. Why should she worry about his health when he clearly didn't care a whit? He must really believe he was indestructible.

Her excitement faded, turning to fear, as a cold lump settled low in her belly. She didn't want to watch, but couldn't tear her gaze away. She held her breath as Mack's bull exploded from the chute and then watched as he was thrown about on the bull's back.

Amazingly, Mack made it to the full eight seconds, but Bindi didn't wait around to see him celebrate. She marched down the bleachers, anger clouding the edges of her vision. How could he be so foolish? They hadn't made any formal arrangement, but Mack would probably assume she'd go back to the bull pens to congratulate him. Well, that wasn't happening.

People milled out in front of the food stands, but Bindi was too angry to be swayed by the delicious smells, she just wanted to get out of there. Not sure what her next move should be, she headed toward Mack's truck. Perhaps she'd grab her swag and take it out under the line of trees beyond the parking lot. Find a nice spot where she could fall asleep under the stars. Because one thing was for sure: she didn't want to sleep anywhere near Mack Diaz tonight.

She was caught up with her own thoughts as she threaded

her way through the crowd on autopilot, head down and mind on other things, not noticing anything or anyone around her.

It wasn't until she was nearly back at the car that she heard footsteps behind her. Glancing back, she saw a large figure looming in the shadows. A man, tall and wide-shouldered. She quickened her steps. Someone was following her. No, that was crazy, there were people everywhere, he was probably on his way back to his own vehicle.

With a sigh of relief, she reached the front of Mack's black truck, but when she turned, the man was still there, getting closer. A frisson of ice slipped down her spine, but she told herself not to be an idiot. This man was probably looking for Mack. All she needed to do was tell this guy he was back at the bull pens, and she'd be fine. There were other people around. Somewhere. Although, she couldn't locate anyone nearby at this particular moment.

She held her ground and waited for the man to step closer.

Stopping less than a foot away from her, he tipped back his hat and Bindi gasped and covered her mouth with both hands. Even in the murky gleam cast by the irregular spotlights, she recognized his features. She stepped backward, but came up against the cold, metal panel of Mack's truck.

"I thought that was you," the man said, voice a deep baritone that sent shivers through her whole body, making the hairs on the back of her neck stand up. "Fancy meeting you here," he said with a menacing grin.

"Mutt!" She could barely utter the word as images of her brother's best friend assaulted her mind. The last time she'd seen him, he'd threatened to kill her for what she'd done to Kai. Did he still feel the same way? "What...what are you doing here?" she asked, hoping her voice sounded steadier than she felt. Mutt should be back in New Zealand. How had he come to be here? Was this just a terrible coincidence?

"I heard you was living near Cairns. I've always wanted to visit Australia. Thought I'd cross over the ditch and take a look for myself. Didn't have nothing else to do. Could hardly believe my good luck when I spotted you back there. It must be karma or somethin'."

His good luck was her bad luck. Because the last person she ever wanted to see was Mutt Waititi.

"Oh. Right." Bindi backed slowly away, down the side of the truck, but Mutt followed her. It was almost seven years since she'd seen him. He'd grown, got bigger and broader, if that was even possible. Surely he wasn't still holding a grudge?

"I haven't forgotten, if that's what you're thinking." Mutt followed her menacingly through the gap between the cars. A whiff of beer fumes met her nostrils. Mutt was drunk. That wasn't good. "Kai died because of you. And you got away with it, ran away to Australia, free as a bird."

She and Mutt had wildly differing points of view when it came to her brother's death. Kai had taken his own life, an intentional overdose when he found out he was going to jail for what he'd done to her. But Mutt blamed Bindi because she'd gone to the police. He'd said that blood should always be thicker than water. Mutt believed she'd forced Kai's hand, that he felt he had no other choice. And a tiny part of her agreed with him. But the rest of her knew she'd done the right thing. Even though Kai was her brother, he'd also been a monster.

"Kai made a choice," she ground out between gritted teeth. "He chose to take his own life rather than face his punishment like a man." Mutt had her backed right up against the rear bed of the truck, but she lifted her chin and stared at the big Maori man, ignoring the smell of liquor on his breath.

"No, you drove him to it, you little slut. You deserved everything, because you led him on, like the little slut that you are."

Anger flared through Bindi. Before she knew it, her hand flew up and slapped Mutt fair across the face. How dare he say that? Kai had been ten years older than her. He knew right from wrong. She'd trusted him; she'd been his innocent and vulnerable younger sister, looked up to him.

Mutt's big hands wrapped around her throat, taking her by surprise. "Don't underestimate me, little girl. I mean to make you pay for what you did to Kai."

She couldn't answer because he was squeezing her neck so tight she could no longer breathe. Panic kicked in, and she began to claw at his hands and face.

"Get off her." A figure darted out of the dark, latching onto Mutt's arm and wrenching him away. "Who the fuck do you think you are?"

Bindi doubled over, wheezing and coughing, dragging precious air into her screaming lungs. The two men were on the ground, rolling and scuffling. Mack had come to her aid, she'd recognized his voice. Even though Mack was quick and lithe, he'd be no match for Mutt's brute strength. He had a typical Maori build, tall, broad, and muscular, bigger than most men. And twice as heavy.

"Help," she wheezed, straightening up. Was anyone even around to hear her? "Help us," she shouted, louder this time. Loud grunts came from the two men, but they were in the shadows between the cars and it was too dark to see who was winning. It looked like Mutt had Mack in a headlock and was using his brute strength to hold him down. But Mack had got in a few good punches, and blood was flowing freely from Mutt's nose. Bindi tried to aim a kick at Mutt's stomach, but Mack kept getting in the way.

Feet thudded on the dusty ground as two men ran up.

"Help," she said, pointing to the two prize-fighters. "He's going to kill Mack if you don't do something."

"Hey, man, what are you doing?" It sounded like this guy knew Mutt. He reached into the fray and tried to pull him off Mack. But it took both of the newcomers to force the two men apart. Mutt lay on the ground, panting and swearing, while one of the men sat on his stomach to make sure he stayed put. Mack scrambled to his feet and stared down at the other two.

"You friends of this idiot?" Mack barked.

"Yeah. Sorry, mate." The one who'd first tried to break up the fight was blond, with a gap-toothed smile. Both the other men looked like city blokes, probably Cairns locals just here for the fun. "He's been hitting the grog pretty hard tonight. We were taking him back to the hotel when he said he saw someone he knew and disappeared all of a sudden."

Bindi wondered how they knew Mutt. How long had he even been in Australia? And was there truly something more sinister to his presence? Like he'd hinted.

"Sorry," the blond man turned to Bindi. "Whatever he did to you, he didn't mean it."

These guys clearly didn't have a clue who she was, or her history with Mutt.

"How are you? Did he hurt you?" Mack came over and tilted her face up, checking for injuries. His fingers were soft on her skin.

Her neck hurt where he'd squeezed her windpipe, and she'd probably have bruises to show for it in the morning. But otherwise, she was unharmed. Physically, at least. Emotionally, she was traumatized as her past came back to haunt her.

"Do you want to press charges?" Mack asked, his eyes never leaving Bindi's face.

She glanced down at Mutt. All the fight seemed to have left him now as he lay on the ground, still trying to get his breath.

"No. I just want him gone," she replied shakily.

"Take him somewhere he can sleep it off," Mack growled menacingly at the two men. "If I see him again, I'll call the cops."

Bindi fell against the side of the truck, her knees starting to wobble as she watched Mutt's two mates hoist him up between them and walk him off into the dark.

But just before they disappeared completely into the shadows, Mutt called back over his shoulder, "Don't think this is the end of it." His dire warning made her stomach clench and her heart race.

Mack took three strides after the trio before Bindi called him back. There was no point in Mack getting any more involved than he already was. She admired his bravado, but she just wanted Mutt out of her face.

As he turned back, she saw his shirt was hanging off his shoulders, where Mutt had almost ripped it to shreds. Mack tugged at the remains with a scornful grunt, and Bindi was suddenly exposed to his naked torso. Even in the shadowy light, Mack's muscular chest and well-defined abs made Bindi stare. Oh, my Lord. He was even more sexy than her imagination had allowed her to believe. She licked her lips, and a different kind of shake overtook her legs until she felt like she might collapse into a puddle of mixed emotions on the ground. For a split second, she was worried Mutt might've hurt Mack, but from what she could see, he seemed to be injury-free.

Mack's face was full of concern as he approached. "You're not okay, are you?" His strong arms wrapped around her, pulling her in close, offering comfort. No, she wasn't. Mutt's sudden appearance had left her feeling vulnerable and shaken. She'd already been feeling worked up after Mack's ride, and now she was doubly distraught.

But his closeness wasn't helping her state of mind. She

raised her hands to his bare shoulders to push him away, but instead found herself pulling him in closer. His bare chest brushed against her breasts, and she closed her eyes for a split second at the thrill she felt, even through the fabric of her shirt. For wild, uncounted moments, she let herself drown in the presence of Mack. He was such a paradox, arrogant and cocky one moment, considerate and kind the next. Protecting her like a knight in shining armor. She wished she knew who the real Mack was. Right now, he felt so vital, so alive, his vibrance infected her, making her want to inhale his presence, and never let him go.

She was supposed to be mad at him because he'd behaved recklessly tonight. And worried that he'd been hurt in the fight. But she was confused; she didn't know if she wanted to slap him, or kiss him.

Kiss him?

Did she really want to kiss him?

Now that the thought had entered her head, she couldn't rid herself of the image. She opened her eyes and found her gaze resting on his mouth, wondering what it would taste like. As if he seemed to sense her change in focus, Mack looked down and studied her face, the light of comprehension replacing concern in his eyes.

He didn't make the first move, however, as she'd expected. No. He merely looked at her, one eyebrow raised, watching. A thrum started deep in her belly. Why did this cowboy have to be so damn sexy? Why was she so temped by him? Like she'd never been with any other man.

Throwing caution to the wind, she stood on tiptoe and reached up to brush her lips against his. His muscled biceps tensed around her shoulders and his firm lips responded to her kiss, meeting hers, opening and inviting her in. She ran her fingers lightly down his side to the waistband of his low-riding jeans, feeling the ridges of the bands of muscles around his hips and across his lower back. She groaned into his mouth and pulled him closer. He smelled faintly of dust and sweat and bull and leather, but it was like an aphrodisiac to Bindi. He was pure male, full of ego and swagger, supremely confident in his ability to please a woman, something she hadn't even known she was craving until right this moment.

And it was her he wanted, of that he made her quite certain. The bulge in the front of his jeans proved he was more than interested. She ran both hands up his naked back, delighting in the warm skin beneath her fingers. Heat pooled between her legs as his tongue delved deeper. Oh, he was so good at kissing. It didn't even matter that he might've kissed hundreds of women before her to become this good. She could stay here all night, just kissing him.

Or… They could do more than just kiss. She hadn't felt this hot, urgent need to have a man between her legs in she didn't know how long. Her fingers found their way to the front of his jeans, where his erection strained to be let free. A sizzle of anticipation ran through her. She gripped the zipper and began to draw it down.

"Whoa." He pulled back far enough so he could look into her eyes. "Are you sure you want to do this? I mean, you seemed quite distraught before. That guy attacked you. I'm not sure…" What? Was he giving her an out? It was the last thing she expected from him, but she shook her head. No, she wanted to get lost in this man for tonight. Forget about Mutt and the dark memories of her brother his appearance had brought to the surface.

As if her giving him permission let loose his last shred of self-restraint, he lifted her up so her back was pressed against the truck and she wrapped her legs around his waist, and he devoured her mouth with his hungry kisses. She tipped his hat off with a flick of her thumb, so she could better access his lips, letting passion overtake her every thought.

This wasn't like her. She didn't do one-night stands. Not ever. Would this even be a one-night stand? Perhaps she was overcompensating for the riot of feelings Mutt had created when he showed up. But it was more than that. She hadn't felt this wild need for so long. If she was giving him permission to take what he wanted, then she was also giving herself permission to surrender to this lust.

"We need some privacy," he groaned into her neck. "So I can get you naked." His words caused shivers to run through her. They hadn't really thought this through. Originally, they were supposed to sleep underneath his truck. But that wouldn't offer them the seclusion they needed for what she had in mind.

"Grab your swag," she said, voice husky from kissing. He put her back on her feet, reached in and did as he was told, first throwing his bull riding gear that'd ended up on the ground into the rear bed. Then she led him by the hand, bare chest and all, through the last line of cars. Ducking under the fence, they made their way toward the line of trees running parallel to the parking lot. Technically, they were probably on private property, but Bindi wasn't worried. They could be back on the other side of the fence before dawn.

The roughened palm of his hand abraded hers, and she itched with the need to get him completely naked, see if the bottom half of him matched the top half, and… Oh. She stopped in the middle of the long grass. She'd almost forgotten.

"Do you happen to have…protection on you?"

"I sure do. A cowboy is always prepared." She caught the flash of his white teeth as he shot her his brightest smile.

Oh, thank the Lord. "Good." Would she have stopped this if he'd said no? She was grateful she didn't have to answer that question tonight.

They made it to the cover of the first row of trees. It was dark out here, the bright lights of the rodeo not reaching this far. The three-quarter moon hung low and full on the horizon, like a porcelain halo in the sky, shedding pale light of its own. No one would be able to see them from the parking lot.

Mack dropped the swag, and she watched as he efficiently unrolled it. His back was lithe and supple as he bent to undo it, all that glorious man-skin glistening in the moonlight. And then, when he stood, she marveled anew at just how chiseled his torso appeared in the weak moonlight.

The walk over had done nothing to cool her eagerness to make love to Mack. In fact, it'd cemented the idea in her head even further. She could have this one night with him, away from Stormcloud, and all the well-meaning, but prying, eyes. No one would know what they'd been up to. He'd been a thorn in her side for days. This sexual thing buzzing between them had been filling her head with absurd ideas. Now, she could get him out of her system, and go back to her life on the station once more. She and Mack could keep a congenial friendship between them, nothing more. She really didn't want a relationship with this American cowboy. He was going back to Montana at some stage, and she would be… Well, not going to Montana, at least. All she needed was for him to scratch this itch for her, then she could go back to being the normal, slightly-boring-but-proud-of-it woman she was used to.

"You still sure about this, Bindi?" His question caught her off guard, as did the two strong arms that swept her up into his embrace.

"Never been surer," she assured him. Her fingers went to the zipper of his jeans, and this time she didn't stop until she had it all the way down and the waistband pushed over his hips. While he shrugged the rest of his way out of the denim, she removed her boots, jeans and shirt, leaving her standing in her underwear.

"I wish we had some proper light," Mack whispered. "Because you're beautiful, and I want to see every single inch of you."

He stepped toward her and lifted her easily in his arms, bending to lay her down on the open swag as carefully as if she were the most precious thing in the world to him. Sighing, she lay back and let desire swallow her up as he lowered his body over hers.

CHAPTER EIGHT

Mack savored the feel of Bindi's curvaceous body beneath his, and let his mouth drift down to hers. She was sweet, just as he'd imagined she would be. But she was also a little spicy, demanding as much of him as he could give. Her tongue delved the depths of his mouth as she tangled her fingers in his hair. He'd never been one to turn down an offer such as Bindi was presenting. Or, at least, he hadn't been until Clarissa had used and abused him and spat him out when he no longer fit her needs. But Mack didn't want to think about Clarissa tonight. So he let himself be pulled under by Bindi's desire, matching it with own blazing craving to hold her tight.

Bindi was cute and sassy and beautiful as hell—he hadn't been lying when he'd said that to her.

But something about this felt not quite right. He knew Bindi was attracted to him, knew from the very first moment they'd met. When he'd seen her trying to rescue that filly all on her own. In the days that followed at Stormcloud, she'd tried to hide it, denying that flare of desire that pulsed between them anytime they got close. But he was well-attuned to the needs of a woman. He liked women. Liked their appealing bodies, and he especially liked the ones with sharp minds, as well. During his time on the pro circuit, he'd had his fair share of women throw themselves at him, batting their false eyelashes, and purring in soft, silky voices. And he wasn't averse to a one-night stand, either. Which was what most of those women wanted. So, he knew Bindi was drawn to him, he could see it in her eyes, watched it in her body language. Felt the buzz of chemistry between them whenever he stood close. Saw the challenge darken her eyes as she fought her feelings for him.

Bindi was different from all of those other women he'd known. Not in the fact that she wasn't beautiful, because with her dark, exotic looks, she could compete with any one of those women he'd slept with in the past. She was more down-to-earth, unaffected; but there was also something ever so slightly melancholy about her. As if a sadness sat just beneath the surface. As if there was a story she wasn't telling anyone. And goddammit, he suddenly wanted to know her story.

Even worse, he was second-guessing whether Bindi would be happy with just one night. Because he wasn't sure he was able to offer her more than that. And suddenly, he didn't want to hurt her.

She moved sinuously beneath him, breaking his thoughts and scattering them like leaves. Her skin was warm and inviting and she ran a hand over his shoulder, down the dip in his lower back and onto his buttock, pulling him harder onto her thighs, letting him know how much she wanted this. Wanted him. Burying his nose in her neck, he breathed in the scent of her silky hair. Grapefruit, or something citrusy, assaulted his nostrils. He liked that wonderful, clean smell.

He went to lower himself onto one elbow and held back a grunt of pain. That big guy had got a couple of good punches in, and the bruises would surely emerge tomorrow. Add that to the workout he'd received riding that bull, and he was going to be sore as hell over the next few days. After all the pain he'd been through after his accident, this was a mere trifle, however. Bindi didn't need to know he'd been hurt. She'd seemed to take his assurances that he was okay at face value. She believed him. Which was one more thing Mack could add to the list of good things about her.

He ran a hand down her hip, feeling the dip and curve beneath his fingers. She sucked in a breath and purred, reaching up to pull his lips to cover her greedy ones.

She reached for his cock, but he stopped her hand, instead guiding it toward the junction of her thighs. Covering her hand with his, he encouraged her to show him what she liked. He was so hard and ready that if she touched him now, he'd explode. It'd been a long while since he'd slept with a woman. This was going to be quick when it happened. He hoped he didn't disappoint her.

She tried to withdraw her hand, but he gently held it in place, stroking his finger against the soft skin of her upper thigh. Gradually, firmly, inexorably, he ushered her hand between her legs, slipping a finger into her hot, wet heat. She gasped and flung her head back, closing her eyes as he moved slowly in a rhythm that belied his hunger for her. Soon, she followed his lead, and he watched her face as she pleasured herself, encouraging her to move faster, deeper, his cock getting harder with each perfect little pant she gave out every time he plunged his finger inside her.

God, he wanted her. His heart was beating like a jungle drum, the thrum taking over his head, clouding his thinking until he could hardly stop himself from taking her. She cried out in deprivation as he pulled away, her eyes springing open in shock as he left her. But it was only for a second. Fumbling for the condom he'd slipped under the pillow, he rolled over to sheath himself and then levered himself so he was hovering on his elbows above her.

"Are you still sure you want this?" He gave her one last chance to say no. Although, whether he'd be able to stop now was debatable.

"Yes. Oh, Mack, please," she replied, breathing hard and staring up into his face. And Mack was only too happy to oblige.

She tilted her hips and groaned deep in her throat, and he couldn't stop himself. He slipped inside her and then held steady for one perfect second, enjoying the exquisite sweetness of her. She moaned and dug her fingernails deep into the skin on his shoulders. Then he began to thrust. It felt so good. She felt so good as she lifted her hips to meet his every stroke. He wouldn't last long.

Her breathy pants came in short, sharp punctuations, driving him on. She moved with him, at one stage lifting her head to bite his shoulder. The pain was keen and exquisite. Oh, God, he was going to come. He could tell by the way she clung to him that she was close, too. But he could no longer hold the tide back and it flowed over him like a tsunami, completely consuming him.

She pressed her forehead into his bicep as he came and then she tilted her head back and let out a primal noise as ripples of her own orgasm washed over them both.

They lay entwined for many long seconds, letting the afterglow sweep them away. That'd been intense. His arms were shaking with the effort of holding himself up. Normally, he prided himself on his staying power. And he'd almost left her behind. But something about Bindi had driven away all his self-control.

Lowering himself, he gently eased away from her and rid himself of the condom.

"Thank you," she said huskily into his ear.

She was thanking him? He was the one who should be thanking her. But her words also felt like a form of dismissal.

As if she was letting him go. As if she expected him to get up and just walk away. Well, she had another think coming, because he was a man who liked to snuggle, and he wasn't going to hide that fact tonight. Not from Bindi. One-night stand or not, he was going to make this count. He drew her into his arms and let her rest her head on his shoulder as he got comfortable in the swag. It was a small space, but it gave him the excuse he needed to keep her close. He wasn't letting go of her anytime soon.

"You don't need to thank me," he replied. "I was a more than willing participant."

"So I noticed," she said with a laugh. Sighing, she snuggled closer.

He turned his gaze skyward and considered the sparkling stars high above for the first time. "Your night sky is almost as beautiful as in Montana."

"Almost," she said with a huff. "There's no place better to see the stars than here. Astronomers from all over the world come to Queensland to study the sky. We have the least light pollution of just about any country. You won't get a better view."

"How about we agree to disagree," he said, running his fingers in a soft arc over her bare shoulder. Bumps of scar tissue from the old wound he'd seen the other day rippled beneath his fingertips.

It was on the tip of his tongue to ask her about it, when she murmured, "Okay. I'd much rather look at you tonight, anyway." Her face was all dark shadows and contours in the small amount of light shed by the moon, but he could make out the curve of her jaw and the glint of moonlight in her eyes. And the hunger was there in her gaze. Again? She wanted him again, so soon? He forgot all about the scar on her shoulder. That could wait for another day.

His mother had taught him to be a gentleman, and he'd

always tried to be chivalrous. Luckily, he was also a well-prepared cowboy, with more than one condom to spare. If she wanted to make love again, who was he to argue? So, he grinned and slipped his hand between their bodies to cup her breast. The first time they'd made love, he's sorely neglected these beauties. He dropped his head and let his tongue wander in lazy circles around her left nipple. She closed her eyes and made a low noise in the back of her throat. Oh, yeah, he definitely wanted to do this again. He'd make sure to do better this time.

CHAPTER NINE

Mack eased his shoulders against the back of the car seat. Just about every muscle ached, either from his ride or from the fight. But it was a good pain, and Mack welcomed it. The lack of sleep was more of a problem right now, with a two-hour drive ahead of them to get back to Stormcloud. But he wouldn't exchange a moment's sleep for what he and Bindi had shared last night.

She'd been wild and even a bit naughty—which had caught him unawares, nothing like the good-girl image she projected—and he'd been a willing participant in her hunger to satiate them both.

Bindi had been the first to stir this morning, wakening him with a light kiss on the lips just as the sun touched the sky. "Thank you," she murmured, and he wondered why there was sadness in her tone. And then she was up and dressed before he could stop her. He was slower, watching her out of the corner of his eye. She glared at him in a way that told him he needed to hurry. It seemed the bubble of intimacy they'd been cocooned in last night no longer surrounded them. A wall had gone up in Bindi's eyes, her face closed and shuttered.

Sounds from the parking lot suggested there were other

early risers about, as well. Time to get up and get moving, before they were discovered in their secret hideaway.

Bindi rolled up the swag as he finished getting dressed, and efficiently tied her hair back in a braid, looking neat and put-together once more, not at all like the untamed woman he'd been with last night.

He wondered if she was thinking about the man who'd accosted her last night. He needed to know more about that man, and what he'd meant when he said he wasn't done with her. But her pale face and the way she strode over the dry grass toward his truck made him decide to leave the conversation for now. There would be plenty of time later.

They'd bought a hurried breakfast of a bacon and egg roll —which'd been damn delicious, especially seeing as how he missed dinner—and then Bindi had requested they head back to the station straight away. He was fine with that; he could check out the woodchopping and the blue-ribbon heifers another day. Bindi had said she'd shower and change when they got home, so he'd swapped his black shirt with the pearlescent buttons and silver thread work on the collar for a clean, black T-shirt, leaving his hat on the console between them. She was still wearing that loose top and tight jeans from yesterday. And now that he knew what resided beneath those jeans, he was even more enamored by them.

The cabin of his truck had been silent for the past fifteen minutes as he navigated through the outskirts of town and ended up on the flat highway back to Dimbulah.

Chancing a glance over at Bindi, he decided it was time to end this impasse that'd inexplicably grown between them.

"You didn't watch me ride last night." His statement was only half accusation.

She gave him a startled look, then narrowed her eyes. "Yes, I did," she retorted. "But I left as soon as I saw you were okay."

"Oh." Okay then. He gave her space to explain why she'd left, but she remained stubbornly silent, staring at the dry floodplains through the windshield. "It wasn't my best ride. I have to admit, I was a little rusty, but I thought I did a pretty good job of—"

"I'm sure you did an excellent job of staying on that stupid bull. The thing you didn't do such a good job of was wearing a helmet." She glared at him, her nose ring flashing nearly as brightly as her eyes.

What did she mean? He never wore a helmet. A true cowboy always stuck to his trusty hat.

"You sustained a serious head injury last time you rode. Or don't you remember that?"

"Of course, I do," he said, frowning as sudden understanding hit him. She was about to lecture him on taking care of himself, looking out for his own safety. Well, he wasn't having that.

But before he could say anything, she went on, "Don't you have any respect for your own life? Why don't you wear a helmet?"

"Because it's my choice not to," he said breezily, trying to take the sting out of his tone.

"Why? Because that stupid hat makes you look cool? Is that it?"

That might be part of it. To be a true bull-rider, you needed to look the part. "I know what I'm doing," he replied hotly. "I use my instincts. All of us riders know how to land, to protect ourselves."

She snorted. "That may be true, except for the one time when it's not."

"That fall wasn't my fault…"

She jumped in before he could explain. "I'm not saying it was your fault. I'm pretty sure none of those riders plan to fall off those big-ass bulls. But it happens all the time. It happened to you." Her dark eyes fixed on him, full of hurt and incrimination.

She wasn't grasping what he meant. "No." He shook his head. "That's not it. My bull rope was sabotaged. Someone sliced almost all the way through it. That fall wasn't an accident. Someone meant for me to get hurt."

His declaration seemed to stop her mid-breath, and she shut her mouth with a click of her teeth, frowning at him. "What?" she asked eventually. "You never mentioned this before. You think someone wanted to see you fall off?"

"Yes, I do," he replied quietly. "And I even know who it was."

Confusion flickered over her pretty face. "But why didn't you report it? Surely the police...or the pro-riding organization who runs the rodeos...someone should do something about it."

"Because I can't prove it. Because I spent weeks in hospital recovering from my injuries and it wasn't until I retrieved my personal belongings from that night that I saw what'd happened to my bull rope." He held up a hand as she opened her mouth to argue. "Trust me, I tried. But no one believed me. They all thought the head trauma had made me paranoid. My gut feelings aren't enough to form a case against the woman who did this."

"Woman?" Her dark eyebrows flew up into her hairline. "What woman?"

"Her name is Clarissa, and she's a real piece of work. A man-eater who'll do anything to climb the corporate ladder. Her company was going to become my major sponsor, offered me a large sum of money." Mack hesitated. How much should he tell her? "I found out the only reason she wanted to sponsor me was so she could manipulate me. Manipulate the results. Anyway, we had a fight, and I stormed out."

"You mean she wanted you to cheat?"

Mack nodded. That was about it in a nutshell. The one thing Bindi probably didn't realize was how much money was on the line if he had thrown his ride, as Clarissa wanted him to do. Not just for him, losing his place in the top ten, but for all the punters who were counting on him out there.

"But you can't prove it was her?" Bindi questioned.

"Nope. But I know it was her. She came to wish me well that night, right before I rode. Wanted to make up for our fight, said that she'd been wrong trying to persuade me to do something I wasn't comfortable with."

Bindi rolled her eyes, but let him go on.

"I had all my stuff laid out on a table, giving it a once-over, like I always do before a ride. Bart, one of the other contestants, asked me a question, distracted me for a few moments, and that must've been when she cut my rope. When I turned back to the table, she was gone." He gave a one-shouldered shrug. "Then they called my name, and I grabbed everything and hustled to the pens." The rest, as they like to say, was history.

"Perhaps this Bart guy was in on it?" Bindi mused.

"I wouldn't be surprised," he grunted in reply. Mack never even made the eight seconds that night. After only the third buck, he inexplicably lost his grip and was sent sailing through the air. Had she been hoping he'd die? Who knew? But Bart had never come to see him in the hospital, unlike most of the other riders from the circuit. Which spoke volumes.

"I spent the first six months after my accident recovering. My leg was broken in two places, and I needed lots of rehab."

"That sounds painful."

"It was." But not half as painful as having to watch the rest of his buddies continue on the rodeo circuit without him. Watch his lead slip away, knowing there wasn't a damn thing he could do about it, because there was no way in hell he was fit enough to get back on a bull that year. He'd persevered, done the work, suffered through the pain, so he was fit enough to start a new season, never mentioning his headaches or dizzy spells after those first few weeks in hospital. Because that was a minor distraction. As long as he was physically strong enough to ride again, he could ignore the minor inconvenience of a headache now and then.

"Then I spent the next six months trying to get back onto the circuit. But it seemed there were roadblocks wherever I went. It was impossible to get a ride, even in the smaller state rodeo circuits. They all said their lists were full. No one wanted to sponsor me, not even the lesser sponsors. It was as if I'd been branded a pariah. I believe Clarissa had a hand in that, perhaps spreading false rumors about me, I don't know. Eventually, I returned home with my tail between my legs, which is when Dean gave me a job on Stargazer."

"That's terrible," Bindi said, brown eyes brimming with sympathy.

"I thought so at the time," Mack admitted. "But when Dean suggested taking some time down under, the idea began to grow on me. Especially when I remembered the pro-circuit, you've got going here. It's nearly as competitive as in the US, and there are definitely some skilled riders here. I decided I may be able to get my foot back in the door that way, instead."

"Hmm, interesting." Bindi's gaze went flat, losing the compassion, her mouth puckering in a pout. "But I still don't understand why you would wilfully endanger your life every time you get up on a bull."

God, was she going to keep harping on about this damn helmet thing? Who did she think she was? His mother?

She leaned over and placed her hand on his knee, surprising him with her intensity. "I mean, surely you can see that a new start here could also mean a new way of riding. Perhaps—" Her words were cut off as a loud bang filled the cabin and then the steering wheel was almost wrenched from Mack's hands. The truck skewed sideways, skidding down the road. Bindi screamed and put both hands on the dash to stop herself from being flung sideways.

Thank God there were no cars coming toward them on the other side of the road, as Mack wrestled with the wheel, trying to pull the car back, stamping on the brakes hard. Suddenly the car responded to his mad pulling on the steering wheel, but Mack had overcompensated and now the rear of the truck swung out the other way.

Almost as if in slow motion, the right wheel caught, and the truck flipped into the air, cartwheeling off the road, rolling over and over until it came to rest with a shuddering thud against a large tree trunk.

CHAPTER TEN

Bindi's ears were ringing. A loud buzz that overrode every other sound. Squeezing her eyes tighter shut, she tasted blood on her tongue. She was completely disoriented. Didn't know which way was up, or which way was down. Her head screamed with pain, and she lifted a hand to touch her temple. But her arm was heavy and slow to respond.

Where was she?

What had happened?

The last thing she remembered, they were talking about Mack's complete lack of sense at not wearing a helmet when he rode. She'd been so mad at him. So disillusioned by his seeming self-indulgence and dogmatic belief he was invincible. When he clearly wasn't.

Then Mack had suddenly grabbed the steering wheel, grappling with it as if it were alive and trying to wrench itself free of his control.

They'd crashed. She could still hear the terrible sound of metal being torn apart like paper as the car left the road and collided with a tree.

Bindi gave a low moan.

"Bindi." It was Mack's voice, loud and urgent, but his words were muffled by the buzz filling her ears like cotton wool. "Bindi, are you okay? Answer me."

She didn't want to open her eyes. Her head hurt. Her chest hurt. Everything hurt.

"Bindi," he said again. There was a sound and Bindi swayed slightly as the truck rocked back and forth, the motion making her feel ill.

Something touched her face, and she flinched. Opening her eyes, she found Mack's tawny gaze boring into her. But he was at an odd angle. He was below her, and she dangled from her seat belt, gravity pulling her down.

The truck was resting on its side. Dirt and debris was spewed inside the cabin from the driver's side window, which had been open when the truck crashed. Mack had undone his seat belt and climbed up through the cabin to reach her. Thank God for her seatbelt. She dare not think where she would've ended up without it. Steam hissed from the engine, but other than that, there was a deathly silence.

"Oh, thank Christ," Mack said with an explosive gasp. "For a second there, I thought..." He didn't finish his thought, merely cupped her cheek with his hand and tensed his strong jaw. There was blood streaming from his nose and his left eye was bruised and already starting to swell shut. He looked a mess. And by the way he was staring at her with such concern, she probably looked no better.

"Are you hurt?" he asked.

Bindi didn't know. She raised a hand to her temple again and felt something warm and wet.

"You have a cut on your head," Mack told her. "But it looks superficial. Nothing much to worry about."

He was one to make light of head injuries. She almost laughed, but he was talking to her urgently again.

"I meant do you have pain in your back, or neck? Can you move your legs?"

Oh, shit. He was asking if she had a spinal injury. She

screwed her eyes shut and tried to block him out. She didn't want to do this. Didn't want to be here. Her brain just wanted to switch off and pretend she wasn't here. Like she used to do when Kai was tormenting her. Abusing her. Her mind had tried to block it all out. Shut her off from the inconceivable thoughts that her brother would want to hurt her. Do things to her that no brother should do to his sister. It was a coping mechanism her counsellor had explained later. It happened to a lot of people when they were faced with trauma too big for their consciousness to absorb.

But this wasn't Kai, she reminded herself. This was Mack, and he was trying to help her.

"Bindi." His voice was deep and commanding. "You need to answer me. Can you move your legs?"

Forcing her eyes open again, she concentrated on her legs, scrunching her toes inside her boots, then working her way up, rotating her ankle and bending her knees.

"I'm fine," she replied at last.

"Good. That's good." The relief in Mack's voice was palpable. "Let's get you out of here."

With surprisingly gentle hands, Mack prised open her seat belt as she held onto the window frame to stop herself from falling sideways. He helped her clamber slowly out of her open widow, and then she sat on what had once been the side door panel of the truck as Mack followed her. He jumped down and then reached up to help swing her down, holding her tight underneath her armpits, then clamping her to his side as they stood back and surveyed the wreckage.

His truck was a complete write-off.

The rear half of the truck was almost unrecognizable. It was wrapped around the tree trunk, almost melded into the rough bark in a tangled mess of metal and wood.

Bindi shuddered and her knees went weak. "I need to sit down," she said. That could've been them, smashed to smithereens. If the truck hadn't spun around at the last second, the cabin would've taken the full brunt of the impact. Mack led her to a spot in the shade beneath a stand of tall ironbarks and she sat heavily, leaning against a sturdy trunk for support. Mack sank down beside her and they both stared at the wrecked vehicle.

Bindi suddenly realized she hadn't asked Mack if he was hurt. "Oh, Mack." She turned to face him, reaching up to touch his face. The blood had stopped trickling and was beginning to dry now. "You're hurt, too."

"What? This?" He swiped at the crusted blood. "It must've been from the airbag deploying. I've had a few broken noses in my time. And more than my share of black eyes, most of them caused by more nefarious things than a car accident." He lifted a cheeky eyebrow in an attempt at gallantry. "I'm fine. Believe me, you look worse than I do." He pointed to her chest.

She looked down to see her white shirt covered in large spatters of blood.

"Here, we need to stop the bleeding." He proceeded to rip a strip from the bottom of his T-shirt and wadded it into a pad for her. "Hold this against the cut, it'll help stem the blood."

"Thanks," she said, taking the proffered cloth, then wincing as she gingerly held it in place.

"You're going to have one nasty black eye, as well," he said thoughtfully. "We'll look like a pair of prizefighters."

A car pulled off to the edge of the road in a screech of dust and flying dirt, and the driver got out, running toward them.

"Are you two okay?" The man shouted. "Do you need me to call an ambulance?"

Mack looked at her for a second, but she shook her head. "Nah, we're okay. Thanks," he said. Then, after a second's hesitation, he asked. "Can we borrow your phone? Ours are lost in that tangled mess somewhere."

"Sure." The man handed his phone over, still staring at the wrecked truck. "Holy shit." The man never took his eyes off the crash. "Man, you two were lucky to get out of that alive."

Bindi only half-listened as Mack called Stormcloud and relayed the accident to Sasha, asking her to get Steve on the line. As he talked, he got up and walked slowly around the crash site, bending down to inspect something, and then continued his perusal. Bindi thought he might've been walking with a slight limp and made a mental note to check his leg for injuries when he returned. Perhaps it was his broken leg, and it was hurting him after the accident, but she wouldn't put it past him to downplay another major injury, just to get her off his back.

"Thanks, dude." Mack sauntered back and handed the stranger back his phone. "Steve's organizing a tow truck to recover the vehicle. He's also reporting this to the cops, he said they'll want to come out and inspect the site. Dale is on his way to pick us up. He'll take us to see the doctor at the clinic in Dimbulah. I think you might need stitches."

Bindi accepted all of this with a nod. It all felt strangely surreal, and for once, she was terribly glad that Mack was doing his take-charge thing.

"So the cops are coming?" The stranger asked.

"Yep. Steve said they should be here in half an hour, or less."

"Well, if you two don't need me to stay here, I might go and keep the traffic moving." He gestured to two more cars that were pulling up by the side of the road. "They mean well, but if people keep stopping, they might cause another accident."

"Good idea," Mack agreed, watching the other man jog back to the stopped cars, waving his hands and signaling to them that everything was okay. It was nice of him. A lot of people would stop out of concern for their welfare. But there were also those dumbasses who just wanted to rubberneck.

Bindi took the wad of material away from her wound and looked at it. There was still fresh blood there, so she replaced it with a sigh. Mack might be right, she probably did need stitches. She'd heard that airbags were a mixed blessing in vehicles. They stopped you from smashing your head against the windscreen or dashboard, but often caused other injuries in the meantime. Like Mack's broken nose and bruised eye, and her cut forehead. Her head throbbed, and she wished for some painkillers.

Mack turned to her, a troubled frown creasing his forehead. "The wheel fell off."

"What? A wheel can't just fall off," she retorted, forgetting her woes for a second.

"Well, it's missing. Take a look." He pointed at the passenger side of the vehicle, where they'd climbed out of the cabin. Just like he said, there was no left-hand wheel, merely a naked axle sticking out of the wheel arch. "That's why I lost control of the car."

"But how…?"

"I think it's been tampered with. The only way a wheel falls off is if the lug nuts are loose. And this is a brand-new truck…" He lifted his shoulders in a shrug. "I guess the cops will be able to tell us more."

The words echoed in Bindi's head, and suddenly she wondered if this hadn't been merely an accident, after all.

The image of Mutt's face, screwed up with hatred as he tried to strangle her, invaded her brain. "Shit. Do you think Mutt might've had something to do with this?" The words were out of her mouth before she could hold them back.

"Mutt? Is that the guy who accosted you last night? Why would he want to…?" Mack shook his head and shot her a look of amazement.

Damn, why had she opened her mouth? No one knew about her life back before she moved from New Zealand. It was better that way; if she left her family and her grief locked away in the past. The last thing she wanted or needed was to be telling Mack her sad story.

Before she could come up with some lame excuse, Mack interrupted her. "That's funny, because I was thinking this might be Clarissa's work. She's certainly got a grudge against me, and she's just crazy enough to do something like this. Or should I say, crazy enough to pay a henchman to do this," he mused.

"Oh." She hadn't even considered that idea. Funny, how they both thought they were the cause of the accident. From what Mack had told her, this lady, Clarissa, sure did seem like a piece of work. And if she had been responsible for tampering with Mack's bull rope…well that put her in the criminal category. But she was back in America. Surely, her reach didn't extend this far. She wanted to dismiss the idea that Clarissa had caused the accident. It seemed much more likely that Mutt had come back sometime last night and tampered with the car. At least, that was what she was going to tell the police when they asked.

Oh.

The thought brought her up sharp. If she told the police that she suspected Mutt, then she'd need to tell them why. And that'd open a whole can of worms she wasn't sure she wanted opened.

Mack came and sat next to her, crossing his legs and leaning in to study her face. "Let me take a look." He gently removed the wadded T-shirt from her temple and stared at the wound. She flinched at his touch, but not because he'd hurt her. His fingers were warm and sure on her skin and sent frantic memories of their night spent together, tumbling through her head. "It's stopped bleeding," he reported. "You might not need stitches after all."

That was good.

His gentle fingers trailed down the side of her face to rest on the skin of her neck. His amber eyes narrowed. "That bastard left bruises," he growled.

Bindi had thought Mutt's rough hands might well have left marks on her neck, but she hadn't been near a mirror to check.

Mack's voice softened, and he said, "While we wait for the cops to arrive, are you going to tell me about that guy last night, then? I think I should know why I shouldn't go back and pummel the shit out of him right now. But more importantly, I want to know why you think he might've tried to kill us."

His questions caught her off guard and stabbed at her like a hammer blow, coming out of the blue like they had. She stared at him blankly, fisting the wad of his T-shirt in her hand by her side.

"It might be a good idea to get our stories straight," he prompted gently. "Before the cops get here."

He was right. And she guessed she owed him some explanation. Perhaps she could try her story out on him first, before she blurted everything out to the police.

She nodded. Where to start? At the beginning, she supposed. "Mutt was best friends with my brother, Kai. They were inseparable, right from when they met in kindergarten. I'm ten years younger than my brother," she explained. "I was one of those *happy accidents*, as my parents like to call it. I was born well after my mother had given up all hope of ever having another baby. So, my brother and I were never really close."

"Mmm," Mack encouraged.

"Kai had always been a bit of a wild child. I knew my parents struggled to keep him in class until he finished high school. Even before he graduated, he'd started hanging out with a gang of boys from the street. My parents kept me ignorant of most of the worst details of what he was up to, but I later found out that his gang was really a bunch of small-time criminals. Peddling drugs to school kids, petty theft, stealing cars, that kind of thing. Kai almost ended up in jail more than once, but I was never told at the time."

Mack screwed up his mouth in a grimace of understanding. It was such a cliché. Kid gets sucked into a dubious group, gives in to peer pressure and ends up on the wrong side of the law. It happened all over the world, to all kinds of young people who were searching for a place to belong, somewhere they fit in.

"Because I was so oblivious to all of Kai's faults, I used to idolize him," Bindi continued. "I always looked up to him, wanted to be like him. But most of the time, it was as if I didn't exist for him. As if I was beneath him. He had his own life with his own friends, and he ignored me. But that all changed when I turned fourteen."

Bindi shuddered as she remembered her fourteenth birthday.

"What happened?" Mack prompted gently.

"Kai turned up to my party with a group of his mates, Mutt included. Mum wasn't happy, but she hadn't seen him in weeks and so didn't want to turn him away. His mates all started to wink at Kai when my parents weren't looking, telling him that his sister was hot. To start with, I lapped up all their appreciation, but it soon turned into something darker, and uglier."

Bindi remembered all the crude comments, made when her parents were out of earshot. About how pretty she was. How grown up she'd become. That she was a hot piece of ass. And how they'd like to take her out the back and fuck her hard. That last comment had come from Mutt, and she'd gasped at his blatant crudeness.

"They started making innuendos to all my friends, as well, and most of the girls excused themselves and left early."

"So, they ruined your party. Bastards."

"Yes, they did, but it was more than that. When Kai and his mates left that night, Kai looked at me as if… I don't know, as if I'd betrayed him somehow."

"What do you mean?" He leaned forward, a little *V* of a frown forming between his brows.

She pursed her lips and tilted her head to watch the blue sky shimmer between the branches above them.

"Later that night, he came home again, after my parents were in bed. There was something angry and mean eating him up inside. He said that I'd shamed him in front of his friends by acting all coy and flirty. Like I wanted it, or something. Mutt had told him that I was coming on to him, giving him the come-fuck-me-eyes. But I promise, I didn't do it on purpose. I was just a fourteen-year-old girl who just discovered boys and was eager for their attention."

"What happened?" he asked, voice cold and flat. The ice in his tone seemed to suck the heat straight out of the day, as if he knew what she was about to say. But she'd started this story, and she knew she had to finish it.

"He raped me," she said in a whisper. "Then told me he'd done it because he loved me, and he was saving me from something worse. And not to say anything to our parents, because if they actually believed me—and he said it was highly doubtful they'd believe my far-fetched story over his word—they'd throw me out of the house for being a dirty little slut."

Mack went incredibly still beside her, like he was suddenly made from stone. "So he was twenty-four when he did this to you? And you were fourteen?" he demanded.

Bindi hung her head and nodded. Yep, he was more than

old enough to know better. To know exactly what he was doing. Even though he tried to blame her; said it was all her fault, that she was so beautiful that he couldn't keep his hands off her. That he was doing this to keep her away from his friends, that he'd needed to be the one to take her virginity because they all wanted to be her first, but if any of them got hold of her, it would've been ten times worse.

"That disgusting piece of shit." Mack spat the words with such venom, Bindi was taken aback for a moment. Mack's lion-like eyes blazed, burning with heat and hate. It'd taken her a while to come to the same conclusion, but Mack was right, her brother had done a sickening thing. It was an act that would change her life forever. But it would also change his.

"Yes," she agreed. "It took me a while to understand he was sick. That his perversion wasn't my fault."

"None of what happened was your fault," he said tenderly, draping a hand around her shoulders and pulling her in close. "That perverted, sadistic prick," Mack growled. Bindi glanced up and saw he was clenching his teeth so tight, she could see the outline of the tiny muscles in his jaw pulse with anger. "I'm not sure I want to find out what happened next," he said. "But I need to know what part this Mutt character played in all this."

Bindi drew in a shaky breath. She'd thought that would be the hardest part, telling Mack about the rape. But there was worse to come. The destruction of her whole family. And she'd been partly to blame.

"I kept his secret for nearly a year, just like he told me," she admitted. Although things had never been the same for her after that. Her parents seemed oblivious to her disenchantment as she slowly withdrew from the world. Her school grades suffered, and she stopped going out with her friends. Her life seemed to drain of all color, but she kept a smile in place for her parents, because they could never know. She felt ashamed and guilty, as if she'd somehow brought the whole thing down on herself. "He stopped coming around to the house, which I was grateful for. I don't know how I would've coped if I'd had to pretend everything was the same in front of my parents."

"So, that was the end of it, then?" He was staring at her intently, as if willing her story to have a happy ending. Except it didn't. She almost felt like she was letting him down as well as everyone else, but the truth needed to be told.

She gave an almost imperceptible shake of her head. "A few days before my fifteenth birthday, he came back, climbed in through my window and raped me again." Mack's arm tensed around her shoulders, but she stumbled on before he could interrupt her. "The first time I'd been broken and sad. This time I got angry. Really, really angry, and I refused to keep quiet."

"Good," he said roughly. "I hope you reported that bastard to the cops."

"I did," she agreed. "I knew I'd only have the strength to tell my story once, so instead of confiding in my parents and having them perhaps try and talk me out of it, I marched down to the local police station and filed a report." That'd been both the best and worst day of her life. She hadn't even turned fifteen at the time, but she'd felt far older than her years, world-weary and scarred beyond redemption. A young constable had taken her statement, and he'd been caring and considerate, as if he believed her. Which made it slightly easier to tell the tale. And then another female officer had taken her to the hospital, and they'd performed a rape kit on her. There was no doubting her story after that.

"But I never imagined the repercussions from that day." Perhaps, if she'd known, she might've kept her mouth shut, like Mutt had kept telling her she should've done. But her story was out and there was no putting the genie back in the bottle afterwards. "The police contacted my parents and then arrested Kai."

At first, her parents hadn't believed her. But once Bindi had tearfully relayed the events following her fourteenth birthday, her father had taken her into his arms and rocked her. Uma, her mother, had been slower to comfort her daughter, and in the following days she had become less and less communicative. Bindi heard her parents arguing late into the night. She couldn't hear what they were saying, but she knew Uma wanted to believe that Kai, her only son, the light of her life, wasn't capable of such an atrocity.

"They released Kai on bail, until his court hearing, on the strict directive that he not contact me, or come within one-hundred meters of me," she continued.

That'd been hard, knowing her brother was out there somewhere and she'd been scared, believing he might try to hurt her again. But instead of her brother showing up at her door, Mutt had come calling.

"One night, about a week before the trial, Mutt turned up on our doorstep and begged for me to hear him out. Kai was staying with Mutt in his share house while he waited for the trial. At first, my father didn't want to let him in, but my mother was desperate to hear anything about Kai. So, my father gave him five minutes to speak." Bindi shuddered at the thought of that night, of watching Mutt's animated face, at how he was so desperate for her to withdraw the charges. "He told us that Kai was terribly remorseful, and he was a changed man."

Mack gave a loud snort of disbelief, but let her continue.

"He said Kai wouldn't survive a stint in jail, and I had to think long and hard about going ahead with the prosecution."

"I hope he didn't talk you out of it?" Mack asked.

"No, he didn't. My father backed up my decision one-hundred-percent. He said there was no place in his family for an incestuous pedophile, and Kai deserved everything he got." Bindi remembered how grateful she'd been for her father, standing behind her, one hand resting on her shoulder, shouting down Mutt's excuses. "Mutt got really angry and told us that we would all pay if anything happened to his friend. How could they defend a filthy little slut and not care at all about Kai's welfare? My dad marched him out of the house, and we thought that was the last of it."

"But it wasn't?" Mack asked when the silence stretched on.

"No," she replied in a low voice, dropping her chin so she didn't have to look him in the eye. "A day before the court case, Kai killed himself. Took a drug overdose. Left a note saying that he couldn't face a life in jail."

"That bastard," Mack grunted with such vehemence she felt the sound echo in his chest. It wasn't quite the response Bindi was expecting. The few people who knew about the situation had all said how sorry they were that her brother had taken his own life. None of them had been angry at him. Except her. She'd been so angry, the emotion had seared away every other feeling, every other sensation and opinion. She was so MAD at him. Like he'd taken the easy way out and left a trail of destruction in his wake. Because her parents were devastated, especially her mother.

"Yes. Everyone was shocked and saddened. But Mutt took it worst of all. He started standing outside our house at all hours of the day and night and screaming obscenities at us; at me in particular. Saying I murdered him, that it was all my doing and I needed to pay for what I'd done."

"That's a little...weird," Mack consented.

"Yes," she agreed. Bindi had had a strange premonition that there was something else going on. Mutt's dogged determination almost bordered on obsession. Almost as if he'd been in love with Kai. Which was crazy, because Kai was as straight as a die. He liked to have sex with women—a fact Bindi could attest to—and showed an outright dislike for anyone from the gay community. If Mutt was gay, then he'd done a damn good job of hiding it, especially from Kai. Because if Kai had caught even a whiff of something like that, he would've kicked Mutt to the curb without a backward glance.

"Anyway, to cut a long story short, my parents' marriage didn't survive the fall-out. My dad walked out about six months after Kai's death, and my mother retreated into herself and stopped speaking to me. I spent a few months sleeping on my friend's couches, not sure what to do or where to go."

"Shit, Bindi, I can't believe what you've had to go through." Mack's arm tightened around her, his gaze compassionate and caring. She liked the feel of his body next to hers. The way the T-shirt fabric stretched nicely over the muscles of his pecs.

"Yeah, well. It was seven years ago. I flew to Brisbane on the day I turned sixteen, and I've never looked back since." Had never seen her family since, either.

"You try to make light of it all, but this is some heavy shit," Mack replied. He opened his mouth to say more, but the faint sound of a siren broke the rapidly warming morning air. The flash of blue and red lights appeared around a bend in the road in the distance. Mack sat up straighter and stared at the fast-approaching squad car.

"We'll talk about this later," he promised, pulling her in for a hug, then standing up and walking toward the road.

She nodded glumly, leaning back against the tree. The last thing she wanted to do was talk about her sad and sorry past. But it didn't look like she was going to escape it now.

CHAPTER ELEVEN

After the squad car had arrived, two cops had alighted, first stopping to talk to the kind passerby who'd stopped to help them and was now moving traffic on. The larger cop, a barrel-chested and bullnecked, shaded his eyes and peered in their direction as the man waved his arms around in explanation. The two cops began to pick their way across the grassy terrain toward the crash site, seeming to be in no hurry. The big cop had come over to greet him and Bindi, introducing himself as Senior Sergeant Johnson, from the Cairns District Police Headquarters, while the woman—much younger, with a long, blonde ponytail beneath her blue hat—went straight toward the wreck, and bent down to look in through the smashed windscreen and then standing on tiptoe to see inside the rear bed of the truck. Probably checking that there were no more casualties.

After the senior sergeant made sure neither of them needed immediate medical assistance, he'd asked who was driving. When Mack volunteered, the man's sharp eyes had narrowed slightly as he asked him if he'd mind doing a preliminary drug and alcohol test.

Mack had agreed, of course. The cop was only doing his job, but his demeanor rankled. Then the senior sergeant had strolled over to stand next to the woman and appraise the mangled truck. As Mack watched, Johnson moved toward the missing wheel, gingerly prodding and poking at the axle. He'd lifted his gaze and seemed to be looking for something. After a quiet word with the female officer, he'd walked—in his extremely unhurried way—down the road, stopping at a black shape around three-hundred meters away. It took a few seconds for Mack to realize what it was. The missing wheel from his truck. Jesus, had they really come that far down the road?

Bindi's story still preoccupied most of his conscience. Her raw admission that her brother had raped her—had committed incest—still left him stunned. And broken. How could she have been holding all that inside for so long?

Clearly, she blamed herself for the family breakdown. For the fact her parents divorced. It was one of the reasons she'd left New Zealand. But there was no time to dissect her woeful tale. Later, when they got back to Stormcloud, he meant to discuss it in more detail. If she let him.

He glanced over to where Bindi was still sitting on the red earth, leaning against the tree trunk. She was a mess, with dried blood caked on her face, combined with streaks of dirt. She looked like she'd been to hell and back. Which she had. But this car accident didn't really compare to the hell she'd been through with her own family. He wondered at her strength. To survive such a thing as what her brother had done, and then move to a new country, completely alone and unaided. She was a miracle. It put his own sorry tale into perspective.

It also made him wonder fleetingly about their time together last night. Bindi had seemed totally unaffected by her treatment at the hands of her brother. She certainly hadn't held back where the sex was concerned. He wished she'd told him beforehand. But then, if he'd known, would he have handled it any differently? She'd seemed perfectly willing to meet him kiss for kiss, stroke for stroke. Last night hadn't been her first time, by any means. Bindi was skilled in the art of lovemaking, that much had been clear. So, he had to assume she wasn't letting the rape affect her now. Or was she? Had she somehow locked it away in a box where it could no longer hurt her, hidden, but not dealt with? He was the master of ignoring pain and suffering. And he thought he recognized the same look in her eyes, as if she thought if she could ignore it long enough, it'd go away, eventually.

After the police had taken a quick statement from the helpful stranger, he'd been given leave to continue on his journey. Now, the female cop, Constable O'Hare, returned from the squad car, handed them both a bottle of water, and stood in the shade beside them.

"Thanks ma'am," Mack said, and she looked at him in slight surprise.

"I'm not sure I'm old enough to be called, ma'am, but I'll take it, anyway." She nodded, her blue eyes sharp and shrewd, even as she smiled at him. Handing Bindi a clean handkerchief from somewhere deep in one of her pockets, she said, not unkindly, "You might want to give your face a bit of spit and polish."

"Thanks." Bindi took the proffered square of material and dampened it with a splash of water.

"Here, let me do it," Mack said, hunkering down beside her. As gently as he could, he dabbed at the crusted blood, while she sat still and trusting, tipping her head up toward him, as innocent as a child, and he suddenly felt strangely responsible for her. Their gazes caught and he couldn't look away. Her pupils dilated and a dusky-pink color spread up her neck as he considered her. Tiny little lines appeared around her mouth as she pursed it into a slowly curving grin. Why hadn't he ever noticed those before? Her bottom lip was fuller than her top, and when she pouted like that, it formed a perfect Cupid's bow. A faint dusting of freckles became visible across her nose as he wiped the dried blood away. Something else he hadn't noticed in the heat of their passion last night. For one stupid second, he wanted to lean in and taste the soft skin beside her eyelid.

He moved closer and her eyes widened, then she said quietly, "My chest hurts. I think it was from the seatbelt when we rolled."

Pulling back a few inches, he shook his head, breaking the spell. He'd been about to kiss her, right in front of the female cop. What had he been thinking? "Yeah, mine too," he admitted. "But I'd rather have bruised ribs than the alternative." Then a sudden thought occurred to him that Bindi was hurt worse than she was letting on. "Dale will take us to the clinic in Dimbulah for a checkup, but if you think you need to go to hospital, I'll get Constable O'Hare to call an —"

"I'm fine," she spoke over the top of him. "It's just bruising. And a few bruises never stopped me before."

"As long as you're sure you're okay," he added, not averting her gaze from his until she nodded again. He'd had more than his fair share of busted ribs and bruises over all parts of his body. But he rode bulls for a living, that was expected. She was a woman unused to that specific kind of torture, albeit a feisty, tenacious woman, but he felt for her, nonetheless. The words *smart* and *sexy* also came to mind.

He stared down at her. She didn't deserve this. Didn't deserve to be caught up in his personal troubles. Guilt roiled in his stomach when he thought she might've been badly injured, or worse, killed in the accident. He wasn't sure he could've lived with that outcome. If he found out Clarissa had something to do with this, she'd better watch her back, because he was going to come for her. Bindi was an innocent bystander in this game of cat and mouse, and he was going to make damn sure she wasn't hurt again.

"My turn to clean you up," she said, taking the handkerchief from him and splashing more water on a clean corner. He settled himself cross-legged in the dirt and tipped his head back so she could reach his face.

"Do your worst," he told her.

She ran the cloth along the edge of his jaw, then under the soft skin below his bottom lip, and her touch felt more like a caress. He narrowed his eyes and watched her as her chin came up and she stared at him with half-closed eyes. Smoky and warm. His heart vibrated in his chest. She seemed to be enjoying this just a little too much. Gently turning his head sideways, she stroked down the side of his temple, and he closed his eyes for a heartbeat, enjoying the sensation of her fingers on his face. They sprang open again, as she swayed forward, bringing her breasts into his eye line. Had she done that on purpose? His breathing grew shallow as his gaze rose from her perfect breasts up to her mouth, which was pursed in concentration as she dabbed at his face, and he mapped the perfect outline of her lips. Her mouth was driving him insane. Had been driving him insane all morning, if he admitted it. And he wanted to take it and claim it again, like he'd done last night. Images bombarded him as he remembered with vivid detail how she called out his name at the height of her climax and dug her fingernails into his back. He wanted that again. And again. If that female cop wasn't standing right there, he might've tried taking her into his arms and kissing her until…

What was happening here?

Apparently, she had the ability to drive him so crazy with just one glance that he lost all logic and reason. He caught her fine-boned hand and ran his thumb gently over her delicate knuckles, stopping her ministrations. They'd shared one night of passion together, that was all. But this was getting too real, too fast. He was starting to care about her. And it needed to stop. Slowly, carefully, he put distance between them.

"Here comes the tow truck," Constable O'Hare stated, and Bindi jumped, as if only now remembering the police office was right there. If the cop had noticed what was going on between them, she was good at keeping her face blank. Mack thought she was probably more focussed on what her boss was up to, as he continued to poke through the wreckage and write in his little notebook.

It was clear the chemistry between he and Bindi burned bright. Perhaps brighter than anything he'd felt for any woman before. But that wasn't a good enough reason to lose all rational thought. He needed to be more careful around Bindi. He would make sure that she remained safe, of course. But this thing that was growing between them—something bordering on obsession, if he let it grow—needed to be shut down. He was into easy and safe, gratifying for both parties, while also being respectful and kind, but never getting stuck on one woman. That wasn't who he was.

"That was quicker than I expected," the cop added, frowning in the direction of the oncoming truck, and shading her eyes against the mid-morning glare. "I'll have to take your statements and do the breath test after we've loaded the car, if you're okay with that?"

Mack extricated himself the rest of the way out of Bindi's grasp. "Fine. But we're also going to report in to the station in Dimbulah, if you don't mind." He stood and squared his shoulders, looking down at the female officer. She might have shrewd eyes and a sharp mind, but she only just cleared five-foot. He wondered how she coped when she had to take down someone much bigger than her, like the guy Mutt, from last night.

"Senior Constable Nash King wants to talk to us," he added. Dale had already confirmed they should talk to Nash, and Mack was happier knowing they had someone they could trust. After his fall at the rodeo and subsequent run-in with the cops in Missouri, who said he had no proof and refused to believe him, he'd developed a wariness of the law. And if this rollover turned out not to be an accident, then he wanted as many good people in his corner as he could get.

The officer narrowed her eyes at him, but merely said, "Nash, huh? Right'o then. Give him my regards when you see him."

"Will do," he replied.

"If you two are okay, I'll go and give my senior sergeant a hand." The woman's focus was already shifting to the truck, now bumping over the grassy tussocks. Mack watched as the vehicle pulled up beside the senior sergeant and the driver hopped out to survey the smash. He shook his head more than once, and Mack had to agree with him. His car was a write off, and he wasn't sure how this guy was even going to get it loaded onto the flatbed. Thankfully, he was insured. He hadn't decided what his replacement truck was going to be, but he'd steer away from the Chevys from now on. He was beginning to learn that large, flashy trucks didn't fit in here in the outback like they did in the US, where the motto seemed to be *the bigger the better*.

Bindi went to lever herself off the ground, and he offered her a hand. She stood beside him, and he had to stop his gaze from skittering to the deep V between her breasts, to where all that creamy, soft skin resided.

"God, I'm stiffening up already," she sighed, wincing as she bent from side to side. "I wish Dale would hurry up and get here."

"Yeah, me too." He could sympathize. It'd be nice to sit in the comfortable seats of an air-conditioned car, rather than continue to stand out here in the increasing heat. But it'd be at least another half an hour before Dale could reach them. Bindi would know that, so instead of reminding her, he decided to tackle another niggling problem on his list.

"Before we get back to the station, there's one question I'd like answered," he said, keeping his tone casual.

"As long as it's not about Mutt or my family. I'm all talked out where they're concerned," she answered wearily, taking a sip from her bottle.

"No, it's not about that." He winced and almost changed his mind. She probably didn't want to think about this right now, either. But he needed to know where they stood. How he was supposed to act around her once they got back to the station. He'd pretty much made up his mind to stay away from her, but he needed to find out where she stood on the matter. "Are we... I mean, will we...?" Suddenly, he wasn't sure how to phrase his query. What he wanted to say was that he'd had a great time last night, and leave it at that. But this morning, as he'd looked into her face, he knew that wouldn't be right. Bindi wasn't some floozy he'd picked up off the street. She was special.

He wanted to nip this thing in the bud, but he didn't want to get Bindi offside, either. He was going to have to work with her for the next six to twelve months. Why he hadn't thought about that when she'd dragged him toward the tree line and set up the swag, he'd never know.

She lifted her dark gaze to meet his. "I've been wondering the same thing," she admitted. She studied him as she tapped the top of her bottle against her front teeth.

He wished she wouldn't do that; it was way too distracting. And sexy, even if she didn't intend it that way. It made him think about running his tongue over those teeth, then plunging in deeper, until...

"Look, you're an incredibly attractive man. And what we

did last night…well, that was fun."

Fun? It was way more than fun. A stupid twinge of defiance spasmed deep in his gut, but he quashed it. This wasn't the first time he'd had this conversation, and just because he was usually the one using that word instead of being on the receiving end, he shouldn't be offended. Apart from being slightly affronted, there was also relief. The tight belt of tension that'd been closing in around his ribs eased slightly. It sounded like they were on the same page. She was going to let him off the hook.

So why did he suddenly feel like he'd been rejected, then? And why did it hurt?

"But we're work colleagues and while I think you're fun, I don't want to jeopardize either of our jobs."

Again, there was that sinking feeling. She'd used that word again. Fun? He was hoping for another adjective, such as amazing, perfect, the best lover she'd ever had. Why was he taking this so personally? Hadn't he just decided he needed to put distance between himself and Bindi? That there was way too much chemistry between them. And here she was offering him a way out on a silver platter.

"I think I was a bit…overwrought last night. What with Mutt appearing and everything. I did something I don't normally do, and I'm sorry if I used you to help alleviate some of my mixed-up feelings. But I—"

He held up a hand to stop her and plastered a smile on his face. One more indecisive word from her would likely drive a dagger into his heart. If she was choosing to ignore the sparks that'd been flying between them merely a few minutes previous, then he could do the same. He needed to do the same. For his own sanity. This was exactly the same thing he'd been telling himself not five minutes ago.

"We obviously have a strong magnetism, but I agree. It'd be much better if we were just remain friends and coworkers, nothing more," he said.

Relief was written in her features. But she quickly shuttered her gaze and turned away, and he wondered if there'd been some other emotion lurking in the depth of her eyes.

"Good. I'm glad that's been decided." She fiddled with the lid of her plastic bottle and wouldn't look at him. "I'm sure —"

"I found a cell phone." The senior sergeant's voice interrupted whatever else Bindi had been about to say. Mack looked up to see the squat man marching toward them through the heat haze beginning to form on the flat plain. "It was on the ground a few feet away from the wreck. Must've been thrown free in the crash."

"That's mine," Mack said, reaching out a hand. But was disappointed when he saw the screen was smashed to smithereens. Damn. He'd need to order a new one.

"What about my phone?" Bindi asked hopefully.

"You're welcome to take a look." The senior sergeant shrugged and pointed at the wreck. "But it's a mess inside. An officer will go through it more thoroughly when it arrives at the police compound. They may well recover it then."

"You're taking it to the police compound?" Mack's head came up. "Does that mean you believe me? That someone tampered with the wheel?"

"It's policy whenever there's a question as to what caused the accident. A forensics team will go over the vehicle. I'm not going to say any more than that at the moment, son." Mack grimaced at the cop's patronizing tone, but at least it seemed he was taking them seriously, so Mack refrained from replying.

"I'll look for you," Mack said, walking toward his smashed vehicle.

"Make it quick then, son," Senior Sergeant Johnson

responded. "The towie wants to get it up on the trailer soon."

Mack hurried over to where his vehicle lay on its side in the dirt. Now that he was looking at it up close, he wondered again how they'd managed to escape relatively unscathed. Jagged cracks spider-webbed their way across the windshield, and the roof was partially caved in where the car had rolled over and over in the dust.

Gingerly, he clambered in through the passenger side window, the same way they'd escaped earlier.

A few minutes later, he emerged, feeling slightly less despondent. He'd found his black hat squashed in between the two seats. It was dusty and creased, but it was still in one piece. For some foolish reason, he was glad his hat hadn't been lost. With any luck, the forensic guys might be able to pry loose his gear bag from the wreckage of the tray, too. He really hoped he hadn't lost all of his bull-riding gear. It'd be hard to replace; he'd have to order it all in from the US. There was no sign of Bindi's phone. It could be anywhere; might've even been thrown free of the wreck like his had been. Looked like they were both ordering new cells.

Bindi had wandered over to watch what he was doing. Placing the black hat on his head, he gave her a rakish smile.

He thought he heard her murmur, "*Men*," before she turned away. But there was a definite smile on her face.

CHAPTER TWELVE

Bindi attacked the batter with the wooden spoon, beating it with gusto, until a deep ache reminded her of her bruised ribs. She'd spent the first two days after the crash supposedly recuperating in her room, although she was perfectly fine and all she wanted was to get back to work. And now Skylar had her on light duties in the kitchen, mixing up a batch of muffins for morning smoko, while Skylar and Julie were down by the billabong with Dale and Steve, helping them with the design of the arch where the bride and groom would stand and deliver their vows. Bindi itched to be down there, helping them. Weddings were such fun. Not that she was craving to get married herself, no sir. But the way love seemed to shimmer in the air on the day of a wedding was intoxicating. And the way friends and family gathered together for a heartfelt celebration, with more food and drink than the guests could handle. That was the fun part.

Hardly any expense was to be spared for this wedding. There were going to be thousands of fairy lights hung between poles and the trunks of trees, or around a raised wooden dance floor that Steve was building, especially for the occasion. On the day before the event, a large white tent would be erected, looking more like a castle from a fantasy book with soaring turrets and dipping white canvas, just in case of rain. It was the beginning of the rainy season, and while December could be deceptively dry, they might also have the first storm of the season sooner rather than later. Fingers crossed that wouldn't happen. With two weeks left before the marriage, the weather forecast was looking good, but that could change in the blink of an eye.

Daniella's brother, Dean, and his wife, Naomi, were flying over from Montana for the wedding. Dean was part owner of Stormcloud, but had only visited twice in the past fifteen years. So this was a momentous trip for more than one reason. Daniella had been rushing around like a headless chook for weeks, wanting everything to be perfect for the wedding, but also perfect for Dean.

With an irritated flick of her wrist, Bindi brushed a loose hair away from her forehead and a spike of pain flared behind her eyes. Bindi winced and closed her eyes for a second. Just as Mack had predicted, she was now sporting a wonderful black eye that any boxer would be proud of. Every now and then, the cut on her head twinged, as well, reminding her she still wasn't completely recovered.

The day of the accident had been long and excruciating in more ways than one. Dale had arrived to pick them up from the crash, and he took them straight to the medical clinic in Dimbulah. Mack had been right, she didn't require stitches; a few butterfly strips, and a bandage were enough to treat the wound on her temple. The doctor confirmed she was only suffering bruising on her torso from the seatbelt, and she'd recover with time and rest. The same went for Mack. And his leg was also fine. Then Dale drove them down to the police station and Nash met them at the door, concern written all over his handsome features. Once Bindi had assured him they were both okay, they recounted the accident to Nash, including the part where Mack thought it might've been sabotage. Then, she told her tale about Mutt and her brother as briefly as she could. Nash could find out the details from the New Zealand police if he needed more information. But he needed to know why she thought Mutt should be a person of interest in his inquiry. Nash's eyebrows rose when she told him about what Kai had done, but that was the only outward sign he was shocked by her brother's abuse. Nash was nothing if not professional with them both, and Bindi was almost glad when he didn't make a big thing over the incest part of her story. She might well have broken down in tears, if he had. Nash agreed to have Mutt found and interviewed as soon as possible.

Then Mack had told a strange tale of a man who'd accosted him after his ride at the rodeo, warning him not to try to get back onto the circuit. It was the first Bindi had heard of it, but now she understood the reason he believed Clarissa might be involved in this thing. He had no proof this thug was in any way connected to his nemesis, but he said his gut told him it was the case. Nash looked dubious when Mack said the words *gut instinct*, but agreed to follow the lead.

Arriving back at the station, all Bindi had wanted to do was crawl into her bed and sleep. Which she'd done a lot of over the past few days.

"Well, hello there." Bindi spun around, startled by the sound of the deep, male voice. Mack was standing in the doorway, flashing a glimpse of his beautiful smile at her. Her heart did a double-tap inside her chest. "How are you feeling?" Mack asked, an unusual awkward hesitancy in his voice. But then he grinned, that charming, handsome smile returning to his face, and her heart did a hundred double-taps all at the same time. He looked damn gorgeous. Today his black jeans were complimented by a sky-blue, Stormcloud work-shirt, with the logo on the left pocket. And his black Stetson, which he'd rescued from the car wreck, was perched at a jaunty angle on his head, the low brim giving him that dangerous, rakish look she was quickly getting used to. Apart from his own black eye—worse than hers due to his broken nose—a rough, day-old growth covered his jaw, and he looked roguish, like a warrior of old freshly returned from battle. And sexy as hell. The bruising only made him look more disreputable and dangerous.

Bindi had hardly seen Mack over the past few days, because they'd both been supposedly recuperating in their dorm rooms. Although, she seemed to have followed instructions better than he had, as she'd seen him from her bedroom window yesterday driving an ATV on his way down the driveway, possibly to retrieve the mail. She'd scowled at him through the glass. Why did he get to break the rules? While she was stuck in her room, with Skylar threatening to march her bodily back to her room if she dared set even one foot in the kitchen before her time was up.

She lowered her eyes, suddenly bashful about meeting his gaze. Then drew in a breath and forced her shoulders back. This would never do. They'd agreed to be friends; work colleagues. And she needed to start seeing him that way. Instead of the naked Mack who'd been haunting her dreams over the past two nights. Naked and doing things to her that friends just didn't do. Shit. She hung her head and closed her eyes. Why had she gone and thought that? Now, all she saw were those mental pictures of Mack doing things to her body all night long, dancing before her eyelids.

"Bindi, are you okay?" She didn't need to open her eyes to know a concerned frown was hovering between his brows.

"Oh, yep, I'm fine," she squeaked, lifting her head and nearly dropping the mixing spoon. Mack was no longer in the doorway. He was striding across the kitchen, an intent look on his face.

"Skylar said you were recovering well, but I should've

come and checked on you myself," he said, slowing his headlong rush, but not stopping altogether. He muttered something else unintelligible under his breath that Bindi didn't catch. Almost as if he was berating himself for leaving her alone.

Oh, God, he was coming around the kitchen island. Reaching for her. If he touched her, she'd melt into his arms, she just knew it. All her hard-won resolutions from the past two days would vanish in a puff of smoke. "No. Nope. You shouldn't have. I'm fine, really. Stay back." Desperate, she raised the bowl and wooden spoon, almost as if they were a shield that could protect her from his physical presence, and waved them in his face.

He stopped, tawny eyes widening in surprise. "Okay," he drawled. "No need to get snippy. I didn't mean to upset you."

Oops. Maybe she'd overacted. But it was too late to back down now. She tried to go for casual indifference. "No, you didn't upset me. I just need to get this batter in the oven, that's all." She bustled around the kitchen, laying the muffin trays with a clang on the solid wood countertop. "Skylar's left me in charge of getting smoko ready, so I'm a bit under the pump." Spooning batter into the moulds, she offered him a bright smile.

He backed away, and the concern faded from his eyes. Replaced by a sheen of hard emotion she couldn't quite pinpoint.

"Sure, you're busy. I'll leave you alone, then. See you around." The last words were thrown over his shoulder.

Ugh, that cocky swagger seemed to be back with a vengeance. She'd thought she'd broken through those barriers, so he no longer found the need to act all egotistical around her. Obviously, she'd been wrong. It was a bucket of cold water over her raging hormones she needed. Who was she kidding? Mack hadn't changed. Wasn't going to change. He was still the arrogant, hot-headed cowboy she'd first met on the road to Stormcloud a week ago. Why did she think that one night spent in a swag with him would alter who he was? Or how he viewed her?

"See ya," she called out, deliberately making her voice bright and energetic. Let him think he hadn't affected her at all. She watched until he disappeared through the doorway, then sagged against the countertop. She was going to have to get her shit together. Next time they met, she needed to be better prepared. Have her defenses well and truly in place, so he couldn't affect her like that.

Without any of the intensity of emotions she'd been feeling mere seconds ago, she apathetically spooned the rest of the mixture out.

The problem was, something was different about her since she'd returned from the rodeo. Something so subtle that she almost couldn't put her finger on exactly what it was. But deep down, she knew. She was different because of the night she'd spent with Mack. He was indelibly printed on her soul, whether she liked it or not. Whether she accepted it or not. There was a connection between them that no matter how hard she tried to ignore, it tugged on her heart every time he appeared. Like right now.

She'd spent the last few days dissecting in minute detail her reasons for sleeping with Mack. It'd been a reckless, spur-of-the-moment decision that was totally out of character for her. But why? And why Mack? Had she done it because she felt indebted to him for saving her from Mutt? Her heart had certainly run through a gamut of emotions that night. She'd been so angry at Mack one minute. Then terrified for her life the next. Then terrified for Mack's life the moment after that. He'd been so courageous, coming to her defense without a thought for his own safety. Savagely beating a man nearly twice his size. No one had ever done that for her before. Stood up for her. Saved her from physical harm. Defended her honor. Even before he knew her dirty little secret.

Least of all her brother. The one person who should've been her protector. But instead had turned out to be her tormentor. The only person who'd stood up for her all those years ago had been her father. Her mother had disowned her, preferring to wallow in her own grief and self-lassitude than to reach out to her only daughter.

It was no wonder Bindi had been drawn to Mack. Some tiny, wasted, girlish part of her brain saw him as her knight in shining armor, come to rescue her. If only he'd been around the night Kai had attacked her. But that was a pure fantasy. No one had saved her from Kai. No one ever would.

Later that night, all the Stormcloud staff were having dinner with the guests. There was only a week left and the last of guests would depart, leaving the station free until the middle of February, when it would all start back up again. Bindi was listening intently to the middle-aged lady on her left, who was explaining that she'd always wanted to visit this area, as it was on her bucket list, and she was so grateful to Steve for taking them up onto the escapement this afternoon so she could see the country spread out in all its glory beneath them. But as the woman, Gloria, expounded on how beautiful this land was, her gaze kept straying over to where Steve sat next to Daniella. Bindi didn't blame Gloria. Steve was a good-looking man. And he was well used to some of the female guests cooing over him. He put up with their attention with mildly amused humor. Daniella, however, wasn't so forbearing, and frowned at Gloria when she glanced once too often in Steve's direction.

Bindi was only half-listening to what Gloria had to say. The reason for her distraction was seated directly across from her.

Mack's scowl was deep and thunderous whenever their gazes met, even while he talked to the man beside him with animated charm. He'd been scowling at her all night, but never actually said a word to her. And she probably deserved it. But his frowning attention was making her nervous and others were starting to notice, as well. He'd removed his hat, and the light from the flickering candles Daniella used to set the dinner-time mood drew his features into sharp relief. A strong, aquiline nose and high cheekbones set off his determined mouth. Bindi hated to admit it, but Sasha had been right, Mack did have a come-hither gaze. When he looked at her with that heavy-lidded stare, it was as if she was the only girl in the world. And he wanted her and no one else. Which her head knew was ridiculous, if only her stupid heart would cooperate.

She wanted to ask him about his injuries, to see if they were healing as well as hers. And more importantly, she wanted to know if he'd had any more headaches or dizzy spells. The crash and the bump to the head may well have aggravated them. She needed to find somewhere private to ask him, but his standoffishness was grating on her, and she couldn't find the courage to open her mouth.

Nash came up and tapped her on the shoulder and she was glad for the interruption. "Will you and Mack come join me in the boardroom when you're finished, please?" He said it loud enough for Mack to hear. It must mean he had some news. Was it good or bad?

Bindi gathered up her plate and those of the guests beside her and took them into the kitchen on her way to the boardroom. Steve was already headed that way ahead of her. Of course, Nash would've invited him, because he needed to stay abreast of everything that happened on the station. A gust of relief left her lips at the thought she wouldn't have to face Mack with only Nash as a buffer. Perhaps with Steve in the room, Mack would stop sending her those glowering stares.

Mack was the last to enter the room, and he shut the door behind him.

"Good evening, everyone," Nash said as Mack took a seat right next to Bindi. And then leaned on the table, so that his arm was mere inches from hers. Couldn't he have sat on the opposite side? She could practically feel the electricity crackle between them. Would it look bad if she subtly moved away? Gritting her teeth, she decided to stay where she was. She was a big girl, and she could handle this small problem of Mack and his ego. Two could play at this game, she decided. Instead of moving away, she moved ever so slightly closer, so she could almost feel the fine hairs on his forearm tickle hers.

Bindi quickly decided that was a dumb move, however, when all her awareness funneled into her left arm, and the corner of Mack's mouth lifted in a smirk.

Before she could determine whether to back down and remove her arm from the table altogether, Nash spoke. "I had a call from Senior Sergeant Johnson in Cairns earlier this evening. And I thought you'd like to hear the update."

Bindi sat up straighter, taking the opportunity to drop her arm beneath the table, where she rubbed at her skin with her thumb to remove the tingle of Mack's proximity.

Mack said, "Damn straight. What's the news?"

"There are a couple of things," Nash said, holding first Mack and then Bindi with his gaze. "Forensics have finished their investigation on your vehicle and concluded the lug nuts were most likely tampered with. It's hard to say exactly once the wheel has fallen off, but it seems they might've been loosened so they were only just holding on by a single turn or two. A brand new vehicle like yours is highly improbably they just fell off by themselves. I'm surprised you got as far down the road as you did."

Mack grunted and tapped the table with his fingers. "Damn, I was stupid not to check my truck before we took off."

"There was no way to predict something like this," Steve cut in evenly.

"Steve's right," Nash said. "Whoever did this had a fair idea what they were up to."

"Yeah, probably hoping both of us died in the crash," Mack answered with a dark frown.

"We've opened an investigation into the crash," Nash went on. "Constable Willow—he's my offsider—will join forces with Constable O'Hare from Cairns and see what else they can uncover."

"Will they be able to interview Clarissa Melman?" Mack demanded. "I told you, she's the one behind all this."

Nash turned his cool, blue gaze onto Mack. "No, not in the first instance. We don't have any jurisdiction in the USA. And we also don't have any evidence she's involved. There has been no sign of this man you said accosted you in the parking lot. No witnesses to the altercation, and without a good description of the man, we don't really even know where to start," Nash said, his eyebrows drooping a little. "But if we can gather enough proof, we might be able to convince our buddies in Texas to bring her in for a chat."

Mack let out a gust of air. Bindi could see he was frustrated, but Nash was right, all they had to go on was Mack's word that this woman was corrupt. It was going to be much harder to prove it.

"Which brings me to the second item on our agenda," Nash added. "We caught up with your friend, Matieu Waititi." He speared Bindi with his sky-blue gaze.

Mack gave her a quizzical glance and Bindi told him hurriedly, "That's Mutt's real name."

"And?" they both chorused in symphony.

"What did he say?" Bindi added.

"And he denies all knowledge of tampering with your truck. His mates back up his story, confirming he crashed out in their hotel room and didn't wake until late the next morning."

"Hmm," Bindi mused. That didn't sound good. Mutt's two friends were giving him an alibi. It seemed they were back to square one.

"We're checking to see if there's any CCTV footage of the area. I believe there was a camera set up to monitor the parking lot at the rodeo." When Bindi raised a surprised eyebrow, he added, "There's a lot of money tied up in some of those vehicles and trailers parked in that paddock. Most councils like the rodeo organizers to keep an eye on things, nowadays. It stops them from getting sued."

Bindi was surprised, but the way Mack nodded sagely, he was obviously well versed in these small technicalities.

"Constable O'Hare also interviewed the stall holders closest to your end of the parking lot to see if they saw anything that night. But a lot of them were already packing up for the night, and now they've moved on to the next show, so it's going to be hard to catch up with them all. She's also talking to a group of the bronco riders who were supposedly drinking with Mutt and his mates before the incident where he attacked you. We're trying to piece together a picture of his movements that night."

That all sounded good to Bindi, who knew very little about police procedure.

"Did you find the missing lug nuts?" Mack asked, his voice rising with frustration. "What about searching Mutt's car? Or his house? At least to rule him out."

"We're working on that," Nash acknowledged. "We need a warrant to do those things, and we need to convince the judge before we can go waltzing on in there." Nash kept his demeanor calm, not letting Mack's exasperation ruffle him. Bindi supposed a cool head was a trait most police officers possessed in spades. Dealing with difficult customers was likely a daily event.

Nash went on, "Mutt doesn't seem to have any fixed address. At least not one that we can find. He appears to be couch surfing around friends' and acquaintances' houses in Cairns. A bit of an itinerant. So it's going to be hard to pin him down."

"How long has he been in Australia?" Bindi questioned, Mutt's words coming back to her. "Because he kind of hinted that he'd come here to find me."

"Really?" Mack turned to face her. "You never told me that."

"He didn't say it in so many words," she admitted. "But he said he'd heard that I was living near Cairns and he had nothing better to do, so he left New Zealand and flew here. I know that all sounds a little vague, but he also said he meant to make me pay for what I did to Kai. Like he's still holding a grudge against me. I know it sounds like a long shot, but did he come to Australia just to hunt me down? Or was it sheer coincidence that he bumped into me at a rodeo?"

"Those are all great questions," Nash agreed. "And ones we mean to get to the bottom of."

Steve spoke up for the first time. "Should we be worried about this Mutt guy?" he asked. "What I meant by that is, should we be worried that he might find his way out to Stormcloud? If he means to do Bindi harm, then…?" Steve didn't finish his thought, but he didn't need to, Bindi felt a sudden shiver run down her spine. She'd never considered Mutt would come out here to find her. She'd always felt completely safe at Stormcloud.

"We're keeping an eye out for him," Nash assured them all. "If he leaves Cairns, or tries to head this way, hopefully

Constable O'Hare will warn us."

That made Bindi feel a little better. Nash was an honorable man, and if he told her she was safe for the moment, then she trusted him.

"Do we even know if Mutt is aware Bindi is at Stormcloud?" Steve asked, ever the pragmatic one.

"Not sure," Nash admitted. "But it probably wouldn't be hard for someone to find out. He knows you were linked to Mack," Nash nodded in Bindi's direction, "and because of Mack's ride on the weekend, his name is on quite a few people's lips."

Silence engulfed the room as everyone digested Nash's words.

Steve was the first to break into their thoughts. "Well, let's cross that bridge if we come to it," he said. "Otherwise, we have a wedding to organize, and it's getting closer every day."

Shit, the wedding. Bindi hadn't even considered Dale and Daisy's upcoming nuptials. Nothing could happen to put that in jeopardy. Steve had probably meant to buoy everyone's spirits, but it made Bindi nervous. She didn't want to be the one to take any of the shine off Daisy's big day.

"Thanks, Nash," Steve continued. "I know you'll be doing everything in your power to sort this little hiccup out." He stood and shook Nash's hand. "I'll let you get back to Skylar, I'm sure she's eager to get out of the kitchen for the night."

"That she probably is," Nash agreed. Nash and Skylar lived in a gorgeous country home that they were renovating together down the road toward town, and Skylar was probably waiting for Nash to come and drive her home. "I'll just say my farewells to Daniella and everyone else."

Mack stood and also shook Nash's hand. "Yeah, thanks for all your help." Bindi couldn't help but notice the small *V* of a frown still hovered between Mack's brows. He was clearly not happy with the information the police had so far, but there wasn't a lot either of them could do about it.

The three men walked out together, still talking amiably as they headed toward the dining room. Bindi trailed behind, her mind racing with all the details—or lack thereof—and not concentrating on where she was going.

She turned into the kitchen and was accosted by Skylar. "There you are," she said, wiping her hands on a dishcloth. Sasha was nowhere to be seen, and the kitchen looked tidy and orderly, which meant they'd probably finished for the night. "Did you learn anything new? Any leads?" She asked, watching Bindi intently. Like everyone else at Stormcloud, Skylar was concerned about her and Mack's well-being after the crash. They all knew of the possibility that it wasn't an accident. But Bindi worried that Skylar's concern might also be skewed slightly by her worry over the upcoming wedding. Skylar didn't like it when things didn't go according to plan. Skylar had told Bindi on numerous occasions that she and Nash never discussed a case he was working on. Nash was particular about not compromising anybody or any case by letting details leak. It was a choice Skylar agreed with one-hundred-percent, being a stickler for the truth herself. But it meant that she'd have to rely on Bindi or Mack to get any particulars on this case.

Nobody knew the whole truth about Kai and what he'd done to her, apart from Mack, Nash and his police colleagues. Bindi knew she should tell Skylar and the rest of the crew, but wasn't ready to reveal the exact details just yet. Not when it still felt so raw. All they knew was that Mutt and Clarissa were two likely suspects, but not even Steve or Daniella knew the full story of Mutt's involvement.

"Not really," Bindi replied, skirting around the island countertop and perching on a stool opposite Skylar. "They've confirmed that the front wheel was definitely tampered with."

Skylar pursed her lips and tapped her chin with her finger. "Of course they did. We all knew Mack wouldn't lie about something like that." Bindi was surprised at Skylar's easy trust in Mack, considering her own reservations she had about the man.

"But Mutt denies coming anywhere near the car, and they can't even really start investigating this Clarissa lady, because she's in America," Bindi continued.

"Hmm. That's no good." Skylar's face took on a faraway look as she stared out the window, deep in thought. "But never doubt Nash, he'll keep going until he gets to the bottom of this."

"I'm sure he will." Bindi was about to lever herself off the stool when Mack marched into the room, and she froze on the spot.

"Goodnight, ladies," he said, sweeping his hat in a low, gallant swish. "I'm off to catch some Zs. Got an early start in the morning." With that, he flashed them one of his ultra-dangerous grins and disappeared out the door. Bindi was still hovering, half off the seat.

God, she needed to get over this stupid reaction whenever Mack walked into the room. Needed to stop the warmth that flooded her stomach at the sight of him. Needed to stop the tingle that started at the back of her neck, hoping that he'd reach over and touch her. Just one touch.

Clenching her teeth together, she flicked her braid over her shoulder with an annoyed jerk of her hand and stood up straight.

"Do you need anything else done tonight?" she asked. "Otherwise, I might head to bed, as well. I'm reading this great book at the moment..." Bindi trailed off. Why was Skylar looking at her like that?

"Did anything happen between you two while you were at

the rodeo?" Skylar asked. "I mean, apart from the accident, of course."

"What?" Bindi took an involuntary step backward. "No. Of course, not. Why do you ask?"

"Because you're as skittish as a long-tailed cat in a room full of rocking chairs when he's around."

"Don't be silly." Bindi gave a smile she hoped passed for amused indifference, even though her heart was racing. Skylar didn't know, did she? There was no way she could know. Mack had agreed they'd keep their little dalliance a secret, and she trusted him with that. He'd been nearly as keen as her not to tell anyone. And Bindi certainly hadn't spoken to a soul. Not that she was ashamed of having slept with Mack. He was a hot stud of a cowboy, and she knew no one would condemn her for one night of weakness. They'd probably cheer her on. Skylar certainly would. She'd been telling Bindi she needed a man in her life for ages. But this was something she was going to keep to herself. For lots of reasons. Lots of complicated reasons she didn't want to have to dissect right now.

"You know he's not my type," Bindi said, adding a breezy wave of her hand. "He's way too much of a pretty boy for my liking."

"Hmm," Skylar said thoughtfully, not sounding convinced as she watched Bindi head for the back door. "But pretty boys can still be fun," Skylar called after her.

Bindi kept going, determined to keep her feelings for Mack tightly under control. No one need know that she was attracted to him. That she might even be falling for him.

CHAPTER THIRTEEN

Mack watched the bright red helicopter lift off from the helipad. That was the last of the guests leaving the station; Aaron was flying them to Cairns in the Bell 505. For a second, Mack envied Aaron and his freedom to flit in and out on a whim. He'd heard the guy was learning the art of cattle mustering from the air—a dangerous job—and Mack decided that he and Aaron were more similar than he'd first thought. Both adrenaline junkies, even if they got their fixes in completely different ways.

The other guests had drifted away from the station in small groups over the past week. It was going to be quiet here without them. Until a different kind of guest descended, that was. Friends and family were due to start arriving in a few days, just in time for the wedding.

Dean and Naomi were going to be amongst them, and while it'd been less than a month since Mack left the US, he was looking forward to seeing a friendly face and catching up with news from home.

It'd been almost a week since Nash had passed on the report that they were opening an investigation into Mack's crash, but there'd been no more news, at least none that Nash was willing to share. Mack was frustrated by their lack of developments, but Steve had told him it didn't mean things weren't progressing, it just meant these things took time. Nash had confirmed that Mutt remained in Cairns and had issued no more threats toward Bindi. In fact, he'd just taken up a job as a cleaner at the local gym, which made Nash think he was going to be no more trouble. But Mack still chafed for answers. And that man in the parking lot hadn't been a figment of his imagination. He'd warned him to quit the rodeo circuit, or he'd suffer the consequences. What did that mean? Because he'd given the man an emphatic no, did it mean the man had escalated his threats that same night? It was a bit of a stretch, but not impossible. He was hoping to have a chat with Dean when he arrived, to see if he might be able to help him dig up some dirt on Clarissa.

Mack knuckled the small of his back and leaned back to stare at the sky. He was helping Steve put the finishing touches to the large dance floor, specially built, tucked into the grassy hill beside the billabong. He had to admit; the setting was magnificent. Pretty much the perfect place to hold an outdoor wedding. Steve had gone up to the machinery shed to fetch a few more screws, and Mack was taking the time to admire the scenery. Jesus, it was hot. He was still getting used to this heat. A mass of clouds sat low on the horizon, but Steve had assured him it wouldn't rain today. Or tomorrow. Or hopefully for the next week, right up until the wedding. But the clouds were adding a humidity that hadn't been noticeable before, and the sweat ran freely down Mack's back. He'd swapped his black dress hat for a more suitable one; a brown, work-stained Stetson he'd brought from Montana when he'd started his job at Stargazer.

A brightly colored bird swooped across the surface of the water, and Mack watched, fascinated by its skill, as the bird lowered its beak and came up with a small fish. He wished he knew what the bird was called. He should ask Bindi... Mack shook his head. Why did his thoughts always automatically go to Bindi?

"Hey, Mack?" Steve's voice drifted down the embankment.

Mack swiped the sweat from his brow and shaded his eyes against the midday glare. "Yeah, boss."

Steve strode down the grassy hill toward him. "We've run out of screws. And I need another can of paint for the arbor." He pointed to the almost-finished bower he and Dale had created for the ceremony. "Would you mind doing an emergency run to Clancy's Hardware in town? I've ordered the stuff over the phone, all you have to do is collect them. You can take my truck, if you like. The keys are on the hook in the kitchen."

"No problem," Mack said breezily. A break from the hard manual labor in this unrelenting heat would be welcome. This would be his third time in Dimbulah; the town was small enough that he just about knew his way around now.

"Thanks, mate." Steve gave a relieved sigh. "I swear, if we get all this finished in time, it'll be a bloody miracle. And even if we do, I'm sure Daniella will come up with a million other half-baked projects that need doing in record time."

Mack nodded, feeling his boss's pain. Weddings were always stressful and pushed most people's tolerance to the limit. Steve had the patience of a saint, if you asked him. If it'd been Mack that Daniella had been yelling at—no, yelling wasn't the right word, perhaps insisting in no uncertain terms described Daniella's demeanor this morning—he would've turned on his heel and stalked away, flatly refusing to add the stupid custom-designed, boho, rustic, wooden book stand thingy for guests' signatures she said was absolutely vital, to his ever-growing list of things that needed to be done.

Really? Was a custom-designed book stand really going to make the day perfect? He very much doubted it.

Mack removed his hat and ran a sleeve across his forehead,

slicking back his hair and knocking the dust from his hat against his thigh.

"I'll go right now," he added. There was still an hour before lunch, he could make the run and be back just in time.

"Great. Oh, and, Mack, ask Skylar if she wants anything while you're in town. I think she was saying she'd almost run out of sugar and flour, and her delivery won't be here until tomorrow."

Skylar had a big order coming in by truck, piled high with all the supplies for the upcoming wedding. But there were always things even the best prepared chef forgot.

"Sure thing, boss." Mack whistled as he headed up the hill toward the lodge. A nice drive in an air-conditioned car with the music cranked right up was just what the doctor ordered.

"Hey, Skylar," he said, tipping the brim of his hat as he strode into the kitchen.

She smiled.

Then he noticed Bindi and Julie huddled together over a recipe book. "Ladies," he said, a touch more circumspectly. "Steve's asked me to grab a few things from the hardware store in town. Do you need me to pick you up anything while I'm there?" He directed his question to Skylar as he reached for the keys to Steve's Land Cruiser.

"Oh, let me think." Skylar's forehead wrinkled with a frown, but then her gaze landed on the two women at the end of the countertop and one eyebrow went up in speculation.

"Actually, I was just going to ask Bindi to head out and grab me a few things."

Bindi looked up, surprised. "You were?"

"Mm-hmm," Skylar assented. "She can go with you? Can't she?"

"What?" Bindi's surprised look turned to one of slight outrage.

At the same time, Mack asked, "Can't you just tell me what

you want?" Damn, he'd been counting on a solo trip to town.

"No," Skylar said a little too quickly. "Bindi knows what I need. You'll get it wrong."

"Oh." He shot Bindi a glance. She looked as peeved as he felt.

Julie's mouth lifted in the slightest hint of a smirk as she watched the interplay without saying anything.

A little voice at the back of his brain told him this smelled a lot like a set-up. And the indignant line of Bindi's mouth, and the way Julie's eyes sparkled with mirth, supported his theory.

"Come on then, let's get going so we can be home for lunch."

Bindi hesitated, her gaze going from Skylar to Julie and back, an ever-deepening frown darkening her brow. Her black eye had faded now to a yellowish light-gray, but it still reminded him of the accident every time he looked at her. Reminded him how close they'd come to losing their lives. His own facial bruising was also fading, and hopefully, they'd both look almost normal by the time the wedding came around.

Bindi had definitely been avoiding him over the past week. Maybe this little plan Skylar had hatched to throw them together might be a good thing, after all. Give him time to find out what was going on behind that tense smile of hers.

Skylar took the lead, scurrying around the kitchen, writing out a list for Bindi—probably a list she dreamed up on the spot—and handing over the corporate credit card for her purchases.

Mack's patience was just beginning to wear thin when Daniella breezed through the doorway.

"Mack, I thought I heard your voice. Oh, and Bindi, you're here, too. Good. I just got a call to say your replacement phones have arrived."

"We're actually heading into town right now, that's amazing timing," Mack replied with a smile. This was great news. He was beginning to wonder if his new phone was ever going to arrive. Things certainly took longer out here in the back of nowhere.

"Good." Daniella waved a brisk hand in the air and turned on her heel to head back to her office.

"Okay, I'm ready," Bindi finally announced, and he led the way out of the kitchen.

In less than two minutes, they were simultaneously sliding into their seats in the car and Mack turned on the ignition. The enclosed cabin suddenly seemed too small and the air between them sparked to life, buzzing with tension. He caught a whiff of her shampoo as she flicked her braid over her shoulder to buckle her seatbelt. Mmm, grapefruit, he remembered it from the other night. Fresh and invigorating. It was certainly invigorating him as the memories took hold. Particular body parts of him, that was. How soft her skin had been. The way she giggled as he licked his way down to the sensitive spot in the small hollow of her hipbone. The way her dark hair fanned out like silk across the blanket as she gazed up at him, watching his face so intently.

Down, boy. He wasn't going to start fantasizing about their one-night stand. She was obviously over it, and he should be, too.

"Was that whole little spiel back there what I thought it was?" Mack asked, reaching over to turn on the air con.

"If you're asking, were we set up? Then yes, I'm pretty confident we were," she replied, raising one dark eyebrow in his direction. "Sorry about that. Skylar seems to think… Well, I'm not sure what she thinks, but whatever it is, she's wrong."

Mack didn't miss the slight pink flush at the base of Bindi's throat, but he pretended to ignore it, as he asked, "I'm assuming you haven't said anything about our little liaison the other night?" It was a relevant question, especially after the way Skylar and Julie had acted.

"God, no," she said, and he wondered at the intensity of her denial. "I don't know where those two get their crazy notions from," she added, almost as an afterthought.

She'd already said she didn't regret sleeping with him, but perhaps she'd changed her mind. Which was a shame, because the way his blood was running hot through his veins right now, he was pretty sure he'd jump at the chance to do it again, if she ever asked.

"You haven't mentioned it to anyone, have you?" she asked sharply, her beautiful eyes narrowing with suspicion.

"Nope. I'm a man of my word," he said, holding his hand over his heart, pretending to be deeply hurt by her veiled accusation. And it had hurt a little more than he liked to admit.

An awkward silence descended over the cabin as Mack guided the car through the main gates and onto the road into town. He wanted to ask her if her thoughts about their one-night stand had changed. Ask her why she seemed to be avoiding him.

"Have you had any more headaches?" she blurted suddenly, catching him off guard. "I mean, since the car accident."

He shook his head. Surprisingly, the answer was no. Like her, he'd half been expecting the dizzy spells to return with a vengeance, especially after the airbag going off in his face. But apart from the normal pain radiating from his broken nose, the more severe headaches hadn't made an appearance. What didn't surprise him was that Bindi was still concerned about his welfare. Because that was just the sort of person she was.

"That's good," she said with an exhale of relief.

"Yeah," he agreed, going for nonchalance.

"How's the insurance claim coming along for your car?"

"What?" Mack was taken aback at the change in topic. "Oh, right. Ah, slowly but surely."

"So, they're going to pay you out for a brand-new car? That's great."

He eased the car up to speed and settled back farther into his seat. Driving on the wrong side of the road still took more focus than he was used to.

"I guess so. Eventually." He shrugged and glanced over at her. She looked no different from any other day working on the station. Slim legs encased in faded denim, brown leather boots and a dark blue shirt with a few dustings of what he assumed was flour on the shoulder. But now he knew what resided beneath those clothes, his imagination wanted to run riot. There was something about her. Something that tugged at a place in his chest no one else had ever touched before.

"Once they wade through all this police red tape," he said, returning his gaze to the road. "I mean, the car is a write-off, there's no disputing that part. But this whole someone-tampering-with-the-car thing is giving them the excuse to drag their feet."

"It's always the same," Bindi agreed. "Insurance companies around the world will look for any loophole, if it means they don't have to pay out."

"Amen to that," he agreed.

"Are you going to get another truck the same as the last one?"

"Not sure yet. Aaron showed me his new Ford Ranger the other day. It looked like a sweet ride. I might think about one of those." Aaron had taken him out for a quick spin after dinner the other night when he'd heard Mack was considering something else to replace his wrecked Chevy. They'd had a lot of fun racing over the gravel roads as Aaron put his vehicle through its paces. Then Mack had his turn and had been impressed by the handling ability and speed of the truck's pickup.

"What, no jet-black, flashy Chevy that screams *look at me*?" Bindi said with a laugh. "Don't tell me you're actually considering function over form?"

"Now, I wouldn't go that far," he countered. "But they seem more...suitable for this type of country, that's all."

"Ah, I see." Bindi stretched out her legs and leaned back into the seat. Relaxing a little, as if they were back on stable ground. The act of mundane conversation seeming to draw off some of that tension leaking from her like she was a live electrical wire.

He decided to leave his inquisition about what was going on between them for now. It was nice to have her acting normal around him, for once.

The rest of the drive into town, they chatted about other brands of vehicle that might suit him. Bindi admitted it was probably time she traded in her old car for something newer. But she liked her yellow ute, it had character and class, something she said was missing from most of the modern, over-the-top trucks nowadays.

Mack dropped Bindi off out the front of the small supermarket and headed to the outskirts of town, where Clancy was waiting for him, the items Steve needed already boxed up and ready to go. Mack chatted with Clancy for a few minutes—the old bloke seemed keen to talk, there weren't a lot of customers that Mack could see—before he hopped back into the Land Cruiser and parked in the main street, waiting for Bindi to return. She was also picking up their new phones from the post office, and he hoped she wouldn't be too long.

He fiddled with the radio until he found a tune he liked and wound down his window, humming along to the tune, watching the small-town locals go about their business. Bindi had told him a lot of tourists travelled through Dimbulah, it was a hub for many tourist sites in the area, and he noticed a couple of big four-wheel-drives parked along the road with vans hitched behind them. But the tourists would wane over the coming wet season as the roads got too dangerous, or became impassable because they were flooded. Mack found it hard to believe this dry, barren land would soon be covered with sheets of water. But everyone kept telling him it was true, so he guessed they couldn't all be wrong.

Bindi jerked the door open and bustled inside. "Quick, drive," she said in a breathless pant.

"What? Why?" he asked, but he was already starting the car.

"I saw Mutt." She was trying to stuff bags of food into the footwell, while glancing through her side window, hat sitting askew on her head. "The guy in the post office took forever because he was helping me set up my new phone, which is why I'm running late. When I came out, I was in a hurry, and I nearly dropped all my bags. And that's when I saw him."

Mack swiveled his head to peer into the rear vision mirror. The street looked normal to him, just people going about their business. Nevertheless, he waited for a four-wheel-drive to pass slowly by and then pulled out onto the main road.

"Are you sure it was him?" Mack maneuvered through the slow-moving traffic, muttering curses under his breath as the line of cars came to a standstill while some old geezer reversed his car into a parking spot.

"Yep. He was across the street. He looked straight at me." Bindi sat forward in her seat, tense, eyes scanning the street behind them.

"What the fuck?" Mack exclaimed. "Nash said his cops were keeping an eye on the guy. How the hell did he get here without someone notifying us?"

"I don't know," Bindi replied tightly. "I just want to get

back to Stormcloud."

Mack agreed, but this traffic was going to be the death of him if it moved any slower. There were too many cars for him to track who was driving what. "Did you see him get into a car?" he asked.

Bindi shook her head. "Nope, he took off running back down the street."

That was odd. But Mack had no time to dissect the other man's behavior as the line of cars finally cleared and he took a right-hand turn to get out of town. They passed the sign for the town limits and Mack sped up, breathing a sigh of relief as the bitumen opened up clear and wide in front. Bindi still gripped the handrail above her head, tension radiating through her body.

A white truck appeared in his rear vision mirror, moving fast, gaining on them.

"Call Nash," Mack said as calmly as he could.

"What?"

"Call Nash and tell him you saw Mutt. Tell him there's a car following us."

"Oh, shit." Bindi swiveled in her seat to peer through the back window. "Do you think that's him?" The four-wheel-drive kept gaining on them, and Mack put his foot down, too.

"Yep," Mack replied with a growl.

"What does he think he's going to do?" Bindi asked, her voice sharp.

"I don't know, but I need you to call Nash, just in case. Okay?" The other car was still gaining, even though he was now going as fast as he dared.

Bindi fumbled through her handbag for her new phone. Thank God the man in the post office had the forethought to help Bindi set up her phone, otherwise they'd have no way to contact Nash. There was silence as she rang Nash's personal number and they listened for his reply. Her knuckles were white where she grasped the phone.

"Shit. Hold on," Mack yelled, as the car careened up and hit them hard from behind. The Land Cruiser jolted forward, but he managed to hold his line on the road.

Bindi squealed and nearly dropped the phone.

"This guy is a fucking maniac," he said, mind racing, wondering what his best options were for getting away from this idiot. If he kept going at this speed, they'd be killed if he crashed.

"Nash," he heard Bindi shout into the phone. "Mutt is chasing us in his car. He's smashing into us. We've just left Dimbulah in Steve's Land Cruiser, but he's following us and Mack's driving as fast as he can, but Mutt has already hit us." Bindi was biting her lip, face pale and drawn.

Mack didn't hear all of Nash's reply, but the man's voice was authoritative and calm. Bindi described where they were and rang off, then stared through the back window at Mutt's car, which was weaving dangerously across the road behind them. "He's at the police station in town, so he won't be far behind us."

"Great." Help was on the way. They just had to keep this madman away from them until it arrived.

"He also said that he was about to call Steve to let him know Mutt had disappeared from Cairns this morning."

"A bit late for that little detail," Mack muttered.

Suddenly, the vehicle rammed them from behind again, and this time the rear wheels swung out slightly before Mack could get the steering back under control, the car swerving dangerously down the bitumen.

Bindi let out a short scream and held on tighter.

He couldn't keep doing this. If the car rolled, they might not be so lucky this time.

He took his foot off the accelerator.

"What are you doing?" Bindi yelled.

"We can't outrun him." Mack tried to keep his voice as calm as Nash's had been. "His car is more powerful than ours. And he seems determined to get to us. I think he's trying to force us off the road. If we crash now…" He knew he didn't need to finish the sentiment. "So the other alternative is to slow this whole race down, and hope that Nash gets here sooner, rather than later."

"But we can't just stop. What if he has a gun? What if he actually wants to kill us?"

Mack hadn't considered that. "I'm not going to stop," he said, moderating his tone to make him sound more in control than he actually was. "I'm going to slow down to a pace where we can hopefully dodge out of his way." Perhaps he might even be able to swing the car around and head back toward town. That might make this fucker run away, he couldn't keep chasing them down the main street. Could he?

"I can't do this again," Bindi whimpered. "I can't go through another car crash. Please, just make all this go away." She hunkered her head down and covered her ears with her hands. She was freaking out, and he didn't blame her.

But he didn't have that luxury, and so he focussed on the road ahead. He made his decision and slowed the car, allowing Mutt to get closer. The idiot rammed the car twice more, and it was all Mack could do to keep the car on the road. Mack considered slamming on the brakes and letting the other car smash into him. That might stop him. It was a good idea. As good as any he could come up with. Just as he was about to tell Bindi to hang on with everything she had, another car appeared on the opposite side of the road, coming toward them. He'd have to wait until they passed, he couldn't endanger other innocent drivers.

But when the car was still a hundred meters away, Mutt rammed them with such force the left front wheel dropped into the dirt at the edge of the road. Mack tried vainly to keep the car on a straight line, but they must've hit something, because the wheel was wrenched from his hands and the vehicle leapt back onto the road, clipping the other car as it careened on its headlong trajectory. Mack grappled gamely with the steering wheel, but the car continued its bearing and went off on the opposite side of the road, sliding sideways, leaving the bitumen and skidding across the wide expanse of dirt. After what seemed like an eternity, the car came to a juddering stop at an angle to the bitumen as the wheels dug into the soft dirt.

Mack glanced back the way they'd just come.

The car going the opposite way had stopped in a flurry of dust a few hundred meters down the road, the driver already stepping out of his car with a look of horror on his face. Thank God that poor man had managed to stay on the road and seemed to be uninjured. The last thing Mack wanted was to be responsible for injuring or perhaps killing an innocent bystander.

Bindi groaned, and he turned his attention to her. "Are you hurt?" He asked urgently. At least the airbags hadn't deployed this time.

"I'm fine," she said.

"Look at me," he demanded. He needed to make sure for himself that she really was okay.

As she lifted her head, Bindi's eyes widened with horror. "He's going to ram us." Her words came out in a strangled gasp.

Mack flicked a quick look over his shoulder out his window and saw the other car stopped in the middle of the road, lining them up. Mutt peered through the windshield, a sneer shadowing his face. Mutt didn't seem bothered about the man they'd nearly run off the road, he was intent on only one thing. He gunned the engine and smoke plumed in the air as he spun the wheels, taunting them, the clownish grimace getting wider as he lined up their car.

Mack turned the key over in the ignition, but the car wouldn't start. He tried it again, never taking his eyes off Mutt, but again nothing. The car was dead. They were sitting ducks. Mutt was watching them like a snake might watch its prey. Knowing he had them cornered, playing with them.

Mutt's grin suddenly widened, and he made a motion of slicing his hand across his neck. Then the wheels stopped spinning, and the car barreled toward them.

Mack threw himself over Bindi, in the vain hope of protecting her, waiting for the impact.

It never came.

Instead, he heard the screech of tires, then looked up to see Mutt backing off as the soft wail of a police siren filled the air.

Mack sat up and saw the flash of blue and red away in the distance. Mutt was looking from them to the police car, and then back. With a grimace of frustration, he took off, wheels spinning on the bitumen, speeding down the road at breakneck speed.

Mack sank back against his seat, letting out a gust of air. "Sweet Jesus, Nash just saved our butts," he said quietly.

CHAPTER FOURTEEN

Bindi tucked her hands between her knees and stared at Aaron across the large boardroom table. He was talking animatedly to Mack, with Steve listening intently, and even though she was supposed to be paying attention, Bindi tuned out and instead took the opportunity to compare the men. Aaron had the physique of a bodybuilder, broad across the shoulders and heavily muscled, with biceps larger than the width of her thigh. When she'd first met him, she'd hardly been able to look away, fascinated by his multicolored eyes; one brown, one blue. But now, she hardly noticed them. He was often serious, rarely smiling—unless Julie was around—and was a man of few words. But when he spoke, everybody listened. Bindi liked Aaron, he'd become a trusted member of the Stormcloud family. Strong, reliable, stable.

Mack, however, was almost the complete opposite. Where Aaron was dark and mysterious, Mack exuded light and charm and warmth. And where Aaron was muscle-bound, Mack was lithe and sinewy. The hard, flat planes of his chest and abs were still well-defined—as she could well attest to after their one night together—but with none of the beefcake that Aaron carried. When she'd first met Mack, she'd passed him off as arrogant, full of corny Americanized glamour. But she come to realize that was more of an act, to cover his more reserved side. His personality went deeper than most people were aware, and his need to please people, to be the best at everything, including his beloved bull riding, was a cover for a lack of self-confidence. As if he felt like he always needed to prove himself. Bindi wondered about Mack's early life. Had something happened to him to make him feel this way? Where Aaron was reliable and stable, Mack seemed vivacious, mercurial, but with a lack of commitment to anything long-term.

Which was the thing that was bothering her right now. Even though she knew she shouldn't be considering it, because she wasn't interested in long-term anything with Mack. Her mind flitted back to this morning before Mutt had chased them.

Once they'd overcome the awkwardness of the first few minutes on the drive into town, they'd developed an easy, friendly banter. It felt natural to talk to him, and as long as she managed to keep her libido in check and her mind out of the gutter so that she could actually listen to what he was saying instead of letting fantasies rule her head. She found he was knowledgeable about a lot of the same things she was interested in. But she was confused how he felt about her. Did he care about her, or not? They were supposed to be friends, but the way he'd looked at her in that moment after Mutt had driven their car off the road; it'd been more than mere concern for a fellow workmate she'd seen echoed in his eyes. And then he'd covered her body with his own when he thought Mutt had been about to ram them. There was no doubt in her mind that he'd do anything to protect her, he was courageous and fearless. But had he done it because he felt responsible for putting her in that position? Or had he done it because he'd cared more than he let on?

It was confusing. He was confusing. And it was all made

even more confusing because she'd already made the decision to stay away from him. One night was all they were ever going to have.

Steve suddenly got up out of his chair and began pacing across the room, drawing Bindi out of her spiraling thoughts. Aaron was talking about the company who used to employ him as a bodyguard, Shield Solutions.

"Timmo said he could be here by tomorrow if we decide we need him. What do you think?" Aaron also stood, watching Steve closely. Timmo, short for Timmothy, was one of Aaron's old teammates, if Bindi remembered correctly.

"I think that's probably a good idea," Steve answered slowly. He turned to stare thoughtfully at her. "The last thing we need is this getting any more out of hand. Not with the wedding coming up, and all our family arriving in the next few days."

Bindi swallowed the bile threatening to rise up her throat. The last thing she wanted was to cause any problems for Dale and Daisy and their family. And that was exactly what she was doing.

"I don't believe this Mutt person poses a threat to anyone else but Bindi," Aaron said. "So, we'll concentrate Timmo's protective services on her." Bindi took it that when Aaron said *we'll*, he meant that he'd also be stepping back into his role of bodyguard for the next little while. Bindi remembered how he'd carried a gun in a shoulder holster when he'd first arrived at Stormcloud. Back then, he'd been employed to guard Julie from her crazed stalker, but he'd never really lost that vigilant demeanor. She guessed it wouldn't take much for him to take up his old mantle for a few days, or weeks, whatever was called for.

"I can still leave," she said. "Then you wouldn't need to take these precautions."

"You're not going anywhere," Steve said with a barely

disguised sigh.

It was the same conversation she'd had many times with him and Daniella, Skylar, and Daisy over the past few hours. They'd all been adamant she wasn't leaving. Daisy said there was no way Bindi was going to miss her wedding, and one stupid psychopath wasn't going to put a damper on her nuptials. Skylar said she couldn't possibly produce the complicated wedding menu they had planned without her— which was possibly true, as Bindi would be an integral part in preparation and then executing on the day. Daniella and Steve had taken it all in their stride, Daniella blithely saying that it wouldn't be a wedding without some form of trouble, and they were getting used to this sort of thing at Stormcloud. Like it was a badge of honor to have something else go wrong.

Bindi felt ill at the idea that Steve and Daniella were having to pay Shield Solutions to protect her. Almost as much as she hated the idea of Aaron having to take up his old role again. Just for her.

"We might also get Jake up here to help on the day of the wedding," Aaron mused. "How many people did you say were coming?"

"A hundred and fifty guests," Steve replied, with a mock eye roll. "I'll never understand where on Earth Daisy and Daniella dig all these people up. If I was organizing this, there'd be twenty people, tops."

The three men all nodded sagely in agreement, but Bindi mentally shook her head. Twenty people at a wedding, how ridiculous.

"Right, I'll go and fill Daniella in on the plan." Steve collected his hat from the table, but stopped in the doorway and turned to face Bindi. "Stop worrying," he said kindly. "None of this is your fault. Nash will hopefully find this maniac before he does anything else stupid, and the wedding will all go off without a hitch."

She pursed her lips. She wished she had his optimism. Steve always saw the good side of people, found the silver lining amongst the clouds in even the darkest scenario. "Thanks, Steve," she mumbled.

Nash had called into Stormcloud, returning empty-handed after pursuing Mutt's vehicle, apologizing profusely to Bindi. He said he'd only got the call through from Senior Sergeant Johnson a few minutes before she called him in a panic, telling him Mutt was chasing them. Nash was livid that the Cairns police didn't seem to take this problem as seriously as they should, and he'd promised Bindi he was going to drum into them that their lack of surveillance had nearly cost Mack and Bindi their lives.

"Aaron, are you ready to take off soon? Dean and Naomi's plane lands in Cairns at five-thirty. I want to make sure we're there to meet them when they disembark," Steve said.

"Sure am, boss." Aaron gave a grim nod.

"Good, I'll go and hurry Daniella along, then."

Oh, God. In all the hullabaloo, Bindi had clean forgotten Dean and Naomi were arriving this evening. Daniella must be beside herself. She hadn't seen her brother, Dean, in over six years, and she'd want everything at Stormcloud to be in tiptop shape for their arrival. She was probably running around in a flap, putting the finishing touches on everything before she hopped on the helicopter with Steve and Aaron to collect them.

"I'd better go and give Skylar a hand," Bindi chimed in. Because if Daniella was in a flap, it probably meant she was harrying everyone else, including Skylar, and she'd need her help.

"Good," Steve acknowledged. "Mack, you right to finish up that dance floor by yourself? There are only a few more planks to go in, and now we have those extra screws, it shouldn't take long."

"I'm on it," Mack promised, also standing and taking up his hat, watching as Steve turned and left the room.

"Anything else you need me to do before we go?" Aaron asked, following Steve down the hallway. Their conversation became muted as they turned into the great room.

Mack surprised Bindi by waiting by the door, hat dangling from one hand.

She glanced up at him. Why was he looking at her like that?

"Stop it," he said gently.

"Stop what?" What was he going on about?

"Stop blaming yourself for all of this." He put a hand on her shoulder. The sudden contact made her gasp quietly. "You're the type of person who takes all that responsibility on your shoulders. You're letting the guilt eat you up inside."

"I am?" she asked, surprised. Not surprised that he thought she was that type of person, but surprised he'd been perceptive enough to see it.

"You are. I know because of what you told me about your brother. The way you acted with him."

Oh. She'd almost forgotten she'd told him that story.

"You're sweet and ingenious. Perhaps a little too trusting, and way too liable to shoulder other people's burdens."

"I am?" she asked again, unable to come up with any other response. Here was the Mack other people rarely ever saw. The insightful, smart guy, full of empathy. It made her want to cross those last few inches separating them and lean against his chest. Feel his heart beating beneath her ear and absorb some of his strength.

"Yes." He ducked his head so he could look directly into her eyes. "You've just been through two extremely scary accidents in the past week. But yet you continue on like the trooper that you are. As if nothing is wrong."

"I do?" Bindi knew she was starting to sound lame, but his words struck a chord deep inside. He was right. She stared up at his handsome face, unable to form any words. His tawny eyes reminded her of a tiger at rest, watching over his domain, all noble and chivalrous, but with a light of danger in their depths.

When he pulled her to his chest, she didn't resist. The need to soak some of his proffered empathy, imbue herself with some of his confidence, was too great. She lay her cheek against his shoulder, put her arm around his waist and just leaned into him. His arm wrapped around the small of her shoulders and she shivered at the safety she felt within his embrace.

"We've been through some heavy shit this past week, you and I," he said softly. "It doesn't make you weak or soft if you need to take a few minutes to process it all. Speaking from experience, it's better not to keep it all bottled inside."

What the hell? It was almost like he was telling her it was okay if she wanted to cry on his shoulder. And to be honest, a lump was forming in her throat at his words. He was right, the past week had been a shock to her system. It was nice that he took the time to acknowledge her situation, but she wasn't about to break down in front of him. It was enough to let him hold her for a few minutes; his touch a balm to her soul.

"You know what I just discovered?" he said, conversationally, his deep voice rumbling through his chest and into her ear. She shook her head. "Steve and Dean are quite alike in a lot of ways. They both value their staff highly —see them as part of the family—and would do just about anything to keep them happy and safe. I admire Steve for getting on top of this so quickly. I have to admit, at first, I was a little surprised that he agreed so readily to Aaron's proposal of upping security." He drew in a deep breath. "What I'm trying to say is that Steve would've done the same for any of his other staff or friends. He cares about you. And remember, he's doing this to protect his own, as much as you."

As he spoke, his hand moved to the slope of her neck, gently stroking the skin just below her collar. His fingers shifted under her hair, his slow, soothing strokes tormentingly sweet, sending goose bumps down her spine. It made her go suddenly weak at the knees, and she slumped a little more against him. A hazy heat slid through her veins, settling between her legs. Holy...how could he do this to her with a simple touch?

"You think so?" she asked, pulling back slightly, so he had to remove his hand from inside her collar. She was both relieved and aggrieved at the loss of his touch.

"I know so," he replied, looking down into her face. His light-caramel-colored eyes locked onto hers.

"Bindi, where are you?" Skylar's voice drifted down the hallway.

Their gentle moment was shattered. Had he been going to kiss her? Did she want him to kiss her? Good thing she didn't need to answer that, as they heard Skylar's footsteps on the slate floor outside.

Bindi pulled away just as Skylar rounded through the door. "Oh good, you're here. I need your help. Daniella has gone completely crazy, and she's trying to tell me we need to order more champagne. She wants me to get six more cases. Come and help me talk some sense into her, will you please?" Skylar was flustered enough not to notice Bindi's own agitation as she straightened her shirt. "Oh, hi, Mack," Skylar added absentmindedly.

"Let's go," Bindi said, practically pushing Skylar out the door, before she had time to put her devious mind to wondering what she and Mack had been up to, alone in the boardroom.

* * *

Dean threw back his head and laughed so hard, Bindi thought he might fall off his chair. The Stormcloud group had finished their late meal and was now sitting around the comfy chairs on the veranda, enjoying an after-dinner glass of sherry. Dean and Naomi were the center of conversation, everyone watching them with barely concealed fascination, as Dean regaled them with tales from Stargazer Ranch.

Bindi let her gaze wander between Daniella and Dean. There was a similarity to their features, something about the eyes, and the long, straight nose. But they were as different as chalk and cheese, personality wise. Dean was as charming and magnanimous as Mack had told her. His round face was always wreathed in a smile, and he had a kind word for everyone he met.

Now that Dean was here, Daniella had settled down and stopped her frantic and often ridiculous nagging, which had everyone else running on the spot. Her newfound calm was in part thanks to Naomi, whose cheerful, but serene demeanor was like a slick of oil over Daniella's troubled waters. Naomi was a petite brunette, pretty, but Bindi detected an inner strength that belied her stature and her smile.

Bindi took another sip of the sherry, letting the warmth of the amber liquid settle in her chest. A full moon hung low over the escarpment, and the stars sparkled in the sky. It was a perfect night, and Bindi was feeling a soft glow of contentment. Her eyes found Mack, and he smiled at her. He was sitting on the opposite side of the group, centered in a semi-circle around Naomi and Dean. They couldn't have picked a better night to arrive. The air was alive with the sounds of night animals, small plops and splashes from the direction of the billabong heralding a fish surfacing or a frog jumping for an insect.

She smothered a yawn just as Sasha stood up. "It was

lovely to meet you," she said. "But I've got an early start in the morning." She picked up her empty glass.

"Lovely to meet you, too," Dean and Naomi echoed together. "Goodnight." They waved, but before Sasha could take two steps across the veranda, Alek was by her side.

"I'll walk you back to the staff quarters, if you like?" He stood close, without touching, hesitantly waiting for Sasha to answer.

"Thank you," Sasha consented. "That would be nice."

Bindi almost choked at their formality. They were so sweet she had to look away, so Sasha didn't catch her grinning like a loon at them. Julie, who was sitting next to Bindi, actually had to cover her mouth to stifle a giggle and then nudged Bindi's arm. She, Julie and Skylar suspected the couple had started seeing each other on the down low, but Sasha wouldn't admit it, her face always blushing a deep red if anyone brought up the subject.

Aaron asked what Julie thought was so funny, and she shushed him with a mock frown. "I'll tell you later," Julie mouthed to Aaron. They were another sweet couple. Stormcloud was abounding with loved-up pairs. Everyone was taking bets that Skylar and Nash would be next to tie the knot. But Bindi was holding out for Julie and Aaron, who'd found love a second time after twelve long years of separation. They were so right for each other, and the way Aaron looked at Julie sometimes, as if she was the only woman in the world, it nearly made Bindi swoon. Made her want something like that. True love that'd last the distance.

Bindi gave another yawn. She was more than ready to get some sleep, but she'd wait another five minutes until Sasha and Alek were well out of the way. All of a sudden, Mack was at her elbow, hunkering down next to her chair. She hadn't noticed him move because she'd been so enraptured by the two lovebirds.

Mack had seemed more attentive since their moment together in the boardroom. As if something had shifted between them. The wall of wary watchfulness she put up when he was around had been lowered by the kindness he'd shown her. He seemed less presumptuous, and she knew she felt less prickly, less in need of protecting herself.

"I'll walk you back to the staff quarters too, if you like?" He raised a wicked eyebrow and Bindi almost swatted him. He demurred and said, "I saw you yawning over here, and knew you'd be heading off shortly, too. But I wanted to talk to you quickly, if that's okay."

What did he want to talk to her about? There was only one way to find out. "Sure," she replied, and stood up. "I'll meet you in the kitchen." She scooped up her empty glass, then weaved between the chairs, retrieving other glasses that'd been haphazardly left under chairs and on scattered side tables. When her hands were full, she stood in front of Daniella. "I'm shattered. I'll see you in the morning."

"Thanks for all your help. We couldn't have done it without you," Daniella replied, waving a hand around at the satisfied group of people lounging on the veranda. "Especially after the day you've had." Bindi knew she meant after her run-in with Mutt. Daniella might have high standards and expect everyone else to step up, but she also was the first one to acknowledge a job well done. She might demand the best of someone, but she wasn't stingy when it came to praise, either. While she and Steve had been off picking up Dean and Naomi, Bindi and Skylar had worked their butts off to make sure the dinner they served up to their American guests was of the highest quality. With everything else going on regarding the wedding, they didn't really have time to create a five-course gourmet menu. But Daniella wanted to showcase the best Stormcloud had to offer, so Skylar had agreed on the proviso that the rest of the meals from here on until the wedding would be nutritious, but simple affairs. Daniella agreed with an airy wave of her hand that left neither Bindi nor Skylar convinced of her sincerity.

There was a chorus of *"Goodnight"* from the others lounging in their chairs as Bindi headed through the French doors into the great room.

No one seemed to have noticed that Mack had disappeared.

He was waiting in the kitchen for her, just as she'd asked. Sprawled against the countertop, he raised one sexy eyebrow in a smoldering look as she entered, and it was all she could do to keep hold of her handful of glassware. He'd dressed up for the arrival of his old boss, Dean, wearing a charcoal-gray shirt with white swirls on the collar and down the arms, teamed with his skinny, black jeans and a pair of dark brown leather cowboy boots. The shirt was unbuttoned to reveal his toned pecs, a smattering of curls appearing in the V of the shirt. Why was he so damned hot? And why was she so affected by him?

"Here, let me help you." He reached out and took some glasses from her hands. She pretended not to feel the thrum of anticipation as his fingers touched hers.

"Shall we take a quick walk up to the stables?" He tilted his head and watched her out of hooded eyes.

She should say no. It was dangerous to be alone with him. Especially the way she was feeling tonight.

"Yes." Her mouth answered, even as her brain cursed her. He motioned for her to lead the way, and she walked down the short hallway to the back door, conscious of him right behind her. They didn't speak on the short trip up the hill to the stables.

They reached the stabling yard, and by force of habit, Bindi went up to the fence and gave a low whistle, calling Sahara over. The horse was a pale wraith in the shadows, placing her warm muzzle in Bindi's hand.

"What did you want to talk to me about?" She kept her focus on the horse. This conversation needed to be straightforward and candid. That way, she couldn't stray into prohibited territory.

"What?" Even in the dim light traveling out through the wide stable doors, she could see his gaze following the length of her legs, up over her hips and finally coming to rest on her face. Then his eyes seemed to clear, but instead of being embarrassed that she'd caught him checking her out, he merely smiled that rakish, pirate smile of his, and said, "Oh, yeah, that."

One night only. One night, that was all she wanted. She didn't need any more from him.

Perhaps if she tattooed that on the inside of her eyelids, she might begin to follow her own rules.

It didn't help that they were standing in the exact same place where Mack had first told her about his injuries and asked her to keep his secret. The same place where she'd first felt the carnal attraction of him, where her body had reacted to his tempting, raw sexuality, even though she tried to deny it. She wished he'd chosen a different spot. One that didn't remind her how much she still wanted him.

"I talked to Dean tonight. And he's going to start his own little investigation into Clarissa Melman."

"Okay, that's good." Was that all? Why did he need to bring her up here to tell her that?

"I told him about the guy at the rodeo, the one who tried to warn me off. And he agrees it's too much of a coincidence. As soon as I show my face at a rodeo, even though it might be in Australia, I'm getting death threats."

"So, he believes you about the damaged bull rope?"

"Yep. But back then, he wanted to respect my father's wishes to not get involved. My father doesn't like to rock the boat. But now, Dean thinks this has gone too far. He's heard rumors about this Bettdorff app, and the word is the company is losing money. Lots and lots of money."

"I guess that's a good thing that Dean's investigating, then," Bindi said, stroking Sahara's neck through the railing.

"Damn straight, it's a good thing. Clarissa needs to know she can't get away with her bullying, dangerous manner. It might go some way to explaining her behavior—Clarissa was always desperate to gain daddy's approval. But just because her company is in debt for millions of dollars doesn't give her the right to behave like a member of the Mafia."

Mack stepped closer, so that he was in her personal space. She had no choice but to look up into his face.

"But that's not the only reason I wanted to talk to you."

"It's not?" Her breathing had become shallow all of a sudden.

"I want to make sure you're really okay after all that happened today."

"Oh, yes, I'm fine." Was that all? It was nice that he was worried about her, but...

"I know you're saying that, but are you sure?" he asked, using his thumb to tilt her chin up, so she was looking directly at him.

Earlier today in the boardroom, she leaned on him, accepted his proffered comfort because she'd needed it. But tonight...? She was telling the truth when she said she was fine. Tonight, part of her wanted something more than benevolent compassion. She wanted passionate kisses from the man who'd made her body come alive that night they'd spent in the swag together. And the other part was screaming that he was no good for her, he would only break her heart into a million pieces and then leave, and to stay as far away from him as she could.

Oh, God, it was like there were two completely opposite

warring personalities residing in her right now.

Mack was still staring at her. He touched her cheek ever so gently.

Every atom in her body demanded that he kiss her. She swayed toward him, unable to resist his tidal pull. A low thrum started deep in her belly.

"I want to kiss you, Bindi. But something tells me I shouldn't, because it would be taking advantage of you. And I respect you. I don't want to hurt you any further."

He respected her? What was that all about? *Yes, please, take advantage of me,* a loud voice shouted in her head. But another voice said that perhaps he was right. She took a step away, out of his sphere of influence, away from his musky, male aroma and muscular body that drove all logical thought out the window.

Something had changed between them. Ever since Mutt had driven them off the road today and nearly rammed them. Something about the way Mack looked at her had shifted. He was more solicitous, tender, almost. When he spoke to her, the layer of pretense was now stripped away. It was as if he were more present with her now, more truthful.

Bugger. Why had he chosen this moment to suddenly become all chivalrous?

CHAPTER FIFTEEN

Mack eyeballed the big dude standing next to Bindi; hovering over her, really. Timmo had arrived yesterday, and Mack had taken an immediate dislike to him. Perhaps dislike was too strong a word. Perhaps it was more to do with that fact that Timmo was all alpha male, dominating a room with his presence. A muscle-bound brute who looked as dangerous as he was purported to be. Clean-shaven, dark hair slicked back, wearing a charcoal-gray suit, Timmo reminded him of a Greek crime boss. And perhaps it also had to do with how close Timmo was staying to Bindi, that was getting his green-eyed monster all worked up. Mack hadn't been able to get a private word in since Timmo had turned up.

The guy was certainly professional, treating Bindi with the utmost respect and always maintaining a businesslike manner around her. The other thing Mack didn't like was the weapon Timmo wore, concealed beneath his suit jacket. It gave him the jitters. He wondered what Bindi made of it? Did it make her feel safer, knowing an armed and dangerous man was around her at all times? Aaron had also taken to wearing his gun in a shoulder holster. Mack decided the weapon gave him more gravitas, a steely glint entering his eyes, and he wouldn't have liked to come up against the man back when he'd been working as a full-time bodyguard. It was his job to guard the family, leaving Timmo to focus on Bindi; and to a lesser extent, Mack. But it seemed neither Nash nor Aaron was taking his suggestions that Clarissa could still be behind the first accident as seriously as they should. Certainly not now Mutt had come after Bindi.

Dale, Steve, and Aaron were taking a delivery of materials for the new cabin. A truck had turned up early this morning, laden with steel girders and stacks of lumber. It was going to be a tricky job getting that large truck maneuvered down the gravel road to where the new cabin was to be built, and he didn't envy the other men in the slightest.

Julie and Sasha were getting cabins ready for the arrival of Daisy's family from Perth tomorrow, as well as Julie's mother and stepfather, along with a raft of Daniella's other relatives. There was an ex-husband, and his two sons—who were actually Dale and Skylar's half-brothers. Daniella had Alek sourcing items for some games she wanted set up for the wedding guests to play after dinner and the speeches—last minute, of course. Aaron was with Steve at the moment, but he also flitted between the scattered family, trying to keep them all safe and accounted for, another task Mack didn't envy.

Which left him and Bindi to take Dean and Naomi on a tour of the station on horseback, along with another couple of Steve and Daniella's friends, who'd arrived early this morning in a cloud of dust and a brand-new Range Rover. Steve's old boss Ron and his wife Marge, from Mitchell River Station, had driven down from up north, and were just as keen as Dean to find out what Steve was doing to make Stormcloud so profitable.

At least Greek God Timmo had exchanged his suit and tie for jeans and a button-up shirt this morning. But those boots wouldn't last the day, the soft leather would be ruined by the time they got back to the stables. The guy probably didn't even know the front end from the rear on a horse.

Ten minutes later, Mack was forced to eat his words as Timmo sat effortlessly on Chico's back, looking like he'd been born in the saddle. Was this guy Superman? Surely he couldn't be good at *everything*?

Mack rode alongside Dean, enjoying the easy banter with his boss. Sitting astride Picasso, he breathed in a deep lungful of outback air. It was getting warm already, but the smell of dry earth and horse sweat was familiar and calming. This country was growing on him. It had a rawness, the open, uninterrupted plains with their red soil and olive trees had a stark beauty. Which was an interesting discovery, because he'd always thought the green grass and towering, snow-capped Montana mountains were the epitome of a divine landscape. He'd never dreamed this Queensland outback would ever hold a candle to the mountains of Montana. But there was something about this place that seemed to have wormed its way into his soul.

Mack shook himself. He was being ridiculous. Tuning in to what Bindi was saying as they rode, he listened intently as she fed them interesting facts and figures about stocking rates, how mustering times varied with how dry the previous season had been, how many weaners were sent to market in one season, how Steve had started reintroducing native grasses and leaving paddocks unstocked for two or three seasons, to help re-establish a natural undercover. She had an in-depth conversation with Ron about the sustainability of running lower numbers of cattle to try and revitalize the natural habitat. It was a delicate balance, but one that Bindi thought was worthwhile, because the old way of farming cattle, where the land was left completely denuded, eventually left the land useless, infertile, and much more open to the effect of drought.

Fascinating as the subject was, Mack found himself watching Timmo nearly as much as he listened to Bindi. Now and then Timmo would talk into an ear comms set, to whom or about what, Mack had no idea, probably Aaron. The guy was so serious about everything. He was making him jumpy with all his hyper-vigilance. His eyes never stopped moving, his back was tense, and he surveyed the land ahead and behind them as if a platoon of armed forces were about to jump out of the low-lying grass and start shooting at them with semi-automatic rifles. Which was laughable because, as far as they knew, Mutt was working alone.

According to the police, Mutt had disappeared. Nash hadn't been able to find hide nor hair of the man or his vehicle after the attempted ramming. Nash had arrived at the crash scene the other day, stopping to make sure he and Bindi and the other driver were all unhurt. Then he'd taken off in a spray of gravel to chase after the fleeing car. But he'd made it all the way to the township of Nychum without a sign of him. The police had been on the hunt for him ever since, without any luck. Mack had heard the Northern Territory border wasn't that far away. Maybe the thug had made a run for it.

Timmo dropped back to ride alongside him. "Hey."

"Hey," Mack replied, lifting one eyebrow beneath the brim of his hat. What did this joker want now?

"Sorry, we haven't had much time to get acquainted."

It was the first time Timmo had said more than two words to him. And Mack was absolutely fine with the distinct lack of communication, but there was no point in putting the guy offside, so he made the right noises. "Mmm. I guess you've been busy."

"Yes, but I make a point to get to know all my clients." Mack's gut churned at the expression. He had no problem with the guy being here to protect Bindi, if that's what Steve and Daniella wanted, but he was quite capable of looking out for himself. He wasn't anybody's *client*.

"Aaron mentioned you have another theory for who might be responsible for the sabotage to your car. I'd like to hear about that, if you don't mind."

Mack flicked a glance at the group in front. Bindi was still regaling them with facts and figures about the station. He figured it couldn't hurt to fill Timmo in on the details. So, he gave him an abbreviated version of his fall from the bull and his theory about the accident. The man's eyes never stayed still the whole time Mack was talking, and he wondered if Timmo even heard a word he said.

"If what you're saying is true, we should take a closer look at Clarissa Melman," Timmo said, finally catching Mack's gaze.

"Really?" Mack was surprised. Maybe he'd misjudged this man, not really bothering to look past the muscle-bound façade.

"Yes, we have connections with another private detective company over in the US. I'll ask them to see what they can dig up."

"Good," Mack agreed. Added to Dean's subtle inquiries, that'd be a big help. Even if all their investigation did was rattle Clarissa's cage a little, he'd be okay with that.

The group of riders pulled up beside a fence, and their conversation came to an end. Bindi pushed Sahara up so she could unfasten the gate, then motioned the other riders through. "This is Portico Paddock," she said. "Over there is one of our bores." She pointed to a clump of trees a few hundred meters away. "I'll show you how the watering system works and how Steve uses state-of-the-art equipment to monitor water levels and stock health."

* * *

Mack reined Picasso to a halt just outside the main door of the stables. The two-hour ride had flown by, and he'd enjoyed talking ranching techniques with the other knowledgeable couples. Enjoyed watching the way Bindi's face filled with vitality as she talked about a subject that obviously excited her.

"Thank you, Bindi. I don't think even Steve could've given us a better tour than that." Dean beamed his trademark smile at her, his face lighting up with animation. "Daniella told me about all of these new innovations, of course. But it's one thing hearing something through an email, and a completely different thing seeing it in real life. You've given me a lot to think about."

Dean dismounted and led his horse into the saddling yard outside the entrance to the stables, without even having to be asked, like the old hand that he was. Then he helped Naomi off her horse and the couple stood by the gate, watching as Ron and Marge did the same.

"Not a problem," Bindi said. "I enjoy showing people around who understand what I'm talking about."

"Yes," Ron chimed in, slapping his horse on the rump to get it moved into the yard. "When Steve told me what he was up to, I was a little skeptical. De-stocking, to help increase productivity, almost sounds counterintuitive. But I think he's proving it works." Ron turned to Dean and gestured an arm to take in the rolling plains.

Mack, too, had been impressed by Bindi's knowledge and enthusiasm. She obviously listened when Steve talked, and had even mentioned at one stage that she'd like to do the same thing one day; turn around a run-down property and make it viable again. Mack fought back a grin as he noticed Timmo dismount awkwardly, and then shake out his legs while he thought no one was watching. Timmo had admitted he'd learned to ride when he was a lot younger—a previous girlfriend had been into showjumping—but he hadn't been near a horse in over five years. The man was going to be sore and chafed tonight.

Dean and Ron were still talking with their heads together, so Bindi raised her voice and said, "If you want to make your way down to the lodge, lunch will be served soon."

"Are you sure you don't want a hand unsaddling the horses?" Naomi asked.

"No, we've got that covered. We'll meet you down there in a jiffy," Bindi replied.

"Thank you. That was a lovely ride." Naomi placed a hand on Bindi's arm and gave her a warm smile. "You've definitely given the men something to talk about." Naomi turned and ushered Dean and Ron down the gravel road. "Come on, you two," she teased. "I'm starving."

The men led the way down the gravel road, still talking animatedly together, while Naomi and Marge followed at a more leisurely pace, taking in the sight of the billabong shimmering in the midday sun below the lodge.

Bindi began to unsaddle Sahara, and Mack did the same with Picasso. She headed inside the main stables to put the saddle away in the tack room, Timmo following a few steps behind. Mack stifled a grimace. Even though he'd changed his mind about the bodyguard, surely the man was taking this all a little too seriously. Bindi shot him a look, and he could see by the glower on her face she was thinking the exact same thing.

But it wasn't until she'd unsaddled Captain and was heading back inside with his tack, Timmo again following in her footsteps, that she said, "You know, I'm sure I'm safe in the stables. You could do something helpful, like unsaddle your own horse." She gestured toward Chico, and Timmo merely grunted, seemingly preoccupied with his ear comms. "Or you could just stay out of my way if you don't want to help," she added with an exasperated sigh.

Timmo ignored her and tapped his ear, but it seemed the

words of whoever was on the other end were indecipherable.

"The tin walls of the shed often block a signal," Bindi said.

Timmo nodded and motioned that he was going outside.

"Bloody hell," Bindi said quietly. "That man is very…shall we say…committed to my safety."

"He's only doing his job," Mack replied with a laugh. It hadn't taken Bindi long to get tired of Mafia Man's presence. He gave a low chuckle. "I would've thought you were enjoying his attention. He is built like a Greek God, after all."

Bindi shot him a dark look. "Not my type," she said, rounding on her heel and disappearing into the tack room.

Somehow, that information made him feel much more charitable. Because he hoped it meant that perhaps *he* was her type.

"Would you mind unsaddling the rest?" she asked, reappearing a few seconds later. "If you finish that, I'll go and organize their feed." She pointed toward the feed room in the back corner of the stables. "Then we can grab something to eat. I agree with Naomi. I'm starving."

"Sure," he said, whistling a tune under his breath as he returned to the saddling yard, letting the gate swing shut behind him. Timmo was leaning against the outside of the yard fence, talking quietly into his comms, which must be working better now. Mack ignored him and ran a hand down Chico's front leg, lifting it to inspect his hoof. The horse had looked slightly lame on the return journey, and he wanted to make sure—

A scream issued from inside the barn.

Bindi.

Not bothering to unlatch the gate, Mack was up the first two rungs of the fence, vaulting over the top and landing on the ground, sprinting into the stables.

Timmo was two strides behind him.

Another scream drove Mack on. Shit. What was going on?

Who was there? Was someone hurting her? The thought almost made his knees buckle beneath him.

He reached the door to the feed store and swung into the room, only to be confronted by a scene from a nightmare.

Bindi was lying on her back on the ground, fending off Mutt with both hands, who was on his knees beside her, trying to drive a knife into her heart. The knife hovered mere centimeters from her chest as Mutt strained to get to her.

With a snarl, Mack launched himself at the man, knocking him onto his back as they rolled together in the hay. This was the second time Mack had fought hand-to-hand with Mutt, but last time, the other man had been intoxicated. Now he was just as powerful, but moved with a lethal grace that hadn't been there before. Mutt might be super strong, but Mack had speed and agility on his side.

He rolled to the side, not letting Mutt get a proper hold on him, but then had to duck his head as the knife landed in the dirt directly where his head had been only a split second earlier. The knife flashed again, and it was all Mack could do to stop it slashing his neck, instead of catching the edge of the blade across his bicep. The pain was immediate and intense, a burning sensation that made Mack grimace.

All of a sudden, Mutt was lifted off Mack and thrown bodily onto the ground a few meters away. The knife went flying as Timmo kicked it from his grasp. Timmo inflicted a few good kicks into Mutt's side, then he landed, knees first, on Mutt's chest, knocking all the air from his lungs.

Timmo stood up slowly and glowered down at Mutt, while he gasped for air and writhed on the ground. "Don't you fucking move," Timmo threatened.

Mack got to his feet, holding his arm where he'd been slashed. Circling warily away from the two prizefighters, he went to where Bindi was backed into a stack of hay bales, watching with terrified fascination.

"Are you okay? Are you hurt?" he demanded.

She turned fear-filled eyes toward him, staring blankly.

"Are you hurt?" he asked again, taking her by the shoulders and shaking her gently.

"No. I don't think so," she finally replied. "He...he came out from behind the hay." She pointed a shaky hand at the stack of bales behind her. "I turned around, and he was just standing there. With a knife."

Jesus wept. How could he have been so wrong about this maniac? Mack had dismissed the Maori man as a crackpot.

She began to shake, and he took her in his arms. "It's okay. You're all right now. Timmo's got him, he won't hurt you again." Surreptitiously, he tried to check her over for blood or other wounds, but it seemed she was telling the truth about not having a scratch on her.

She grabbed him tightly, and pushed her face into his shoulder, as if she wanted to burrow into him; shut out the rest of the world. Small tremors wracked her body, but she wasn't crying. There were no hysterics, just a quiet trembling. He hugged her tighter, ignoring the pain in his shoulder. Right now, Bindi needed him, and that was all that mattered.

Over the top of her head, Mack watched the bodyguard flip Mutt onto his stomach and fasten a set of handcuffs around his wrists. Hauling him up by the scruff of the neck, Timmo dragged the man against the far wall and pushed him down onto his butt on the concrete floor.

"Sit there and don't say a fucking word," Timmo growled.

Mutt was doubled over in pain, and Mack doubted he had enough air left in his lungs to speak. But then a strange sound issued from within the form huddled next to the wall. A wet, gurgling noise from deep in his throat. Almost as if the man was...

"Are you crying?" Timmo said, disgust clear in his tone.

The noise increased, even as Mutt curled into the fetal

position and lay on the ground.

The big Maori dude was crying? Mack found it hard to reconcile the idea. What the hell did the man have to cry about? It was Bindi who should be crying. The shudders running through her seemed to have subsided somewhat. She lifted her head and turned to study the hunk of quivering muscle lying adjacent to the wall.

Mack glanced down and saw that her beautiful, brown eyes were red-rimmed, but dry.

"What's wrong with him?" Bindi demanded of Timmo.

"I dunno." The bodyguard shrugged. "I need to call this in," he said, looking straight at Mack. "You be right to keep an eye on him while I take this outside again?"

Mack lifted his chin in acknowledgement. Mutt wasn't going anywhere in a hurry, not in the state he was in. As if to punctuate his point, the wailing sound issuing from the big man got louder.

Bindi pushed away from Mack. "Thank you," she said. "But I'm fine now."

Reluctantly, he let her go.

"Here. Use this to stanch the bleeding." Timmo threw a piece of material toward Mack, who caught it and turned it over in his hand. It was a large, clean handkerchief. Of course, the bodyguard carried a clean handkerchief on him at all times. The man was a walking embodiment of the motto, *always be prepared*. Timmo stalked out of the feed room without a backward glance.

"What bleeding?" Bindi eyed him sharply.

"It's nothing." Mack turned, and they both inspected his bicep through the slash in his sleeve.

"Bloody hell, Mack, why didn't you tell me?"

He was about to say he'd been too busy comforting her, but decided she might not appreciate his sarcasm. And his wound seemed to galvanize her, give her something else to think about than her own near-death predicament. The in-charge version of Bindi seemed to be back with a vengeance.

"Give me this." She snatched the hanky out of his hand and ripped open the shirt so she could inspect his wound. After a few seconds, she said, "I don't think it's too bad. It's not deep, you were lucky."

Mack thought the word skilful would be better applied to him; if he hadn't ducked and warded off the knife blow, it'd be sticking out of his neck right now. But again he kept his thoughts to himself, and instead smiled indulgently at Bindi, who was wrapping the hanky tightly around his arm. The tip of her tongue came out from between pursed lips as she worked the fabric around his bicep, and he was suddenly fascinated with her mouth. Her very pouty, kissable mouth.

"There," she said, patting his shoulder. "That should hold it until we can get you to a doctor."

A deep moaning was still coming from the man curled up on the floor, and Mack felt a sudden urge to get out of the room, away from this man who was clearly having some sort of breakdown. Not that he didn't deserve everything that was coming to him; he'd just tried to kill Bindi. Again. Mack could easily inflict damage on Mutt for that. But something about the way the guy was losing his shit was making Mack uneasy.

"Bloody hell," Bindi said from between clenched teeth. "His sniveling is driving me crazy." She headed across the room toward Mutt before he could stop her.

"Bindi, wait," Mack called, but to no avail.

CHAPTER SIXTEEN

"Oh, will you just shut up?" Bindi marched across the room and stood in front of the lump of quivering man flesh. "What the fuck do you have to cry about? I'm the one who nearly died. Mack is the one with the stab wound. You don't even deserve to feel sorry for yourself."

She was so mad she was practically vibrating. The anger had surged up from deep in her gut, possibly in response to the hot flashes of other emotions searing through her veins over the past few minutes. She'd been scared out of her mind when Mutt attacked her, then adrenaline had kicked in as she did everything in her power to ward him off, and that'd morphed into sheer relief when Mack and Timmo had arrived. So she became a quivering mass of unspent hormones and feelings. Which left her irrationally, irredeemably mad. She was mad for lots of reasons. Mad because she'd become complacent enough to let Mutt ambush her. Mad because he had the audacity to attack her with a knife. Mad because the crazy Maori had slashed her man across the arm. And mad because this stupid person lying on the floor in front of her continued to blame her unfairly for her brother's death. Well, she was going to set the record straight, once and for all.

Wait…

Backup a second.

She reversed all those thought bubbles until she came to the one that'd caused her to pause.

She'd called Mack *her man*. Admittedly, it was only in her head—thank God—but was he? Her man? She didn't have any claim on Mack. They'd agreed to be friends, that was all. Even if he was sweet to her now, kind and respectful. All things he hadn't been when she first met him. That didn't mean—

"I'm sorry," Mutt sobbed, breaking her absorption with her convoluted feelings for Mack.

He was sorry? He had no right to feel sorry.

Mack walked over and stood next to her, almost pushing her out of the way, as if perhaps he thought to make a human shield of himself. Well, she wasn't having that. She wanted to hear what Mutt had to say, so she stood her ground.

Mutt sat up slowly. The man was a mess, tears and snot streaked his face, and his vain attempts to wipe the streaming mucus away did no good with his hands firmly tied behind his back. He sat on the ground staring up at her, eyes imploring, like a dog who'd just been beaten.

"I'm sorry," he sobbed again. "I should never have done that."

"Done what?" she snapped. "Tried to kill me?"

Mack slipped his hand into hers. Whether to hold her back, so she didn't strangle Mutt, or as a form of comfort, she wasn't sure.

"Yeah, I shouldn't have done that. I really wasn't aiming to kill you." He looked up at her, blinking like an owl.

"It certainly looked like it from my angle," Bindi spat. "A knife aimed at your heart only means one thing, as far as I'm concerned."

"I know, I know," Mutt sniffed. "But it was like something

came over me. Some kind of evil spirit took me over, you know."

"No, I don't know," Bindi said. What was going on with Mutt? He'd never apologized to her in the whole time she'd known him. "You've had it in for me ever since Kai died," she went on. "That was seven years ago. I can't believe you still hate me so much."

Timmo re-entered the room, but hung back when he saw them talking. Seeing Mutt was no threat, he remained watching and listening from behind Bindi's left shoulder.

"I don't hate you, not really." He dropped his gaze to the ground, and Bindi stood, waiting for Mutt to explain himself. "It's true. I needed someone to blame when Kai died. I was so destroyed when he took his own life. I couldn't understand why he'd do something like that. And leave me all alone." Bindi's heart softened slightly at the torment in Mutt's voice. Then he muttered the words she'd suspected all along. "I was in love with him. He never knew it, because he would never have accepted it." The truth was finally coming out. Mutt was gay, but had never admitted it, not even to the man he'd adored. It was a little sad, really. Love made people do strange, surprising things sometimes.

"So, why did you attack me?"

"When I saw you at the rodeo, it was a complete surprise," Mutt continued. "I didn't plan that meeting. I made it all up on the spot to scare you. Because when I saw you, it brought all those buried feelings flooding back. And I hated you so much at that moment."

"So, you didn't come to Australia to track me down?" Bindi asked.

"Nah. To tell the truth, I'd nearly forgotten about you. I moved away from Nelson a few months after Kai died and you left. Tried to start anew in Auckland, but that didn't go so well for me, either."

Bindi could just imagine. Mutt and his gang had been involved in drugs and petty theft. And a leopard never changed its spots. Just because Mutt moved towns, it probably didn't mean he'd climbed any higher up the socio-economic ladder.

"But when I saw you again, it was like something clicked in my mind. Like a white-hot heat took over, and I was completely devastated by Kai's death all over again. I wanted you gone. So I didn't have to keep feeling this way."

In a twisted way, Mutt's explanation made a strange kind of sense. It didn't excuse his behavior, or in any way justify it. But it added a level of understanding. "Go on," she prompted, needing to hear the whole story. "Because you clearly followed me out here to finish your dastardly deed."

He grimaced, then said, "It took me a few days to track down where you lived. And a few more days to come up with a plan. I got a new job, you see, and I didn't want to just up and leave. So I waited until I had no shifts rostered and came up here to find you. I'd been waiting all day in the main street of that shitty little town, when you happened to walk out of that supermarket. It was as if the Gods smiled on me."

"Yeah, I bet it felt like that to you. It was a little different from our perspective." Her hand jerked convulsively in Mack's as she thought about the look on Mutt's face, right before he went to ram their car. She was sure he'd meant to kill them. And he'd been prepared to go through Mack to get to her. Mack would've been collateral damage, and Mutt wouldn't have cared one jot. Mack was doing a good job of not interrupting her questioning of Mutt, as if he sensed this was something she needed to do.

"Well, you can tell your sob story to our friend, the senior sergeant. He's on his way, and I'm sure he'd love to hear your justifications for all of your murderous intents," Timmo interrupted.

Bindi nodded with satisfaction. Nash would deal with Mutt. He'd spend a long time in jail, where he could cogitate on all the things he'd done wrong in his life. And be as remorseful as he liked, as long as it was far away from her.

Mack's warm fingers curled around hers, reminding her that he was still standing beside her. It made her wonder. Did she really blame Mutt for fixating on her? Maybe not as much as she'd once done; not now that she knew the full extent of his obsession with Kai. How would she react if the one person she loved most in the world took their own life? Would she blame someone else for her lover's failings? Bindi couldn't answer those questions, but she turned to stare at Mack as he squeezed her hand again.

How would she feel if Mack died?

The idea made her toes curl inside her boots with dread, and her stomach clenched so tight she almost doubled over. It wasn't a thought she ever wanted to entertain.

"I should've known something was up," Timmo went on. "When my comms went on the fritz and I had to go outside, Aaron was trying to tell me he and Steve had found a white ute parked up by the new cabin site. He wasn't sure if it was abandoned, or what. I'd just worked out from his description that it might belong to this fellow when I heard you scream." Timmo looked crestfallen, as if he should've worked it all out much sooner. Taken more care of Bindi and not allowed her to wander around the stables alone. But it was her fault. She'd been the one to send him away, he'd been doing everything right.

"I'm really sorry, Bindi. I want you to know that," Mutt continued from his seat on the ground, as if determined to gain Bindi's forgiveness. "When I followed you out of Dimbulah, I know it looked like I was going to do it. Try and hurt you, I mean. And I wanted to. I really did. But even before I heard that cop siren, I'd lost my nerve. I just couldn't go through with it. I was so mad at myself. So, I came back to finish it today, but instead…" He shrugged, those big shoulders rolling with the effort. "In a way, I kind of expected to be caught. If I'd truly wanted to stick that knife in your heart, do you think you would've been able to stop me?" he asked, looking her directly in the eye for the first time.

His question brought Bindi up sharp. He had a point. He was so much bigger than her. Would her puny arms really have had enough strength to hold him at bay? She went over the scene in her head, but in the end couldn't decide. Perhaps she'd never know.

"All right, enough of this self-exoneration," Timmo said, taking two strides past Bindi and levering Mutt to his feet with a hand under his arm.

"Wait." Mack released her fingers and held up his hand. "Can I just clarify something, before you take him away?"

Timmo nodded, but didn't let go of his grip on the Maori's collar.

"You've talked about the time we saw you in Dimbulah and then today. But what about tampering with the front wheel on my car? Did you have anything to do with that?"

Mutt tilted his head to the side and regarded Mack with sad brown eyes. "I'm not sure what you're talking about."

"My truck. The one parked at the rodeo that night. Someone tampered with the front wheel, and we crashed on the way home the next day."

"Nah, sorry, mate, I don't know anything about that. Like I told the cops, I was really drunk that night. Me mates took me back to the hotel room, and we all crashed out until morning."

Mack looked at Bindi, and she finally grasped the importance of Mutt's words. "So, if you didn't sabotage Mack's truck, then who did?"

"I don't know." Mutt stared at her, and for some mad

reason, she believed him. A chill of apprehension slid up her spine. Just when she thought this whole saga was over, solved so she and Mack could move on, maybe it wasn't.

"Come on, mate." Timmo hauled on Mutt's collar. "You two need to come down to the lodge, as well," he said. "Nash will be here soon, and he'll need your statements. You also need to hightail it into town to get that injury seen to."

Oh, shit, for a second Bindi had forgotten about Mack's knife wound. "Yes, let's go," she urged. But just as they exited the tack room into the stables, three figures exploded around the side of the open front. Julie, Sasha, and Alek skidded to a halt in front of them, all out of breath from their sprint up the road from the lodge.

"Dale just called us on the two-way and told us what happened. Holy shit, are you two okay?" Julie punctuated each few words with a short pant.

Before Bindi could tell her they were fine, Alek added, "We came to help as soon as we heard." He was eyeing the big Maori man as if he wanted to go a round in a boxing ring with him. "Aaron, Dale, and Steve are on their way, too."

"It's all right, I have everything under control," Timmo growled, pushing Mutt, so he began to walk down the length of the stables. Alek followed him, taking up position on the other side of Mutt, just in case. Bindi had to smile. She hoped Sasha appreciated this masculine act he was putting on, because it was as much for her as it was to keep Bindi safe. Alek had this impression of himself as a tough Polak, with Viking blood running through his veins, who could keep up with any of the other ringers and stations hands who worked at the station. In reality, Alek was more of a pussycat, but Bindi liked him just the way he was. And she was sure Sasha thought much the same. She couldn't say that to Alek, however. Male egos were fragile things, sometimes.

Julie and Sasha crowded around Bindi, but when she

assured them—five or six times—that she was unhurt, they focussed on Mack, Julie demanding to see his arm, because she knew first aid.

The next hour was confusing and frenetic. The one thing that Bindi remembered, though, was that Mack stayed by her side the whole time, refusing to be separated from her.

Nash and his offsider, Constable Willow arrived in a spray of gravel from the wheels of his police Land Cruiser only fifteen minutes after they escorted Mutt to the lodge and Timmo sat him down in a corner of the dining room, handcuffing him to the table. Dale, Aaron, and Steve had also arrived, all scowling at Mutt like a bunch of SAS troopers, as if daring him to move even one finger. Bindi almost felt sorry for Mutt. He'd become a sort of exhibit, as everyone crowded down the opposite end of the dining room, come to stare at the criminal and get up to date on Bindi and Mack's story. Bindi felt a little like an animal at the zoo herself, with so many people asking her questions, swarming around her, wanting to touch her. She had to keep reminding herself it was because they were concerned for her well-being, not because they'd come to rubberneck at this sudden and unexpected drama on the station.

After they'd given their statements, Constable Willow had bundled Mutt into the back of the Land Cruiser, and he and Nash had driven him to the station to formally book him, and lock him up.

Steve took it upon himself to personally drive Mack and herself into the clinic in town so they could both get checked over. He was so upset that he hadn't been there to protect Bindi, that he said it was the least he could do. Bindi had been about to protest that she was fine, but a chance to get away from the throngs in the dining room and to spend some time alone with Mack was too much to turn down. He was so sweet, he held her hand all the way into town, as they sat in the back seat of the car. And he chatted to Steve amiably, so she could lay her head back against the seat rest and stare out the window to process everything that'd just happened.

She glanced down at their fingers locked together. Such a simple gesture, and yet it could mean so much. Sure and strong, his tanned hand grasped hers, his thumb occasionally running over her knuckles. A physical connection that led to an emotional connection. It felt natural and easy, as if they'd been doing this all their lives, like they were an old couple in their sunset years and still remained terribly in love.

Shifting her gaze from their hands, she looked up to trace his profile. Alluring lips turned up at the corners, as he smiled at something Steve had said. Then he spoke, saying something about Madonna and how she and her filly were doing nicely now. Bindi wasn't really listening, she was intrigued by his face. A vestige of dust still lingered on the edge of his nose, probably from where he'd rolled in the dirt and hay when he attacked Mutt. His designer stubble roughened his jaw, making him look sexy, like he'd just got out of bed. But he was aware of her scrutiny. He winked at her out of the corner of his eye, without even turning his head, tawny eyes sparkling in the mid-afternoon sun. Still that cocksure, slightly dazzling guy she'd first met. So full of himself and his own bravado. But that part of Mack was growing on her. Because she knew what lingered beneath that layer of swagger. And she could see now that it was part of the act of being a bull rider, competing in a cut-throat contest with other men who'd gladly see him land in the dust on his backside. But there was a camaraderie there as well, even though the other riders were his opponents, and a charming and friendly demeanor was also necessary to get along with the rest of his peers. Someone—she wasn't sure who—had mentioned that Mack had been the Golden Boy of the PBR at one stage. It was a long way to fall from grace, but Mack seemed to have done it with equanimity, and at least his self-respect was still intact.

Bindi wanted to know more about Mack. Wanted to delve deeper, get to know more than just the bull-rider. But what was the point, a tiny voice asked? If he was indeed heading back to America? That was the plan, at least. Things could change; they often did. But it'd be foolish of her to live on a false hope. And foolish to let hope persuade her to open her heart to Mack. Even though he was tugging at the gates guarding her heart with just about everything he did and said, she'd be a fool to let him in. Wouldn't she?

He finally looked over at her and smiled. Bugger. It didn't seem like her heart was listening to her reasoning, because it jumped like a frog in a sock at that smile, meant only for her.

CHAPTER SEVENTEEN

There was a fierce debate going on when Mack walked into the lodge later that afternoon. He glanced at Bindi and then at Steve to see what they made of the scene in front of them. Aaron and Timmo sat at the main table, glaring at each other like stalking panthers.

"I think you should stay. At least until the wedding is over," Aaron said, leaning over and banging his fist on the tabletop to emphasize his point to Timmo, who was sitting opposite him.

"And I don't disagree with you, but Jake wants me back in Sydney. He has another case that he says takes priority." Timmo leaned back in his chair, man-spreading, hands behind his head and looking as cool as a cucumber. While Aaron looked about ready to chew stone.

"This thing isn't over, and you know it," Aaron said, raking a hand through his already ruffled hair.

Of the rest of the Stormcloud team and the wedding guests, there was no sign. Perhaps they'd gone back to their duties, or perhaps Daniella had removed everyone from the room, so they weren't party to this conversation.

Julie entered through the hallway off the kitchen. "Oh, thank God you're here, Dad. Maybe you can talk some sense into Aaron." She waved a dishcloth in his direction. "He's being mulish about Shield Solution's decision to recall Timmo. They seem to think the perpetrator has been caught, and we no longer need his services."

"I can see why they'd believe that," Steve said, walking over to join the other two men at the table. "Nash is almost of the same mind."

"Except for the fact that Mutt didn't cause the first accident," Bindi muttered under her breath.

Mack agreed with her wholeheartedly. There might well still be someone else out there who meant either him or Bindi harm, namely Clarissa. But Mack wasn't so captivated by the idea of Timmo staying as Aaron seemed to be. He wasn't exactly sure how much good Timmo had done. It was Mack who'd first tackled Mutt to the ground, while Timmo had been too busy on his comms set. He hadn't even suspected there was anyone else in the stables, and his mere presence certainly hadn't dissuaded Mutt from coming onto the property, as it was supposed to. A bodyguard was a big waste of time, he decided. But he wasn't about to utter his theory to the three men at the table. So, he caught Bindi by the hand and towed her toward the kitchen. They'd missed lunch with all the shenanigans going on, and his stomach was about to turn itself inside out.

Julie watched them walk past, giving an exasperated sigh. "Men. Why does everything have to come down to banging on tables?" She shook her head and flicked the dishcloth a few more times. "How's the shoulder, by the way?" she asked, as she turned to follow them down the hallway.

"Not bad." Mack rolled his arm over a few times. "The doc gave me a local anesthetic so he could put the stitches in, and I'm feeling no pain right now."

"Ew, stitches. How many did you get?"

"Only seven," he replied with a shrug.

"Only," Julie quipped. "That's not an only. That's a goddamned battle scar, that is. You're a warrior with a war wound. You leapt in a like a knight in shining armor to protect your woman. I'd call that pretty spectacular."

"I'm not—" Bindi began to say.

At the exact same time, Mack said, "Yep, that's me. A knight in shining armor." He draped an arm around Julie's shoulders. "Anytime you need rescuing, darlin', you just let me know."

Julie gave a girlish laugh and slapped him on the arm just as they entered the kitchen. Mack stepped back and said, "But my stomach could do with some rescuing right now. We missed lunch."

"Did you now?" asked Skylar, looking up from where she was julienning a pile of carrots. "There are leftover sandwiches in the fridge. I'll make you and Bindi a plate each."

"Thanks, that'd be great." Mack pulled out a stool and planted himself at the island countertop, watching from the corner of his eye as Bindi did the same.

Bindi had been about to deny it. But he'd jumped in before she could finish her sentence, turning on the charm to re-direct Julie. The last thing he needed right now was Bindi being spooked by Julie's over-anxious need to make everyone happy. He'd noticed a seismic shift in the connection between them recently. And he didn't want to damage that fledgling relationship. It was too precious.

Even as he talked to Julie, bantering easily back and forth with her, he was assaulted by the image of Bindi lying on the ground, Mutt on top of her, driving the knife toward her chest. But in his replaying of the moment, he hadn't been able to get to her in time, and the knife plunged into her chest. He shuddered at the thought. That moment had been an epiphany for him. All of a sudden, the only thing he cared about was saving Bindi. Nothing else mattered, not even his own security. Mack was self-aware enough to understand that he'd never been a very altruistic man. He was all for existing in the moment, live fast, die young and enjoy everything that came your way in between. He could never do what Timmo or Aaron did, put other people's lives and wishes before his own. But in that moment, he would've given anything, so that Bindi lived. Which was an interesting concept, and one he needed to ponder further in private.

This change had been taking place over the past few days, but today had cemented it in his head. Bindi was worth more to him than he cared to admit. And he had no idea what to do about it.

He took the proffered plate of sandwiches from Skylar and gave her a wink, burying his innermost thoughts down deep. He'd figure it all out later. He hoped.

* * *

"Timmo's leaving in the morning," Bindi said, stalking into the staff shared lounge later that night. "Aaron couldn't stop him from going."

"Oh, well." Mack shrugged from his spot on the sofa where he'd been watching TV because his mind wouldn't stop whirling enough to let him get some sleep. He didn't believe the station would be any worse off for not having the big brute of a man around anymore. But clearly Bindi didn't hold the same view as she scowled down at him.

"How can that stupid boss at Shield say he's needed back in town? Timmo has been here less than forty-eight hours. Even if they think they've got their guy, surely he should stay until the wedding, just in case." Bindi stood, tapping her booted foot, and he couldn't help but take an appreciative glance at her trim thighs and small waist, cinched in by her well-worn jeans.

He patted the sofa seat next to him. "Yeah, I see what you

mean." He didn't want to outright disagree with her. "Come and sit down," he requested, leaning back and giving her his best sultry smile. Alek and Sasha had already retired to their own rooms over half an hour ago, and he had the staff room to himself.

"It's late. I'm on my way to bed," she replied, her gaze shooting between him and the hallway behind her.

"Me, too," he agreed. "I'm just winding down a bit before I hit the hay. Come and join me for a few minutes."

"You're probably not wrong about needing to wind down. There's been a lot to process today," she replied thoughtfully.

"Exactly." He patted the seat more firmly. Would she sit next to him? He held his breath, watching her waver. "We can talk about anything that's bothering you, if you like."

"Yeah, well, I wouldn't know where to start," she replied, plopping down in the seat next to him. Trying not to show how elated he was, he casually leaned back into the sofa and lay his arm along the armrest. The movement caused a sharp sting of pain and he winced. Reminding him that the local had worn off a few hours ago and he should probably take some pain killers so he could sleep tonight.

Bindi must've noticed his grimace, because she said, "Oh, how's your arm?" Her mouth twisted in a conciliatory grimace. "Does it hurt a lot?" She leaned in, as if to take a look at his shoulder, and he obligingly lifted the sleeve of his T-shirt to show her. She screwed up her face as she studied the bandage and the tip of her tongue came out, the same way it had when she'd been tying on the handkerchief earlier this morning. The action had nearly driven him wild then, and now parts of his body were reacting before he could stop them. He wanted to taste the tip of that tongue.

"Well, does it?" she prompted, and he refocussed his mind away from her tongue.

He should play it up a little, get more sympathy. That's

what he would've done once. But this wasn't a normal situation. His feelings for Bindi weren't normal.

"It's a bit sore," he conceded. "But I'll live. It's just a scratch, really." Besides, it was a small hurt to bear, if it meant Bindi remained unharmed. His gaze met hers and he almost drowned in their dark depths.

"I haven't actually thanked you," she said, gaze never leaving his. "You know, for saving my life, and all."

"Pshaw." He waved a hand in the air. "Big, brave Timmo was only two steps behind me. He would've saved you if I hadn't."

"Maybe. Maybe not." She was looking at him with her head tilted to one side, as if considering him. "It's interesting," she said slowly.

"What?" he asked, forcing a lazy smile onto his face. Did he really want to know what she thought was interesting about him?

"I'm wondering why you don't want to take credit for your amazing feat? Why you're being so self-effacing. It's not every day you fight off a man with a knife and save some damsel in distress."

He snorted. She'd got it all wrong. It wasn't that he didn't want to take credit for tackling Mutt. It was that her safety meant more to him than some stupid knife wound. He'd do it all again in a heartbeat. But how did he tell her that without sounding like a complete sap?

"The Mack I met three weeks ago would've been the first to blow his own trumpet. Back then, you would've been swaggering around, telling anyone who'd listen what you'd achieved."

Whoa. Her comment stung. Had he really been that bad? "I'm not sure that's completely true," he said with a shrug, trying not to let his pique show. But she'd hit a raw nerve with her perceptive comments. It made him unsure of his next move. Perhaps he had come across as being overly sure of himself when he'd first arrived. But that's how a star bull-rider was supposed to act. To be larger than life. To not be afraid of anything. Or anyone. But now…?

She smirked and said, "You really don't remember how pompous you were, do you? You strutted around like you owned the place, even the first day on the job. I thought you were so arrogant. I guess you did help me with Melody and her filly, but that was a small compensation, as far as I was concerned."

"Oh, really?" He was lost for words. She'd caught him off balance and he didn't know how to respond.

"Yes, really. But I think the time here at Stormcloud has softened some of that pretentious shit. Let the true Mack shine through."

He stared at her as she sat on the sofa next to him. Mack was unsure if losing his *pretentious shit*, as she called it, was a good or bad thing. He wasn't about to give up his Golden Boy crown just yet.

Bindi reached up and touched his arm, just below his stitches. "I think this proves how much you've changed." She glanced up at him, dark eyelashes fluttering. "I know you're trivializing this wound, and if I push it, you'll probably say something like, you've had worse plenty of times. And because you ride bulls for a living, I'd probably agree with you. But I want you to know how much I appreciate that you did this for me."

For a second, he was lost in her gaze, watching her expressive face as she talked. Heat radiated from her hand, which still rested lightly on his upper arm, and tension buzzed between them.

He raised an eyebrow. "Well, if you really want to show your appreciation, how about you come to my room, and we play a little doctors and nurses? You can look after my wound, and cool my fevered brow, among other things." He'd meant it as a joke, but the words came out more candidly than he'd meant them to. She'd rattled his equilibrium, made him second guess who he was, who he was supposed to be. Falling back on old habits was a way to stop him from feeling so nonplussed. It was a tried-and-true technique that he'd used on countless women before. A little shameless flirting lightened the mood and usually got him exactly what he wanted.

Removing her hand from his arm, she sat back, away from him. "Doctors and nurses?" Brow furrowed, she glared at him. A tingle of chagrin ran down his spine. But it was too late to back out now, so he shot her his best charming grin.

"Well, you know what I mean."

"And should I also refer to you as My Knight in Shining Armor from now on? Perhaps you haven't changed as much as I thought you had." She gave a little snort and turned away. She was going to leave. But he didn't want her to go. Not with this simmering tension between them, bordering on displeasure. He didn't want her to be angry with him.

Without thinking, he grabbed her arm just as she rose from her seat. Pulling her back into his lap, he took her mouth in a kiss, grabbing the back of her head to keep her from drawing away. Her surprise changed in a second to hunger as he slipped his tongue between her lips, and she kissed him back with raw, unrestrained desire, relaxing into his body, letting passion overcome any resistance.

This. This was what he was good at. What he and Bindi were good at. He seemed to be unable to put his feelings into words when it came to her, but his body language was excellent at telling her what he wanted, how he felt about her. They had chemistry. Their physical connection was immediate and sizzling. Like nothing else he'd had with any other woman.

She moaned and nuzzled the corner of his mouth, letting her lips graze down his jaw. "God, you taste so good," she said, letting her lips come back and claim his mouth once more. "I could spend the rest of my life just kissing you," she mumbled, as his tongue ran over her teeth.

She must be able to feel his bulging erection from where she was sitting in his lap. He wanted to make love to her. Right now. Right here. But someone might walk in at any moment. Alek or Sasha might get up to see what the all the noise was. They should go to his room. Yes, that was a plan. But he didn't want to let go of her lips. Carry her to his room, that'd be the best option. Repositioning his arm around her shoulders, he used his other arm to pick her up underneath her knees, all without letting go of her mouth. Hoping like hell he didn't split his stitches, he stood up with Bindi in his arms.

She broke their kiss.

"What are you doing?" Her lips were soft and wet from his kisses, her pupils dark with desire.

"Taking this to the bedroom," he answered seductively.

She shook her head. "Put me down."

"But we don't want someone to walk in on us." Surely, she didn't want to stay here? He wasn't opposed to continuing their scorching session, as long as he got to kiss her. But out here in the staffroom? Really?

"Put me down, please," she said more forcefully.

"What? But I thought…" What had he done wrong? He'd assumed that this was leading to another night of extraordinary sex. Perhaps even better than the first time. He knew they'd both agreed there wouldn't be a next time. But, really… How could anyone resist this type of temptation? He knew he couldn't.

"I'm not going to your bedroom, Mack," she said softly.

Was that regret in her voice? Or censure? He couldn't tell.

Gently, he lowered her feet to the floor, and she stepped away from him. She kept her chin down and wouldn't look at him.

"This can't go any further. I'm sorry, Mack, but you will ruin me." She turned on her heel and disappeared through the doorway, leaving him standing alone in the middle of the room. Feeling slightly foolish. And destitute.

What did she mean by *ruin her*?

Mack turned and punched the back of the sofa, immediately regretting it, as the painful reverberations from his wound shot up his shoulder. He was so damned confused. This woman was turning him inside out. And he didn't know if he wanted what she was offering, or not.

How was he supposed to keep working with Bindi, with all these bewildering emotions roiling around inside him? He thought perhaps they could take up where they'd left off the other night, have a bit of fun. They were both clearly attracted to each other; they could scratch each other's itch, so to speak. Friends with benefits. She was so damn tempting. Irresistible. But she'd just made it crystal clear that wasn't an option. What did she want from him? A little voice in his head said that he already knew the answer, but it was impossible, he didn't do commitment.

Perhaps he should go back to Montana. He didn't think he could stay here for another day longer. Not if he had to be so close to Bindi, yet not be allowed to touch her. Maybe he'd have a word with Dean, see if he'd take him back. He'd stay until the wedding. But after that... Montana was looking like a better option all the time.

* * *

Mack paced quietly across the grass, getting as close to the edge of the billabong as he dared in the dark. The tranquil sounds of night insects filled the air, but they didn't help to calm his roiling emotions. After Bindi rejected him, he knew there was no way he'd be able to sleep, so he'd slipped out to walk the perimeter of the lodge and think, hoping the exercise and fresh air might sort out his confused feelings. It was after midnight, and not another soul was around. Everyone tucked up in their beds asleep.

The moon was out, and it cast a serene glow over the glassy surface of the water. The soft plunk of a fish rising to capture an insect that'd risked flying too close to the surface sounded, attracting his attention. He stopped and turned to stare at the billabong. It sure was pretty. If only his mind would stop racing, he might even be able to appreciate it.

His cell phone vibrated in his back pocket, making him startle. Who in the hell would be calling him this late at night? Retrieving his phone, he stared at the screen. A private number. Curiosity finally got the better of him, and he answered the call.

"Hello." He kept his tone neutral and brusque.

For many long moments, there was silence on the other end.

"Mack, it's so nice to hear your voice again," a familiar voice sounded seductively in his ear. An image of long, auburn hair falling over a beautiful face as a woman arched her back in pleasure assaulted his memory.

Clarissa. He was so surprised he took a step backward, tamping down on the image of them in bed together. Why had that totally inappropriate thought come to him the moment he heard her voice? More importantly, why was she calling him?

"I heard you moved to Australia. I don't know what time it is there. I'm sorry if I woke you," she purred, her voice low and provocative. He knew she wasn't in the slightest bit sorry, and anger began to churn in his gut. Why did this woman think she had the right to pick up the phone and call him?

"What do you want, Clarissa?" Time to cut to the chase.

This wasn't a personal call, and they both knew it. She wasn't calling to ask him to come back and start up where they'd left off. He needed to remember she'd tried to kill him; or, at the very least, seriously injure him. "I'm not interested in your bullshit. Either tell me why you called, or I'm hanging up."

"What do I want?" She dropped all pretense of sweetness, her voice taking on a nasty edge. "I want you to call off your dogs. I warned you already, but you didn't seem to listen. I want you to stop telling lies about me and setting the cops on me. You can't prove anything." She stopped and drew in a deep breath, as if trying to calm her rising anger. "And if you keep annoying me, I might get really angry and do something I'll regret. Or maybe I won't regret it, but you surely will." She gave a sly giggle.

"What are you talking about? Call my dogs off. What does that mean?" But Mack had a feeling he knew exactly what she was talking about. Dean had spoken to him earlier this morning, saying he'd called in a few favors back home in Montana, and Clarissa Melman was now being investigated by no less than three private detective agencies; fraud and embezzlement high on her list of crimes. Plus, the local cops in Texas were reopening his complaint about sabotage to his bull rope. She was feeling the squeeze, just like he'd hoped.

"Don't act stupid, Mack, it doesn't become you," she snapped.

Mack decided to ignore that jibe. He wanted to rile Clarissa, and he thought he knew just the way to do it.

"Why, Clarissa, you sound positively peeved," he said with a laugh.

"Shut up! You cost me millions of dollars, you fuck," Clarissa hissed. "Everything started to go wrong the day I employed you. All you had to do was throw that one ride. Then you could've gone right back to winning your precious little rodeos. But no. You were stupid enough to let your morals interfere with your career."

"Yeah, right. Until the next time you wanted me to cheat, so you could swindle more of your customers out of their hard-earned cash," he retorted with a snort. It sounded like Clarissa was blaming him for all her woes. Typical, she never liked to admit defeat. Never took responsibility for her actions. Her father's company was in financial trouble, and it was all her fault.

"If you'd just done what I asked, I wouldn't be this deep in the shit. I could've pulled Bettdorff out of the quagmire and Daddy would—" She cut off mid-sentence and breathed deeply on the other end of the phone.

He gave a wry smile. He'd just love to be a fly on the wall to hear what Clarissa's *daddy* had to say about all this. He'd trusted her to take their family money and build up Bettdorff. Now it was going broke, Mack wondered if he was threatening to strip her of the CEO position and regain control himself? Or worse. To disown her.

"This is all your fault," she ground out, sounding less hysterical now, and more like the ice queen he knew her to be. "I'm warning you, make this little…problem go away, or else."

"Or else what?" he asked, sarcasm dripping from his tone. She didn't scare him. He was done with her interfering in his life.

"Or else it's not going to be just the wheel that falls off your car," she taunted quietly.

Mack went completely still. Had she just confessed to being involved with the sabotage to his truck? A feeling of surety grew in his guts. That guy who'd threatened him at the rodeo had indeed been connected to Clarissa. He was sure that big fucker had been the one to loosen his wheel lugs now. Shit, he should've recorded this call, or something. He needed to pass this information onto Nash. Clarissa was so determined that he was responsible for her life spiraling out of control, she was prepared to kill him to get her revenge. She was completely crazy.

"How is your little girlfriend?" Clarissa went on, her voice silky smooth. "I hear you were both unhurt after your car mysteriously ran off the road. If you want to keep your little slut that way, you should call off your dogs." With a loud click, Clarissa hung up.

His blood turned to ice in his veins. It was one thing for her to threaten him, but a whole other level of viciousness to threaten Bindi.

CHAPTER EIGHTEEN

"We're not going to be ready in time," Skylar moaned, leaning her elbows on the countertop and putting her head in her hands. "There's still too much left to do." Her words came out muffled, with a slight edge of hysteria. Bindi was at a loss. Skylar never let stress get the better of her, but it seemed that catering a wedding stretched everyone to the limit.

"Of course, we will." Bindi lay a soothing hand on Skylar's back. The wedding was still two days away yet. And Skylar had everything planned down to the last second. She was the queen of organization. Ms Perfection, herself. "Look." Bindi walked over and tapped the schedule Skylar had taped to the refrigerator, written in her neat handwriting. "It says here, we need to ice the cake this morning, and make the native pepperberry crackers for the entrée and put them in the freezer, ready for the big day." That didn't sound too bad. As long as they broke things down into small steps, everything was achievable.

Skylar gave a moan and lifted her head. "Yes, but that list doesn't take into account the lunch we need to prepare for all the hoardes of people Dale and Daisy have invited. I don't know why I ever agreed to do this," she ended on a wail.

Oh, God, what was she supposed to do with a boss that was losing her shit? It was supposed to be the bride who had the meltdown before the wedding, wasn't it?

Just as Bindi wavered between going over and patting Skylar on the back, or leaning her own elbows on the countertop and joining in her misery, Julie waltzed in.

"What's going on?" she asked in her usual bright, chirpy voice.

"I can't do this. I don't know why Daniella has put all this on my shoulders. It's too much, I'm telling you." Skylar slammed her hands down on the countertop with a smack, making Bindi jump.

"Oh. Right." Julie's astute gaze shot between Bindi and Skylar. "It's like that, is it?"

"Like what?" Skylar asked, narrowing her eyes at Julie, who held her hands in the air and backed away.

"Time for a little emergency break, and something to eat," Julie said, approaching her stepsister as if she were a rabid dog. "Low blood sugar can turn everyone a little crazy. And I know you haven't eaten anything this morning. Have you?" She reached Skylar and took her by the shoulders, spinning her around to face her. "Come with me and we'll have a little chat."

"No, I can't leave—" Skylar protested.

"Codswallop." Julie exclaimed. "You need a break, little sister. Five minutes to have something to eat and get some fresh air."

"Did you just say codswallop?" Skylar asked. "Surely you didn't just use that word?"

"I did, and I'll say it again, if you don't come with me right this instant."

Skylar gave a low chuckle. Then she tilted her head back and gave a long sigh. "You're right. I'd kill for a Diet Coke and a muffin."

Julie drew her into an embrace, and the two sisters hugged. Bindi was so glad that Julie was around to handle Skylar at her worst. She wasn't sure what she would've done without her.

"Good, girl. Then I'll get in the kitchen and give you two a hand," Julie replied. "Daniella has had me folding bloody napkins all morning." Julie gave a theatrical sigh. "But I'm here now, ready to do your bidding."

"Thank you," Skylar said, removing her apron and throwing it on the countertop. "How about we grab a soda and a snack and take it into my garden for a few minutes?" She opened the smaller walk-in cool-room and grabbed two cans of drink and two muffins left over from yesterday's smoko. "Will you be okay for a few secs?" she asked Bindi as she backed out of the door.

"Sure. I'll start making sandwiches for lunch," Bindi said helpfully. That would be one less thing Skylar had to think about. At least Skylar had agreed to keep all the daily meals simple on the lead up to the wedding, and she wasn't expected to produce the gourmet meals that she was renowned for.

All the cabins on Stormcloud were now full of friends and family here for the wedding. Bindi had lost track of who was who. As she got to work buttering a stack of bread she grabbed from the freezer, Bindi reviewed the names of the guests she knew. Daisy's family from Perth were here, of course, including her parents, elderly grandmother, and her brother, River. Bindi still couldn't quite get over her aversion to River after he'd got Daisy into so much trouble when they'd first arrived in the area. Plus, a gaggle of four of Daisy's best friends—also from Perth, three women and one man—who'd commandeered a lot of Daisy's time over the past few days. The rest of Daisy's extended family—aunties, uncles, and cousins—were making the trip down from the

Northern Territory, but had opted to stay at the Koongarra Station, in the indigenous community, less than an hour's drive away.

Dean and Naomi, along with Daniella's ex-husband and his entourage of wife and two sons—both stepbrothers to Dale and Skylar—were here. Along with Steve's old boss and his wife, who were an absolute hoot; Bindi had loved talking to them on their ride the other day.

The station was bursting at the seams. There were so many people coming that the overflow had to be housed at the hotel and van park in Dimbulah. The rest would drive in from Cairns or the surrounding country areas on the day. It was touted to be the event of the year.

Steve and Daniella had been kept busy entertaining their family, and Daisy and Dale were kept equally busy handling the million-and-one little emergencies that always came up when there was a wedding to plan. Like, could they sit Aunty Sharia at the same table as Aunty Polly, because of their long-standing feud that no one really remembered how or even when it'd started? Or the white flannel flowers Daisy had ordered for her bouquet were delayed, and Daisy might have to go with ordinary old chrysanthemums, which had almost made her cry.

But as long as the weather held out, all of those minor details would fade away on the day. The weather gods seemed to be smiling on them, as there were still no predictions of rain, at least until Christmas. Actually, the weather remained unseasonably hot and dry.

Bindi worked methodically until there were nearly a hundred slices, buttered and ready. She'd make a selection of fillings, which would be simple, but tasty. She laid out slabs of rare roast beef from a haunch Steve had slow-cooked on the barbecue himself the other day, combined with some of Skylar's special homemade relish. Bindi had just started on the Swiss cheese and pickle sandwiches when Skylar and Julie came back into the kitchen.

"Oh, good, thanks," Skylar said, looking much less frazzled.

"Tell us what's left to do, and we'll help you finish up," Julie added.

"If you could whip up a bowl of egg mixture to make the last of them, that'd be great," Bindi replied. "There's a heap of hard-boiled eggs in the cool-room." She pointed at the larger of the two refrigerated rooms.

The three women worked efficiently, side by side, until all the sandwiches were cut and stacked neatly onto five large platters and placed in the cool-room until they were needed at lunch time.

"One job down, twenty-million more to go," Skylar said, but her voice was no longer cynical, and it held a lighter note, which hadn't been there before. Julie had obviously worked her magic.

Skylar decided she wanted to make the royal icing for the wedding cake—because it had to be perfect, of course—and Julie and Bindi had just set to work making the pepperberry crackers, when Mack bust into the kitchen.

"Madonna and Melody have escaped again," he said breathlessly.

"What?" Bindi looked up from where she was turning out the dough onto a floured board, ready to be rolled really thin and cut into squares.

"I was just up at the stables. One of Daisy's friends left her jacket up there yesterday after their ride, and I went up to see if I could find it. As soon as I went through the entrance, I noticed that Madonna's stall was wide open. There's no sign of either of them."

"Shit," Bindi swore, and the other two women stopped what they were doing and looked up. "Have you told Steve?"

"No, he's gone to Cairns with Daniella, Dale, and a raft of Daisy's family, so they can pick up the best men's rental tuxedos and buy any last-minute items they need before the wedding. They won't be back until late this afternoon." Mack's face was flushed, as if he'd run all the way down the hill and straight to the lodge. It'd been two days since that fated kiss on the sofa. Two long, torturous days, where Bindi had avoided Mack as much as she could. Which hadn't been hard, as they were both being run off their feet. She hadn't even had time to ask him how his arm was doing; if his stitches were healing okay. But something had been bothering him, she could tell by the tense little lines around his tawny eyes. She'd caught him and Dean in deep conversation yesterday morning, but they'd broken apart as soon as she'd stepped foot on the veranda, Mack giving her a guilty smile. Come to think of it, Dean had looked decidedly edgy yesterday, too. But Bindi didn't want to know what was going on, she was over all this drama. Her mind went back to the task at hand.

"Shit," Bindi said again. "We need to find them before they get too far away. Steve would hate to lose his prize horses."

"I know," Mack replied. But he seemed to be waiting for her to say something, as if he were unsure what to do next. Today he was wearing faded blue jeans and a blue Stormcloud shirt, set off by his brown work Stetson, which he'd forgotten to remove in his rush to come inside. He looked gorgeous, and it was all Bindi could do to keep her mind on what he'd just said.

Bindi glanced at Skylar, who swiped a strand of blond hair away from her face and stared back. Then, with a scowl and a nod of her head, she said, "You two had better go look for them. Julie will have to finish up the crackers on her own."

"I can manage," Julie sang out, but Skylar ignored her.

"I thought Dale was going to fix the stall, so that damned

mare couldn't pull these Houdini acts," Skylar added. "This is the last thing we need today."

"So did I," Bindi shot back, already washing the last of the dough from her hands under the kitchen faucet.

"I told Steve and Dale about these new latches we've been using at Stargazer," Mack said, almost apologetically. "I think Steve ordered some, but they haven't arrived yet."

"We'll have to do something to fix them temporarily before then once we get them back. Even if we have to padlock the stable door shut," Bindi huffed. Joining Mack in the doorway, she grabbed her Akubra off a hook near the door and said, "I think we should take the horses. We can track them easier that way."

"I agree." Mack gestured for her to precede him to the door.

"Don't forget to take a radio each," Skylar called after them, and Bindi gave her a wave and took two radios and two shoulder holsters out of the cupboard just inside the door. It was Dale's job as leading hand to make sure all the radios were returned every day, as well as keep them charged up and ready for use, so at least she knew these radios would be in perfect working order.

Their conversation was non-existent as they raced up to the stables, slipping into the shoulder holsters as they went, Bindi trying to figure out which way the mare could've gone. She saddled Sahara quickly, while Mack did the same with Picasso. Then she led Sahara out of the saddling yard and studied the ground in front of the main entrance. The earth was dry, the rust-colored dust churned up with all sorts of footprints. She couldn't tell if any belonged to Madonna, or her filly. Would the mare take off in the same direction she'd gone the last time? Toward Dimbulah. Bindi walked down the gravel roadway, leading Sahara behind her. If she had gone toward town, then she should be able to find footprints farther down. But here was nothing, and Bindi wasted precious minutes investigating the earth on both sides of the roadway for any signs. Mack stood, waiting for her without a word, Picasso's ears flicking forward and back as he also waited for the word to get going. Mack had tied a couple of lead ropes and a spare bridle to his saddle, Bindi noted. At least one of them was thinking straight.

On a hunch, she led Sahara around the back of the stables. Two trails led off almost at right angles from here, one toward the old gold mine, and one following the ridge of low hills, then winding upward onto the top of the escarpment. Dale and Julie had taken a contingent of wedding guests up onto the escarpment yesterday, but no one had ridden out to the gold mine in nearly a week. Most of the time, they took the ATVs to the mine; it was easier and quicker, and you could carry more supplies—like lunch—on the back of the little four-wheel-drives.

Bindi walked slowly down the track, head down, eyes trained on the red dirt, with Sahara trailing obediently after her. There. A single hoof print. Smaller than any of the others. Made by the little filly, if she wasn't mistaken.

"Over here," Bindi sang out, mounting up. Mack, who'd been hanging back, so he didn't mix his own footprints in with the ones she was studying, rode up behind her.

"Which way?" he asked, tawny eyes intent and focussed.

"Toward the old mine." She raised a hand and pointed. "Although, I'm not sure why Madonna would head in that direction. There's very little feed, all the pasture areas are back toward the road." It was confusing. But then, who knew exactly what went through the mind of a horse? Mack had yet to visit the mine, which might put him at a disadvantage. She gave him a quick rundown of the layout as they walked briskly along the gravel path. Hopefully, they'd spot the two runaway horses well before they made it to the mine. Bindi kept her eyes on the ground in front, making sure they were still following the horse's hoofprints.

Hang on. Something was wrong. Bindi leaned down in her saddle, slowing Sahara so she could double-check the marks on the path. There were Madonna's hoof prints, with little Melody's smaller ones, showing her trotting dutifully alongside. But there was another set. Slightly larger than Madonna's.

Bindi sat back in her saddle, just as Mack said, "Do you see three sets of prints?"

"Yes," she agreed. But what did that mean?

"Did someone steal Madonna?" Mack voiced her fears, even before she could properly form them.

Surely not. "Why would anyone do that?" she asked, incredulous.

"You told me yourself that she and her filly were worth a pretty penny," Mack replied.

She pondered that for a few seconds. He was right. But a horse thief? Way out here? The idea bordered on the ridiculous. Especially during the middle of the day, and with all the people around for the wedding. But then, maybe the thief was counting on them being distracted, and had chosen his time more carefully than she first thought.

"Should we let the lodge know?" Mack asked.

"Not yet," Bindi decided. They needed to make damn sure that Madonna had been abducted before they raised the alarm. She urged Sahara into a trot, a frisson of panic running down her spine. They needed to find those horses. Mack kept Picasso trotting by her side, but neither of them said anything. She tried to keep her eyes on the road in front, and away from Mack's long fingers resting lightly on the reins just above Picasso's neck. He had an easy, laid-back riding style and the horses all responded well to him. Their knees touched now and then, as their horses came together and she had to remind herself to concentrate on the tracks in front, just in case the thief strayed from the path, and not on how tingles of awareness shot up her thigh every time they came in contact. Occasionally, he'd glance at her and grimace, then look away, as if he had something to say, but wasn't sure of himself.

Finally, he spoke. "There's something you should know."

Uh-oh. She didn't need any more drama right now. What else could possibly go wrong? She clenched her teeth and stared at him from beneath the brim of her hat. "What?" she ground out.

"I had a call two days ago..." He hesitated, as if not sure how to say whatever he needed to say. "From Clarissa."

"Oh." Her mouth made an *O* of surprise. That was unexpected. She slowed Sahara to a walk so she could concentrate fully on what he was saying.

"She practically admitted that she was behind the crash on our way home from the rodeo."

"Wow! So, what did you say? Have you told Nash?" This was good, wasn't it? The breakthrough they needed to finally get all the answers. It meant that Mack could stop looking over his shoulder.

He waved her questions away. "Yes, I've talked to Dean and Steve. Dean and I had a meeting with Nash yesterday. But that's not what I'm trying to tell you."

He'd had a meeting with Nash already? Without her? That realization stung. Perhaps he was trying to shelter her from the unpleasantness. It was Mack that Clarissa wanted to hurt, not her, after all. And God only knew how busy they'd been. But stupidly, she felt left out. It'd would've been nice to have been told what was going on. But then another idea snuck into her head. Was it because he'd been avoiding her? Because she'd rejected him? Was he punishing her?

Perhaps her thoughts showed through in the squint of her

eyes, because he hurriedly added, "I'm sorry I didn't tell you before now, but I didn't want to worry you unnecessarily, and…" He waved a hand, as if trying to snatch the right words out of the air. "Anyway, I'm sorry, but I'm telling you now."

"Right," she answered tightly. "So?"

"So, she threatened me. Told me to stop the investigation, or else. But I told Dean and Nash that was the last thing I wanted. So the investigation is still going ahead."

This Clarissa sounded like a real bitch. Who did she think she was, some sort of Mafia Queen? But there wasn't a whole lot she could do from all the way over in Texas.

"Good. This woman deserves to go down," she said. "I'm glad you're standing up to her. But that doesn't stop the fact that we still have two horses to find." She was getting tired of this conversation. Mack could fill her in on the rest of the details later. She clucked at Sahara to get her moving up again, but Mack called out to her.

"Wait, Bindi. The reason I'm telling you all this now is that I'm not the only one Clarissa has in her sights."

Bindi reined Sahara to a halt, a sudden sliver of fear worming down her spine.

"Clarissa was trying to blackmail me, and she used you as the bait. She's threatened to hurt you, as well."

"And you didn't think to warn me before now?" she asked coldly.

"It was Nash and Steve's decision," he said plaintively. "I thought we should, but they decided that with so much going on for the wedding, there was no way anyone would get close to either of us in the next few days. Nash hoped he'd have an answer from his colleagues in the US by that stage." He held up his hands in supplication. "I'm sorry Bindi."

It suddenly dawned on Bindi, the whole reason Mack had brought this up now. "Do you think this horse thief has something to do with Clarissa?"

"I really don't know." He shrugged. "This could be random. A coincidence, because as you say, Madonna and her filly are worth a lot of money. But I needed you to know, just in case. We have to go in with our eyes open."

"Fine. You've made me aware of the danger, now let's get going." She kicked Sahara up into a fast trot. This was great. Just perfect. Not only did they have to worry that the horses had been stolen. But now there might also be an ulterior motive behind it all. Which seemed a little ridiculous to Bindi. This was surely an elaborate plan, if it was meant to trap Mack. And her.

There was no mistaking the three sets of tracks now, and they continued to lead them straight toward the mine. Almost as if the horse thief were holding up a sign, telling them exactly where he was headed.

After a while, Mack asked, "Why take them to the mine site?"

Bindi had a few theories, but the one that made the most sense was probably the best one. "I'm guessing they may have a truck parked somewhere up there. It's a well-known tourist destination, and the road runs right up to it. All they'd need to do is load Madonna and Melody onto the truck and they could disappear down one of the many roads leading out of here, never to be seen again."

"Makes sense," Mack grunted. "But if it's a tourist site, won't there be other people around? Surely they wouldn't do it where there might be witnesses?"

Bindi shook her head. "The rangers closed the site a few days ago over the Christmas period, for scheduled maintenance. It's the low season, and they don't get many tourists at this time of the year, especially not when the rains start. Even Stormcloud isn't allowed to take our guests out there at the moment."

"Aha." Mack twisted his mouth into a bow of concentration. Fascinated by the firm line of his lips, she had to force herself to look away. Why did he have to be so bloody gorgeous? "But how would whoever has the horses know that? Unless they're a local. Or at the very least, they've been talking to a local."

She hadn't considered that aspect, but it was a reasonable assumption. If it were locals, it also explained how they knew about Madonna and her filly, and what they were worth, as well.

Bindi quickened their pace, and within another fifteen minutes, she spotted the dry riverbed that heralded the outskirts of the mine site. They slowed, so the horses could more easily navigate the rocky bottom of the river.

Bindi swiveled in her saddle and peered back the way they'd come. "Do you smell smoke?" she asked, standing up in her stirrups to get a better look.

Mack reined in Picasso and turned a worried glance backward. "Look." He pointed skyward, where a plume of smoke drifted just above the tree line. Even as they watched, the white wisp grew in size and became dark gray, expanding from a small finger of smoke to a larger cloud, to a billowing, angry mass. Sahara gave a nervous whicker, as she got wind of the flames.

"Holy shit," Bindi could hardly believe her eyes. This was bad. Especially now, when the land was as dry as a chip. The dehydrated grass and underbrush would go up like a bonfire someone had thrown gasoline on. "We need to let Skylar know," she said a little breathily. Her heart was beating fast, and it was almost as if she were hyperventilating. She tapped the button on the two-way, and said, "Bindi to lodge. Acknowledge. Over." Then waited for someone to reply.

The main radio comms unit was in Daniella's office, and neither she nor Steve were there. But a smaller unit was situated in the kitchen, where Skylar might hear it, in case of emergencies. The two-way radios had their limitations, and could only be used over smaller distances and only on flat ground, as they used line-of-sight frequencies. If any of the staff went to the other end of the station, or on a muster, then satellite phones were a must, but this close to the lodge, the radios should work. Skylar would know it was up to her to answer this call, and to Bindi's relief, her voice crackled down the line a few seconds later. Mack moved in closer, so he could hear the conversation. Both horses shuffled nervously, ears twitching and eyes wide with alarm. They didn't like the proximity of the fire any more than the humans did.

"Skylar here. Have you found them?"

"No. But you need to call the fire services. We're at the perimeter of the mine, but we can see smoke behind us. There's a fire between us and you, closer to the mine. Say around half a kilometer away." As she said the words, it also dawned on her. They were now cut off from the lodge. The fire was directly in their path. Unless she wanted to cut across country, which she could do if pressed, but that fire seemed to be spreading quickly. She had been considering backtracking, to see if she and Mack might fight the fire themselves, but the amount of smoke now billowing around them put paid to that idea. And now she could see flames licking the tops of the taller trees. There was a slight breeze, but it was carrying the fire away from them, which was one small mercy. Until she remembered that if it were being blown away from them, it meant the fire was heading straight for the resort. Was this purely a coincidence? Or was there something more sinister going on here? Or should she say *someone* more sinister?

"Oh, shit. Not good. Not good at all." Bindi could hear scuffling noises, as if Skylar were juggling the radio, then she heard her say something indistinct. "Julie's on the phone to the fire brigade right now. I'll round up Alek and Sasha, and we'll grab the fire truck and jump on the ATVs. See if we can keep it from spreading any closer to the lodge. I'll leave Aaron here to look after the guests."

Stormcloud had a dedicated fire truck they kept on station for just such emergencies. It was an old four-wheel-drive truck that Steve had converted to house a large, stainless steel Furphy water tank on the rear bed. The engine drove a small pump, which allowed them to spray a strong stream of water from a long hose. It'd come in handy more than once over its lifetime, although Bindi had never encountered a fire in her time on the station.

Bindi could hear the worry in Skylar's voice. The absolute last thing they needed right now was a wildfire threatening Stormcloud. Not while their cabins were full of people, and they had a wedding in two days. Bindi couldn't even think about what might happen if this fire reached the lodge. Of course, they had an escape plan in place, and Bindi knew Skylar and Julie would make sure the guests were evacuated to safety, if need be.

"What about you? Are you safe?" Skylar demanded.

"Yes. We're going to keep going to the mine site." She glanced at Mack as she said this, and he nodded his consent. It was the only real option, anyway. And she was determined not to let some thieving asshole take Steve's prized horses. Which reminded her, Skylar needed to be told the rest of the story. "The reason we haven't found the horses yet is that we think they may have been stolen and taken to the mine site. Perhaps to be loaded onto a truck." Should she tell her about Mack's little revelation, as well? That not only had the horses been stolen, but he thought there might be a connection to someone who wanted him dead? Deciding that it wouldn't make any difference to how Skylar responded to the emergency if she told her or not, she rushed on, not letting Skylar's gasp of surprise deter her. "But if the fire gets any worse, we'll ride north, we'll come out on the main highway around the turnoff. We won't put our lives at risk for the horses," she consented.

"Good idea," Skylar agreed. "Did you take a sat phone?" she asked suddenly.

"No." They'd left the kitchen in such a hurry, she'd clean forgotten to take one. At the time, she hadn't really thought they'd need it. But if the fire spread, and they had to keep going north, they might get out of range of the two-ways. It was a mistake, but there was no point in beating herself up about it now. "But like I said, we'll head to the highway. Someone will pick us up there."

There was a moment of silence, and then Skylar said brusquely, "Okay, we'll have to deal with that eventuality, if it happens. Stay safe. Out." The radio went quiet.

She and Mack stared at the mushrooming fire behind them. "We'd better get moving," she said, at last.

"I just had a thought," Mack said, as they reined their horses away from the rising flames. "This fire may not be a coincidence. It may be a diversion. To stop us looking for the horses."

Again, he was thinking one step ahead of her. It was an interesting idea. One that held merit. Whoever was doing this had come up with a way to distract everyone at Stormcloud. As well as a way to cut her and Mack off from any rescue.

Bindi studied Mack for a few moments. Back when she'd first met him, she'd compared him to Wazza, and found him seriously wanting. She'd decided that he'd never be able to fill Wazza's boots. But maybe she'd underestimated him back then. While Wazza would certainly have taken charge; known exactly what to do and been able to direct people in his calm, efficient way, Mack wasn't backing down from this challenge. His face was deadly serious, and she recognized that look from the time he'd been about to mount the bull at the rodeo.

Completely focused and deadly. There wasn't a single sign of the cocky, flirty cowboy persona he usually projected. He may not have Wazza's experience from many years of working at Stormcloud, but he was using his sharp wit and intelligence to guide them both. He had her back, and the glint in his eye told her he'd do whatever it took to get those horses back and get out of this predicament alive. If she had to face this frightening scenario with anyone, she was glad it was Mack by her side.

"We need to find Madonna," she said, determination coloring her voice. "Then we need to get the hell out of here." She clucked at Sahara, who required no urging to move away from the fire, and took off with a bound up the dry riverbank.

"Well, at least let me go in first," Mack said grimly, spurring Picasso into a canter so that he was in front of her.

Blasted men and their blasted egos. Bindi urged Sahara to keep up with him.

CHAPTER NINETEEN

Mack glanced back to make sure Bindi was right behind him. She glowered at him from beneath her hat, but didn't say a word. They'd slowed down as they approached the first ruined building, keeping to the tree line and out of sight as much as they could. Bindi had hissed at him that she needed to lead, because she knew her way around the scattered buildings and pathways.

Begrudgingly, he acknowledged this was true. But he didn't want Bindi out in front, because they could be heading straight into danger. He wanted her behind him, where he could safeguard her. Call him an old-fashioned, macho male, but where Bindi was concerned, his protective instincts had soared to twenty out of ten the moment that fire had started. Actually, if he were being truthful with himself, his level of concern had been that high since Mutt had tried to stab her.

The second Mack realized what the three sets of hoof prints meant, he'd been as agitated as a nest full of ants. It felt like his skin was crawling. He knew he had to tell Bindi about the phone call, he'd had no other choice. All the reasons he'd kept the truth about Clarissa from Bindi dissolved in a puff of self-recrimination.

Remorse wasn't a strong enough word for what he was

feeling right now. Gutless and dumb were two words he might use, but even they didn't accurately describe what a thoughtless human being he was. The simple fact was that he'd kept the information from Bindi because he was mad at her. She'd rejected him, and it hurt like hell. He was being a sore loser. But he now understood by making that decision, he'd been gambling with her life.

He could use the excuse Nash and Dean had persuaded him to keep it under his hat, but something in his gut had told him they were wrong.

Why hadn't he listened to his gut?

Mack reined Picasso to a halt beneath the wide, spreading limbs of an old gum tree and put his finger to his lips, taking in the lay of the land. Bindi had already given him a few hurried facts about the place.

The local Shire had set it up as a museum, to give tourists an insight into how things might've been back in the twenties and thirties when the mine was in its heyday. There were a few abandoned miner's cottages scattered around the old township, but Bindi had indicated that they were unsafe to enter. The layout of the old township remained the same as when it'd been alive with people, with a wide, gravel road running down the middle, smaller pathways branching off toward ruined buildings. The old gold mine was situated at the base of a small escarpment, a blunt finger of rock, part of the larger range, of which Mount Mulligan escarpment was also a part. Red rock abounded here. Tufts of dried grass broke through the red gravel. It felt completely deserted, the only sounds that of the frenzied buzzing of the cicadas. It was more than a tad spooky. The temperature was becoming intense, a heat haze shimmering off the gravel on the main road. The humidity was debilitating, and he wiped ineffectively at the sweat on his brow. He glanced over his shoulder and gauged the size of the fire behind them. It was definitely growing in size, but thankfully not coming in their direction, the slight breeze blowing it backward, just as Bindi had predicted. But the wind could change at any second, then they might be in real trouble. Smoke filled the air behind them in an angry cloud, but here in the township, it was surprisingly clear.

One building, directly in front of them, had been restored. The manager's cottage housed information about the gold mine. People were encouraged to enter, to read about the history. Mack studied the building, looking for any signs of… he wasn't exactly sure what. Just in case someone was hiding, lying in wait for them.

"The rangers will have locked the manager's cottage up at the end of the season," Bindi whispered to his back. She must've noticed him staring at it. That didn't mean some reprobate wouldn't think twice about breaking into the building to use it as a lookout, so Mack kept gazing at the windows, watching for movement. "There's an old elevator shaft off to our left, behind those trees." She lifted a hand and pointed, and he turned to follow her finger, making out the top of a large, wooden structure. "The old mine shaft is boarded up, and you can't go down it anymore, it's too dangerous. There are also two or three inspection shafts toward the back of the township, but they've also been covered over up to make them safe."

Mack nodded thoughtfully.

"My guess is that they've taken the horses to the other end of town. There's a big, wooden building, like a barn, called the main battery, where they used to crush the quartz stone and process it to remove the gold. If a thief wanted to hide the horses, that building would be big enough. The parking lot is at the rear of the building, so that's where they'd take them if they wanted to load them onto a trailer and get out of here," she continued in a whisper.

He was glad of Bindi's intimate knowledge of the place. It'd save them a lot of bumbling around. And time was of the essence, especially with a wildfire on their tails.

"Some horizontal mining tunnels run directly into the escapement farther along, but they've been shut off, as well. Too dangerous to go into, they might collapse."

"Hmm." Mack considered these options.

"I think we should head toward the old battery," Bindi whispered impatiently, when Mack took too long to answer. "That's the most likely place they'll be."

He agreed, but he was still loathe to move from their hiding spot. The place was too eerily quiet for his liking. Too still, like everything was holding its breath, waiting for something to happen.

With a huff of exasperation, Bindi pushed Sahara past him, heading to the left, toward where she'd pointed out the elevator shaft, staying off the track and weaving behind clumps of bushes and underneath low hanging tree branches. Mack hurried after her, clamping his lips together over the urge to shout at her. This wasn't a game they were playing. But he followed in her wake, keeping his head tucked down by Picasso's withers, and making sure they stayed camouflaged behind the trees as best he could.

They followed the gentle curve of rising ground, moving parallel to the escapement, which got lower as they progressed farther north. Nothing moved in the abandoned township—the bits he could make out through the brush, anyway. But the skin on the back of his neck crawled, and he wondered what they were going to find when they reached this wooden barn structure Bindi was talking about.

Finally, Bindi came to a halt behind a clump of acacia bushes, at the edge of a large, cleared section. A hundred meters away, an old building loomed close to the cliff-face.

"I think we should leave the horses here," she said,

hunkering low over the pommel and staring at the building. "We can sneak around the side of those boulders there." She lifted her chin in the direction of a pile of large rocks jumbled around the edge of the clearing. Probably pushed there when the first miners had cleared the area.

Again, her idea made sense. If they rode the horses across the clearing, they'd make a large target and surely be spotted if anyone was watching for them. For a second, Mack felt foolish. Was all this cloak-and-dagger stuff really necessary? The idea that someone was lying in wait for them seemed fanciful and stupid.

Nevertheless, he dismounted and patted the piebald's neck, while Bindi did the same.

There was a small sound. It made him lift his head and peer through the shrubbery. What was that? It was like the whoosh of air… Followed by a faint crackling noise, like…

"Fire," Bindi said softly, her eyes fixed on the roof of the old building, Sahara's reins forgotten in her hands. It was true, he could see a hint of smoke rising from the right-hand corner of the old battery. Even as he watched, the smoke became thicker over the top of the roofline and he could imagine flames devouring the aged wood like a hungry beast. Had someone set the structure on fire on purpose? This wasn't good. It became crystal-clear to him in that instant that they needed to get out of there. Now.

"Bindi, let's go," he commanded, remounting in one swift movement.

She glanced up at him and then back at the half-ruined building.

"Bindi, we need to get out of here. Something isn't right," he said, raising his voice.

She tore her gaze away from the quickly growing cloud of smoke and even though she didn't look convinced, she bunched Sahara's reins on her neck, ready to mount.

A loud, terrified whinny erupted from inside the building. Mack's eyes flew to where the noise had come from.

"That's Madonna," Bindi yelled. "We have to get her." And without a backward glance, she took off at a sprint over the red gravel. Sahara pivoted and reared at Bindi's sudden movement, probably already spooked by the smell of smoke and the sound of another terrified horse. She crashed into Picasso's shoulder, sending him stumbling, the two horses almost falling as they came together. It was all Mack could do to stay in his saddle, and he lost sight of Bindi as Picasso regained his feet, then tried to bolt. Mack leaped out of the saddle and onto the ground, managing to keep hold of the reins as Picasso reared away in panic. Sahara stood a few feet away, snorting her agitation, eyes wide with growing fear, as if she, too, was ready to dash away at any second.

He couldn't leave the horses untethered. They might take off into the bush, the smoke spooking them, and they'd be left without a means of getting out of there.

But what about Bindi?

She was almost to the other side of the clearing.

Shit, shit, shit.

He reached for Sahara's bridle, speaking in a soothing tone. If he could capture her, then he'd swing up into his own saddle and gallop across the clearing, reaching Bindi before she did anything more foolish.

"Hey. Shit-for-brains." The voice startled Mack, so he dropped his horse's reins. What the…?

He turned to see a big man bearing down on him, face set in a grimace of intent. The man had massive shoulders, like a weightlifter, with a huge, black, ten-gallon hat rammed on his head. Mack recognized him immediately. It was the guy who'd accosted him in the parking lot at the rodeo. And he had a gun. Pointed directly at Mack.

Behind him, Sahara took off in a panicked clatter of hooves

on gravel, unable to deal with this new threat. Mack didn't blame her. Picasso also sidled away from the approaching man with the gun, leaving Mack standing alone and uncertain.

"Put your hands where I can see them," the man demanded.

Mack vacillated. What to do? The man had a gun pointed directly at him. Out of the corner of his eye, he saw Bindi approach the large open end of the wooden structure. Then he lost sight of her as she dashed inside the burning building, totally unaware that he was in trouble. *Fuck. Fuck. Double fuck.* His pulse pounded in his neck, his heart threatening to leap out of his chest.

Was it a good thing Bindi was now out of sight? Not a good thing that she'd run into a burning building, but at least this man couldn't shoot at her.

Mack raised his arms into the air.

"Who are you? What do you want?" Mack demanded.

"I'm your worst fucking nightmare," the man spat back. "Now turn around."

"What? Why?" Mack didn't know what else to say, but he knew he needed to buy time. Let his brain catch up with this shitstorm of a scenario.

"Just do as you're told," the guy in the black hat growled.

He was close now. Close enough not to miss if he pulled the trigger. Mack chose prudence over valor. At least until he knew Bindi was safe. So he turned around.

"Hands behind your back."

He did as he was told and felt the man slip a plastic tie over his wrists and pull it tight. Mack's thumping heart lodged in his throat. He hated the feeling of powerlessness that washed over him. He was used to being in charge. How was he going to save Bindi if he couldn't even save himself?

A tug on his shoulder holster was the only warning he got

as his two-way radio was pulled out and thrown on the ground, the guy stomping on it four or five times for good measure. Shit. Mack angled his body slightly away from the big man, hoping and praying he'd leave it at that. But Black Hat reached over and patted the top pocked of Mack's shirt, almost as if he knew where his phone was kept. That, too, was thrown on the ground and stomped upon. Not that it would've done him much good, there was no signal out here.

Glowering from beneath lowered brows, Mack tried again to engage the guy in conversation.

"Why are you doing this? If it's the horses you want, then take them, I don't care." That wasn't strictly true, but if he had to bargain his and Bindi's lives for the two horses, he would.

"It's not about the horses. Although, they made good bait." The man smiled at him. Actually smiled, like this was some sort of joke. But his words brought all of Mack's fears to the surface, and he suddenly knew this wasn't going to end well.

"I know you're working for Clarissa Melman," Mack said as calmly as he could.

"Never heard that name," the man replied lightly. "All I know is a lady with a very sexy voice asked me to do her a favor, and she offered to pay me well enough that I can probably retire somewhere out on the coast. So, who's to argue with a lady?" He shrugged, as if this was an everyday occurrence for him. And perhaps it was. Then he waved his gun at Picasso, yelling, "Ha. Ha. Get outta here, ya dopey animal!"

It was too much for the piebald horse, and he took off in the same direction as Sahara. Somewhere in the back of his mind, Mack hoped the horses were smart enough to stay away from the wildfire.

Refocussing on the man in front of him, he tried to figure out what to say that'd make him let Mack go? And where was

Bindi? He hadn't heard anything from Madonna since she'd entered the building. Had she found them and was leading them to safety right at this moment? He fervently hoped so. Perhaps if he could delay this bozo for even a few moments, it'd give Bindi the time she needed.

The midday sun beat down on Mack, and he wanted to wipe the sweat from his brow, but couldn't with his hands tied behind his back, so he lived with the torment of it dripping into his eyes as he blinked it away.

"At least be man enough to tell me what your plans are." Mack demanded. "Am I a dead man walking?" he asked darkly. It'd be nice to know if Clarissa wanted him dead, or was merely sending him another, stronger message. Perhaps if he got out of this alive, he might even heed her this time.

Black Hat simply snorted.

"I can pay you." Mack was grasping at straws now. It was true, he had enough money stashed away to buy this guy off, but somehow he doubted his ploy would work. There was no way he'd pay a scumbag like this guy, anyway, but he needed to sound convincing. "I can double whatever Clarissa is paying you."

"Move," the man commanded, waving him forward with the loosely held gun, then pushed Mack in the back when he refused to budge, sending him off-balance. Mack barely stayed on his feet, with his hands behind his back, he almost landed face-first in the gravel. The man pushed him again, and Mack began walking toward the piles of rocks at the edge of the clearing, where the guy indicated he should go.

"Hey, Whip, you out there?" a voice echoed around the clearing. Shit, there was another one. He hadn't counted on Black Hat having an accomplice. Mack swiveled his head to catch a glance at this new threat.

"Yeah, come on out, I got our boy leashed," the man called Whip answered in a loud voice.

A figure emerged from the shadows of the open side of the building. He was carrying something, staggering slightly under the weight. A body. He had a body slung over his shoulder.

No.

Mack's knees nearly gave way beneath him.

It was Bindi, her head hanging loosely down the other man's back.

Was she dead?

Please, please, please, don't let her be dead.

The man walked toward them, shuffling his feet through the dust. As he got closer, Mack saw he was a rotund man, nearly as wide as he was tall, and was perspiring profusely, large sweat patches staining the light blue T-shirt, the bottom of his shirt riding up to reveal a flabby paunch. He, too, was wearing a black, ten-gallon hat, but it didn't seem to have the same menace that Whip's leant him. He squinted at Mack through piggy eyes, his round face blotchy from the heat.

"It worked like a charm," Paunchy Man said. "She came running in, so worried about the horses, she didn't even see me until it was too late."

"Good," Whip replied. "Is the fire out? The last thing we need is to get penned in by another wildfire."

"Yeah, of course. It was just a whole lot of green branches. They smoked like shit, but didn't really burn, just like you told me." The fat man gave a satisfied grin.

Mack was desperately trying to see if Bindi was still breathing, so he was only partly listening to the men's conversation. *Bindi, look at me*, he pleaded silently. But she remained motionless.

"What have you done to her?" Mack snarled. "If she's dead…" He clenched his fists in his bindings and turned to face Whip.

"You'll what?" The other man laughed in his face. "You

aint' got much of a say in anything right now, fella."

"Oh, she's not dead," Paunchy man piped up. "I only hit her with a bit of wood, she's still breathing. See?" He turned helpfully to the side, so Mack could get a better look at Bindi's face, which bounced bonelessly off the man's fleshy hip.

"Don't be a fucking idiot," Whip snapped at the man. "Chuck her in the shaft. Then meet me at the car. We need to get outta here," he commanded.

"Oh, yeah, right boss." Paunchy man's face fell for a second, then hardened, taking on a look of resolve. This guy might be an idiot, but he was still dangerous. He took off at a forced trot over the red ground toward the pile of large boulders to the left, Bindi's arms flinging around like she was a rag doll as Mack stared helplessly after them.

Suddenly, Blue T-shirt stopped in his tracks and looked back over his shoulder. "What about the horses?"

"Shoot them," Whip replied, after a moment's contemplation. "Bit of a pity, they're some fine horseflesh, but I'd never be able to sell them, they're too recognizable. May as well make these stupid assholes understand who they're dealing with. Make 'em sorry they ever crossed us." Whip turned to grin at Mack.

No. Mack wanted to shout the word. The poor horses were innocent in all of this. Steve would be devastated by their loss. But then again, knowing Steve, he'd be more devastated knowing his staff were in danger. And Bindi *was* in danger. Terrible danger, if Mack couldn't do anything to help her.

Mack rounded on Whip. "What are you going to do with her?" He'd mentioned throwing her down a shaft. That didn't sound good. Bindi had told him all the old inspection shafts were boarded up, but he guessed it wouldn't be hard to jimmy one open, if you were intent on mischief.

"You'll find out soon enough," Whip replied cryptically.

Mack was desperate to follow Paunchy Man and took a few steps in that direction.

"Stay where you are," Whip growled, menace clear in his tone. Then he narrowed his eyes and glared at Mack thoughtfully. "Stand still," he commanded.

Mack tensed as Whip walked around behind him. What was he up to now? All his senses were screaming for him to follow the man and Bindi, who'd now disappeared behind the rocks, and he hardly noticed when Whip cut the tie binding his wrists, until he walked back in front, waving a small flick-knife in the air.

Mack rubbed his wrists and glowered at the thug, eyeing the knife in one hand and the gun in the other. The other man was close enough that if he kicked out, he'd be able to send the knife flying. But that still left the gun. Mack considered the consequences of taking a bullet. If it meant he could escape Whip, the price might be worth it. But there was also Bindi to consider. If he was injured or incapacitated, how would he help her?

"Raise your hands in the air and walk backward," Whip commanded.

"What? Why." Mack wasn't ready to do as he was told.

A bullet ricocheted off the gravel, not a foot from where Mack was standing, and he jumped in fright. "Because I said so, that's why," Whip said, the corners of his mouth twitching upward in a vicious snarl.

Mack slowly raised his hands, showing that he was obeying, but taking his time about it. What was this guy up to? Mack wanted to glance over his shoulder, to see where Paunchy Guy had taken Bindi, but he didn't dare take his eyes off Whip.

"Your lady friend asked me to pass on this little gift, courtesy of her. To make sure you'll never ride any damn bull ever again."

Before Mack could even react, Whip had raised the gun and shot at him. Pain seared through Mack's right hand, and he stumbled backward, landing on his butt, cradling his hand to his chest. The bastard had shot him. Right through the hand. He gritted his teeth together to stop the howl of pain from emerging.

"That's just a little reminder," Whip laughed, as if he was enjoying this immensely. "But I doubt you're going to need a reminder. Because you ain't going to make it out of here alive."

Blood roared through Mack's ears, pounding so hard, he barely heard the other man's caustic words. His hand was on fire. He wanted to look at the wound, assess the damage, but Whip was prodding him with the gun, telling him to get to his feet. The man had shot him through the hand to make sure he'd never be able to hold a bull-rope again. It was wickedly cruel, and ultimately simple. It also showed him that Whip wasn't a man to be trifled with. He would shoot Mack again without a second thought, if he had to.

Mack stumbled in front of him, trying to staunch the bleeding by pushing his hand hard against his chest as well as concentrating on staying upright. He wanted to wail in anguish and pain. And anger. The anger was building inside him so he felt his blood might sear his veins, turn them to liquid metal. The world turned red in front of his eyes. This guy was going to pay for his crimes. Pay dearly.

"Around to the right," Whip directed, as they passed by the first pile of enormous boulders. There was a faint path winding through the haphazardly strewn rocks, and Mack picked his way along. It was the same direction Paunchy Man had taken Bindi, and Mack kept his eyes trained on the ground in front, hoping to find any sign of her.

But there was nothing. No guy in the blue T-shirt, and no Bindi. The ground ahead was open and clear, apart from a heavy metal grate lying alone on a cleared area of gravel. As he got closer, Mack saw a large, unguarded hole opening like a yawning maw in the ground. Whip pushed him until they were standing next to the shaft. He could barely see more than ten feet down the hole before the light was swallowed up and darkness took over. He certainly couldn't see the bottom. How deep was it? The metal grille had obviously been pried off the top with bolt cutters and a crowbar.

Whip took a small flashlight out of his pocket and shone it down the shaft, careful to keep the gun pointed at Mack. "Oh, look, there's your girlfriend," he crowed with glee.

What the…? Mack leaned over to peer down the shaft. The flashlight might be small, but it was powerful. The beam showed a hole around thirty feet deep, and there was Bindi's body lying crumpled at the bottom. Paunchy Man must've dumped Bindi, then retreated to the car as Whip had ordered.

"Bindi," Mack called urgently, but the only answer was a snort from Whip.

"Now, it's your turn." Whip took a step toward him, as if meaning to push him down the shaft, as well. "If the fall don't kill you, that fire might stop anyone coming to rescue you," Whip crowed, jerking out a hand and catching Mack by the shirtfront.

"No," Mack howled, and bent his knees low, then sprang upward, shoving his shoulder into Whip's gut. He heard the air leave the other man's lungs in a whoosh, and then Mack karate chopped at Whip's right hand with his own good hand, sending the gun twirling through the air to land in the dust ten feet away. Mack grabbed Whip in an arm lock around the neck, and the two men were entwined in mortal combat. Hampered by his wounded hand, Mack used his sheer desperation to stay alive and keep on top of Whip. He grappled with the man, and they rolled over and over in the dirt. He needed to defeat Whip. Then he could rescue Bindi out of that hole.

They rolled over and over, Mack fighting with every ounce of his being. If he could only subdue the man long enough, he could perhaps reclaim the gun. Pain shot through his wounded hand and up his arm; it was practically useless, he couldn't use it to grab Whip's clothing, or even punch him. Dust and spittle clouded the air as they struggled together on the ground. Suddenly, Mack felt the earth give way beneath his shoulders. Shit, they'd rolled too close to the edge of the hole. He struck out with his legs, trying to stop his trajectory. Whip seemed to notice at the same time, and he let go of Mack and grappled for the crumbling edge. Mack felt himself slowly, inexorably, slipping, being drawn into the gaping hole, while Whip still teetered on the edge. At the last second, he jerked, and clasped Whip's shirtfront in his good hand. If he was going down, then he was taking this bastard with him.

Together, they tumbled down, down, into the darkness.

CHAPTER TWENTY

Something jerked Bindi out of unconsciousness. A heavy weight draped across her legs. She was lying on the ground, but the weight pinned her down.

"Whaaaa…" she murmured, totally confused. Where was she? Dark shadows swallowed the surrounding area, but a square of bright sunlight hovered high above. Cool earth was gritty beneath her cheek. She lifted her head off the ground to get her bearings. Pain ignited behind her eyes, so excruciating she cried out and raised her hands to cradle her temples, falling back to the earth.

After the pain subsided, she considered her surroundings once more. She must be down one of the old inspection mine shafts. That was the only thing that made sense. Had someone thrown her down here? The idea was horrendous, but it seemed more and more likely. Slower this time, she moved her arms, testing for injuries. Her whole body ached, as if she was covered in one giant bruise. All down her left side, hip, ribs, shoulder and thigh burned with a bone-deep ache. Now she was concentrating, she could feel scrapes on her elbows, and when she raised a hand to her face, there was a nasty graze down the side of her temple. Was the pain in her head from the fall? Had she hit it on the way down?

Walking her fingers gingerly over her skull, she found a large lump at the back of her head that might account for her splitting headache. The weight was still pinning her from the waist down, and she had no idea if her legs had sustained any damage, or not.

A loud groan issued from out of the darkness, making her startle.

"Who's there?" she hissed, still holding her head. No one answered, and she tried pushing at the warm weight on her legs, wanting to struggle free, but it was useless. What was this…? She felt around and then recoiled as she touched skin. Skin rough with stubble. A man. It was a man on top of her. Bindi began to struggle, panic clawing at her throat. She needed to get out from under him, he was pinning her to the ground. He hadn't moved yet, but…

Another groan issued from the shadows, and there was movement. Some of the suffocating weight suddenly lifted, and a darker shadow moved in the dim light.

Pushing her hand against her temple, she raised up onto her elbows and kicked at the man still lying partially across her legs. Which meant there were at least two other men down here with her. Who were they? The last thing she remembered was running into the old battery shed. Madonna and Melody had been there, tied up in a back room, and she'd run toward them, then… Nothing. She couldn't remember what happened. Bindi's breath came in ragged gasps. Had someone hit her from behind? Knocked her unconscious?

"Bindi," a voice croaked. "Bindi, are you there?"

It was Mack. Utter relief flooded her veins. If Mack was down here with her, then they'd be safe. He'd make sure she was safe. Her eyes were adjusting to the dim light in the shaft, and she could make out the softer shape of the body lying over her lower legs. It wasn't Mack, because this body was motionless. In fact, hadn't moved at all. And certainly hadn't spoken.

"Mack, I'm here," she said, but was surprised when her voice came out as a squeak. "I can't move, there's...someone on top of me."

"I might be able to help with that." She heard Mack grunt and the rasp of clothes being dragged over the earth and suddenly her lower torso was mercifully free.

She sat up, testing her legs to make sure they worked. Her muscles complained loudly, shooting sparks of discomfort up and down the length of her thighs, but once that first shock was over, she knew no bones were broken.

"Thank you," she said, getting onto her hands and knees and crawling toward the sound of his voice. "What about you? Are you okay?"

He was sitting with his back against the rock wall. The light was too dim to make out his facial features in detail, but she got a gleam of reflected light from his eyes when he turned to look at her.

"Not sure," he answered after a few seconds, and Bindi could hear pain lacing his voice.

"What's wrong?" she asked urgently, crawling the last few feet to where he sat.

"My ankle isn't good. Not sure if it's broken, but it sure as hell hurts."

"Oh, no," Bindi whispered, fear wrenching her stomach painfully. If he was injured, how were they going to get out of here? She reached out to touch him, needing to feel the surety of his presence, and his hand clasped around hers, fingers warm and strong.

"It's okay, we'll be okay," he murmured soothingly, pulling her into his chest. She nestled into his muscular, male body, laying her head on his shoulder, and took the comfort he was offering as he wrapped one arm around her. She pushed down the overwhelming urge to cry. Tears wouldn't help now. She was alive, and Mack was alive, she needed to concentrate on that. Mack continued to murmur soothing words of comfort and Bindi got lost in the honey-velvet tone of his deep voice, his American accent so familiar and calming, now. Drawing in his strength, she stirred after a few minutes, bringing herself back to the reality of their situation. They couldn't stay here forever, they needed to get out.

Mack felt her move and released her, so that she leaned against the rock wall, too.

"At least I fared better than our mate here. I think he's dead," Mack said.

She reared back from the dark lump resting on the other side of Mack. She'd almost forgotten about the other man. "Dead?" she squeaked. "How do you know? And who is he? Why is he down here?"

"It's the guy from the rodeo. The one who warned me off taking up bull-riding again. His name is Whip, and he all but confessed to the fact that he's working for Clarissa. I'm betting all my money he was the one who tampered with my car, too."

"Oh." Bindi couldn't find any words.

"Seems like he came back to finish the job," Mack said dryly.

Her mind turned over these new events. "So, he stole the horses to what? Lure us out here?"

"Looks that way," Mack answered. "There were two of them. The other guy must've ambushed you as you went into the old building. Did he hit you over the head?"

Lifting a hand, she felt the lump at the back of her head and nodded as the pieces of the puzzle started to click into place. That probably explained her headache. "How did he know it'd be us...you...who chased them out here?"

"Don't know." Mack lifted one shoulder in a half shrug.

"But I think I ruined his plans when I pulled him down this hole with me," he added with a grim smile. Then he tried to shift his position and grunted with pain, reminding Bindi about his ankle.

"Let me take a look." She shuffled on her bottom down the length of his leg.

"I'm assuming the other guy took your radio and phone?" Mack asked as she felt around until she found the fabric of his jeans.

"Oh, shit." Why hadn't she thought of that? But both communication devices were missing, when she patted her shoulder holster and front pocket of her jeans. "Yeah, he did," she replied in disgust. This duo had certainly been thorough, making sure all the bases were covered. But this guy hadn't counted on falling down the shaft with his intended victim. Which reminded her of the man Mack had called Whip.

"How did we survive that fall, and he didn't?" She didn't dare glance in the direction of the unmoving lump.

"Don't know the answer to that one, either," Mack admitted. "You were unconscious when the fat man threw you in, so maybe that played a part in keeping you alive."

"Maybe," she muttered, not sure. She'd heard of other people miraculously surviving falls like this one. Ten meters was a long way down, but perhaps not quite far enough to kill her.

"And I landed on top of Whip, who landed on your legs. I think he must've broken my fall. A soft landing, so to speak. But he must've broken his neck, either when he landed, or on the way down."

Bindi drew in a soft breath of regret. This man was a nasty piece of work; had tried to do them both harm, but it was still hard to comprehend he was now dead because of his actions.

She tried to forget about the guy lying mere feet away from her, and concentrated on Mack's ankle, instead. Without good light, she gingerly felt down his jeans to the top of his cowboy boot, pushing her fingers inside the leather, gently palpating the area until she got to his ankle and he sucked in a sharp breath.

"Sorry," she apologized. As carefully as she could, she felt around his lower leg. She should probably remove his boot, but that would cause him too much pain, so it stayed, for now. His leg seemed to be lying at the correct angle, his foot pointed up toward the light. If it was broken, it wasn't a bad break, the bones hadn't pierced the skin or anything equally sickening. "I think your boot might've stopped the injury being too bad," she said calmly.

"Maybe it did. But even so, I don't think I'll be able to walk."

Not good. It meant Mack wasn't getting out of here without her help.

Bindi, whose eyes had now fully adjusted to the dark, tipped her head to the side and could just make out an opening on the opposite side to where they were sitting. A passageway running directly to the main mine. She could even detect a faint breeze coming from that direction. It might be possible to walk out that way. Although where this tunnel led was anyone's guess, and even if it led to the surface, the odds were that the opening would be boarded up at the other end. And what if she got lost? A small shudder ran through her. Without a flashlight or light of any sort, those tunnels would be pitch black. If she got lost, she might never be found. Nope, they needed another plan.

Tipping her head back, she studied the opening above them. "This hole must be an old shaft the miners used to access the main mine, which runs horizontally out from the escarpment," she said, thoughtfully. "They might have once hauled out the ore on a windlass system through here. Or used it as an inspection point." She squinted upward, trying, but failing, to make out anything helpful up there. Any remnants of a windlass were now long gone. No roped dangled helpfully down the rocky walls. The shaft had been covered and made secure by the local rangers. But now this thug, Whip, had removed the grating, they were free to get out through the top. Which meant she'd have to climb out. Could she even do that?

"I believe his plan was to throw us both down here and then reposition the grate on top. Even if the fall didn't kill us, we'd never be able to escape," Mack said, as he noticed her staring upward. "But now the grate has been removed…" He didn't finish his sentence. They both knew what he was hinting at.

Could she really climb up there? The edges of the shaft were rough, small ledges and grooves carved into the side where the old miners had blasted their way through the rock. It was a possibility. Not one she was completely happy about. What if she fell? Maybe she wouldn't be so lucky this time.

"There's something else you need to know," Mack said quietly.

"What?" she asked, dreading this newest problem. What else could possibly go wrong?

He held up his right hand and she could see in the dim light that it was all misshapen, as if he had something wrapped around it. "Whip shot me. My hand is practically useless," he said matter-of-factly.

"Oh, God," she breathed. "I'm so sorry. What…? Why did he do that?" She imagined a scuffle. Had Mack tried to escape and Whip had shot him?

"He said it was a message from Clarissa. To remind me never to take up bull riding again. Even though he never meant for us to survive this encounter."

"He did what?" she could hardly believe what he was saying. How could someone be that…callous? That cold-hearted. This Clarissa woman was a piece of work. Her blood began to boil at the thought of it. The injustice. The entitlement. Who did this woman think she was? If Bindi ever had the chance to meet her, Clarissa better watch out. Bindi normally abhorred violence, but right at this second, she felt quite capable of harming this woman.

"I'm so sorry." She shuffled back up along his leg and took his good hand in hers. Clarissa had effectively taken away his dream. Bull riders relied on the strength in their hands to hold on to the bull rope with all their might, to keep them steady and secure on the bull's back. Mack wouldn't be able to do that now.

"Yeah, me too. But it's the least of my worries right now. What it does mean, is that, added to my ankle, I won't be able to climb out of here."

His dark eyes found hers and held them. His gorgeous hair, normally slicked back in a classic style, hung in limp curls over his forehead and she reached up to push them out of the way.

He continued to stare at her, compassion in his gaze, and the reality of their predicament hit home to her with the force of a steam train. It was up to her to get them out of this place. Mack clearly saw the moment the reality of their situation struck her, because he grasped her fingers with his good hand and squeezed them.

"We don't know what's happened to the accomplice." Mack kept his tone neutral, as if talking about moving a herd of cattle to another paddock, rather than about a man who might be out to kill them. "The Fat Man may have taken off when Whip didn't show. The guy seemed a bit slow and weak-willed. But he could also still be up there. I need you to be careful." He squeezed her fingers again, but his face kept that bland expression. He was trying to make this sound like one more everyday task she needed to complete. But it wasn't.

Bindi tilted her head toward the sky and shook it uncertainly. She couldn't do it. Climbing had never been one of her strong suits. The rock walls were rough, not smooth, and probably offered a lot of good handholds, if she were to try. And she wasn't afraid of heights, so much. But she *was* afraid of falling. Her breath began to come in sharp little panicky pants as she stared up at the high walls.

"Nope." She shook her head more forcefully. A surprising tear leaked from the corner of her eye. She couldn't do this. The familiar paralysis took over her mind, blocking out the bad thoughts. Lethargic and useless, that was how she felt. The same as when Kai had molested her. This wasn't happening. If she kept telling herself that, over and over, it'd all eventually go away.

Mack's fingers entwined in hers, warm and strong. Not condemning her, just waiting, broadcasting his faith in her ability.

His faith made her realize that fear never really went away. It only got worse if you didn't confront your feelings, eventually.

Her counsellor had given her methods to fight this. To help her claw her way through the terrible sensation of slowly drowning. She'd thought she was past it all, wouldn't need those coping mechanisms ever again. But twice now, she'd reverted to old habits. After the car crash and now with Mack.

Because everything was on the line here. If she couldn't do this, then they were both stuck down here indefinitely.

"What if I fall?" she said in a small voice.

"You can do this," he said, gently grabbing her chin and turning her face toward him.

"And if you fall, I'll catch you," he said.

She laughed at the ridiculousness of it, but his gaze was

deadly serious. Maybe he didn't mean he'd physically catch her—she wouldn't put it past him to try—but maybe he meant he was there for her emotionally. He had conviction in her ability and her strength to complete this. It felt good to have someone believe in her so utterly.

"I don't want to leave you on your own." She made one more attempt to convince him—convince herself—not to do this. "You're hurt. What if something happens to me? No one knows where you are. What if I—"

"It's a risk we're going to have to take," he said, pulling her gently onto his chest. She avoided his injured hand as she lay her head on his shoulder.

"I don't think I could go on without you," she said suddenly.

Where had that thought come from? But she had no time to dissect the idea, all she knew was it was true. He'd become special to her. Someone she didn't want to live without. The word *love* hovered in her mind, but she brushed it away. That word was nearly as scary as the idea of climbing out of this shaft. Too big and too unnerving, if she admitted that, it would take over her whole being, and she needed to concentrate on the here and now.

"Of course, you could," he replied, lifting his hand to stroke her hair. "You're much stronger than you know. That's one of the many things I admire about you. You've rocked my world, Bindi, and I intend to show you just how much you mean to me once we get out of here."

His words both astounded her and made her heart flutter with excitement. She rocked his world? Never had she thought to hear that sort of sentiment from him. Hugging him tightly, she looked up into his face.

His lips touched hers, and she raised up to meet his mouth. Firm and insistent, she got lost in the feel of his lips, the touch of him, his body pressed into hers. Eyes closed, she traced her finger down the side of his face, enjoying the rasp of his stubble, finding the jut of his jawline and tracing it backward, up toward his ear. Kissing Mack took over her body as she melted into him. Took over her all her thoughts, ideas and sensations, until it was just him and her. Suddenly, she felt unbelievably possessive. He was hers. Her cocky cowboy. All that bold, cheeky, gorgeous man was hers. Giving in to the sweet surrender of him for a few more seconds, at last she moved back slightly, breaking their contact.

It was time to climb.

CHATPER TWENTY-ONE

Bindi took a chance and slowly peeked over the rim of the hole. Her toes were balanced precariously on a small lip of rock, and she was hanging onto a protruding root that stuck out of the edge of the shaft with one hand. With a wary gaze, she searched the surrounding area. No one was waiting to nab her as she emerged, as she'd half feared. If this other man Mack had warned her about was still here somewhere, at least he wasn't lurking around the shaft.

Pulling herself the last few feet, she flopped, belly first, onto the red dirt and lay there, panting. She'd made it to the top. But there was no time to congratulate herself. Mack was still down there, waiting for her to find help. Sweat ran profusely down her back and between her breasts, mainly due to her exertion from the arduous climb. But some of it was because she couldn't quite rid herself of the image of herself hurtling back down the hole to land all broken and bent on the hard ground beneath. The thought that Mack was directly below her, and she might hurt or even kill him if she did fall, was one of the main incentives that'd kept her going up. Cowboy boots were not the best climbing equipment, she'd discovered quickly. But the climb itself had been surprisingly easy, once she'd made up her mind to do it.

There'd been a few scary moments, when she'd overstretched for a handhold, or her foot had slipped unexpectedly, but she'd always made sure her other holds were secure and she'd proceeded slowly, but surely, up the rocky wall. It hadn't helped that her body had been battered and bruised by the fall. But once she'd got moving, her muscles had warmed up, and all she needed to do now was to keep moving, so she didn't seize up. Because as soon as she stopped, there was no doubt in her mind her body would shut down.

"I made it," she called down the hole. It was pitch black down there, the sunlight not making it all the way to the bottom, so she couldn't actually see Mack.

But his voice drifted up to her. "Told you, you could do it." She could hear the pride in his tone. "Is it safe?" he asked urgently.

"There's no one around," she said, getting slowly to her knees, and lifting her hand to shield her eyes. Nothing moved. The sun beat down mercilessly, just past its zenith. Only half an hour had passed since they'd arrived at the mine site. Placing her hands on her knees, she levered herself to standing with a groan.

Now she was out, what was she going to do? There was no real plan, apart from climbing the wall and go and get help. Turning in a full circle, Bindi spotted the smoke. Shit, she'd nearly forgotten about the fire with everything else going on. The pall of smoke hadn't got much bigger, and as she studied it, she saw some of it was turning white, rather than the ominous gray it'd been earlier. Which meant someone was fighting the fire. Smoke only turned white if water was being poured on it. That was good, the fire was less of a potential threat, at least for now.

Bindi continued to stare at the sky as the light and dark plumes mixed to cover the blue, tangling together and causing a sinister twist to spiral through her belly. The tangled skies were a reflection of her knotted emotions. She had to find a way to rescue Mack. He was down there, hurt and waiting for her, and part of her wanted to jump back down the shaft just so she could be with him, hold him, comfort him. He drew her body and soul, a gravitational pull as strong as if she were the moon and he the earth. That pesky word hovered just outside her consciousness again. *Love*. Did she love him? She let out a groan of fear. If she couldn't get him out of the shaft, it might not matter if she was in love with him, or not.

Continuing her slow rotation, her gaze landed on the old battery building. An idea grew in her head. "I'll be back in a minute," she yelled down the shaft. "I promise, I won't be long."

Mack yelled something back, but she didn't catch it as she was already striding purposefully across the clearing. Madonna and her filly could still be in there. She might be able to use them to help get Mack out.

Firstly, she crept around the rear of the battery building until she could make out the gravel parking lot. It was empty. Which was good, but that could mean a lot of things. Mack had said there were two men. One was dead, and the other was unaccounted for. At least one of them had been on horseback when they stole Madonna and her foal. Mack had said Whip had told the other guy to wait for him in the car. Had the other guy now driven away in the car, taking the horse and trailer with him?

Entering the building with a lot more care than she'd taken the first time, she snuck around a wooden post at the edge of the open siding, keeping to the shadows. Mack had told her the fat man hadn't really been planning on burning the building down, he'd just flooded it with smoke to scare the horses. Standing just inside the doorway, she hugged the wall and used all her senses to search the interior. It was dim in here, after the bright sunshine, and she gave her eyes time to adjust. Dust motes hung in the air, suspended in the odd ray of sunlight that filtered in through a break in the roof. The large, ten-head gold stamper used to crush the quartz ore as part of the gold mining process, took up most of the far side of the building. Two enormous metal wheels stood on either side of two boilers, which once would've provided the steam to drive the whole battery. It was the section behind and to the right of this industrial machinery that Bindi was interested in.

Bindi heard a noise. A soft snuffle. Then a louder snort and a tapping sound, like tiny hooves on a wooden floor. The sounds were coming from the other end of the big, open-plan building, from behind a walled off section. The same place Bindi had been heading when she'd been hit over the head earlier. A small frisson of excitement ran through her. Madonna and Melody were still in there.

Still taking care, Bindi weaved her way around the walls, not daring to go out into the open. The old concrete floor was buckled and broken in places, so Bindi picked her way carefully around, until she was in a position where she could peer through the slats of wood in the wall separating her from the dingy space beyond.

Putting her eye to the gap, she peeked into the room. It was empty. But when she swiveled her head to the left a little, she caught sight of movement. Madonna's hindquarters swung into view. But the angle of her little peep hole didn't allow her to see any farther into the dark corner. What if the man was lying in wait for her, just behind the door?

Madonna gave a snort, and whickered loudly, as if she'd suddenly scented Bindi close by. Oh, well. Her cover was blown now, anyway. There was nothing for it. At the last second, she picked up a long piece of wood lying on the floor a few feet away and wielded it like a baseball bat as she reached for the door handle.

Easing the door open, Bindi winced when it squealed in protest on its rusty hinges. She jumped into the doorway, stick raised, ready to strike. But there was no one there. Except the two horses. Madonna stamped anxiously, and Melody hovered behind her mother, clearly fearful.

"Hey," Bindi crooned. "It's okay. I'm here now." She placed the wood on the floor and reached out a hand to Madonna, who snuffed her fingers in welcome. "Hiya, baby," Bindi said softly, running her hands down the mare's shoulder, checking for any injuries. Apart from the horse's obvious displeasure at being kept in this dark, dusty place, and being manhandled by two strange thugs, she was otherwise unharmed.

Madonna was wearing a halter and was tied to a post in the corner by a long, lead rope. Melody also wore a halter and lead rope, but she didn't really need one, as she would follow her mother anywhere.

So, the horses were safe and in one piece. The first part of her plan to rescue Mack had fallen into place. Now, she needed a piece of rope or something similar to help her haul him out. But there was nothing. The room was completely bare. Her plan wouldn't work if she had nothing long enough to reach to the bottom of the hole.

Leaving the horses where they were, she went back into the main building, searching for anything that might serve her purpose. A few minutes later, she returned with arms laden with items, none of which was exactly what she wanted, but they might do. There was an electrical extension cord—someone must have left that, perhaps a workman patching up the building recently—a couple of pieces of thick leather cord that were old and covered in dust, but still strong, some copper wire, and a handful of twine.

"Come on, baby," Bindi clucked to Madonna. "You're

going to work for your hay bag today." She led the mare carefully out through the door, making sure the filly was following close behind.

It only took a few minutes to get back to the open hole. Mack must be wondering where she'd got to.

"I'm here," she sung out, leaning over the edge but making sure Madonna didn't get too close.

"Oh, thank God," Mack's voice echoed up to her, and in these few words, she understood just how worried he'd been.

"I've got Madonna and Melody," she told him. "I'm going to try and pull you out."

"What?" Mack sounded stunned. "But Whip said…" He stopped, as if considering his words. "Never mind. That's good. Really good the horses are still alive."

Still alive? Had Whip's plan been to kill the horses? What a horrible thought. It just made the man even more reprehensible.

"Give me a few minutes," she hollered back, and threw her stash on the ground, sorting through it while Madonna looked on with interest. "No, there's nothing to eat here," Bindi scalded gently. But a plan was beginning to form in her mind. Lifting her head to glare at the smoky sky, she decided the fire was no more of a threat at the moment.

Ten minutes later, she had a rude harness fitted around Madonna's chest, using a piece of leather as a breast strap running across the horse's chest, with two bits of twine looped around her neck, and another piece of leather under her tummy as a sort of belly band, to hold it in place. The electrical cord was tied to the left-hand side of the breast strap. Bindi prayed it was long enough to reach to the bottom of the hole, but she only had the one piece, so Madonna would have to pull to the right to compensate. She'd tied a loop on the end, so Mack could put his foot through it, and— if everything went right—she'd pull him to safety. Madonna wasn't happy with the contraption around her chest, and sniffed at it suspiciously, but she was a good stock horse, one of the best, and Bindi didn't doubt she'd do as she was asked. Steve had trained her up from a foal, there was no doubt that if any horse could do this, then she could. Bindi had no choice but to tie Melody up to the nearest shrub. She couldn't have her trotting around and accidentally falling down the shaft. The filly gave a nervous whinny, but Madonna ignored her for the moment, as if realizing her baby was safe, and there was work to be done.

Backing Madonna right up to the edge, she called down, "Heads up. I'm throwing down a rope."

"Okay," Mack answered, but she could hear his voice tinged with pain. She had to get him out of there and to a hospital as quickly as possible.

As carefully as she could, she lowered the cord, watching it snake its way down the rock face until it vanished into the gloom below. She heard Mack grunting and the echo of the rasp of boots on gravel. He must be levering himself to his feet. She could just imagine how hard that would be with only one hand and an injured ankle. But there was nothing else she could do to help him, so she waited, wincing in sympathy as she listened to his stifled, inarticulate sounds of pain.

"I can see it," Mack called out eventually. "But can you swing it back and forth, it's all the way over on the other side of the shaft and I can't reach it."

"Sure." She wriggled the cord and got it swinging in a slow circle. Suddenly, the cord jerked, and she gave a small clap of glee. "Have you got it?"

"Yep. Just give me a sec to get settled."

She waited with bated breath, until he finally called. "All set."

Bindi went around to Madonna's head and slowly led her

forward until the all the slack was gone from the cord. "Hang on," she sang out. Then she clucked loudly, urging Madonna forward, pulling hard on her halter. At first, Madonna balked at the strange weight pulling her sideways and backward, but Bindi kept her gaze trained on the horse and angled her head to the right, encouraging her with her words and her body.

"Come on, girl," she said, her breath coming in short pants as she strained to pull Madonna forward. "You can do it. Good, girl."

Step by step, the horse dragged Mack out of the shaft. Bindi was afraid to let her gaze leave the mare, in case she decided the weight was too much to bear. She couldn't let Madonna go, or she might drop Mack right back to the earth below. She had no idea how close Mack was to the edge. She just kept Madonna moving, inching forward, one hand on either side of the halter, almost as if she might pull Mack up all by herself.

"Stop, stop," Mack's voice rang out, echoing off the pile of boulders. "I'm out," he puffed, and Bindi dared to let her eyes leave Madonna's face to glance back toward the hole. Sure enough, Mack was lying prostrate on the ground a few feet from the lip, dragging in huge gulps of air.

"Whoa," Bindi called to Madonna. As soon as the horse stopped, she ran back to where Mack lay on the dusty ground. She slipped the hook of cord from around his foot, just in case Madonna took it into her head to move off again, and crawled up to cradle his head in her lap. His beautiful, tanned face was pale, sweat running freely down his temples, his eyes pinched and lined with pain.

"Oh, Jesus, are you okay?" She stroked his sweat-soaked hair away from his face.

"I'm great." He tried to raise a smile for her, but it was missing that cocky tilt that she'd come to love. She wanted to lean down and kiss all the pain and hurt away from his face.

Kiss him until he no longer felt anything but her in his arms.

"Let me help you sit up," she said gently.

But he grimaced and let out a groan from between gritted teeth the moment she moved him, then fell back onto the earth. It seemed that the act of being pulled out of the shaft had drained most of his energy and ability to fight down the pain. Her half-baked plan of perhaps helping him onto Madonna's back and both of them riding out of here disappeared in a whoosh of air. He wasn't going anywhere in a hurry. She needed another plan. It looked like she might have to leave without him and go and find help. Which was the absolute last thing she wanted to do, but she may not have an option. She needed to get him into the shade, at least. This blazing heat would do him no good. They were both already dehydrated, and they'd brought no water.

"What have you done with Whip?" a tremulous voice asked from behind her.

"What the fuck?" she said, turning around slowly to see a large man in a blue T-shirt pointing a gun at her head.

CHAPTER TWENTY-TWO

Mack was in a world of pain. The effort to hang onto that cord as he was lifted out of the shaft had cost him his last remaining ounce of strength. His hand was on fire, as if there were literal flames consuming his skin, and he cradled it protectively against his chest. It was hurriedly wrapped in a strip torn from the bottom of his shirt, but that wouldn't stop the bleeding for long. And the agony had spread up his ankle, through his calf and up his thigh, so that his whole leg was throbbing. Everything was hazy around the edges. It was almost as if he was no longer one-hundred-percent part of this world. The only thing that anchored him to reality was Bindi's hand softly stroking his hair as he lay in her lap. He concentrated on that feeling, nothing else.

A voice inside his head was ranting at him that he was a weak, spineless coward. He'd been through worse than this during his time riding bulls. Suffered broken bones before, bruising, dislocated fingers, torn ligaments, and a litany of other injuries. Admittedly, he'd been unconscious the last time when he'd received his most serious injuries. But for all of his internal ranting, he couldn't seem to rouse himself from this stupor.

Suddenly, Bindi's soothing hand left his brow, and he

frowned. Why had she stopped?

Mack lifted his head, but the world spun and he knew the dreaded dizzy spells were back.

A man's voice sounded faraway and distant. Who was speaking? Bindi answered, he'd recognize that sweet voice anywhere, but who did the other voice belong to?

Had someone come to their rescue? Mack sure hoped so. A nice, soft hospital bed and a syringe full of drugs would be more than welcome.

But no, the deep voice got louder. He screwed his eyes together and concentrated on the words.

"You killed Whip?" The man's tone took on an incredulous edge. "You're gonna pay for what you done."

Bindi's soft lap was suddenly yanked away from him, and his head landed hard on the ground. He forced his eyes open, but the bright sunshine nearly blinded him.

"Leave me alone, you fucker," Bindi yelled, and this time Mack ignored the fact the world was spinning and managed to lift his head and look up. Straight into the face of Paunchy Man. He had Bindi by the hair, dragging her away, a gun pointed at her head. What was he doing here? Bindi was sure he'd gone, got in the car and driven away, but Mack should've warned her to be more vigilant.

"I didn't kill him," Bindi pleaded. "He fell down the shaft when he was trying to push Mack in. It was an accident."

"It wasn't no accident," the fat man growled. "But I'm going to finish what he started. You're going back in. And this time I'm gonna make sure you stay down there." The fat man struggled with Bindi. He had hold of the base of her long braid and was pulling her along as she kicked out, fighting to get to her feet. He was dragging her toward the lip of the open shaft with one hand and in the other, he held a gun.

"My, my, you're a feisty one, ain't ya?" the Fat man drawled, seeming to enjoy the struggle.

"Let me go," Bindi screamed.

"Ooh, I like it when a woman fights back." The man's tone had become excited, a sleazy glow entering his eyes. "Especially a pretty one, like you. Maybe I'll take a little somethin' for me troubles before I throw you down that hole."

"No." Bindi's reply was soft, almost helpless.

Mack tried to refocus his eyes through the world whirling around him. What was going on? The sounds of Bindi struggling on the ground and lots of inarticulate grunting reached his ears.

"Ow, you bitch," the fat man yelled, then Mack heard the distinctive noise of a man's hand slapping a woman's face. Then everything went quiet.

With a huge effort, Mack levered himself up onto his elbow. He needed to know what was going on. Needed to help Bindi.

Paunchy Man stood over Bindi, who lay on the ground, unmoving. His black hat had fallen off in the scuffle and his stringy hair was plastered to his skull with sweat. His belt buckle was already undone, and he was fumbling with his zip. Why wasn't Bindi fighting back? It was almost as if she'd become comatose.

Mack watched the scene unfold before him like he was watching a hazy movie replay in slow motion. As if it wasn't really happening.

How was he going to help her? The fuzzy shape of Madonna hovered in the background, but he ignored her for now. There was no way the horse could help, it was all up to him.

Paunchy Man got his zip undone, and was wriggling his jeans down to his ankles. Then he got down on his hands and knees, hovering over Bindi, who lay as still as a corpse.

What was going on? Her eyes were open, but it was as if

she'd checked out of her own body. Then it hit him. Bindi had told him about the way she used to shut down when Kai did those terrible things to her. And now this man was about to rape her, she was doing it again. Blocking out the bad stuff, pretending it wasn't happening. Well, *he* wasn't going to let it happen. *He* wasn't going to take it lying down.

Mack had to do something. To save Bindi. To save the love of his life. She'd saved him. Now it was his turn to return the favor. He'd rather die than see her get hurt. He'd give his life for hers, he knew that now. It wasn't even a decision; it was a foregone conclusion. Written in the stars. An absolute. Because he couldn't live without her.

With slow, deliberate movements, he got to his knees. The sun was a furnace on top of his head. His vision swam and his head felt fit to burst as he blinked sweat out of his eyes.

"Hey, asshole," he croaked.

The man looked up from where he knelt over Bindi, surprised. The bastard was enjoying it. Enjoying the domination. Enjoying humiliating her.

"Why don't you pick on someone your own size?"

"Don't you worry," the other man jeered, his double chin wobbling unattractively. "You'll get your turn." He returned his focus to Bindi, licking his lips and saying, "Now you're gonna know what it's like to have a real man between your legs."

"Hey," Mack said, louder this time. Still on his knees, he picked up a rock with his left hand and ditched it at the man. It missed its mark, which'd been the spot right between his eyes, but struck the man on the shoulder, instead. Not a bad shot, considering. Then Mack hauled his good foot out in front, balancing for a second on one knee, until he pulled himself to standing. The other man didn't know about Mack's ankle. If he could bluff him long enough, it might give Bindi a chance to break free.

"Bindi," he yelled. "Bindi, do something. Don't let this asshole win."

Bindi turned her head to look at him, but otherwise, didn't move.

Come on, he pleaded silently.

"Bindi, you can do this. Get up. Move," he implored. "Please. Do it for me."

The other man got to his feet, and pulled up his jeans, the gun in his right hand.

Mack swayed on his feet, putting as little weight as possible on his injured foot, but hopefully making it look like he was about to make a charge at the man with the gun. If he could just distract him long enough…

Bindi twitched, and then sat up as if suddenly coming back to life. Like an internal switch had been turned back on.

Elation surged through him. She was listening to him. Fighting back.

"Mack, don't," Bindi squeaked, terror flooding through her beautiful, brown eyes. "He'll kill you," she warned.

"Yes, I will," the man confirmed, raising the gun and pointing it at Mack. Which was exactly what he wanted him to do. Paunchy Man wasn't real bright, was he? Because if the gun was pointed at him, then it wasn't pointed at Bindi.

Mack sought her gaze, fixed his eyes on her face. *Run*, he pleaded silently. *Just get out of here.* He'd dragged her into this whole sorry mess. The least he could do was to offer his life to let her gain her freedom. Bindi's eyes went wide as sudden understanding flooded through her. But instead of relief, her lips pursed in determination. No. What was she thinking? She needed to run. Mack took a step forward, forgetting for a second about his ankle, he was so intent on her. But his step-hop became more of a stumble and the fat man laughed.

"You can't even walk, can you?" The man leered at him, showing a missing tooth. "Like I said, I'll get to you in a min

—"

The man's words were cut off as he landed heavily on the ground, butt first. Bindi had taken him out at the knees, sweeping her feet low and catching him behind the soft spot in the middle of his legs. But Bindi didn't stop there, she scrambled up and punched the guy full in the face, blood spurting out of his nose. Her move took him so much by surprise, the fat man howled in pain and covered his face with both hands, forgetting he still held the gun in one hand, so that it clashed against his cheekbone and he let out another howl of pain. While the thug fumbled with the gun, trying to get it pointed in the right direction, Bindi kicked it out of his hand, where it landed close to Mack. With a supreme effort, Mack conquered his pain and dizziness enough to bend down and retrieve the gun.

"Maybe I should push *you* down the shaft instead," she growled.

That was his brave girl. He was so proud of her, he could almost burst. He watched with interest to see if she would indeed follow through with her threat, holding the gun by his side. The threat of it should be enough to keep the other man compliant.

Bindi glared so hard at the man, Mack thought he might well burst into flames. "But I won't," she finally said, and retrieved some of the twine she'd used to make a harness for Madonna and bound his hands behind his back, tying his feet, as well.

Then she stood and smiled at Mack, a smile so bright and triumphant, his heart leapt into his throat. That was it, they'd won. She was safe, and so was he.

Mack collapsed in a heap on the ground, his legs no longer able to hold his weight.

CHAPTER TWENTY-THREE

Daisy looked resplendent in her cream wedding dress. The simple V-neck bodice clung to her curves, while layers of pleated chiffon fell from a high waistline to the floor, swishing gracefully, as Daisy walked down the aisle. The olive green of gum leaves in her bouquet, studded with simple white flannel flowers—they'd arrived on time after all —and cream grevilleas, were crowned with a single, rare white Waratah bloom. Accompanied by the haunting sound of a single didgeridoo being played by an Elder from the Kuku station, Bindi thought the scene was dreamlike.

Daisy's father looked about ready to burst as he took her arm and lead her toward the flower-festooned bower in front of the first rows of seats. Bindi had the best view of the whole proceedings from her chosen spot, standing at the rear of all the chairs. It gave her the perfect prospect over the top of the heads of the crowd of seated family and friends, directly down to where Dale was waiting at the makeshift altar.

The billabong sparkled like a diamond behind the arbor, such an amazing backdrop for this amazing event. A few cotton-ball clouds studded the teal-blue sky, but the rain had held off, at least until tomorrow. And the Stormcloud crew had managed to hold off the bushfire until the local fire services had arrived, and together they'd stopped it well before the flames threatened the lodge or any of the smaller cabins. So, thankfully, the guests didn't have to look at charred, blackened bushland as a detraction to the wedding Daisy had planned so carefully. The fire had burned a large chunk of country between the mine site and Stormcloud, however, so they might have to find another route for when the guests came back in February, until the regrowth was back up and it was considered safe from falling tree trunks or burned branches.

Skylar was up at the altar with Julie, standing off to the side, waiting for Daisy to join them. Skylar surreptitiously brushed away an errant tear, and Julie just beamed at Daisy like a brilliant, one-hundred-watt lightbulb. They both looked spectacular in their dove-gray dresses, as simple and elegant as Daisy's, hair caught up in soft chignons that showed off both women's faces. Aaron and Nash stood next to Dale, also looking elegant—if a tad uncomfortable—in their dark-gray tuxedos, with smoke-colored ties that matched the bridesmaids' dresses to perfection. But both men couldn't hide how their eyes devoured the two women standing opposite. Nash's blue gaze was as bright as the sky as he stared at Skylar, and only at her. And Aaron's broad shoulders twitched in an effort to keep his hands calmly behind his back as one corner of his mouth lifted in a grin meant only for Julie.

Who would be next to tie the knot? Her money was on Skylar and Nash. Those two were just so good for each other.

A lump formed in Bindi's throat, which surprised her immensely. She wasn't the sentimental type. But seeing Daisy and her dad so close made Bindi think about her own parents. She hadn't talked to anyone in her own family for seven years. She'd thought it best at the time when she'd left, and she'd never even let her dad know where she was, or how she was doing. Even though he'd said he was on her side, it was too painful, and she didn't want to rehash the past over and over, so she'd decided a clean break was best for all.

But that'd all changed when she'd spoken on the phone to her father, Henri, last night, after Daniella had finally persuaded her to get in touch. At first, Bindi had completely disagreed with Daniella, ignoring her protestations that her father was her flesh and blood and he deserved a second chance. But Daniella was very persuasive; when she wanted something, it was very hard to say no. Daniella said that if a near-death experience wasn't enough to put aside old quarrels, then nothing was. So, Bindi decided to give him five minutes, and if he said anything disparaging or abusive or tried to make her feel guilty in any way, that'd be the end of it. But Henri had sounded so...broken, so desperate, that she'd given him five minutes, then ten, and surprisingly by the end of an hour she was feeling almost jubilant. Her father had never stopped loving her, had been shattered when she'd taken off without a word, he'd tried to find her many times, but Australia was a big country, and he had no idea where to start looking.

A fragile connection had re-formed between herself and Henri over the course of their hour-long phone conversation. It was too late to go home to New Zealand this Christmas, but perhaps next year. Her mother was a different matter; Bindi wasn't sure she'd ever forgive her daughter for what happened to Kai. Which was a shame. But Bindi was finally over taking the blame for his death. If Uma wanted to wallow in her grief and accusations, then Bindi wouldn't allow herself to be dragged down to her level any longer. It was Kai who'd destroyed her innocence. Who'd destroyed their family. Not her. She needed to lose the mantle of guilt that'd been weighing her down for so long. And Mack had been partly responsible for her seeing through the darkness into the possibilities of the light.

She reached for Mack's good hand and his warm fingers closed around hers. Mack had chosen to stand at the back as his single crutch and bandaged hand made it hard to maneuver down the aisle, and it was easier not to have to make excuses to everyone he knocked on his way past. So, she'd chosen to stand with him. Of course. As if there were any choice at all. Bindi dared not look at him, because if she did, she'd be a goner. The waterworks would come then, she just knew it. And she had a lot of work to do yet. She, Skylar, and Sasha would be run off their feet putting together the meal for the reception later, which was to be held in the large marquees, erected farther around the edge of the billabong.

Bindi spied Wazza and Kee sitting a few rows in front of her, Kee's daughter Benni, wriggling on a seat between them. Bindi had been so glad to see Wazza when they'd arrived at the station yesterday.

A hush fell over the congregation as Daisy arrived at the altar. Her father leaned in and kissed her cheek, unable to hide his pride in his wonderful daughter, then took his seat in the front row.

The celebrant looked up from her notes and surveyed the silent crowd. Dressed in a simple black sheath dress, her long, gray hair tied back in a neat bun, the celebrant then turned her direct gaze onto the couple now standing in front of her.

She cleared her throat. "Hello, everyone." The aura of the crowd was filled with anticipation, and Bindi squeezed Mack's hand even tighter. "First, Dale and Daisy would like to acknowledge the traditional custodians of the land of the Kuku-yalanji tribe on which we meet today and pay their respect to Elders, past and present."

There were murmurs of acknowledgement from the crowd, then the celebrant motioned for Dale and Daisy to face each other and hold hands in front of her, then began the ceremony in earnest.

Mack stirred slightly beside her, and she turned her sharp gaze on him. "Are you okay?" she mouthed. It was less than two days since their clash with Whip, and Bindi was worried about Mack. He'd only been discharged from the hospital this morning, and that was only because he said he was going to be at the wedding come hell or high-water, and he'd discharge himself and walk all the way to Stormcloud if need be. So, Aaron had flown to Cairns specially to pick him up.

"All good," he whispered back.

The little Stormcloud helicopter had made quite a few trips back and forth to Cairns in the past few days, keeping Aaron busy.

When rescue had finally come in the form of Steve and Dale roaring into the mine site in one of the station's Land Cruisers, she and Mack had immediately been airlifted straight to the Cairns hospital, where Mack had undergone surgery on his damaged hand, and had his fractured ankle set in a cast. At least it wasn't badly broken, much as Bindi had already guessed, but Mack would still be out of action for the next four-to-six weeks. Bindi's injuries had been much less severe, mainly scratches and bruising, but the paramedics had wanted her checked out thoroughly, anyway. And then she'd demanded she be allowed to stay until she could see Mack was fine. When he finally came out of surgery and woke up, gifting her with one of his stunning smiles, it'd taken her breath away, and she'd clung to him, not wanting to leave him ever again. She'd spent that first night in the hospital, sitting in a chair by his bedside all night. It took a lot of convincing by the doctors, Steve, Daniella, and Mack himself, that he was in safe hands, and she really should return to Stormcloud to help with the wedding preparations.

Madonna and Melody were ensconced safely back in the

stables—with a new tamper-proof lock attached—enjoying the extra attention from the Stormcloud crew. Steve had been eternally grateful to get his prize mare back, but even more grateful that she'd been instrumental in helping to save Mack from the shaft. Every time he popped up to the stables to check on his beloved horses, there were always a few extra carrots in his pocket, a delicacy that Madonna would crunch up with sheer delight, basking in the glow of everyone's appreciation. That horse really was every bit of a princess—or perhaps diva might be a better description. Bindi was never happier to pamper a horse in all her life, and she, too, had been up to the stables more than once to offer her never-ending gratitude to her.

And best of all, Picasso and Sahara had been found by the owner of an adjoining property a day after the fire. They'd been terribly thirsty after their flight from Whip and the fire, but otherwise unhurt. Bindi was so grateful the two horses had stuck together and survived the terrible events together. Bindi had spent a good hour at the stables yesterday grooming and fussing over the pair.

"Did I tell you just how breathtaking you look in that dress?" he whispered, gaze traveling appreciably down to her bare legs beneath the short, flirty hemline, then back up to meet her gaze, tawny eyes alight with mischief. And something more. Hunger. Deep, and ever so slightly savage.

She shivered at his look, but answered as flippantly as she could, "At least ten times already today." They both still looked worse for wear. Mostly hidden by her dress, dark bruises covered her hip, thigh, and shoulder where she'd landed at the bottom of the shaft. And they both had grazes and bruises on their faces and arms. Those injuries would fade soon, and right now, Bindi didn't mind that they reminded her they'd both come through a terrible event, and lived to tell the tale.

Then there were the internal scars. Maybe the best part of the whole sordid episode was the way Mack had helped her to battle her way out of her self-imposed mental constraints that Kai's mistreatment had forced upon her. She still remembered, with vivid detail, how the fat guy had threatened to rape her and her whole world had shut down, just like it had when Kai raped her. But then she'd heard Mack's sweet voice. Urging her to get up; to resist her tormentor. He'd awoken her from her torpor, helped to banish all her demons. Reminded her she was a strong, independent woman, and she had the right to fight back. And fight back, she had. She'd done it as much for Mack, as she had for herself. Nothing had ever felt quite so good as when she knocked that bastard to the ground.

"Yeah, well, I meant it every single time," he whispered in her ear pulling her back from her musings, and she couldn't hide her delight at the effect her new dress was having on him.

It'd arrived in the mail a few days ago, a spontaneous purchase online, a baby-pink, A-line style, with a plain, chiffon skirt and scattered rhinestones and embroidery as decoration on the bodice. It looked perfect with her buffed-up cowboy boots—no stilettos for her today—and she wasn't sure if it was the dress or the boots Mack was appreciating the most.

"And I'm probably going to say it at least ten more times," he warned.

Someone in the back row shot them a frown and Bindi smothered her smile, clutching his hand tightly, before turning back to the ceremony. She needed to concentrate. But it was damn hard when she could feel the heat of Mack's purely masculine body burning into her skin, even through his suit jacket and shirt. The second Bindi had seen Mack alight from the helicopter this morning, she'd rushed to hug him, not able to get enough of him. The day and a half she'd spent without him had been like a slow form of torture. But as soon as he'd taken her into his arms, dropping his crutch on the ground and pulling her into his chest, she knew. Knew that she hadn't imagined her feelings for him. Or his feelings for her. They still needed to talk about it. Where they saw their relationship going. But she was in no doubt they would have a relationship, that they had a future together. It was something unwritten between them. Ever since they'd been thrown down the shaft, their bond had become like glue. She'd felt a seismic shift in him. He'd been prepared to give his life so that she might go free. No words were needed after a gift such as that.

Bindi tried to tune into the words, as Dale repeated his vows after the celebrant, and watched as Daisy stared into his eyes, a love so pure and strong evident in her face. Then she repeated her vows, holding the gathering in a hushed awe at the beauty of her words. Bindi had to brush away a tear, so intense was the moment when Dale finally lifted the veil and kissed his new bride.

Then the Kuku Elder stepped forward. Wearing only a traditional loincloth, his body and face were decorated in the lines, patterns, and motifs specific to his tribe. Holding a piece of flattened bark, on which a pile of herbs and leaves smoldered, he wafted the smoke over the newlywed couple, speaking the traditional words of praise and fidelity.

The white-bearded Elder finally stepped back, and the celebrant said, "You may now come up and congratulate Mr and Mrs Williams." With a theatrical wave of her hand, she beckoned people forward. Daisy's family were first to surge from their seats and embrace the couple, who were both beaming so wide, they looked ready to burst with happiness. Dale's family wasn't far behind.

"That was beautiful," Bindi said wistfully to Mack.

"You're beautiful," he replied, taking the opportunity to snag her around the waist and pull her in for a kiss while everyone else was focussed on the newly-wed pair up front.

* * *

Mack lowered himself with a sigh into a chair at a table beneath the marquee. It was a blessed relief to sit down. Easing his leg out underneath the table, he leaned back and blew out a breath. He hated this terrible weakness, but he also knew the doctors had warned him about not exerting himself too soon. It'd been all he could do to remain standing throughout the ceremony, which had shocked him. Bindi's hand in his, the only thing keeping him upright. That and sheer force of will. Because he wasn't going to miss this wedding for anything. He certainly wouldn't give Clarissa the satisfaction of knowing she'd had any effect on him. But as soon as he possibly could, he'd hobbled toward the tables and chairs set up in the shade of the large tent. Easing out of his suit jacket, he slung it over the back of his chair. God, that was better. The back of his shirt was damp with sweat; he'd felt like a roasting leg of lamb inside an oven in that thing.

"Are you sure you're okay?" Bindi asked, worrying at her bottom lip with her teeth. Such a sexy action. Did she even realize what she was doing to him right now? She'd followed him over to the tent, a frown marring her beautiful face.

"I'm good," he replied. "I just wish I could be of more help." He grimaced and tilted his head up so he could stare into her face. Everyone else on the Stormcloud crew was rushing around; he was the only one not pulling his weight, and it rankled more than he liked to admit.

Bindi touched his shoulder. "You sit there and behave," she said, using her teacher's voice. "Everyone is just glad you could be here today. Nobody expects you to do anything else but sit and enjoy. After what you've been through…" Her gorgeous face wrinkled with concern. He'd much rather see her smile. They'd survived their ordeal, that was the main thing, and all he was clinging to, at the moment.

"I'd feel much better if you could sit with me for a few minutes." He patted his lap, raising an eyebrow suggestively.

"You're incorrigible," she said, slapping him lightly on the shoulder. But her smile told him that she appreciated his flirtation, nonetheless.

"I really do need to get into the kitchen," Bindi said, lifting her head to stare at the dwindling crowd still surrounding Dale and Daisy. Most people had congratulated the newlyweds by now, and were drifting toward the bar set up on the veranda for a much-needed drink and to get out of the mid-afternoon heat. But Mack would have to pass on his good wishes later. There was no way he could've stood at the back of that queue for any longer. His leg was aching like a bitch. It was hard work, only being able to use one crutch to hobble on. His other hand was wrapped in so much gauze and bandages it was next to useless. The doctors had wanted him to wear a sling, but he'd refused. At least give him the dignity of looking a little less like the useless cripple he was.

"Off you go." Mack patted her behind gently. Then immediately regretted it, as the feel of the soft globe of her butt cheek set off explosions of sensations through his body. It was all he could do not to reach up under her short little skirt and run his fingers over her smooth thigh. He was desperate to touch Bindi. As often and as much as he could. He'd fantasized about her the whole time he'd been in hospital, and now that she was here in the flesh, he had to keep reminding himself there were other people around.

"I'll bring you a glass of water," she promised. "This heat is a killer."

"And something a little stronger," he called out hopefully as she walked up the grassy slope toward the lodge.

"Nuh-uh." She waggled her finger at him, walking

backward, a solicitous frown wrinkling her brow. He half wished he hadn't told her the doctors warned him to stay away from the booze for a few days, while he was still on the strong painkillers. He'd kill for a cold beer right now. The ceremony might be over, but he still had to get through the reception and the speeches, yet.

Mack watched Bindi until she disappeared inside the large French doors off the veranda, enjoying the sight of her slim, brown legs for as long as he could. Once she'd vanished from sight, he let his gaze drift over the gathered crowd scattered along the grassy slope above the billabong. Dale and Daisy were still at the center of a knot of people, all leaning in to shake their hands or wish the new couple well on their future happiness. The rest of the bridal party stood off to one side, the two men having removed their jackets and slung them over their arms. Mack didn't blame them, this heat was almost unbearable while encased in a tuxedo. Every so often, Dale went to reach up, as if to tip the brim of his hat, which wasn't there, and it made Mack chuckle. Cowboys were always a little lost without their hats; he knew exactly how Dale felt. Skylar kept glancing up toward the lodge, and Mack knew she'd be itching to get into her kitchen, and was just waiting for the word from Daisy to release her from her bridesmaid duties. But Bindi, Sasha, and to a smaller extent, Daniella would handle it for her until then. Daniella had hired a raft of waitstaff to help keep the guests well watered, and fed.

Dale and Daisy's cabin wouldn't be finished for a month or more, yet. Mack hoped he got to do some work on it, at least. In a few weeks, he'd be able to get rid of the crutches and walk around in a moon boot, which would give him much more mobility. Still wouldn't be able to ride a horse, though, and that part irked him the most.

But the newlyweds would be on their honeymoon for the

next three weeks, so Steve would employ another couple of builders to help him get it well on the way to completion. Then Dale—and hopefully Mack—could help him finish it up when he returned.

Mack's gaze continued to swing around the gathered people. He noticed Alek standing over by the DJ, giving him instructions on the next set he was to play. But the DJ only had half of Alek's concentration. Mack watched Alek's gaze follow Sasha as she walked around the edge of the infinity pool with a harried look on her face, heading toward Skylar. He sure was smitten, that man. Mack wondered how long it'd take for those two to finally become an official couple.

A tall guy threaded his way through the crowd, heading in Mack's direction, carrying two glasses of what looked like lemonade. Bindi had pointed out Wazza to her earlier in the day, and he sat up a little straighter as the ex-leading hand approached. Mack was well aware that, as Wazza's replacement, the man would probably want to check him out.

Wazza put the drinks on the table, pulled out a chair and then held out his hand in greeting. "Nice to finally meet you," the big man said. "I've heard a lot about you."

"All good, I hope," Mack said, holding his arm out for an awkward left-handed shake.

Wazza grimaced and said, "Sorry, dude, I forgot you were..."

Mack waved his apology away.

"Bindi asked me to bring you over a drink," Wazza said, sliding one of the glasses toward him.

"Thanks. Cheers to the newly married couple." They both held their glasses high and Mack drank deeply. He was parched, and while it wasn't a beer, the lemonade would have to do for now.

Wazza smiled broadly. "I'm so glad Dale and Daisy got the happy ending they deserve," he said thoughtfully. "They went through some tough times to get where they are." Wazza's face took on a faraway look.

Bindi had told Mack a little of Wazza and Kee's story. It sounded like they'd been through some tough times, as well, on their road to find love. And he knew Wazza had lost someone special a while ago, around the same time as Dale and Daisy had got together. It seemed that Stormcloud had had its fair share of heartache, as well as happy endings.

"How's life in Cairns treating you?" Mack asked.

"Great. Better than I expected." Wazza raised his glass again, and Mack suspected that had a lot to do with the petite, dark-haired beauty and her daughter, standing talking to Steve and Daniella. Especially when he saw the way Wazza's eyes kept darting to follow her, watching her with open tenderness. Then Wazza's face sobered slightly, and his blue gaze came back to Mack's face. "How are you faring?" Wazza waved in the general direction of Mack's hand, barely hiding his grimace. Most hard-working men would understand the torture Mack was going through, not being able to do what needed to be done; to be relying on others to help him do the simplest of tasks.

"I'll get there eventually," he replied. "The plastic surgeon said I'll need to give it four or five months, and then he'll have a go at reducing the scarring, and hopefully I'll get almost full use of my hand back within a year."

"Wow," Wazza said with a sympathetic nod. "That's good news, I guess."

"Yeah." Mack shrugged. He was philosophical about his fate. Whatever would be, would be. As long as he had Bindi, he could endure just about anything.

"What about the villain? Bindi mentioned it was some old girlfriend of yours back in The States who had it in for you. Sent some local thugs after you. I heard one of them died, and you caught the other one, but have they got the woman yet?"

Wazza asked.

Mack gave a smug grimace as his mind went back to the mine site two days ago. He'd been pretty much out of it by the time Nash and his constable turned up. A medivac helicopter was on the way to collect him and Bindi, and people were crowding the area, while he lay on the ground with his head in Bindi's lap. But Nash had taken the time to come over and make sure they were both all right. And while not altogether happy with the dead body at the bottom of the shaft, he quietly congratulated them on their escape and capture of the accomplice.

Of course, there'd been many long interviews and statements given while he'd been laid up in hospital, but Nash had dug up the dirt on Whip and Fat Man—whose name turned out to be Neil. Neil had sung like the proverbial canary, confirming that Whip had indeed loosened the lug nuts on Mack's truck. Neil had also given Nash the name of a farmer who lived on the other side of town, who'd given Whip the info on Madonna and Melody. It seemed this farmer had asked if he could buy Melody when she was old enough to be weaned, as he wanted to add an Australian Stock Horse to his raft of other horses, and had even called at Stormcloud to talk to Steve. But Steve had turned him down, as he considered the man slapdash with his training and there were rumors he was violent toward his horses, something Steve would never condone. At least they knew where Whip had found his local information now, but the farmer probably wouldn't be charged, which was a shame. The locals had their own way of dealing with people like him, however, and he was already being shunned by the community any time he dared to show his face in town.

Nash also had the financial team tracing payments made to Whip's account to see if they could track them back to Clarissa, using their police counterparts in America to help. It seemed that after Mack's phone call with Clarissa, where he'd told her she'd have to kill him to stop him, she'd sent Whip after Mack again, this time with more deadly intent. If only he'd managed to record that conversation.

"Not exactly," Mack replied. "Clarissa Melman is a slippery one. But Dean assures me the police in the US are working up a case on her as we speak. It's only a matter of time before they prove she ordered Whip to kill me and Bindi. Now the IRS is involved, because of the rumors of fraud and misuse of sponsor's money. She's not under arrest yet, but they've seized her passport, as they believe she's a flight risk."

"That sounds promising," Wazza said with a positive nod.

"Sure does." Mack took a swig of lemonade, and considered his last conversation with Nash earlier this morning, after he'd arrived at Stormcloud. He'd told him that Clarissa was supposedly trying to bluff her way out of the accusations, and when that hadn't worked, she'd called in Daddy and his big-gun lawyers.

Nash had confirmed that the Beffdorff company was on the brink of collapse, and had indeed lost millions of dollars due to Clarissa's mismanagement. It seemed she'd recruited other bull riders to her corrupt plan to cheat on her own gambling app, and they were now coming forward to tell their stories. The pro circuit was in disarray as more allegations came to light of the betting scandal. Nash surmised perhaps Clarissa thought if she could silence Mack once and for all, she'd be able to keep her subterfuge quiet. He also seemed to think that Clarissa would be kept far too busy from now on to try any more attacks on Mack or Bindi. She was being closely monitored. Mack enjoyed a quick few seconds imagining Clarissa in an orange jumpsuit, being dragged through the halls of some large prison, the other women catcalling to her through the bars of their prison cells. He really hoped she got her comeuppance. Especially because Clarissa had dared to hurt Bindi. It was one thing to have a go at him, but how dare she try and touch his woman?

"I hear Steve has hired a new stock hand," Wazza added, conversationally.

"Yeah." Mack nodded. Steve had already passed on the good news. "With me out of commission for a while and Dale heading out on his honeymoon, they're certainly short-staffed right now." In truth, Stormcloud had been running on fewer staff than it should for a while now, as Steve had never replaced Karri after she died. It'd be good to have the extra help, and it was a great time for the new stock hand to start, while the station was resting over the wet season. They could learn the ropes and be ready to hit the ground running once the guests returned in February.

"Do you know much about them?" Wazza asked, gaze flicking to where Kee was now talking to Julie, waving her arms around animatedly.

"Only that her name is Indy, and she comes highly recommended. She's been working on another cattle station up the top end of Western Australia. Bringing two horses and two dogs, and she's supposedly arriving right after Christmas."

"Another woman joining the team, huh? I hope she makes it down here before the rains start," Wazza added. "I'm sure Steve has done his homework on this lady. Here's hoping she fits in with the team as well as you have." Wazza raised his lemonade and Mack touched the rim of his glass to Wazza's, surprised at the other man's praise.

Mack had never really thought about it before, but now that he did, he could see he *had* slotted into the Stormcloud crew easily. It wasn't something that would've bothered him before, because he'd only ever thought this would be a temporary stay. The crew had made him more than welcome, but he could see now his skills were also valuable. He picked up where Wazza had left off, where the horse and cattle side of things were concerned. Of course, Dale, as the leading hand was technically his boss, and technically he handled the decisions about how the stock should be run, but now Mack was here, he could take a lot of that day-to-day responsibility from Dale's shoulders. He still had a lot to learn, but now that he was thinking of staying on indefinitely, that knowledge would become second nature soon enough. And, of course, there was Bindi. Admittedly, she hadn't always made him feel welcome. At the beginning, she'd been downright antagonistic. And when he thought about it, she'd had every right, because he'd acted like a total ass. But now, she was the one who made him feel most welcome. Who made him want to stay. Forever, if that was believable.

Thinking about Bindi seemed to conjure her. As if by magic, she appeared by his side, looking slightly frazzled and bearing a tray of hors d'oeuvres. Her nose stud sparkled in the sun, as did her eyes, and he thought he'd never seen a more beautiful woman in that particular moment.

"Hi. I see you two have met," Bindi said, a little out of breath.

"Yes," Wazza replied. "I needed to check out this guy who's stolen your heart," he added candidly, winking at Bindi. "I hope you're going to look after my girl?" His gaze strayed to Mack.

Mack was a little taken aback at his direct question, but he wasn't going to shy away from his answer.

"Hey," Bindi started to protest, slapping Wazza lightly on the shoulder. "That's enough—"

But Mack jumped in to answer the question. "Yes, sir, I most definitely am," he replied, sliding a possessive arm around Bindi's waist, and she leaned into him slightly.

"Good. Because Bindi's special. I'd hate to see her get

hurt." Wazza slitted his eyes at Mack and Mack met his gaze with his own level stare.

Wazza may well have heard about Mack's philandering ways, he wouldn't be surprised if his reputation had preceded him when he first moved to Queensland. Bindi and Wazza had worked closely together and Wazza was looking out for a mate, and Mack understood that. Hell, he was already feeling the same about the crew here at Stormcloud, he'd jump in and defend every single one of them after only a few weeks, and Bindi and Wazza had worked side by side for over three years. But Mack had changed, and it was all because of one woman, and he wanted her to know that. He was no longer scared of commitment, and he meant to show it.

"I promise, I won't hurt her," Mack replied levelly. It was the truth. Bindi meant more to him than… Hell, she meant more to him than bull-riding, more than regaining his reputation as the golden boy of the circuit. She meant everything. They still had a lot to work out, but he knew now he'd be sticking around for as long as she'd have him.

"That's good enough for me." Wazza clinked his glass against Mack's once more, giving Mack his stamp of approval, and they both drank.

"Hey, I'm right here," Bindi complained, bumping her hip against Mack's shoulder, while both men smirked at her. She might not understand exactly what'd just transpired, but Mack did. And so did Wazza. Now he just needed to convince Bindi.

CHAPTER TWENTY-FOUR

Rain drummed on the tin, sounding like a herd of fleet-footed horses galloping across the staff quarters' roof. Ominous, dark-gray clouds had rolled in yesterday afternoon—the day after the wedding—and most of the guests still lingering had fled in their four-wheel-drives, or Aaron had flown some out in the helicopter in the nick of time, the storm hot on their tail. The wet season had hit with a vengeance, but at least it'd held off long enough to make Dale and Daisy's day perfect.

Bindi knocked on the door to Mack's room and waited until she heard his deep voice tell her to come in. The curtains were drawn against the morning light and the room was dim, but not dark. He was propped up on his pillows, arms behind his head, blankets pulled up to his chin. Mack was still healing, and attending the wedding had knocked him for six, even though he refused to acknowledge it. Both Steve and Daniella had ordered him to take some bed rest for the next few days, especially now the rain was here, as it made it hard for him to get around on his crutch when the huge puddles of water turned the red dust to mud all around the lodge.

"Your breakfast, my master," she said, placing the plate of food on his bedside table, feigning tugging at her forelock and bowing low. It was only just after eight in the morning, but Bindi had been up for hours, helping Skylar clear away the remnants of the wedding so that the workspace was finally resembling a modern, gourmet kitchen once more. It was going to take them the rest of the day yet to get it all cleaned and put away properly, but they'd made a huge dent in the work over yesterday and this morning. Just in time for Christmas, in two days' time. It was going to be a wet celebration, but Skylar was well prepared, and had stocked up even before the wedding to make sure they could still celebrate in style.

Bindi shook her head, water droplets flying from her wet braid, scattering over the floor rug, some landing on the bed where Mack was just throwing back the blankets and emerging to put his feet on the floor.

"Hey," he complained, ducking his head away from the water.

Bindi's breath stalled in her throat. Mack was shirtless. Actually, he was only wearing black boxer briefs, and as he sat on the side of his bed, running his good hand through his sleep-mussed hair, she drank him in. Well-defined chest, with a sprinkling of curls leading her gaze down his flat stomach and impossible abs to narrow hips, where the waistband of his boxers revealed a dart of hair leading lower. Muscular thighs tapering down to strong calves, one of them encased in a cast that came halfway up to his knee, reminding her he was convalescing, and she shouldn't be looking at him like he was some delicious dish she wanted to consume in a single gulp. Memories of their one time together swirled through her, eliciting a purely physical response, as her heart rate increased and butterflies tumbled in her stomach. Her hand flew to cover her pounding chest, and she held in a gasp of appreciation. He was one damn beautiful man.

"You weren't kidding when you warned me about the rain," Mack said lightly, then stopped as he looked up and saw her staring.

Tawny eyes darkening in an instant, Mack stood, balancing on his uninjured ankle, and stretched out his hands for her. She meant to take a step back, out of his reach, but impossibly, she found herself stepping into his arms instead. She'd left him alone for the past forty-eight hours, even though every molecule in her body was screaming that she needed to go and see him, touch him, be with him, find out what was going on in that complicated mind of his. Now, touching him gave her the sweet relief she'd been craving. As if by its own volition, her fingers traced over the curve of his shoulder, delighting in the heat of his skin, then trailed down his arm, pulling his hand farther around her waist, moving in to him so she was pressed hard up against his chest.

"I've wanted to do this ever since you landed back here for the wedding," she muttered. Admittedly, they had kissed when Mack had first disembarked from the helicopter, a welcome-home, I've-missed-you-terribly kind of kiss. Then Mack had flirted shamelessly with her the whole way through the wedding, but by the time evening had rolled around, his face was pale and pinched, his smile had waned, and Bindi knew he needed rest, not the hot night of debauchery she'd been dreaming of. It'd all been highly unsatisfactory, but Bindi had kept busy and upbeat, telling herself they'd find time sooner or later.

It seemed it might *finally* be that time, and Bindi burned with longing. Her lips searched for his, locking onto his firm mouth as if she were drowning and he was her only air. He panted into her mouth, his tongue dancing with hers, devouring hers, demanding more, hands all over her body, running over her back, up her stomach, cupping her breasts through her shirt.

Hopping on one foot, he maneuvered them until they could sit on the edge of his bed together. Then he began popping the buttons on her shirt, one by one, never taking his mouth away from hers. Her shirt landed in a heap on the floor and for a second she groaned and leaned into his hot hands that were all over her body. Then the gauze on his bandaged hand brushed her skin, and common sense returned as she recoiled away.

"Wait." Pushing on his chest, she turned her head, so she had room to breathe. "We can't do this," she protested. "You can't do this," she amended, making a point by lifting his hand at the wrist and pointing at his bandaged hand.

"That?" he scoffed. "Don't you worry about me. I'm invincible." Mack knelt up on the bed, and raised both his arms above his head and flexed his biceps like he was Thor, the God of Thunder, and Bindi couldn't help but laugh.

But that wasn't all. "What about your head? Have you had any more headaches?" she demanded.

"Nope," he replied, raising a seductive eyebrow. "Not a single twinge."

Bindi studied him. When Mack had been admitted to the hospital, Bindi had persuaded him to tell the doctor about his headaches. The doctor had run some tests, and they were both relieved to hear there was no permanent damage to Mack's brain and that lingering headaches could indeed be an ongoing symptom of a heavy concussion. The doctor's advice was that the dizzy spells and pains would fade over time, especially if Mack rested and didn't overexert himself. Bindi had laughed outright at that, startling the doctor. But it'd put both their minds at ease to know the headaches would eventually get better. Even if it took the next year or two, Mack would be okay.

"Like I said, I'm invincible." He gave her his best smile.

Right at that moment, Bindi almost believed he was.

The cocky smirk left his mouth as their gazes locked and the gold flecks danced in his eyes, which suddenly turned serious. With great deliberation, Mack got slowly off the bed, hobbled over to the door and flicked the lock.

"I've been wanting to do this for days. No, scratch that. Ever since that moment you got out of my swag at the rodeo, I've wanted you back in my bed. I'm not letting you get away from me now," he growled, pulling her down onto the mattress with him.

"Really?" she squeaked. "But you said…we said…"

"I was an idiot. What I said and what I felt back then were two very different things," he murmured against her mouth. "God, you taste so good. Like coffee and warm muffins, and… You. You taste like you." They kissed again, lying sideways across the bed, Bindi enjoying the nearness of him, the heat of him, the strong male presence that was doing all sorts of things to her insides. His hand snaked around the back of her neck, releasing her braid and combing his fingers through her damp hair, so that it fell over the blankets in a sheath.

One of the best things about living at Stormcloud Station was Daniella and Steve hadn't skimped when it came to building and outfitting the staff quarters. They were as luxurious as the main lodge, and every room had a queen-sized bed. Bindi welcomed that indulgence now; no more making love within the confines of a single swag under the stars, they had a whole bed to themselves. Luxury.

"Skylar is expecting me back." She tried one more time to stop this before it went too far. "She might come looking for me."

"You give Skylar too little credit," he said. "She'll guess exactly what we're up to. And no, she won't come knocking."

"Oh, God," Bindi groaned.

"What? Are you ashamed of being with me?" he asked, drawing back a little.

"No. No, not at all," she exclaimed. Although part of her

squirmed a little at the idea, everybody probably knew what they were up to. She didn't like people knowing her private business. But then again, everyone had seen them at the wedding, and knew they were a couple; knew they'd been through a terrible ordeal together and had grown incredibly close because of it. Knew that she was madly in love with him.

Hold that thought.

The word *love* had drifted around her head when they'd been trapped down the shaft together, but she'd pushed it away, not ready to examine the feeling. It looked like the word had lodged in her brain without any conscious thought, after all. What was she to do with that notion? Should she just come out and tell him? Was it too soon to be admitting to such a massive sentiment?

"Good," he said, covering her mouth with his own, and driving all errant thoughts out of her head. Later. She'd tell him later.

Warm lips left a trail of hot kisses down her neck, across her collarbone and then covering her breasts—still encased in their bra—and stomach, sending shivers of anticipation through her. He stopped at the belt on her jeans, teasing his tongue around the waistband as he undid the buckle one-handed. She'd almost forgotten about his wounded hand in the depth of her desire, and she reached down to help him undo the button and zipper. Deciding he'd never get her boots off, she sat up and quickly disposed of boots and jeans, leaving her panties and bra on, then lay back on the bed, giving him a come-hither smile. But he didn't come back to her mouth, as she expected. Instead, he continued his warm kisses, this time trailing them along the tender skin of her inner thigh. Her limbs went all quivery at his touch and a liquid heat built low in her belly. Mack's tongue slipped around the edges of her panties, and she almost held her breath as he eased them aside with one finger and then let his tongue find her most sensitive parts. She wriggled out of her panties as he slid them lower. Her fingernails dug into the skin on his shoulders, and she threw her head back onto the pillow.

Gently parting her legs, he buried his face in her and she gasped, raising her hips against his hot mouth. His skilful tongue found the center of her core and he began to lick and suck with such talent that her breathing quickly became rapid and labored, and she twisted the sheets between her fisted hands. It only took moments for the swell of sensations to build to a crescendo and her body strained towards his mouth, seeking the heat of him, until she cried out in ecstasy, and he pressed himself into her as she rode the spasms of climax.

Her body relaxed and her short gasps slowed to deeper breaths of satisfaction.

Bindi stroked his back, her body still a quivering mess from her incredible orgasm. "Oh, Mack," she sighed, feeling the muscles in his back and shoulders bunch as he lifted himself up and brought his lips to hers.

Sucking gently on the corner of her mouth, he groaned, "Bindi." Her name on his lips made her chest expand as if it were a balloon inside her ribcage. "I love you so damn much," he said softly, meeting her gaze. "And I want to make you happy."

"You do make me happy," she agreed hoarsely. "Very, very happy." She could hardly speak as he began to move his lips across her body. Kissing and tasting, in slow, sensuous strokes until she felt as if she'd lost all control. But she needed to say the words, too. Tell him she loved him, too.

His mouth found the edge of her bra and he tugged it down, running his tongue slowly around each nipple. Sliding his good hand under her shoulder, he unsnapped the fastener and released the bra with a flick of his wrist. With one hand still cupping her breast possessively, he captured her mouth again, pulling her beneath him, so he hovered over her, chest crushing hers, thighs pushing her into the bed, erection burning a brand into her stomach. She could hardly believe it, but even after that earth-shattering first climax, she wanted him inside her, could feel the need building in her again.

With a groan, she reached for him, drawing her hands down the ridges of his back, but suddenly he was gone.

"What...?" she gasped like a stranded fish.

"Condom," he said, voice hoarse, the word barely distinguishable from a groan of pleasure. Rolling over, he reached for his bedside draw and had sheathed himself in seconds. Mack was back, covering her with his body once more, the heat of him burning right through to her soul. His ankle in a cast didn't seem to hinder him at all as he pushed into her, moving with long, deep strokes that sent her toward the edge of oblivion again. She couldn't stay silent, and he covered her mouth with his as she cried out in rapture and they rode the growing ripples of orgasm together. In that moment of sweet, blinding pleasure, she felt light-headed, almost disconnected from her own body.

He kissed her gently, caressing her, loving her, naked bodies entwined in the now tangled sheets as they lay panting and satiated. He rolled off her and disposed of the condom, then curled into her body from behind, spooning her, running his fingers up and down her arm gently.

This morning had been different from the first time they'd made love. Mack was a skilled lover. And the first time Mack had been attentive to her needs and had brought her to orgasm easily with his amazing body and his sensuous hands. Today, Mack had still been attentive and sexy as hell, but there was one major difference; he held her with intention, as if he never wanted to let her go. He not only loved her body, he cherished her soul, as well.

Bindi let her thoughts drift and soar, but she kept coming back to the words Mack had uttered earlier. He'd said he loved her. And he'd meant it, there was no doubt in her mind. She felt the same way, even although she hadn't uttered the words. Yet. But there was a problem. Something they needed to sort out. Mack had said, over and over, that he was only here for six months—twelve at the most. Then he was heading back to the US. Should she even bring it up now? Perhaps she should let sleeping dogs lie. But when would it ever be the right time to address this obstacle between them? If she left it, her thoughts would fester, drive a wedge between them. How could she possibly be with Mack, give her heart to him, if he only stomped it into the mud when he decided to return to America? That was where his home and his family were. There was no reason for him to stay here.

But before she could open her mouth, Mack beat her to it. "I could get used to this," he said, lazily stretching his legs down the mattress. "Get used to being here with you in my bed."

"Really?" There were a million questions all clamoring in her head to be heard. "Me, too," she replied, ignoring all the obvious ones and going for heartfelt confession, instead. "But, Mack..."

"It feels good. Right. Like it was meant to be," he plowed on. "Like we should be together, forever."

Bindi rolled over slightly so she could peer into his face. What was he getting at? "But you said—"

"I'm thinking I might stay on for a while. I had a word with Steve yesterday, and he's happy to keep me for as long as I want. What do you think?" His words stunned Bindi too speechlessness for a few seconds.

"Stay here? At Stormcloud? What, you mean for a whole year? Or longer?" She was still confused.

"Indefinitely," he said with a grin.

"You mean, not go back to America? Forever?"

"Well, I'm not committing to forever. That's asking a bit too much of a bloke, don't you think?" he asked, rising up on one elbow so he could look down into her face. He smiled, but it never made it fully to his lips, as if something else was weighing him down. Like he was waiting for her to say something. Waiting for those words she wanted to say, but couldn't seem to force them out between her lips.

"I...I don't know," she stammered, instead. "Really?" she repeated. Was he really saying he was going to stay? Here? With her?

"Steve even mentioned that he'd been thinking about combining the two rooms at the end of the hall and converting them into a couple's suite. Said that we could try it out for size if we liked."

"Oh. He did?" Bindi could barely keep up with this conversation. She sat up, brushing her still-damp hair out of her face, ignoring the fact that her breasts were now bared, and stared at Mack.

"Let me get this straight. You're offering to stay here. In Australia. At Stormcloud. For me?"

"Yep." His tawny eyed sparkled. "And for me." His face sobered, and he sat up next to her. "I want to stay, Bindi. I can see now that I can build a life here. With you. Away from all that pressure and hype of the bull-riding circuit. And who knows, maybe in a year, we can go for a visit. See my folks. I can show you around Montana. Truth be told, I don't really care where I live, as long as you're there."

Wow, this was all so fast. And astonishing. But fast. Ideas of Mack and her living together, loving each other was almost too much to handle.

Bindi took hold of Mack's injured hand and stroked her fingers over the tips of his, which poked out from beneath the bandages. "What about riding bulls for a living? I know that was your dream, and while Whip tried to maim you so badly that you could never ride again, the surgeon seems to think there's hope you could regain full strength in your hand. Don't you want to give it one more try?"

"Yeah, nah." Bindi nearly laughed at Mack's use of the Aussie vernacular. "There's one little detail that Whip overlooked when he shot me, and I don't think anyone has realized yet."

"What's that?" Bindi asked.

Mack held his uninjured hand in the air and wiggled his fingers. "I'm left-handed. I don't need my right hand to ride bulls."

Bindi stared at Mack, digesting this newest piece of information. "You mean...?"

"Yep, once my ankle heals, and my headaches subside, I could get back on the circuit, if I wanted to."

"Oh." She tried not to let her confusion show. "Are you absolutely sure?" When Mack had first arrived, riding bulls was all he thought about. All he lived for. Could he have changed so much in such a short time?

Mack placed a finger under her chin and lifted her face until he could look into her eyes. "But I don't want to," he said softly. "I mean it, I want to stay here with you. As long as you'll have me," he whispered.

"Have you? Of course, I'll have you. I love you, Mack."

"You do? Oh, thank God. I thought... I was prepared to put everything on the line for you, because I knew we had an undeniable connection. And I know my feelings for you are the most intense I've ever had for a woman. But I wasn't one-hundred-percent sure you felt the same way."

"I've always had strong emotions when it comes to you. I admit, when you first arrived, I was a little mixed up about my feelings for you." She gave him a wry smile, still playing with the fingers of his bandaged hand, then looked away, trying to find a way to explain how she felt.

"Love and hate are both powerful emotions in their own rights," he said, capturing her hand in his other one and bringing it to his lips.

"Yes, they are. But I never hated you," she clarified. "You just annoyed the hell out of me. Rattled my cage, infuriated me, brought out the worst in me. And the best." At this, she raised her gaze and met his.

"I tend to have that effect on people." He lifted a cheeky eyebrow, and she stared into his familiar amber eyes. "But I'm incredibly glad you've decided you love me, because I'd hate to have to take back all my resolutions and my offer to stay. I'd hate to have to go back to the US with my tail between my legs. I was really looking forward to my first Aussie Christmas here at Stormcloud."

"You won't have to do any of that," she laughed.

"Oh, good. And besides, there's always the Aussie circuit, if I want to keep my skills up," he added with a twinkle in his eye.

"Only if you promise you'll wear a helmet." She lifted her chin and looked him directly in the eye. Some things were non-negotiable.

"Awww. Do I have to?" He sounded like a petulant little boy. At least he did, until his gaze dropped from her face to her naked breasts, and it turned decidedly naughty.

"Okay, on one condition. That I get to play with these as my consolation prize." He took her nipple in his mouth and sucked, and she gasped at the unexpected pleasure of it.

She never dreamed she could feel this happy. So fulfilled and serene, yet on fire at the same time.

"Bindi, you're the best thing that ever happened to me. I'm going to make you so happy, you'll think you've died and gone to heaven."

"I already do," she smiled, and took his mouth as her trophy.

Want to know more about Stormcloud Station?
Get your FREE and EXCLUSIVE Prequel Novella
MISTY SKIES
Read Steve and Daniella's story.

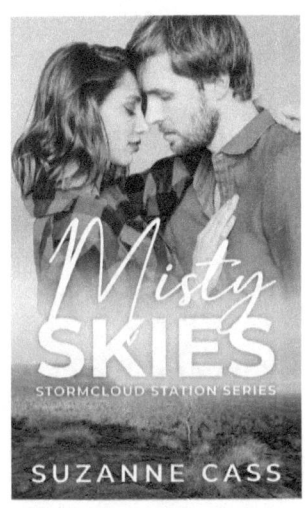

GO TO THIS LINK FOR YOUR FREE
BOOK
https://dl.bookfunnel.com/xyuua14lyp

Stay in touch via my website
www.suzannecass.com

Facebook: www.facebook.com/suzannecassauthor/
Instagram: www.instagram.com/suzanne.cass/
Pintrest: www.pinterest.com.au/suzanne_cass/

If you liked Tangled Skies, you'll love;

Clear Skies

Fate and flooding rains brought them together. Secrets may tear them apart. Book 1.

Starlit Skies

They're polar opposites, with only one thing in common…
Book 2.

Crystal Skies

Her heart was shattered the night he disappeared…now he's back. Book 3.

Dawn Skies

When you love someone…you'll do anything to protect them. Book 4.

Outback Skies

His heart it the only thing he can't afford to risk. Book 6.

Also by Suzanne Cass
NEW
Stormcloud Station Series
(A Stargazer Spinoff Series)
Small Town Romantic Suspense
Clear Skies
Starlit Skies
Crystal Skies
Dawn Skies
Tangled Skies
Outback Skies

Stargazer Ranch Romance Series
Small Town Romantic Suspense
Combustion: Prequel Novella
Wildfire
Firelight
Snowbound: A Christmas Novella
Snowfall
Cloudburst

Island Bound Series
Mystery Romance (on an Island)
Books can be read as stand-alone
Bound by Truth
Bound by Silence
Bound by the Stars

Colors of the Earth Series
Small Town Romantic Suspense
Books can be read as stand-alone
Shadows in the Dust
Shadows in Deep Blue

Shadows of Red Earth

Romantic Suspense
Single Title
Island Redemption
Glass Clouds
Chasing Bullets

Love in the Mountains Novella Series
Small Town Short Romance
Novellas can be read as stand-alone
Rain on a Tin Roof
Lost and Found
Rescue his Heart

Please Leave a Review

The greatest gift you could ever give an author is to leave a review. You will be helping other people to discover this book and making a difference to me as an Independently Published Author. If you liked this book and want other people to read it too, please leave a review.

About the Author

Suzanne Cass is an Australian author who writes rural romance and romantic suspense abounding with passion and danger.

Her debut novel, Island Redemption, won the Romance Writers of Australia Emerald Award in 2016. Suzanne was also a finalist in the 2019 Romance Writers of Australia RUBY award.

She had always had a fascination with the tough resilience of people who live in our amazing red-dirt outback country. When not writing about the characters that inhabit her head, Suzanne can be found roaming the Perth beaches with her border collie, or encouraging from the sidelines as her two sons play sport.

Stay in touch via my website

www.suzannecass.com

Acknowledgements

Tangled Skies is the fifth book in the Stormcloud Station Series. I decided that adding a cocky, American cowboy would mix things up a little for the more laid-back Aussie characters. I hope you like Mack as much as I do. He has a lot to learn about humility, but Bindi is more than willing to help him along that path. I have to admit, the wedding between Dale and Daisy (the couple from book1) at the end of this story was especially heart-melting to write. It brings Mack and Bindi closer together and I know they will go on to have as special a relationship as D & D.

To my beta readers and my ARC team, who are essential to an Indie Author like me, I'm sending you all big (virtual) hugs across the globe. Thank you for reading my books and taking them into your hearts.

Big thanks to my editor, Tanya Saari for polishing my writing so it shines like it should.

My hubby, Gary needs a special mention, as do my two beautiful sons. They do not read romance, (I hear them shudder at the mere thought) and they don't try to understand what it is that I do, but they love me wholeheartedly, and that's all that matters. And to my beautiful Dune Dog, may you always chase butterflies and balls over the rainbow.

I'm so very grateful to all the readers who have bought and enjoyed my books and touch my world with your comments and words of wisdom.

www.ingramcontent.com/pod-product-compliance
Lightning Source LLC
Chambersburg PA
CBHW020345120726
47904CB00002B/460